PRAISE FOR

Between

An ALA Best Fiction Book for Young Adults
Texas Tayshas Master List
A Booklist Top 10 SF/Fantasy for Youth Pick

★ "Liz runs the gamut of strong emotion throughout this
compelling backtrack of a short life punctuated by early
grief, parental failings, and honest, flawed love."
—*BCCB*, starred review

★ "A compelling tale."
—*Booklist*, starred review

"A rich and compelling character study wrapped around a mystery."
—*Kirkus Reviews*

"Warman seamlessly blends romance, mystery, suspense, and the
supernatural in this exploration of innocence, guilt, and morality."
—*Horn Book Magazine*

"A suspenseful whodunit."
—*SLJ*

PRAISE FOR

where the truth lies

★ "Unflinching, multilayered narration and realistic
dialogue capture the wishes and fears that drive teens.
A page-turner to the bittersweet ending."
—*Kirkus Reviews*, starred review

"Warman sensitively portrays the sibling-like tensions
and intimacy of boarding-school friendships. . . . Memorable."
—*Booklist*

"A smart, sensitive melodrama."
—*BCCB*

"Insightful and touching."
—*SLJ*

PRAISE FOR

breathless

An ALA Best Book for Young Adults

"Poignantly honest and real. . . . Exudes authenticity
and is told with depth, intelligence, humor, and affection."
—Todd Strasser, bestselling author of *Give a Boy a Gun*

★ "Achingly realistic . . . with rare, refreshing
honesty and flashes of wry humor."
—*Booklist*, starred review

★ "Vivid and exquisite. Katie is achingly real, and her relationship
with her ferocious, guarded, and superbly faithful roommate, Mazzie,
is one of the most tender and intimate platonic friendships in YA lit."
—*BCCB*, starred review

★ "Warman treats Will's schizophrenia with stark honesty as
seen through his sister's eyes. . . . Provides an important look
at an extremely difficult illness and its effects on a family."
—*SLJ*, starred review

Between

jessica warman

WALKER & COMPANY

New York

BOOKS BY JESSICA WARMAN

Breathless
Where the Truth Lies
Between
Beautiful Lies

For M. C. W.
Because we fit.

First published in the United States of America in August 2011
by Walker Publishing Company, Inc., a division of Bloomsbury Publishing, Inc.
Paperback edition published in August 2012
www.bloomsburyteens.com

For information about permission to reproduce selections from this book, write to
Permissions, Walker BFYR, 175 Fifth Avenue, New York, New York 10010

The Library of Congress has cataloged the hardcover edition as follows:
Warman, Jessica.
Between / Jessica Warman. — 1st ed.
p.   cm.
Summary: By weaving through her memories and watching the
family and friends she left behind, eighteen-year-old Liz Valchar solves
the mystery of how her life ended in the Long Island Sound.
ISBN 978-0-8027-2182-2 (hardcover)
[1. Afterlife—Fiction. 2. Dead—Fiction. 3. Family problems—Fiction.] I. Title.
PZ7.W2374Bet 2011   [Fic]—dc22   2010040986

ISBN 978-0-8027-3386-3 (paperback)

Book design by Nicole Gastonguay
Typeset by Westchester Book Composition
Printed in the U.S.A. by Quad/Graphics, Fairfield, Pennsylvania
2 4 6 8 10 9 7 5 3 1

This living hand, now warm and capable
Of earnest grasping, would, if it were cold
And in the icy silence of the tomb,
So haunt thy days and chill thy dreaming nights
That thou wouldst wish thine own heart dry of blood
So in my veins red life might stream again,
And thou be conscience-calmed – see here it is –
I hold it towards you.
—John Keats

One

It's a little after two a.m. Outside the *Elizabeth*, things are relatively quiet. Boats—yachts, really—are tied to the docks, clean white buoys protecting their fiberglass and porcelain exteriors from the wood. The *slosh* of the Long Island Sound, water beating against boats and shore, is a constant in the background. In most of the other boats—with names like *Well Deserved*, *Privacy*, *Good Life*—there is peace.

But inside the *Elizabeth*, there is persistent unrest. The boat is a sixty-four-foot cruiser, equipped with a full kitchen, two baths, two bedrooms, and enough extra space to sleep a total of twenty people. Tonight there are only six, though. It's a small party—my parents wouldn't have let me throw a big one. Everybody is asleep, I think, except for me.

I've been staring at the clock for twenty minutes now, listening to this annoying *thump, thump, thump* against the hull. It's late August. The air outside is already cool, and the water is undoubtedly frigid. Connecticut's like that; the water gets warm for a month or so in July, but near the end of the summer it's already cold again. Sometimes it seems like there are only two seasons around here: winter and almost winter.

Regardless of the water's temperature, I'm pretty certain there's a fish out there, stuck between the dock and the boat, pounding against the fiberglass, trying to free itself. The noise has been going on for what feels like forever. It woke me up at exactly 1:57 a.m., and it's starting to drive me nuts.

I finally can't take it anymore. *Thump. Thump-thump.* If it's a fish, it's a *stupid* fish.

"Hey? Do you hear that?" I say to my best friend and stepsister, Josie, who's sleeping beside me on the fold-out couch in the front of the boat, her highlighted dirty-blond hair plastered against the side of her face. She doesn't respond, just continues to snore softly, passed out since a little after midnight from an alcohol-marijuana combination that sent us all to bed before the late show came to an end. That's the last thing I remember before falling asleep: trying to keep my eyes open, mumbling to Josie that we had to wait for 1:37 a.m., which is exactly when I was born, before we fell asleep. Nobody made it. At least, I know I didn't.

I stand up in the near darkness. The only light in the boat is coming from the TV, where there's an infomercial for the SuperMop! running with the sound turned off.

"Anyone awake?" I ask, still keeping my voice low. The boat rocks against the waves coming in from the Long Island Sound. *Thud-thud-thud.* There it is again.

I look at the clock. It's 2:18. I smile to myself; I've officially been eighteen for over a half hour.

If it weren't for the thumping, the rocking of the boat would feel like being tucked inside a lullaby. This is just about my favorite place in the world. Being here with my friends makes it even better, if that's possible. Everything seems peaceful and calm. The stillness of the evening feels almost magical tonight.

Thump.

"I'm going outside to liberate a fish," I announce. "Somebody please come with me."

But nobody—not one of them—even stirs.

"Bunch of selfish drunks," I murmur. But I'm only kidding. And anyway, I can go outside by myself. I'm a big girl. There's nothing to be scared of.

I know it sounds hypocritical, since we've been drinking and smoking, but it's true: we're good kids. This is a safe town. Everyone onboard has grown up together in Noank, Connecticut. Our families are friends. We love each other. Looking around at all of them—Josie in the front of the boat, Mera, Caroline, Topher, and Richie in sleeping bags on the floor in the back—life inside the *Elizabeth* feels like a hazy dream.

Elizabeth Valchar. That's me; my parents named this

boat after me when I was six years old. But that was a life-time ago. A few years before we lost my mother, before my dad married Josie's mom. My dad got rid of a lot of my mom's stuff after she died, but he was always adamant about keeping the boat. See, we have so many happy memories here. I always felt safe here. My mom would have wanted it this way.

Still, it can be eerie so late at night, especially outside. Other than the sloshing of the waves, the dull thumping against the hull, the night is dark and silent. The smell of ocean salt water, algae dried onto all the thick rock formations this close to shore, is so overwhelming that, if the wind catches it the right way, it can almost make me nauseated.

I'm not particularly keen on trying to figure out where the mystery noise is coming from all by myself, even though I'm almost certain it's just a fish. So I give Josie one more try. "Hey," I say louder, "wake up. I need your help." I reach out to touch her, but something stops me. It's the oddest feeling—like I shouldn't be disturbing her. For a minute, I think that I must still be drunk. Everything feels kind of fuzzy.

Her eyelids flutter. "Liz?" she murmurs. She's confused, obviously still asleep. For a second there's a flash of something—is it fear? Am I freaking her out?—in her gaze. And then she's out again, and I'm standing by myself, the only person awake. *Thud-thud-thud.*

The docks are like a wooden jigsaw puzzle. Waves break in from the ocean, and by the time they reach the Sound they're usually gentle enough, but tonight they seem stronger than normal, rocking us all to sleep like a bunch of babies. Despite my attempts to be brave, I feel small and afraid as I tiptoe out the open sliding glass door, my shoes making light *clacking* sounds against the fiberglass deck of the boat. Each arm of the docks has only two overhead lights: one at the middle and another at the very end. There is no visible moon. The air is so chilly that I shudder, thinking what the water must feel like. Goose bumps rise on my exposed flesh.

I stand on deck, frozen, listening. Maybe the noise will go away.

Thump. Nope.

It's coming from the stern, between the dock and the boat, like something heavy and alive, persistent, stuck. We're the last boat on this arm of the dock, which means the back of the *Elizabeth* is almost fully illuminated by the light. I don't know why I feel the need to be so quiet. The noise from my shoes against the deck is jarring, every footstep making me cringe, no matter how carefully I step. I make my way along the side of the boat, holding tightly to the railing. Once the sound is directly beneath me, I look down.

Wet. It's the first word that comes to mind before I scream.

Soaked. Waterlogged. Facedown. Oh, shit.

It isn't a fish; it's a person. A girl. Her hair is long and so blond that it's almost white, the pretty, natural color shimmering beneath the water. The wavy strands, moving back and forth like algae, reach almost to her waist. She's wearing jeans and a short-sleeved pink sweater.

But that's not what's making the noise. It's her feet; her boots, actually. She's wearing a pair of white cowgirl boots, encrusted with gemstones, steel-toed decadence.

The boots were a birthday gift from her parents. She'd been wearing them proudly all night, and now the steel toe of her left boot is lodged awkwardly between the boat and the dock, and with each passing wave it's kicking against the side, almost like she's trying to wake people up.

How do I know all this? Because the boots are mine. So are the clothes. The girl in the water is me.

I scream again, loud enough to wake everyone for a mile around. But I get the feeling nobody can hear me.

Two

I've been sitting on the dock for how long—hours? Minutes? It's hard to tell. I stare down at myself, stuck in the water, my body waiting for someone living to wake up and discover me. It's still dark.

I've been crying. Shaking. Trying to come up with any possible explanation for what's happened tonight. For a while I tried to wake up myself, convinced I was having a nightmare. When that didn't work, I went back through the open door of the boat—making no attempt to be quiet this time—and tried to wake everyone else. I stood in their faces and shouted. I tried to shake them, to slap them; I stomped in my boots and cried for someone, *anyone*, to open their eyes and see me. Nothing. When I touched them, it was like there was a thin layer of invisible insulation between my hand and their bodies. Like I simply could not reach them.

Now I'm outside again, looking at my body. I'm officially freaking out.

"Elizabeth Valchar," I say out loud, in the sternest voice I can muster, "you cannot be dead. You're sitting on the dock. You're right here. Everything is going to be okay."

But there is doubt in my voice, which trembles as I say the words out loud. I feel so young and alone, so incredibly helpless. It is beyond a nightmare. It's like a hell. I want my parents. I want my friends. I want anyone.

"Actually, it's not going to be okay."

I look up, startled. There's a boy standing beside me. He can't be older than sixteen or seventeen.

I put a hand to my mouth, jump to my feet, and clap my hands in excitement. "You can see me! Oh yes! You can hear me, too!"

"Obviously," he says. "You're standing right in front of me." He looks me up and down. "You were always so hot," he says. Then he glances at my body in the water. In a voice that almost makes him sound pleased, he says, "But not anymore."

"Excuse me? Wait—you can see her, too?" We both stare at my body. All of a sudden I feel exhausted and very cold. Beneath the light on the dock, I can make out enough of the boy's face to realize that I know him. But for some reason, I can't remember his name. My mind is fuzzy. I'm so tired.

"Obviously," he repeats.

I bite my lip. It doesn't hurt. I take a deep breath and try to blink away my tears. As I'm doing so, the action feels ridiculous. I've already been crying. Something awful is happening; why am I embarrassed for this boy to see me crying? If there was ever a time to cry, it's right now. "All right. *Obviously* something strange is going on. Right?"

He shrugs. "Not strange, really. People die every day."

"So you're saying . . . I'm"—I can barely force the word from my mouth—"dead."

"Obvi—"

"Okay! Okay. Oh Jesus. This is a nightmare. It has to be. This isn't really happening." I stomp my foot in frustration laced with panic. My boots are a shade too tight; pain shoots up my calf, stinging all the way to my hamstring. Pain! My feet hurt! I must be alive if I can feel it, right?

"I can't be dead." I put my hands on his shoulders. "My feet are aching. I feel it. And I can feel you. I couldn't really feel them in there," I say, meaning everyone on the boat. "Can you feel me?"

"Obviously." He kind of flinches away from me. "I'd actually prefer that you don't touch me, if it's all the same to you."

"You don't want me touching you?"

"Obvi—"

"Say 'obviously' one more time. Go ahead and do it." I try to give him a mean look, but my heart isn't in it. He's the only person who can see me. And the emotion feels confusing; why do I want to be mean? Isn't he trying to help me? But he doesn't want me to touch him. What is his problem?

He just stares at me, his expression blank. He has messy

brown hair. His face is young and smooth, his eyes a penetrating shade of gray. Why can't I remember his name?

"You're Elizabeth Valchar," he says.

I nod. "Well, actually, it's Liz. Everybody calls me Liz." As I'm speaking, I get the strangest feeling—it's like I'm not exactly sure about anything, not even my name. I have this sense of uncertainty, and it occurs to me that I don't remember much about the night before. I'm sure there was a party; that much is clear from looking around the boat at all the empty beer bottles, the half-eaten birthday cake. But the details are unclear. Did I really have that much to drink?

Before I can question the boy about any of this, he says, "And that's you down there in the water. The very cold water."

I stare at the girl in the water. *That's me. I'm dead.* How? When? I was in the boat all night, wasn't I? I am *so* frustrated that I can't remember exactly what happened. My memory of the previous night is broken into many bits and pieces, each so small and fleeting that I can't force them into any cohesive whole. I remember blowing out my birthday candles. I remember posing for a photograph with Caroline, Mera, and Josie. I remember standing alone in the bathroom, trying to steady myself as the boat rocked in the water, taking deep breaths, like I was attempting to calm myself down. But I can't remember what I was upset about, or if I was even upset about anything at all. Maybe I was just drunk.

When I speak, my voice barely breaks above a whisper. I

can feel myself starting to cry again. "It would appear that way. Yes."

"And you're not moving. You're not breathing." He leans forward to peer at me in the water. "You're white. I mean corpse white."

I look at my bare arms. Standing there beside him, I'm not nearly as horrific a sight as the girl in the sea. I am still put together, still beautiful. "I always had such a great tan."

The thought doesn't make sense to me. Why do I remember being tan? And who needs to be tan at a time like this?

He nods. "I remember. Those are some killer boots, too." He pauses. "So to speak."

"It's okay. It's just . . . they're so pretty." And somehow I feel certain they were very expensive. "You know, I learned in history that the Egyptians used to bury their dead with lots of personal possessions to take with them to the afterlife. Can I take them with me?" I pause. "Is there an afterlife?" I look down at my pricy footwear as I stand there next to what's-his-name. "I'm already wearing them," I murmur. They're *so pretty*? Who cares? They're only boots, for God's sake. And they're pinching the hell out of my toes. I don't want to *keep* them; I want to take them off.

But they look so good. I feel disoriented, overwhelmed, almost like I'm going to pass out. Before I can focus on anything else, the thought continues. *They totally complete the outfit.*

I feel unsteady, like none of this is really happening. It can't be. It's like I barely know who I am. I feel a flicker of new hope that this is all just a bad dream, that I'll wake up, wiggle my bare toes as I lie in my bed, and later on my friends and I will go out for coffee together and we'll all laugh about the crazy nightmare I had.

Except maybe not. The boy shakes his head. "Slow down. You're getting way ahead of yourself." He takes a breath. "I don't want to talk about boots. First of all, aren't you curious as to why I can see you? Aren't you wondering why I can talk to you?"

I nod.

"Take a guess," he says.

I put my face in my hands. My palms feel cool and clammy against my cheeks. "Because I'm not dead. Because this isn't happening." I peer at him from between my fingers. "I'll do anything. Please. Just tell me this isn't real."

He shakes his head. "I can't tell you that. I'm sorry."

"Then what happened? I'm not dead. Do you understand?" I take a step closer to him. I scream as loud as I possibly can, loud enough to wake everyone on the boat, to wake everyone who might be sleeping on all the neighboring boats. "I am not dead!" Something occurs to me. "There were drugs. We were doing drugs, I think. Yes, I remember—we were smoking up. Maybe I did some hallucinogens. Maybe I'm all tripped out, and this is just a side effect."

He raises his eyebrows. He clearly doesn't buy the possibility. "Did you do any hallucinogens last night? Really?"

I shake my head in disappointment. "No. I wish I had, now. I wish I'd eaten more cake, too." I frown. "I don't know how I remember that. I can hardly remember anything. Why is that?"

"You can see me," he says, ignoring my question, "because I'm dead." He adds, as though to drive the point home, "Like you."

A gentle feeling of sleepiness washes over me as he speaks. For a moment, the penetrating cold leaves my body and I feel warm everywhere. Then, just as quickly as the feeling came over me, it's gone. And suddenly I recognize him.

"I know who you are," I tell him. The realization excites me. I want to hold on to it tightly; every new thought making me feel more steady, more in control. It's funny; *of course* I know who he is. I don't know why I didn't remember his name immediately. He's gone to school with me since kindergarten. "You're Alex Berg."

He closes his eyes for a minute. When he opens them, his gaze calm and even, he pronounces, "That's right."

"Yes. I remember you." I can't stop glancing at myself in the water, looking from Alex to my body, unable to feel anything but numb horror. As I'm staring, my right boot—which has been loose on my foot ever since I first saw myself—finally slips off. It fills slowly with water. And then it sinks beneath the surface with a gurgle, disappearing as I reach for it halfheartedly. In the water, my bare foot is exposed: bloated and shriveled at the same time.

Aside from the fact that we went to school together forever, I remember something else about Alex. His face has been all over the newspapers for the past year. Last September, just after school started up again, he was riding his bike home from work after dark—he worked at the Mystic Market, just down the road from my house—when a car struck and killed him. His body was thrown into the sandy brush along the street; even though his parents reported him missing right away, he was thrown so far from the road that they didn't actually find him for a couple of days. It wasn't until a jogger happened to go past, noticed the smell, and decided to investigate that he was found.

"How gross," I whisper. Again, the thought surprises me. What is the matter with me? Aside from the obvious, it's like there is no filter between my brain and my mouth. *Be nice, Elizabeth. The poor kid is dead.* Trying to correct myself, I add, "Well, you don't *look* like you got hit by a car." And he doesn't. Aside from his mussed hair, there isn't a mark on him.

"You don't look like you just drowned a few hours ago." He pauses. "You drowned, right?"

I shake my head. It's the first time it's occurred to me to wonder. "I . . . I don't know what happened. I don't even remember falling asleep. It's like all of a sudden I woke up because I heard a noise outside." I pause. "I couldn't have drowned, Alex. You have to understand that. It isn't possible. I'm a good swimmer. I mean, you know, we practically grew up at the beach."

"Then what happened?" he asks.

I stare at my body. "I have no idea. I can't remember anything. It's like . . . some kind of amnesia or something." I look at him. "Is that normal? Did it happen to you? I mean, can you remember anything from before you . . . died?"

"I remember more now than I did right after I—right after it happened to me," he says. "I'm not an expert or anything, but my guess is that it's normal for your memory to be sort of fuzzy for a while. Think of it this way," he explains. "People usually get amnesia after some kind of a trauma, right?"

I shrug. "I guess so."

"Well, death is one hell of a trauma, isn't it?"

"Dead. Shit." I bite my lip and look at him. "I'm sorry, Alex. I just can't believe it. It's a dream . . . right? I'm asleep, that's all. You aren't really here."

He stares at me. "If it's a dream, why don't you pinch yourself?"

I stare back. I feel so small and desperately sad, I can barely speak. But I manage to shake my head a little bit, to coax a single word from my mouth. "No."

I don't want to pinch myself. I'm afraid that if I do, I won't wake up. Deep down, I know I won't wake up.

I take a deep breath. I can feel my lungs filling with air; I *feel* alive.

"You're definitely a goner." He's so flippant about it, so matter-of-fact, that I almost want to slap him.

"Okay. Let's say, for the sake of argument, that this is all real. If I'm actually dead, why don't you prove it?" I narrow my eyes in defiance at him. "Seriously."

He's amused. "The sight of your corpse floating in the water isn't proof enough for you?"

"I'm not saying that. I'm saying there's another explanation. There has to be."

"Put your hand on my shoulder," he says.

"I thought you didn't want me to touch you."

"I don't. But I'm making an exception."

"Why don't you want me to touch you?"

"Would you just—"

"No. I want to know, Alex. Why don't you want me to touch you?" And then I can't help myself; the words are coming out before I have a chance to think about them. "A boy like you? You're a nobody. I'm *Elizabeth Valchar*. Any guy would give his pinky finger to have me lay a hand on him."

Why am I treating him this way? We're here together, with no one else in the world to talk to, and I'm being mean to him.

He stares at me for a long time, but he doesn't answer. I know I sound conceited, but it occurs to me that what I'm saying is true. That's right—I'm pretty. Beautiful, actually.

Alex stares past me, at the water. "You say you feel like you have amnesia. But it's interesting what you *can* remember. You know I was a nobody. You know you were popular." He brings his gaze back to me. "What else do you remember?"

I shake my head. "I don't know."

He shrugs. "It doesn't matter. You will eventually."

"What does that mean?" I demand.

But he doesn't answer me. Instead, he says, "Just do it, Liz. Put your hand on my shoulder."

So I do. Then he closes his eyes, which leads me to do the same. I feel like my whole body is being sucked into a gelatinous vacuum. I almost yank my hand away from his shoulder, but just as I'm about to pull it back the vacuum is gone, replaced by—oh God—the cafeteria of my high school.

It's crowded with students, but right away I spot my old table: it's next to the potato bar, on the far end of the cafeteria near the double doors leading to the parking lot.

"There you are," Alex says, pointing at me. "You and the cool crew."

I can see myself; it's almost like being in reality, except not. There I am, and here I am, watching. I'm sitting with my closest friends: Richie, Josie, Caroline, Mera, and Topher. They were all on the boat with me last night. They're still inside right now, sleeping.

"Oh God," I murmur, "look at my hair." Even as the words are leaving my mouth, I know they sound ridiculous.

"Your hair is fine." Alex sighs. "It's exactly the same as everyone else's."

I realize that he's right: my girlfriends and I are all wearing our long blond hair with the sides pulled back, a slight pouf at the top of our heads, the result of a good twenty minutes of painstaking teasing and hairspraying in the morning. The look is called a bump, I remember. It was popular a few years ago. The only variation on the look is Caroline's hair, which is decorated with red and white ribbons, whose shades exactly match the colors of her cheerleading uniform.

"What year is this?" I ask. "We can't be older than—"

"Sixteen. This was sophomore year. You know how I can tell?"

"How?" I hate to admit it, but even though we might be ghosts, even though I know nobody can see us, I feel awkward being here with Alex. It's as though I'm afraid my friends will look over at any moment and see me with him, and immediately brand me as an outcast. My God—what would Josie say?

Why do I feel like this? And what kind of a person was I, anyway? I know that I was popular, but it's so odd—I don't remember exactly why, or what I was like in my everyday life. And all of a sudden, there's a part of me that really, really doesn't want to know.

Alex stares at us. "I know we can't be older than that, because I'm still alive." He nudges me. "Here I come."

I watch as he walks into the room alone. He's carrying his lunch in a plain brown paper bag.

"Why didn't you just buy your lunch?" I ask. "Nobody brown-bags it in high school."

He gives me an exasperated look.

"What?" I ask. It seems like a perfectly legitimate question to me.

"It's four dollars a day to eat lunch at school," he says. "We didn't have the money."

I gape at him. "You didn't have four dollars a day?"

"No. My parents were strict. They were really tight with money. If I wanted to spend something—even to buy lunch at school—I had to earn it myself. The Mystic Market, where I used to work, paid minimum wage." He shakes his head. He almost seems to pity me. "You don't know how good you had it. Not everyone just gets whatever they want handed to them. And besides, I wasn't the only one who brought his lunch." He points. "Look."

We follow Alex across the room, to an empty table not far from me and my friends. At another table nearby, also sitting alone, is Frank Wainscott. Frank is a year older than we are, which would put him in eleventh grade here. He has bright red hair and freckles. He wears a blue T-shirt and ill-fitting jeans that are too short for his legs. And he is, I remember, a *major* dork. Like Alex, Frank has brought his own lunch. But on the outside of his brown bag, somebody—presumably his mother—has written his name in black marker and drawn a *heart* around it. I almost cringe with embarrassment for him.

As Frank unpacks his lunch, Alex and I start to eavesdrop on my friends.

Caroline is gazing longingly at a shiny red apple, passing it back and forth between her hands. "I've already eaten six hundred calories today," she says. "How many calories are in an apple?"

"Eighty," I say to myself. *How do I know that?*

"Eighty," my living self informs her. "But apples are good, Caroline. They have fiber and nutrients. Go ahead. Eat it."

She gazes at my willowy body, visibly very thin even though I'm sitting down. I'm wearing a sleeveless shirt, my arms skinny and muscular. "You don't have to worry about getting fat, Liz. You've got good genes."

Josie snatches the apple from Caroline's hands. "I thought you were trying to stick with twelve hundred calories a day. If you eat this, that's almost seven hundred calories right there. And you know you'll be starving after cheerleading practice."

Caroline frowns. "I'll eat a light dinner."

"The last time I ate dinner at your house," Josie reminds her, "your mom made homemade pizzas. On white bread." She pauses for emphasis. "With *full-fat* cheese." Josie takes a big bite from the apple herself. "I'm doing you a favor," she tells a forlorn Caroline, talking with her mouth full. "Trust me, you'll thank me later." Josie looks around. "Think they've got peanut butter up there? I love apples with peanut butter."

"You," I inform my stepsister, "are going to get chunky if you don't watch it. Peanut butter has two hundred calories for every two tablespoons, and it's all fat."

Josie stops midchew, staring at me. "You heard what Caroline said. We've got good genetics."

I don't respond. I just kind of glower at her, silent. The rest of the table falls into a momentary hush, the awkwardness almost palpable.

"I thought she was your stepsister," Alex says to me.

"She is."

"Then why would she say you've got good genetics? You aren't blood related."

"Right. *I* know that. But Josie thinks . . . oh, never mind. It's ridiculous."

"I want to know," he presses. "Josie thinks what?"

I shake my head. "Come on, Alex. You've lived in Noank your whole life, right? You must have heard the rumors." But I don't have a chance to expand beyond that.

Alex and Frank are sitting at the only empty tables in the whole lunchroom. Alex starts to unpack his lunch. He slouches in his chair, almost like he's trying to seem invisible. Frank does the same.

It works for Alex, but not for Frank. Right away, Topher notices him.

"Hey, look. It's our favorite mama's boy." Topher's grin is

wide, his teeth an almost glowing white. "Frankie," he calls, "what did Mama pack you today?"

Frank doesn't answer.

"He's being so mean," I mutter. "Why is he doing that?"

"Because he can. Because he's a bully," Alex replies.

"But Frank's not doing anything wrong. He isn't bothering anyone."

Alex stares at me, like he can't believe my confusion. "Liz, the lunchroom was like a war zone. You and your friends used to sit at that table like you were the freaking rulers of the school." He pauses. "Keep watching."

Caroline, Josie, and I exchange subtle smiles as Topher continues to rip on Frank, but we don't say anything. Only Richie looks uncomfortable.

"Come on," he says to Topher. "Cut the kid a break already. It's not his fault that—"

"Oh my God." Topher leans his chair back on two legs, clapping his hands.

"I wish he would fall on his stupid face," Alex says quietly to me.

He doesn't. Instead, he rights himself, gets up, and strolls over to Frank's table. Topher turns a chair around, straddles it backward, and sits down next to Frank. He starts picking through the contents of Frank's lunch.

My stomach feels hollow with guilt and shame as I watch my younger self, and all of my friends, giggle while Topher torments Frank.

"Look at this," Topher says, holding up Frank's sandwich for everyone to see. "Mommy cut it into the shape of a *heart*. Does Mommy wipe your bottom for you when you go poo-poo, too, little guy?"

Sitting at the table, Frank's face turns a deep red. I can tell he's trying not to cry. At the next table, Alex is clearly listening, his expression stoic. He's bothered by what Topher is doing to Frank, I can tell. But it would be social suicide for him to get involved.

I put a hand to my mouth. "Alex," I say, "I'm sorry. We were all being mean, I know. But you have to believe me, I don't remember this."

"It doesn't matter if you remember, Liz. It doesn't change what happened."

"But it's not like I really did anything . . . I mean, it was mostly Topher—"

"You're right," he interrupts, "you didn't do anything. You never did *anything* to help him. You wouldn't have dared; it might have made you less cool."

I blink at him. "You didn't do anything, either."

"What was I supposed to do? Speak up and get my ass kicked?" He shakes his head. "No thanks. It was enough work just to keep your friends from making *my* life misera-ble. I wasn't going to get involved with Frank's problems. I had enough of my own, trust me."

For a moment, I'm at a loss for words. Finally, I ask, "You don't like me, do you? Everyone likes me."

He stares at me. "You're right. I don't like you, Liz."

I stare back at him. When I speak, the harsh tone of my voice surprises me. "Then why don't you leave me alone?"

"Take your hand off my shoulder."

So I do. And just like *that*, we're standing beside the boat again, the docks rocking gently beneath us as we glower at each other.

"What are you doing here?" I ask him. "If I'm really dead, then why are you here?"

He shakes his head. "I honestly don't know. Because I'm dead, too, I guess. Because I've been around for a year, just waiting for someone else to show up. Believe me, I don't want to be here either. I'd rather be with *anyone* but you."

For the first time since I've found my body in the water, the truth seems real. It seems indisputable. I am not dreaming. This isn't a nightmare that I'm going to wake up from. I'm dead.

And then something occurs to me—I don't know why it wasn't my first thought. The moment the words begin to come out of my mouth, I can feel myself starting to cry again. Dead people can cry. Who knew?

"Alex," I ask, "are there other people . . . over here? Can we see other people?"

"What do you mean?"

"Other people who are . . . you know . . ."

"Other dead people?" He shakes his head. "I don't think so."

"But you can see me."

"I know. You're my first." He pauses. "Why do you want to know? Why are you crying?"

"Why am I crying?" I wipe my eyes, even though I'm not embarrassed for Alex to see my tears anymore. I think of my parents—my dad and stepmother, Nicole—of my friends inside the boat, wondering when they'll wake up and find me. But more than anything, I'm thinking of my mother. My *real* mother.

"My mom," I tell him. "She died when I was nine. I was just thinking that maybe . . ."

"You'd see her?" He shrugs. "I don't know, Liz. Hey—don't cry, okay?" His tone is less than comforting. If anything, he seems a little annoyed by my display of emotion. "You don't need to feel sad. I'm not an authority or anything, but I get the feeling this situation—you know, being stuck here—is only temporary."

I continue to cry. "And then what?" I demand. "Are you supposed to be my guide or something? Because you're not doing a very good job, if that's the case. You haven't really answered any of my questions." I pause. "Except for the one about my memory. And you only sort of explained it. But other than that, you're horrible." I'm almost hysterical. I don't *feel* dead. I feel alive and helpless and *so* cold. I want to go home. I want my dad and Nicole. And if I can't have them, I want my mom. Where is she? Why isn't she here? And how the hell did I end up in the water?

"This cannot really be happening," I say, even though I know it *is* happening. "It's my *birthday*. People aren't supposed to die on their birthday! Especially not me. I'm Liz Valchar." I'm almost shouting. "I'm very popular, you know! Nobody will be happy about this."

His voice is bone dry. "Yes, Liz. I'm aware of your social status."

"This isn't possible." I shake my head. "No. It's not real."

"Yes. It is." His tone is flat, bored. "Come on. Take deep breaths. Maybe I can . . . maybe I'm supposed to, I don't know, *help* you."

I breathe. I can taste the salt in the air. I can feel the dock swaying beneath my feet, my legs unsteady in my boots. If it weren't for my own body, not ten feet away, everything would seem normal.

"I don't know that much about what's going on here," Alex says. "Nobody gave me a rule book or anything. Pretty much the same thing happened to me that's happening to you. I remember being on my bike, riding home from work. It was a little past ten at night. It started to rain really hard. I could barely see. And then nothing—I woke up in the sand, lying next to my own body." He shudders. "I was a mess."

I wipe my eyes. "You don't remember anything? Not the car that hit you? Not what happened right before? You don't remember hearing or seeing anything?"

He shakes his head. "I told you, nothing." He hesitates. For the first time since we've been together, his tone softens just a bit. "I was alone, Liz. Not like you are. I didn't have anybody to help me. I'm sorry if I've been cynical, but you have to imagine—I've been by myself for almost a year."

"What have you been doing?" I ask. "You're here, so obviously you can go places. Have you seen your family? Your parents?"

He nods. "Sure. I've gone home now and then. But trust me, I'd rather be anywhere else. My house is not exactly overflowing with laughter at the moment. My parents practically haven't left church in months, they're so busy praying for my soul. And when they're home, my mom pretty much stays in bed." He pauses. "When she's not wandering around the house, holding vigils for me, crying."

"I'm so sorry," I whisper.

"It's okay." He half smiles. "Not your fault, is it? Anyway, I can go places, but it's not like there's a whole lot to keep me entertained. For the most part, I've just been staying near the road where I died. And then, all of a sudden—here I am." He shakes his head. "I don't know what I'm doing here. Honestly, I'm almost as confused as you are."

I stare at him. "But we can go places. That's what you're saying. I can go home if I want to."

He nods. "Yes. But you won't want to, not after the first couple of times. It's horrible, watching everyone cry and mope around, watching them suffer. Knowing you can't reach out to them and make them feel better, or even let them know you're all right."

"But we're not all right," I say. "Not really. Are we? I mean, we're trapped."

He appears to think about it. "Yeah," he agrees. "I guess you're right. Trapped."

"And you've just been stranded like this? For a year?"

"Well . . . not exactly. There's something else." He hesitates. "It's like I showed you. You can go into memories. You can go back and see yourself. You know how you don't remember everything from when you were alive?"

"Yes. Why is that happening? Do you know?"

He appears to be thinking. "I'm not sure. But I have a theory."

I stare at him. He doesn't say anything for a while.

"Well?" I demand. "Are you going to tell me, or are we just going to stand here?"

He sighs. "Okay. But it might sound strange. Like I said, it's just a theory."

"Tell me."

"Well, we're here. On Earth. We're not . . . somewhere else."

"What do you mean? That we're not in heaven?"

Alex nods. "Heaven, hell . . . you're getting ahead of yourself. My point is, we're stuck here for some reason. We both died young. And we both want to know why, right?"

"Of course," I say.

"Well, when I really started to think about what I could

remember, something occurred to me. It was like I could only remember mundane facts. I knew who people were. I knew about some things that had happened. But I couldn't remember anything . . . significant. Not at first." He takes a deep breath. "I think we're supposed to learn something. Not only about how we died, but I think we're supposed to—I don't know, to gain some kind of deeper understanding. Before we can move on." He pauses. "Does that make any sense?"

Nothing makes sense to me right now. But I don't want to admit that to him. "Okay," I say. "You've been dead for almost a year. What have you learned so far?"

He averts his gaze. "A few things."

"Did you see what happened to you the night you died?"

"Not yet."

"What?" I almost screech the words. "After a whole *year*?"

"It might be different for you! I don't know. I'm just telling you what I think, okay?"

I glare at him. The last thing I want is to remain in some kind of Earthly limbo for the next year. There has to be something more. Doesn't there?

"I can tell you other things," Alex offers.

I'm so frustrated that I feel like I might start crying again. "Like what?"

"Well," he says, "do you feel tired at all?"

I nod. "Really tired."

"Yeah, me, too. But you'll learn—at least, this is what it's like for me—that you can't sleep. Something different happens instead."

"What? I'll go into more memories? I'll remember things?" The sun is starting to come up. Time is moving quickly; it feels like I've been out here for ten minutes, when it must have been hours.

Alex scratches his head, thinking. "Well, you know how they say that, when you die, your life flashes before your eyes?"

I nod.

"It's kind of like that. Except it's much . . . slower. You get really tired, like you're going to fall asleep. You close your eyes. But you don't sleep. Instead, you see things."

"What kinds of things?"

"Things from your life. Sometimes they're just random memories. Other times, they're more important. It's like you're putting together a puzzle. You watch things happen, and when you're seeing them from the outside, you can understand them better. It's like what I showed you in the cafeteria."

"But you don't know who hit you yet?"

"No. Not yet."

I pout. "Are you even close to finding out?"

He nods. "Yes. I'm close." Then he adds, "But it might be different for you. I don't know."

"Oh, you're a big help. Thanks a whole lot."

"Want some real advice?" he offers.

"Oh, please. You've done so much already." My voice simmers with irritation and sarcasm. I'm over the shock of my initial rudeness. Alex and I are not a good mix. There's no point in pretending to get along, is there?

Alex nods at the boat. "There you go. Things are about to get interesting."

I turn around. Standing on the deck, wearing nothing but a pair of plaid boxer shorts, is my boyfriend, Richie Wilson.

"Richie," I say, starting to cry again. I raise my voice to shout at him. "Richie!"

"He can't hear you." Alex sighs. "You aren't the sharpest sheep in the barn, are you?"

"That's not even the right metaphor," I snap, my attention still focused on Richie. "It's sharpest *pencil* in the *box*."

"Right." Alex nods. "Except you *are* a sheep. I'm not stupid, I just adjusted the metaphor to fit your persona—"

"Oh, shut up. Richie!" I scream again. Alex shakes his head.

"Liz?" Richie calls softly, looking around. He wraps his arms around himself, shivering in the cool morning air. "Liz, are you out here?"

I scream his name, over and over again, until I'm so tired that I feel like I'm going to collapse. He obviously can't hear me.

Richie looks around for a few more minutes. He doesn't

seem concerned; why should he? My parents' house is less than a two-minute walk from our boat. For all he knows, I woke up early and went for a run. The last thing he's thinking, I'm sure, is that I'm standing less than ten feet away, practically right beside him. Or that I'm also in the water, beneath him.

He waits a few more seconds. Then he walks inside, probably to go back to sleep, sliding the door shut behind him. Richie and I have known each other since we were toddlers. We grew up on the same street. We've been a couple since seventh grade. We love each other. Somehow, from deep within myself, I know all this. These aren't the kinds of facts that I can imagine ever forgetting.

"Damn it," I whisper, watching as he slips back inside the boat, wiping more tears from my eyes.

"Don't worry," Alex says.

"Why not?"

"He'll know soon enough."

"He'll never be the same," I murmur. "None of them will."

"You're probably right. How will any of your friends function without you?"

I decide to ignore his sarcasm for the moment; I have more important things to deal with. "What do we do now?" I ask. The sun is growing brighter, reflecting against the water. Beyond the boat, beyond the docks, I can see the town of Noank beginning to illuminate.

"We wait," he says. His gaze follows mine. Together, we

stare at our little town, where everything used to feel so safe. "It won't be long now," he says, "before someone finds your body."

"And then what?" I whisper.

He pauses, considering the question. "Then we find out what happened to you."

"We do?"

"Yeah." Another pause, this one longer than the last. "Maybe."

Three

But it does take a while for someone to find me. And when it finally happens, it's terrible. Alex and I waited until the sun was all the way up before we decided to go inside the boat. I don't know why it took us so long to get the idea. As we were sitting on the dock, watching my friends move around inside, I said, "I wish I could hear what they're talking about in there."

"Oh, we can," he said. "We can go in."

I looked at him, not saying anything. I just got up to walk inside.

But when I reached the sliding glass doors to the boat, I stopped. "The doors are closed, boy genius," I said. "How am I supposed to get in?"

"You're dead, Einstein," he replied drolly. "You don't exist in the physical world anymore. The rules don't apply. Just walk through."

I hesitated. I reached out a hand, tentatively, and gasped when I saw that Alex was right—there's a feeling of coolness where the door is, but my hand goes right through.

My physical body is still in the same place, lodged awkwardly between the boat and the dock, except now both of my boots are long gone. And I'm not looking so hot anymore. Not that I was when I first saw myself, but a few more hours in the cold salt water has not been kind to my skin. I'll leave it at that.

Alex follows me onto the deck of the boat. "Go ahead," he says. "Walk in."

So I do. Just like that. Like there's no door or anything. As terrified as I am, I can't help but feel the slightest bit exhilarated. I'm *supernatural*.

As we step into the boat, all of my friends are huddled in the back, sitting quietly together.

"Should we go to her house and check?" Mera asks.

"Good timing," Alex says. "They're talking about you."

We take a seat on the steps and watch. I stare at Richie, who's sitting right across from me on a sofa. My purse is in his lap. My cell phone is in his hand. So they've obviously gotten this far—they know I'm missing, and Richie looks worried now. He probably knows I wouldn't go home without taking my purse. And there's *no way* I'd leave my phone.

It's like my umbilical cord to the outside world, has been since I first got one at age ten. I'm lost without it.

Oh, Richie. I want to go to him, wrap my arms around him. I close my eyes for a moment, imagining his touch.

All of a sudden the uncomfortable feeling of cold is yanked away, and I feel like I've been submerged in a warm bath, except I can breathe. It's just like before, when I put my hand on Alex's shoulder and followed him into his memory of us at school. My surroundings kind of swirl into oblivion, and I find myself standing at the edge of the community playground in Noank. Two grown women are side by side in front of me. They're each pushing toddlers on swings. One boy, one girl. The girl is me. I can't be older than two.

"She's adorable," the little boy's mother says, nodding at me. She smiles at my own mom.

My mom! I stare at her, trying to take it all in. Aside from photographs, it's the first time I've seen her in nine years. I want to hold on to her, to curl up beside her, to hear her whisper in my ear. My whole body aches with the knowledge that I can't do any of those things. I want to tell her how much I love her, even though she left us. Even though she left *me,* her little girl. I was nine years old and she left me alone, to be raised by my father, at least until he and Nicole got married.

I used to feel so angry that she'd let herself die. But I recovered from my loss; I forgave her. Now, more than anything, all I want is to be with her—to *really* be with her—even if it means I'm not alive anymore.

My mother was only twenty-four when she had me, which would put her in her late twenties here, and she's beautiful. She has long blond hair, almost exactly the same shade as mine. She's tall at nearly six feet. She gives the other woman a nervous smile. I never remembered that much about my mom, even when I was alive, but I do remember my father telling me she was always very shy around strangers.

"I'm Lisa," my mom says, "and this is Elizabeth. My husband and I just moved from the far side of Mystic into his father's old place, on High Street."

"Oh! You're our new neighbors!" The other woman is not nearly as shy, not around strangers or anyone else. "I knew I recognized you. I'm Amy Wilson. This is my little boy, Richie."

For an instant, I see Amy's gaze flicker down the length of my mother's body. Despite her height, she can't be more than a hundred and twenty pounds. Her hip bones are visible through her shorts. And even though she's smiling, obviously happy to have met a neighbor, there is something sad about my mother's gaze. She looks tired; there are dark half-moons beneath her eyes. She looks hungry.

Already, Richie and I are friends. I smile as I stare at us, tears pricking the corners of my eyes. We hold hands as we swing. He has dark curly hair and full red lips. Someday they'll be my first kiss, when we're both four years old. And then again, when we're both twelve—he'll be my first *real* kiss. The only person I've ever kissed like that. As I stand there watching the four of us, I realize that I don't remember everything about Richie and me, especially anything too recent. But I remember enough to know that I loved him. I'm sure of that.

"Liz? Hey—are you there?" It's Alex's voice. Like before, I feel the sensation of being sucked through a vacuum. As quickly as it began, the memory is over.

"I saw him," I say, breathless. "And I saw my mom, and Richie's mom. We were toddlers."

Alex doesn't seem surprised. Again, he's blasé. "Really? You saw all that?"

I nod. I'm still crying. It feels like I'm never going to stop. My breath is ragged; I'm overwhelmed with emotions that are coming so quickly I barely have time to process them. It's all too much for one girl to comprehend, on what would have been such a lovely summer morning. "I was looking at Richie, thinking about him, and all of a sudden there I was. It was the first time we met, on the playground."

"Oh." Alex blinks. "How nice for you." But then he pauses. "They won't all be good memories, Liz. You know that, right?"

I cross my arms. "Why would you say something like that? I was happy for a second, and you had to go and ruin it." I feel defensive, even though I'm not sure why. All I know is that Alex Berg is not turning out to be my favorite person on this plane of existence. "What's wrong with you? I'm *dead*, Alex. It's already a pretty bad day."

"All right, don't have a conniption." His tone is annoyingly light, like this is all just a distraction to him. "I wanted you to be prepared. That's all."

I shrug. It doesn't really matter; I've just seen my mom again! And she was so young, so . . . alive. She was touching me, taking care of me. Loving me. Her only little girl.

"What did I look like?" I ask Alex. "You know, when I spaced out just now?" The feeling of intense coldness has returned. I don't think I'll ever get used to it.

Alex only shrugs. "It was nothing weird. You were just kind of staring at him. At Richie, I mean."

"Oh." I pause. "For how long?"

"A few minutes."

"Really?" I ask. It didn't feel like that long. "What did I miss?"

"Well, they sent Mera up to your house to look for you."

The words are barely out of his mouth when we hear a very loud scream coming from outside.

All of my friends sit up straighter. They look scared. For a moment I study their faces, trying to figure out if any one of them looks different, maybe a little guilty. But as quickly as the idea materializes, I dismiss it. These are my best friends. Nobody killed me.

But then, how is it possible that I drowned?

Mera doesn't stop screaming, not even after my friends have gone outside after her. And then I hear them, all of them, reacting as they see me.

It's pure horror. I close my eyes.

"Do you want to go out there?" Alex asks, his tone tentative. He already knows the answer.

I shake my head. When I speak, the words come out fast and frantic. "I want to go home. You said I can go home. How do I do that?"

"They'll be calling your parents soon, Liz." He shakes his head. "It's not a good idea."

I stare at him. Who is *he* to tell me what I should and shouldn't do right now? "I don't care. I want to go home."

"But do you really want to see that? I'm telling you, it will break your heart."

"Now," I tell him firmly. "Before it's too late. Before they get the call."

"Okay . . . ," he says, obviously reluctant. "It's just like earlier, when you went into the memory with me. Just close your eyes, and imagine that you're already home." He pauses. "Do you want me to come with you?"

My breath is shaky. I don't want him with me; I don't even *like* him. But more than that, I don't want to be alone.

"Yes," I admit. "Will you come?"

He almost shudders. "You'll have to touch me again."

"Oh, how terrible for you." With force, I clasp my hand onto his shoulder. "Close your eyes," I order. "Let's go."

My parents are still asleep in bed. I call them my parents; I've been calling my stepmom, Nicole, "Mom" for the last eight years, which is as long as she's been married to my dad. I know it might seem strange that she fell into the role so quickly—my mom wasn't dead a year before Nicole and my dad married—but I was so young. And like I said, I was angry with my mother for leaving us. Nicole had always been nice to me. And when I got her as a stepmom, I got Josie, too. I had a sister. We were best friends. It was like a slumber party every night.

I try not to think about what's happening on the boat. I stand at the foot of the bed for a few moments, gazing at them while they sleep peacefully, watching their easy breathing, knowing it will likely be their last night like this for a very long time.

My father looks like a bear; he's a big guy, heavy, who likes scotch and cigars and rich food. Even though it's a Sunday, I'm surprised that he's home; I remember him working almost all the time. He's a corporate attorney, which is a pretty high-stress job. Sometimes I think he's a workaholic; he had a mild heart attack when I was only fourteen years old, and he was back at work less than two weeks later.

It's funny; after my mom died, I was always so worried about my father's health. I used to try and imagine what life would be like without him. I think that after losing one parent so young, I was always kind of bracing myself for the other shoe to drop. So to speak.

It never occurred to me—not for a moment—that I could die before my dad. I'm only eighteen! Eighteen-year-olds aren't supposed to die.

But Alex did, and when he was only seventeen. And now me. I can't stop wondering—why are we together? I barely knew him. He was quiet, shy, obviously a loner. Nevertheless, despite our apparent character differences, I have to admit it's much better to have someone to talk to than it would be to go through this all alone, like Alex has been doing for the past year.

As Alex watches me, softly—as though I'm afraid of waking them—I crawl into bed between my parents, on top of the comforter. It's something I haven't done since I was very little, and only with my real parents—never my dad and Nicole—but right now it feels like what I need to do.

I lie between them and listen to their quiet breathing. Just like it was with my friends, I can't really touch them. It's as if there's something invisible preventing me from fully making contact, no matter how hard I try.

I stare at my father's full, aging face, and try to focus on it through my tears.

"I love you, Daddy," I whisper.

Nicole's cell phone rings on her nightstand. I don't have to look to know who it is. Her alarm clock says it's 8:49. Before nine on a Sunday morning, it doesn't take a genius to guess that something's wrong.

"Don't answer," I murmur. "Come on. Don't answer, don't answer, don't answer."

Nicole's eyelids flutter open. "Marshall," she murmurs. That's my dad.

"Hmmm? Who's calling?" He doesn't open his eyes. He yawns. "What time is it?"

I am sobbing now, willing to do anything to keep them from having to hear this news. "I'm right here, Dad," I whisper. I put my hand on his arm, knowing he can't feel it. But even though there's that odd space between us, preventing me from making full contact with him, I can *almost* feel him, and it's enough to bring me some small comfort. I can sense his warmth beneath my touch. I can sense the blood running through his living veins. Oh, Dad. Once is enough to have your heart broken. He's already lost my mother. And now this.

Nicole stretches her arms, reaches leisurely for the phone. She squints at the caller ID. "It's Liz." She glances at my dad. "Why would she be calling this early?"

He yawns again. "Beats the hell out of me. Answer it. See what she wants."

It's Liz? How is this happening? I'm right here—and back there, I'm in the water. Then it dawns on me: whoever's calling is using my phone.

I feel slapped, terrified. It's not fair for things to be happening this way, not fair for my parents to lose this last brief moment of peace before everything bursts into chaos.

Nicole answers the phone, her voice tired but cheerful. "Liz, honey, what is it?"

There's a long moment as she listens. The voice on the other end is male. I recognize it immediately as Richie's.

"Wait—Richie, slow down. You're scaring me. Okay. All right, we will. We'll be right there."

She closes the phone. She stares at my father. Her face is the color of death. I know from experience.

"That was Richie," she tells my dad. "He says the police are on their way to the boat. He says there's been some kind of accident, and we need to go down there right now."

My father sits up. "What kind of accident?"

She shakes her head. "He wouldn't say."

They stare at each other.

"Why did Richie call? He used Liz's phone? Why not Liz or Josie?" my dad asks.

Nicole doesn't say anything at first. Then she puts a hand to her mouth. "Get dressed, Marshall."

I can't watch anymore. I get out of bed and cross the room to Alex, who is standing there wordlessly, waiting. He doesn't seem surprised when I put my hand on his shoulder and close my eyes again.

In an instant, we are on the boat, inside, and outside there is wailing, five voices working all at once, heartbreak upon horror.

There is no place to go that doesn't hurt. There is nothing to do but wait.

Four

The police have called divers. When they arrive, I see that it's two men and two women, dressed in full wet suits. They climb down the ladder at the back of the boat and work together to free my body from the space between fiberglass and wood. While they work, the police—there's a slew of them—push the boat away from the dock to create more room. My body rolls onto its side and then onto its back, from the waves created by all the motion. Then, so quietly, so slowly, the divers hold on to me and guide me toward the rocky shore. Once I'm out of the water, they place me—carefully, as if they're afraid I'll break—into a shiny black body bag. A *body bag*. Me. On my freaking birthday.

My parents see it all. My friends look on, silent and numb. None of them are crying, not now. Nothing feels real.

"Liz?" Alex asks, his voice just a tad beyond indifferent. "You're being so quiet. Are you . . . you know . . . okay?"

I glare at him. "Oh, I'm fantastic. The police just dragged my body from the ocean. I looked like shit. It's my birthday, and I'm dead, and if that weren't bad enough, I'm so bloated and disgusting from being in the water that they probably won't even be able to have an open casket for me. I'm *ugly*. Am I okay? No, Alex, I'm not freaking okay."

"You will be," he says calmly, ignoring my rant. "You'll get used to it." He pauses. "You just died, Liz. Is that really what you're most concerned about? How your body looks right now?"

I bite my lip. It would certainly seem that way, wouldn't it? Was I really that superficial? There's so much else that is more important. I don't know how to respond to him.

I notice Alex's gaze drifting across the crowd to the periphery, where the female divers have stripped off their wet suits and are pulling sweats on over their one-pieces. "Look," he says.

The divers are standing together, talking. One of them is crying. She says something to the other woman.

"I want to hear what they're talking about," I tell him. "I'm going over there."

The first woman has short brown hair. Her fingers are pruny from being in the water. She keeps her head down, like she's trying not to let other people notice that she's crying.

"I have a daughter her age," she tells the other woman, a tall blonde. "She lives with her father in Vermont."

The blonde shakes her head. "What the hell happened here?" She lowers her voice a tad. "What the hell kind of parents let their kid throw a party on a boat? With alcohol? And you know there was dope in there. Those kids were wasted last night."

But we weren't! Okay, maybe a little bit. Obviously too much. But my parents didn't know we would be drinking. They never would have *let* us drink. My parents are good people. And like I said, we're good kids. At least, I thought we were; Alex obviously feels differently, and I'm starting to think he might be right. Again, the thought flashes bright as neon in my mind: *how did this happen?*

The blonde shades her eyes with one hand; with the other, she reaches down to grip the crying woman's arm. "You can watch your kids all you want. You can almost never let them out of your sight. It doesn't matter. Things happen for reasons we can't understand."

The brunette wipes her eyes. She gives the blond woman a sharp look. "You mean God?"

The blonde nods. "Giveth and taketh away. We can't control it."

There's a long pause. Then the brunette says, "You know, I think that's a load of bullshit. Those parents could have prevented this if they had half a brain."

And like that—without any sense of motion, without willing it to happen—I'm at my father's side.

My dad and Nicole are standing among my friends. There are four policemen with them. I only recognize one of them— his name is Joe Wright, and he's the town sheriff. It's funny; I have this vague sense that I know him somehow, aside from just recognizing his name and face. So I close my eyes and try to let myself slip into a memory, and almost immediately I see it happening, right there in front of me. There's Richie and me, having a run-in with him just a few months earlier, after the junior prom. We'd gone parking down by the beach at Groton Long Point in Richie's dad's SUV, which he'd borrowed for our Big Night. We were in the back of the SUV, under a blanket, when Joe Wright tapped at the foggy window with his flashlight.

He seemed like a nice enough guy at the time. He took our names and told us to go on home. It was after four in the morning, way past curfew for kids under eighteen in Noank. But it was prom night, so he cut us a break.

Instead of going home, though, we just went up the road, parked in Richie's driveway, and walked down to my parents' boat. We spent the rest of the night in each other's arms, talking about what it would be like to be seniors, about what college we might go to together. There was never any question, not for either of us, that we'd stay together after high school. Richie Wilson was the love of my life.

"So that's your stepmom," Alex says, yanking me out of the memory. He's still at my side.

"Yeah," I say. "Her name is Nicole. She's Josie's mom."

Alex lets out a low whistle. "Man, she is *hot*."

"Would you shut up?" I give him a shove, so hard that he almost loses his footing on the dock. Not that it would matter. What's the worst that could happen to him at this point?

"How can you treat all of this so lightly?" I demand. "These are people's lives. My parents, my friends—their lives are probably ruined."

Alex gives me a look. "Somebody sure thinks highly of herself."

"Alex. They just found my body in the water."

He nods. "That's true. But they'll move on eventually."

I look at my father. His gaze is lowered. I can't imagine what he must be thinking. "No, they won't," I say. "Not all of them. Not my dad."

"Death is a part of life," Alex murmurs. "Everyone dies."

"Not like this." I look toward my body, zipped and concealed on the shore. Why are they just *leaving* it there? Why aren't they taking it somewhere, like, now? *Small-town cops*, I think to myself, *are incompetent*. What do they know? It's not like there's ever any real crimes in Noank for them to solve.

A local news crew has arrived. People from the other boats are awake and staring, hands over their mouths. Looking past the docks, I can see my neighbors standing on their front porches or peeking out from their windows. Watching.

Fascinated. It's probably like a movie to them, something to dish about over coffee all morning, a gruesome story to share with their friends who might have missed the big show. Beyond the latest hot gossip, people in Noank care about *things* above all else. They might be upset that I've died, sure, but I'd bet anything that they're all wondering what my death will do to their property values.

Joe Wright looks like he's doing his best to keep things from dissolving into total chaos. He's gathered my friends and my parents on the front deck of the boat, and they're heading inside.

I look at Alex. He nods. "Let's go."

Inside the *Elizabeth*, there's a mess kind of suspended in time: sleeping bags still unrolled on the floor, the coffee pot filled with grinds but no water, empty beer cans scattered on the kitchen countertop. Above the captain's seat there is a photograph, taken only a few months before my mother died. Ironically, it was my stepmom, Nicole, who took the picture—she and her husband were always close with my parents, and Josie and I were always best friends. I'll never forget that day on the boat, both of our original families together and happy for what was probably the last time. At least, we were as happy as we could have been, considering the circumstances. See, my mom was really sick by then. In the picture, I'm eight, almost nine, and am wearing my dad's captain hat. My parents stand on either side of me. We are all smiling. My mother is so thin that her cheeks are sunken into hollows. Her arms are like rails. Any fool could have seen she wasn't well.

Mommy. I want to be with her so badly right now. I would give anything. I close my eyes, trying to imagine her from a better time, before she got so sick.

And like magic, there we are: I stand watching the two of us in the bathroom of the elementary school. I'm wearing a black ballet leotard, pink tights, and pink ballet slippers. My light blond hair is pulled into a tight bun, secured with bobby pins. It must be the evening of a dance recital. When I was a little girl, I took everything: ballet, tap, jazz, gymnastics—even acting lessons with our community theater for a while.

"I'm afraid I'll mess up," I say to my mom; I'm clearly nervous. I'm maybe six years old. My mother is still painfully thin—I don't remember a time when she wasn't—but she looks happy. She always seemed to enjoy my recitals. Beside her, balanced on the lip of the sink, is a makeup bag. She kneels in front of me, her eyes narrowed as she carefully swirls blush onto my young cheeks.

"You won't mess up, honey. You know all the steps. I've seen you do it. You'll be great."

"Can I wear mascara?"

She smiles. "Sure you can."

"Will Daddy be mad?"

"Because I'm letting you wear makeup? No, he won't be mad. You look like a princess. You look beautiful."

"Daddy says I don't need makeup to be pretty."

My mom bites her lip, hard. She fumbles through the makeup bag, pulling out a yellow tube of mascara. "Open your eyes wide," she tells me. "Look up. I'm going to show you how to do this."

After she's finished doing my makeup—blush, mascara, even lipstick and eye shadow—she puts her hands on my shoulders and stares at me. "You're perfect," she says.

"Really?" I fidget in my slippers.

"Yes, really." She kisses me on the tip of my nose. "My perfect little girl."

I want *so badly* to be inside my younger self, to feel her touch. But all I can do is watch.

"Mrs. Greene says it doesn't matter what a person looks like on the outside. She says the only thing that matters is being beautiful on the inside." Mrs. Greene was my dance teacher. I pause, thinking. "But I think it's important to be pretty on the outside, too. Isn't it, Mommy?"

My mother hesitates. "It's important to be pretty on the inside," she says. "It matters a lot, Elizabeth. But you're a girl. It's different for girls." And she gives me another kiss on the nose before she stands up and takes me by the hand, leading me out of the bathroom.

As I follow, I see that my dad is waiting for us in the hallway, where there's a crowd of other parents with their little ballerinas, getting ready for the recital to start. When he sees me, when he notices my heavily made-up face, his own face turns a deep red.

"What are you doing?" he whispers to my mom. He's obviously angry.

"She'll be on stage, Marshall. I want her to stand out."

"She already stands out. She's half a foot taller than everyone else, and she's rail thin." My dad flashes me a forced smile. "Like a real ballerina."

"It's just a little blush." My mother frowns. "It's nothing. Just to bring out the color in her cheeks."

"She looks like a goddamned geisha," my father mutters.

"What's a geisha?" I ask, gazing up at them. "Are geishas pretty?"

My parents stare at each other. My father positively glowers at my mother, who is expressionless now, her blank look defiant and final.

"Geishas are pretty, yes," she tells me, "but not as pretty as you." And she kneels down again, leans close, and whispers in my ear. As I'm watching the three of us in the memory, I have to step closer and strain to hear what she says.

"You're the prettiest girl here," she whispers. "You always will be."

My father walks away from us, into the auditorium.

I've seen enough. I blink and blink, willing myself to be back in the present.

"Where'd you go?" Alex asks. "What did you see?"

"None of your damn business."

He smiles widely. "Well, it's good that you're back. You were about to miss the show."

I start to cry again as my friends quietly find seats inside the boat. I'm crying because I know that this is real, that I'm truly dead, but also because of the aching that remains inside from the memory I've just seen. I'd never realized before that my parents had problems. Everybody's parents fight sometimes. But I get the feeling the tension I witnessed between the two of them—in our whole family, really—was nothing new. As difficult as the memory was to witness, though, it made me want to be with my mother even more.

Everybody's parents fight, I think again. My dad and Nicole fight sometimes. It's not like my parents' marriage was a disaster. Sure, I can remember the rumors clearly, even though I wish I couldn't, but I know they aren't true. No matter what anybody else might think.

"Would you pull yourself together?" Alex asks.

"Shut up."

He raises an eyebrow but he doesn't say anything. Instead, he turns his attention to the scene unfolding inside the boat. Together we watch.

A couple of my friends—Mera and Topher—are openly smoking cigarettes, their fingers shaking, silent tears running down their cheeks. Everyone is white, shocked into paleness, their summer tans nowhere in sight.

Without a word, my stepmom, Nicole, goes first to Mera,

then to Topher, taking both of their cigarettes. She drops one of them into an empty beer bottle and keeps the other one for herself. Nicole quit smoking a few years ago, when my dad had his heart attack. I guess she figures now is as good a time as any to start up again.

Once everybody is sitting down, Joe Wright takes a seat in the captain's chair. He's holding a tiny spiral notepad and a pen. It seems like an impossibly small tool for solving the mystery of how I ended up dead. There's another cop standing beside him, also holding a notepad. His name tag reads SHANE EVANS.

Joe Wright clears his throat. "Okay, kids." He takes a deep breath and rubs an invisible spot on his forehead, like this whole situation is giving him a headache. "Let's start at the beginning, all right? Tell me what happened."

Nobody says anything for a good long minute.

"I know you kids were partying here. It was her birthday, right?"

"Liz." Richie stares at the hardwood floor of the boat. "Her name is Liz."

"And you are? That's a good place to begin, actually—let's get all your names, and you can tell me what you remember from last night. One by one."

"It's fascinating," Alex whispers, as though they might hear us.

"What is?" I can't stop looking at my dad and Nicole. They are both trembling, probably from shock. I would do anything to put my arms around them right now, to really feel them, and to have them realize my touch.

"I've never seen the cool kids in such disarray. Your friends don't even have on makeup. They don't look so hot without it. Don't you think?"

I scowl at him. "When would they have had time to put on makeup? Do you think they're really that shallow?"

"It wouldn't surprise me." He squints. "Especially Josie and Mera. You three were the most superficial people I'd ever met. You know what my friends and I used to call girls like you? Girls who had everything handed to them on a silver platter, who only cared about how they looked and who was dating the most popular guy?"

"What?"

His grin grows wider. "We called you bitches. You girls were straight-up bitches."

The comment stings. Coolly, I say, "Funny, I thought it might be a trick question. I assumed you didn't have any friends." Right away, I'm sorry for saying it. I almost want to apologize, but the silence dangles between us, so palpably uncomfortable, so thick with other emotions, that I don't know what I'd say.

"I had friends," Alex says. "You just didn't know them."

"Who were your friends, Alex?"

"I worked with them. At the Mystic Market." He pauses. "They were older. Mostly college kids. But they were nice. They liked me. They were different from you and your group.

They understood that there was life beyond high school, that there were other things that mattered besides what brand of purse you carried or who you were dating."

I shrug. "But high school *was* life. It was all we knew. So even if those things wouldn't matter forever, they mattered then."

Alex opens his mouth to respond. But before he has a chance to reply with what I'm sure would be another one of his biting observations, Mera starts to talk. As she speaks, my memory of who she is becomes clearer and clearer.

Mera Hollinger: eighteen years old. Blond hair, long and highlighted, just like all of my other friends. She's a swimmer, and a very good one at that. She's also kind of stupid. She's all beauty and athletic prowess, no brains whatsoever. Out of all my friends, I like her the least. I'm almost disappointed that she's the one who found me; aside from her other flaws, Mera can be melodramatic. Once school starts, I'm sure she'll be taking full advantage of the fact that she discovered my body, using every opportunity to tell the story, making sure to mention what I looked like when they pulled me out of the water.

Then there's Mera's boyfriend: Topher Paul, also newly eighteen, who's sitting beside her now, holding her hand. They were the first couple I knew of in our school to have sex, back in the tenth grade. They're joined at the hip. They'll probably get married someday. Topher is a real high school celebrity, a football star, the only son of wealthy parents who dote on him like he's God's gift to the world. He is prone to fits of anger, sometimes difficult to get along with, but deep down he's a nice guy. We have known each other since pre-school.

"We were just having a regular party," Mera says.

"There was nothing out of the ordinary," Topher echoes.

"And you are?" Joe Wright is frantically taking notes; there are visible beads of sweat on his forehead even though it's cool inside the boat.

"Topher Paul. Christopher. My father is Dr. Michael Paul." Topher pauses for effect. "The dentist," he adds. "He's Noank's most popular dentist and oral surgeon."

Joe gives Topher an odd look. He says, his tone dry and sarcastic, "Well, then. I suppose that would explain your beautiful smile."

"His dad's a dentist? I don't see what the big deal is," Alex says, confused.

"Hey, that's my friend," I tell him. "And it kind of is a big deal. His dad is on the board of directors for the country club. And, you know, Topher's mom was Miss Connecticut once, too."

"Hmm. How important and meaningful. She was really contributing to the betterment of society, wasn't she?"

"Just be quiet. I'm trying to pay attention here."

"So it was a normal party," Joe is saying, "and 'normal' for you kids involves drugs and alcohol?" He raises an eyebrow in my parents' direction. "Who bought the alcohol?"

When nobody says anything, Joe lets out a long sigh. "This is serious, now. I need to know where you got the booze."

"It was on the boat," my dad whispers. He squeezes his eyes shut. A single fat tear drips down his white, whiskery cheek. "We keep the bar stocked." He looks up, glances around at my friends. "We trusted them," he says.

Caroline Michaels, who has been sitting silently on the floor until now, finally speaks up. "We weren't that drunk," she says. "Liz wasn't a big drinker. It was just something to do."

Caroline: seventeen years old. As sweet and naive as they come. She is the youngest of four girls. She made head cheerleader at age sixteen. Her claim to fame is the ability to do a triple back handspring, which she does often and with great enthusiasm at football games, flashing her perfect, Lycra-covered ass at the adoring crowd in the bleachers. Her parents travel frequently, and most of the time they go to exotic places like Vienna or Athens or Egypt. She's well known for throwing the most amazing parties—I somehow know this, even though I can't remember anything specific from any of them. It's like somebody has taken my memory and deleted entire sections, simply wiping it clean, while leaving other simple details untouched. The effect is unsettling, frightening, and intriguing all at once. I don't even know who I am. Beyond that, I don't *like* who I seemed to be all that much. And I don't know what happened to make me that way. But I get the feeling I'm going to find out.

"Right," Joe says, writing in his notebook. "And what about the drugs? Pot? Coke?"

"Jesus," Richie blurts. "No coke. Nothing like *that*. A little weed, that's all."

"So you were partying," Joe continues, "getting drunk, getting stoned . . . and then what happened? Someone get in a fight with the birthday girl?"

"No," Richie says. "I don't know what happened. We went to sleep. We all went to sleep."

Richie Wilson: almost eighteen. Also known in school as Famous Richie Wilson. He's my only friend who's never worn braces; his teeth are naturally perfect. He is the smartest person I've ever met. He exudes confidence. I might have been pretty and popular, but I understand—I *always* understood, even in life—how lucky I was to have Richie. He is an all-around nice guy and the love of my life. I feel more drawn to him than anyone on this boat.

Right now, though, his confidence, that self-assured coolness that drew everybody to him, is nowhere in sight. Instead, he looks deflated. He is shaking. Somehow, I know that he's dying to go home, to lock himself in his bedroom and smoke weed until he can barely remember his own name. Richie has a drug problem—it's his major flaw. But it didn't matter much to me; I couldn't help but love him regardless.

"And when we woke up, Liz was gone," Josie says. "We thought maybe she went up to the house, for food or something. She gets spacey when she doesn't eat. She gets hypoglycemic." Josie's gaze flickers to my dad and Nicole. "She's had problems with passing out. She's been in the hospital because of it."

Josie Valchar: seventeen years old, a full six months younger than me. Even though she's my stepsister, she and her mom took the last name when our parents got married. Although some people don't believe we're stepsisters. People who don't know any better. Other than Richie, she has been my best friend since elementary school. Josie believes in ghosts; like her mother, she frequently goes to the Spiritualist Church in Groton. She claims she's always felt a connection with the spirit world, but it's obvious to me, right now, that she's full of it. She's just a scared kid, like the rest of my friends, devastated and horrified. I don't know what she'll ever do without me.

"Hypoglycemic?" Alex asks. "What's that?"

"It's nothing," I say. "It's just low blood sugar. It happens when I don't get enough to eat."

"You mean like diabetes?"

"Sort of. I'm not diabetic, though. But I get dizzy a lot. Like Josie said, sometimes I pass out."

"Well, that's interesting."

"Yeah," I agree, "it is. I was in the hospital last year because I fainted on my stairs. I got a concussion," I say, almost brightly, encouraged that I remember the detail. "And I was drinking last night—I'm not supposed to drink."

He nods. "And now look what's happened. You're dead. Did you learn nothing from health class?"

I give him a cool stare. "It's no wonder you weren't popular. You aren't very nice."

He stares right back. "Being nice doesn't have anything to do with being popular. You of all people should know that."

I close my eyes for a minute. He's right. I should try to be nice. As politely as possible, I say, "Well, I've asked you twice now. Please shut up. I'm trying to listen."

Joe is looking over the notes he's made in his tiny spiral notebook. "So . . . all right. Is everyone telling the same story here? You fell asleep, and when you woke up, Liz was gone."

"That's right," Mera says.

"And then someone decided to go look for her?"

Mera nods. "I did."

"After how long? Ten minutes? An hour?"

My friends stare at each other. Finally, Richie says, "It couldn't have been longer than maybe fifteen minutes. We sent Mera up to the house." He swallows. "But she didn't make it. She walked outside, and she saw Liz right away."

Joe takes a long moment to consider each of my friends. He stares at my parents. I notice a softness to his eyes, a watery quality. This isn't easy for him, either. He knew who I was; I wouldn't be surprised if he remembers me and Richie from that night a few months ago. Two kids in love, steaming up the windows of a car after prom.

"So we've got ourselves a little mystery," he murmurs. "Isn't that something?"

Silence. The calm inside the boat is unnatural, buoyed by silent horror and heartache.

Joe closes his notebook. "All right. That's it for now, kids. I'm going to be in touch with all of you, though. So, you know, don't go too far." He glances at my parents. "Mr. and Mrs. Valchar, we're gonna need you both at the station directly."

They don't say anything. They only nod.

Alex and I follow Joe and his partner, Shane, onto the dock. Once they're out of earshot from the boat, they stop.

"You believe that?" Shane asks.

"Do I believe what? That an eighteen-year-old girl fell into the water and drowned in the middle of the night without anybody noticing?" He takes a long look at my parents' boat. "I don't know. She had a history. I guess we'll see what the medical exam says." He appears to be thinking. "It's probably an accident. That's my best guess."

"But it sounds kinda fishy," Shane prods, "doesn't it? Like a bunch of liars in there with a lousy story they're trying to keep straight."

"Fishy," Joe repeats. "Ha." He pats Shane on the shoulder. "You watch too many *Law and Order* reruns, you know that? This isn't New York City. I'm sure her friends didn't just decide to up and kill her."

Five

Before people knew me as a dead girl, they knew me as a runner. I remember this fact as clearly as I remember my own name or my mother's face. I was on the cross-country team. I wasn't all that fast—I usually clocked around an eight-minute mile—but I could run for hours. And I did; every morning, even during the school year, I'd roll out of bed before sunrise, tug on my running shoes, and go up and down the Sound, along the road leading to Mystic—which is the larger community that neighbors Noank—sometimes all the way to the outskirts of town before turning around to come home. It wasn't unusual for me to do ten miles in a day. It is such a comfort that these memories are still with me, to know that they are ingrained within my being. At any time, I can close my eyes and almost hear the rhythm of my footsteps against the road.

It's funny—my parents used to worry about me, running alone in the mornings like that. Water everywhere, all around us, and they were always worried about my safety on dry land.

For right now, everyone's version of the events from that night seems to point to the conclusion that I drowned. The story is this: I was drunk, had low blood sugar, and I went outside to get some air. I stumbled and fell off the docks. Nobody saw anything. Nobody heard anything.

And people seem comfortable enough with that version of the truth. My parents seem to accept it; my friends seem to believe it. It's the Official Story. Case closed.

But unofficially, Joe Wright is standing in a suit and tie at the back of the funeral home, watching with quiet eyes as the crowd shifts in the room.

Getting around with Alex is easy enough; all it takes is for me to close my eyes as I make some kind of physical contact between the two of us, and he can come with me anywhere. Even though we don't like each other, I can tell that we're both grateful for the company. Regardless, aside from the memories that I visit on my own, when I choose to leave him behind, we've been practically inseparable since the day I died, bonded by an unseen force that I don't have a name for.

We're at my funeral. It's the same funeral home where they held services for my mother when I was nine years old.

"She's not here," I murmur, tears coming to my eyes.

"Who isn't?" Alex asks.

Even though I know nobody can see us, I feel strangely out of place with Alex, both of us so casually dressed among all the mourners in black. I gaze down at my boots. Their gemstones shimmer beneath the light from the chandeliers that hang in the funeral home. They hurt my feet so badly; all I want is to slip into a pair of sneakers, to wiggle my toes freely, but I died with these boots on, and it seems as though they're here to stay. It's weird; I can't feel any pain aside from my feet. I don't understand why.

"My mother," I say.

"Hmm." Alex's gaze drifts across the room. "Everyone else is here, that's for sure."

It's true. As I've reminded him more than once, I was very popular; it looks like practically the whole school has turned up to cry over me. But my close friends have the premium seats. Mera, Caroline, and Topher are seated in the second row, behind my immediate family. The other two—Richie and Josie—are seated with my dad and Nicole. Richie's parents are there, too, a few rows behind my friends, sitting with Caroline's and Topher's parents. I haven't spotted Mera's mom and dad yet, but I'm sure they're here somewhere.

Death is tricky. My personal experience, I've learned, is different from Alex's in a few ways. For instance, I still have sea legs; everywhere I go, even on dry land, I'm bothered by a persistent rocking feeling. And I'm freezing all the time, chilled almost to my bones. It feels like being submerged in cold water. Alex tells me that he feels cold most of the time, too, but more like he's alone in the wind, in a wide-open space. It makes sense, when I think about it: death by sea, death by land. What follows really should be similar. Sometimes, when I concentrate on the taste in my mouth, it almost feels like I'm swallowing salt water.

And it's tricky in other ways. In the first day or so after I died, I had to really concentrate to bring myself into a memory. And when I was watching one, it felt very separate from my consciousness in the present. But what were initially so pronounced as flashbacks into my old life come quicker now, drifting almost like memories unfolding before me, the past and the present beginning to blend together—except that I'm not living the memories this time; I'm only a spectator.

Like my mother's funeral. All of a sudden, in a blink that I'm not anticipating, I see my nine-year-old self sitting in the back row of the funeral home, watching as my father stands before a closed oak casket. Inside the casket, I know, is my mother.

My hair is long and shimmering; I look oddly pretty and docile among so many mourners, their faces somber, an almost palpable grief saturating the room. My head is down. I'm staring at my feet. At nine years old, I am wearing small, black patent leather high heels. At *nine.* Now, at eighteen, this choice of footwear—did my father let me wear those shoes? Did he buy them for me?—seems embarrassingly improper. Who lets their nine-year-old wear heels?

Josie's mother, Nicole, comes up behind me and puts her hands on my shoulders. She leans over to whisper in my ear. "Elizabeth. Sweetheart. How are you?"

When she touches me, I flinch. I look up, gazing in confusion at the crowded room. My face is red and tear streaked. I look like I have no idea what's going on, like a lost little girl who only wants her mommy back. Watching myself, I feel a pang of sadness, of grief so deep that I realize now it never went away, that it has always been with me somewhere inside.

Back then, I knew Nicole as Mrs. Caruso, Josie's mom. And while it feels like a struggle to recall specific events from my childhood, which is overall sort of fuzzy and indistinct in my mind, I remember the basics: At age nine, Josie and I had already been best friends for years. Our parents used to spend a lot of time together before my mother died. Then Josie's dad left. What happened after that between my dad and Nicole almost seemed natural. Years ago, they'd been high school sweethearts. After my mother died, and after Nicole and her first husband got divorced, Nicole seemed to fall seamlessly into my life as a mother figure, and I never thought much about it; it was simply the way things were. My father needed a new wife; Nicole needed a new husband. I never felt like she was trying to replace my mother. And I've never believed any of the rumors that were spread around school, and throughout town, about my dad and Nicole having an affair before my mom died.

Other people believed it, though. People close to me believed. Josie believed. It was a topic she and I tried not to broach much, and I never dared to bring it up with my dad. It occurs to me now that it isn't that I was always certain there was no truth to the rumor; it was that I didn't want to acknowledge the possibility that there *could* be any truth to it.

"I'm okay," I tell Nicole, attempting a smile. It seems obvious, now, how seriously Not Okay I was.

Nicole kneels beside me. She holds my hands. Even as an observer, I can smell her. She's wearing the same perfume she's worn for as long as I've known her.

In an instant, the thought occurs to me—who wears perfume to a funeral?

"Josie is here," she says. "She doesn't want to come in, honey. She's in the hallway. Would you like to come see her?"

The nine-year-old me only nods, fresh tears filling my eyes. *Where's Mr. Caruso?* I wonder. I don't see him anywhere. It's not all that surprising—he and Nicole got divorced a few months after my mom died.

I follow my younger self and Nicole as they walk toward the back of the room and into the hallway. As I'm watching us, I notice several of the funeral attendees shooting glances at Nicole. They're almost glaring at her. She doesn't seem to notice; her arm is around my shoulders, guiding me toward the door as I take shaky steps in my high heels.

Josie stands in the hallway, her back pressed into a corner that is covered in gaudy purple wallpaper.

I can't help but smile when I see her. She is so young, so innocent and pretty. She's missing one of her front teeth. Her hair is pulled into two long, light-brown ponytails. An odd fact surfaces in my mind: Nicole didn't let Josie start highlighting her hair until she was twelve.

We hug each other tightly, holding on for a long time. Her hands are clenched into little fists around my neck. Out of total coincidence, we are wearing the same dress: black and dark green stripes on our full, knee-length skirts, black crushed velvet bodices tight around our tiny waists and chests.

"Josie, honey? Do you have something you want to tell Liz?"

Josie nods. She stares at me, wide eyed. "I wanted you to know," she begins, her voice small and scared, "that you can come to our house whenever you want. You can even sleep over on school nights." She glances up at Nicole. "Right, Mom?"

"That's right." Nicole smoothes her daughter's hair, winding a strand around her finger in thought. "If Liz's dad says it's okay."

"Thank you," I tell her.

"I got you something," Josie adds. She looks at her mother again. Nicole reaches into her white suede purse and removes a long, narrow velvet box. Inside, there's a slim gold bracelet, a single charm dangling from a loop. It's half of a heart.

"Best friends. See?" Josie holds up her left wrist. She's

wearing another bracelet, the matching half of the heart dangling from the chain. Nicole removes my bracelet from the box. Carefully, she puts it on my wrist. Josie and I hold our arms side by side, pressing the hearts together so they form a full heart that says "Best Friends."

"I love it." I smile at her. "Thank you."

"You're welcome." She beams. For a moment she is too cheerful, as though she's forgotten where she is. *It's not her fault,* I think to myself now. *She was only nine.* "Come over soon, okay? We got a new Slip 'n Slide."

Leaving Josie alone in the hallway, Nicole guides me back through the double doors, back to my seat inside the viewing room.

She leans forward to give me a long hug. "We loved your mom so much," she whispers. "And we love you, too."

"Mrs. Caruso?"

"Yes, sweetie?"

I gaze at her, searching her face for answers. "Where is my mom now?"

Nicole doesn't miss a beat. "She's safe, honey." She gives my hands another squeeze. Whispering again, she says, "Next time you come over, I'll show you."

I get a kiss on the forehead. Then she walks away, toward my father.

I leave my younger self and follow her. When I was a child, I didn't have a chance to observe so much; now it seems crucial that I pay close attention. I'm not sure why.

But I'm here, aren't I? There must be a reason for this memory. It's like Alex said: I'm trying to put a puzzle together. But I have no idea what the picture will look like when it's finished, which makes it hard for me to know quite where to start, or what pieces to pay attention to.

"Marshall," Nicole says, putting her arms around him. With her mouth beside his ear, she murmurs, "She'll never be hungry again."

And like that, I'm back at my own funeral, watching as Mera and Topher walk hand in hand toward the front to stare at my closed casket. They are both crying. At eighteen and a half, Mera is older than everyone else—she got held back a year in preschool for what she calls behavior problems, but everyone knows the real problem was that she wasn't potty trained in time for kindergarten. Anyway, for her eighteenth birthday, her parents bought her breast implants. Even if I didn't remember the fact, it would be obvious just from looking at her. To my *funeral,* she's wearing a low-cut black sweater and a push-up bra that really show off the twins.

When she and Topher turn around, Mera notices Joe Wright standing in the back. She nudges Topher and whispers something under her breath.

To anyone else, it could seem suspicious. But Mera didn't have any reason to hurt me. Mera is the epitome of her breast implants: friendly, welcoming, and—at least according to the FDA—harmless. For that matter, I can't imagine Topher killing anyone, either. He can be tempermental, but he's actually a pretty calm guy. He's a senior in high school, and he still has a pet rabbit that lives in his bedroom and is litter-box trained and sleeps beside his bed at night. People like that don't kill their friends.

"Bitches and jerks," Alex says, stretching his legs out in front of himself, crossing his arms behind his head in a casual pose. "Honestly, Liz. How could you be friends with those people?" Then he smacks his forehead, as though it were a stupid question. "What am I saying?" he asks. "You were their leader. You were the worst of them."

"I don't think that's fair," I tell him. "A few of us went to your funeral, you know. Lots of people went."

"Really?" His tone is cool. "I guess you *were* there." But he doesn't seem willing to give me any credit for the fact.

There are still flyers up all over town, posted to the telephone poles. Alex's parents are offering a ten-thousand-dollar reward for anyone with information about what happened the night he died.

"I changed my running route," I tell him. I'm surprised that the memory, from just about a year ago, has come to me seemingly from nowhere.

And while I'm talking, I tug off my left boot—I'm not wearing socks—to stare at my foot. My big toenail is almost completely gone. My piggy who went to market. The piggy who stayed home isn't looking too good, either. It's not because I drowned, though—it's because of all the running I did. The rest of me might have been beautiful, but my feet were always downright ugly. Oddly enough, it never bothered me much.

Well, it bothered me a little bit. My friends—Mera and Caroline and Josie—used to love to get mani-pedis all the time, but I usually opted for just a manicure. I was too embarrassed by the condition of my feet to let anybody else see them. Hence the ostentatious footwear; I guess you could say I was overcompensating.

I smile as I stare at my left foot. Around my ankle, there's the same "Best Friends" bracelet that Josie gave me nine years earlier. Once she and I got to middle school, we decided it wasn't cool to wear them on our wrists anymore, so we had extra links added to the chains and wore them around our ankles. We almost never took them off. It occurs to me that, at the front of the room, lying in my casket, I'm probably still wearing it.

"You changed your running route?" Alex asks. "When?"

"It must have been after they found you. I used to run past the Mystic Market every morning, and once they found your body, I couldn't bear to go there anymore." I shudder, slipping my boot onto my foot. I have no choice but to put it back on. More than once I've tried to leave them off, but the boots simply reappear in place a moment later. The shoes are a part of me now. I'm stuck with them.

"What happened to you was terrible, Alex."

But he's busy gazing at Mera's chest as she walks back to her seat.

"You've got quite a collection of friends, Liz. All the hot girls. All the pretty boys." He shakes his head. "I never imagined I'd get to spend so much time with them."

I shrug. "Well, I was beloved. You're lucky to get to spend time with them now, I guess." I pause, remembering that it's not good manners to be boastful, embarrassed by what I've just said. "I don't know if I was all *that* popular, though, now that you mention it."

He glares at me. "Oh, you weren't? Let me ask you something, Liz. Did you ever have to eat lunch in the library?"

"What do you mean?"

"You know what I mean."

I blink at him coolly. "No, I don't."

"You do. I showed you the memory. You saw Frank in the lunchroom, getting bullied by your . . . friends. You saw me, eating by myself."

"Alex. I told you I was sorry about that."

"Sorry for what? For doing nothing? It happened almost every day, Liz. I knew it was only a matter of time before Topher, or one of your other friends, noticed that I was all alone, too, and that I packed my own lunch. So you know what I started doing?"

"What?" I have a feeling I don't want to know.

"I used to take my lunch into the library and eat in there. All by myself."

"You didn't have to—"

"Yes, I did. I needed to be invisible. I knew what your

group was capable of from watching Frank. You and your friends were . . . you were empty. You could be like monsters."

I don't say anything. I stare at the front of the room, where my friends sit together, all of them red-eyed and crying. They certainly don't look like monsters right now.

"Richie's the only one of you with half a conscience," Alex says. "But he never did much to stop it. He was still right there by your side, no matter what you did. It was like, in his eyes, you could do no wrong." Alex shakes his head bitterly. "You sure had him wrapped around your little finger, didn't you?"

"Alex, I already told you I feel bad about that."

But he's not finished. "You don't know what it was like to be uncool. To be alone. It wasn't fun, Liz. It was hard."

I don't know what to say to him. I don't know how to make him feel better, or if there's anything I can do that will help at all. So I blurt out the first thing that comes to mind. The only thing that's been on my mind since the moment we walked into the room.

"Do you know how my mother died?"

He shakes his head. "Beats me. Champagne and caviar overdose?"

"She was anorexic, Alex. She starved herself. She used to take cold medicine to control her appetite. She'd take handfuls of pills at a time." I remember it so clearly now: my mother standing at the sink, her mouth *stuffed* with pills. Is there no mercy for a dead girl in the afterlife? Out of all the memories from my childhood, the ones surrounding my mother and her illness are what I'd love to forget. But they're there, rooted, holding on tight.

And then she died.

"She had a stroke when she was thirty-three," I tell him. "She collapsed in the shower." I pause.

"What?" Alex asks. "You look like you're about to say—"

"I'm not about to say anything. That's what happened to her. Now you know."

If Alex feels sorry for me, he isn't showing it. "And then what? Your dad married Josie's mom?"

I nod. "Yeah, he married Nicole."

She's safe, honey. Next time you come over, I'll show you.

"Want to hear something weird?" I ask.

"Sure."

"A couple of weeks after my mom's funeral, I went over to Josie's house for a sleepover. Do you know what Nicole did?"

"What?"

"She brought out a Ouija board. I was *nine,* Alex, and she brought out this Ouija board to try and contact my mother for me."

We both look at Nicole. Alex was right when he said that she's gorgeous; Nicole is the walking definition of a blond bombshell. She's also flaky and superstitious. She believes in the afterlife, in UFOs, and in all things mystical. After she moved into our house, she had a feng shui expert come over to rearrange all the furniture. Nicole doesn't work—instead, she takes frequent yoga and tai chi classes, spends a lot of time volunteering, and keeps herself otherwise occupied by continually redecorating the house. My dad doesn't seem to mind.

Josie is just like her mom. She goes to the Spiritualist Church with Nicole all the time. They both believe in ghosts. For a second, I consider approaching them, trying to touch them, to see if they can sense me. As quickly as the idea materializes, though, I dismiss it. Like my father, I'm much more pragmatic. I might be a real ghost now, but I'm still not convinced that anyone could be able to sense me. The possibility seems ridiculous.

"Did it work?" Alex asks. "The Ouija board?"

I close my eyes, trying not to cry again. "Yes. She asked how my mother was, and it spelled 'safe.' Just like Nicole promised me she was."

"That seems so inappropriate," he says. "A grown adult shouldn't be playing with a Ouija board with kids. Especially nine-year-olds."

It's funny—it never occurred to me before now just how inappropriate it really was. And her words to my father, at my mom's funeral—who *says* something like that?

Before we can talk about it further, Alex and I are

interrupted by the sound of canned organ music coming through the speakers in the corners of the room.

"Show's starting," Alex says.

My friends grip each other's hands. Richie puts his arm around Josie. The two of them are crying so hard that they're shaking.

I turn in my seat to look at Joe Wright, who's still standing in the back. His arms are crossed, his gaze steady on my casket. As far as I know, there's absolutely no evidence to suggest that my death was anything but accidental. So why is he here, watching everybody so closely? He might as well be jotting down notes.

Local cops, I think. *He probably has nothing better to do.*

As my gaze moves past him, taking in all of my friends and family, it occurs to me that my death is not a peaceful one. Here I am. Still on Earth, with Alex, watching and waiting—but for what? Why are we still here? What are we supposed to be doing? Piecing things together, according to Alex—but into what? Again, I try to reassure myself that none of my friends would have harmed me. What reason could any of them possibly have had?

I try to swallow. I taste salt water. As though I'm still on the boat, the room seems to rock gently back and forth. Suddenly it's hard to breathe.

Six

Everyone is leaving as Alex and I get to Richie's house. Topher and Mera are climbing into Topher's car. Caroline is getting ready to catch a ride with them; she stands on the front porch with Richie and Josie, buttoning her black jacket, hugging herself in the cool air. My friends all look so solemn and grown up in their funeral clothes, their eyes red and puffy from crying.

The weather seems especially dreary for late August, considering that it's still technically summertime. Caroline wraps a Burberry scarf around her neck and rubs her hands together, trying to warm them. She picks up her purse from the floor of the porch and holds it close to her body.

"I have to get home," she says. "My parents have been lunatics the past few days."

Josie nods. "I guess I should get going, too." She glances at Richie. He sits on the floor of the covered front porch, staring at the space between his shoes. He looks like he hasn't slept in days. There are circles under his eyes. His skin is broken out. His lips are chapped. He rode home from the funeral in his dad's car, which is nowhere in sight on the street; his parents probably dropped him off and left. The fact makes me angry, but it doesn't surprise me. I don't even have to go inside to guess that they left some money for him on the kitchen counter. Like that can take care of everything. Like he'll be just fine without them.

I walk over to Richie, sit beside him on the floor, and put my head on his shoulder. I'm expecting that I won't be able to genuinely feel him, like it is with everyone else.

But it's different. I still can't feel him—not truly feel him—but I *almost* can. It's like he's just a shade out of reach. I can sense him profoundly, right down to the threads of his shirt and the warm flesh beneath his clothing. And I can smell him. His parents are both sculptors, hippies like you can't even imagine. So Richie always smells like wet clay. Wet clay and patchouli.

"Alex," I say, "something's different. I can almost touch him."

Excited, I press my hand to Richie's cheek. I try to really concentrate, but it doesn't help much; there's still an invisible barrier between us. But I feel like if I try hard enough—if

I really, *really* want it—I might be able to break through. Maybe it will take time. But I would do anything to make real contact.

Despite my heightened senses toward him, Richie doesn't give any sign that he can detect me. Closing my eyes, focusing on the love I feel for him, I can sense every whisker, the imperfect texture of his sweet face, the angle of his jawline. I'm so certain that we are still connected somehow that I begin to tremble. For a moment, my body feels so electric that I almost forget about the pain in my feet, my toes curled in my boots. Almost. But not completely.

"Calm down," Alex says. "You're probably just imagining it."

"I'm not imagining anything. Alex, I mean it! It's different with Richie. I feel like I could reach him if I really tried. I'm so close. What do you think that means?"

He shrugs, uninterested. "Probably nothing. You're dead, Liz."

"Josie," Caroline says, squinting at my stepsister, "you must have left your coat in Richie's room." I wasn't here to see it, but I can guess that my friends were probably all up there earlier, smoking cigarettes. Even when Mr. and Mrs. Wilson are home, they don't pay that much attention to their son; all Richie has to do is open one of his bedroom windows and lean his head out to smoke. He never gets in trouble for it. His parents have a "live and let live" kind of attitude. They don't believe in imposing too many rules on their son.

"Oh." Josie stares down at her bare arms. Her skin is a deep, lovely bronze that is the result of hours spent in a tanning salon. Unlike her mother, Josie isn't a natural beauty; she has to really work at it. She exercises a lot, takes spinning classes and lifts weights just to maintain an okay figure. And her hair is naturally much darker than mine, almost brown; she gets it highlighted every six weeks to keep up the illusion that she's a natural blonde. "I guess so."

"Want me to come with you?" Caroline offers. She holds up a single finger, gesturing for Topher to wait before leaving without her.

Josie appears to be studying Richie. "No," she says. "That's okay. I think I'll hang around for a few more minutes, actually."

Caroline shrugs. "Whatever. I'll be at home if you need me." She pauses. "Just make sure you call first. My parents aren't letting me out without, like, advance notice."

Richie and Josie—and Alex and I, for that matter—watch without saying anything as Caroline walks down the steps and climbs into the backseat of Topher's car. After the three of them pull away, Richie says, "Well, I guess you should go get your coat."

Josie nods. "I guess so."

"I'll come with you," he says.

Walking into Richie's house feels like going home in so many ways. I can't count the number of afternoons I've spent here, the weekend sleepovers—in the basement, with all of our other friends—and of course, all the time Richie and I spent alone, in his room.

Like I said, his parents are hippies. It's funny; Nicole is such a free spirit, but Richie's mom and dad never seemed to warm to her after my mother died. My real mom and Richie's mom were close, and his parents always liked me— but it wasn't like our families were particularly close. Even though everybody thought Richie and I would eventually get married. Even though we lived two doors down from each other practically our whole lives.

"So this is where the magic happened," Alex says, looking around Richie's room. He glances at my body.

I raise an eyebrow. "What?"

"Nothing."

"No, it's not nothing, Alex. What did you mean, 'this is where the magic happened'?"

He blushes. "You know. All the sex." He bites his lip, still gazing at me. He might hate me, but I know it doesn't change the way I look. "I bet you two did it, huh?"

Alex is wrong, though. Despite all the time we spent alone in Richie's room, when his parents weren't even home, I remember now that we never went all the way. The night in his car after prom—and later on, in the boat—was as close as we ever came. Even then, it wasn't that close.

When I tell Alex this, he looks shocked. "You dated him for how long?"

"Since we were twelve," I say. "Almost six years."

He shakes his head, laughing. "Man, he must have been *frustrated.*"

"No," I say firmly. "Richie wasn't like that. He never would have pressured me to do anything I wasn't ready to do."

"Still," Alex says, "you guys were going to be seniors, and Richie could have had any girl he wanted. I mean, he's *Famous Richie Wilson.*"

"I know that," I snap. "We were *going* to do it. Just not yet."

Alex gives me a long stare. "Are you sure about that? You're sure he felt the same way?"

"Yes, I'm sure." I look around the room and feel overwhelmingly sad. It's the same room where he gave me my first real kiss, the same room where we sat on his bed and talked for hours, sometimes well into the night, so many times. The bedroom is big and warm and filled with light. It's on the far right side of the house, and it takes up the whole length of the place, so there are three windows: one in front, looking out on the street; one on the side, facing the neighbors' house; and one in the back, which allows Richie a clear view of the Long Island Sound and the *Elizabeth*. "Why would you ask me something like that?"

"Because," he says simply, "it looks like he sure has moved on quick."

"What do you mean?"

"I mean they look awfully friendly. Don't they?"

Before I can argue with Alex, I notice that Richie has closed his bedroom door. Josie stands close behind him, beside his bed. She has her hands on his shoulders. She tugs him closer to her.

He turns around. He stares at her for a moment. And then he kisses her.

I didn't know it was possible, as a ghost, to feel like I've been punched in the stomach. But as I stand just inside Richie's doorway, watching the two of them together, I actually feel like I'm going to be sick.

Richie's room is practically a shrine to the two of us. On his desk, below the back window that looks out over the Sound, are several framed photographs of us at different ages. There's one of him and me standing at the bus stop together on our first day of kindergarten. We're holding hands, both of us wearing those backpacks that look like stuffed animals. Richie's is a lion; mine is a unicorn. Our fingers are laced together.

In another photo, we're sitting on the bleachers after a cross-country meet. Richie isn't a runner, but he was always there to support me. In the picture, I'm wearing my running uniform, my long hair falling over my shoulders in two braids. I'm flushed and sweaty, obviously exhausted, but I'm smiling. So is Richie. His arm is slung casually around my tanned shoulders. It was Josie, I believe, who took the picture.

The last photo—the biggest one, in a shiny silver frame—is of the two of us at homecoming last year. We look so happy. We loved each other. Like plenty of events, I don't remember any details from the evening. But I'm willing to bet it was one of the best nights of my life.

And now here he is—my boyfriend kissing my stepsister. They wrap their arms tightly around each other. Richie is crying a little bit. Still kissing him, Josie reaches for his face and wipes away a tear. Her hand lingers on his damp cheek. Josie's fingernails are painted a sparkly shade of deep purple, which I happen to know matches her toes exactly. I was there with her, the week before, when my friends and I went to get our nails done. My own nails are the same exact shade—but not my toenails, of course.

We'd chosen it on purpose—the nail polish, I mean. We were always coordinating like that. We loved being sisters.

"This can't be real," I whisper, wiping my eyes. I don't want to see what's happening, but it seems impossible to look anywhere else. The kiss goes on for what feels like forever. With his open mouth against Josie's, Richie begins to back her *toward his bed*.

"I'm going to be sick," I say, finally turning away, putting my arms around Alex and burying my face in his chest.

He shrinks from my touch. "No, you're not. You're a ghost. You can't throw up."

"I'm not so sure."

I squeeze my eyes shut. For a moment, there's darkness. Then something changes.

I'm in the past, standing in a corner of Richie's room. He's lying in bed, on top of the covers, in nothing but a pair of black boxer shorts. He is pale, hair plastered to his face with sweat. His breathing is deep and ragged.

I know this day. Seemingly out of nowhere, the memory comes into sharp focus as I watch it unfold before me.

It's the spring of tenth grade. Richie's parents are in Prague. They have been there for almost two weeks. The Wilsons left money for Richie to buy food while they were gone, and he'd stocked up on bread and lunch meat from the supermarket. Three nights ago he accidentally left a package of turkey on the counter overnight. He ate some anyway the next morning, and now he has food poisoning. He hasn't been to school in two and a half days.

The entire time, I've been skipping school to take care of him. Every morning, Josie and I walk down the street together, heading toward the high school. Then I double back, taking alleys and side streets so my dad and Nicole won't see me going through the porch door into Richie's house.

Now I watch my younger self as I push Richie's bedroom door open. I am holding a steaming bowl of broth in one hand, a glass of water in the other. He's in so much discomfort that he barely acknowledges me. There's a bucket beside his bed. I can smell the room; it reeks of sweat and vomit.

"Hey," my younger self whispers. Even though Richie is the only one around, I'm still dressed to the nines, with a full face of makeup, my hair wound into a carefully tousled fishtail braid that hangs over my shoulder and dangles at my side. "How are you doing?"

"Uhhh," he moans. He pauses, taking deep, labored breaths. Then he says, "Better. I feel a little better."

I take a careful seat beside him on the bed. For just a second, my gaze flickers to the bucket, noting its contents, but it doesn't seem to bother me a bit. I put the bowl and glass on his nightstand and press my palm to his forehead. When I pull it away, it's almost dripping with his sweat. Without any hesitation, I wipe my hand on my black capri pants.

My sixteen-year-old self stares at Richie with what can only be described as real love. As a ghost, I watch the two of us, so touched by the palpable tenderness in the room that I almost forget to breathe. Not that it would matter.

"Can you sit up?" I ask, touching him lightly on his back. He glistens with sweat as he lies on his side.

"Yes." He nods. He sits up. With a shaky hand, he lifts the glass of water from his nightstand and takes a few sips.

Wordlessly, I slip my arm around his bare waist. I press my free hand to his forehead. "You feel warm," I murmur.

"It's just food poisoning. I don't have a fever, Liz. I'll be fine."

I pull him a bit closer. "You should go to the doctor."

"No." He takes one last swallow of water, returns the glass to the nightstand, and falls back against the mattress, pulling me with him. "I'm getting better. I have to. I've got a ton of homework to catch up on." He pauses. "So do you, by the way."

I ignore the comment, clearly unconcerned about homework. "We could have someone come over and check you out. What about Sharon Reese's dad? He would stop by, I'm sure of it."

"Elizabeth." Richie half smiles. "He's a veterinarian."

I sigh as I lie down behind him, my body curled against his frame, our arms wound together, hands interlaced against his stomach. "What can I do to help you?"

He closes his eyes. "You're doing it. You're here. But Liz, you have to go back to school tomorrow. You know they'll call your parents if you miss three days in a row."

"Mmm. It won't matter. My dad will be at work. Nicole never answers the house line. If they leave a voice mail, I'll delete it." I close my eyes, tugging our bodies closer together. As I watch the two of us, I can remember the way his body felt. I remember that I could see each individual pore on his shoulders and back, the tiny hairs growing down his neck, the way his skin seemed to breathe in relief from exposure to the cool air. I remember it all so clearly.

"But you're missing class."

"Shhh. I'm not leaving you."

He takes another deep breath. A light wheeze sounds from his chest. "Thank you."

"Don't thank me. Sleep. I'll be here."

"Liz?"

"Hmm?"

"Why do you care about me?"

The question seems to startle me. It's uncharacteristic for Richie, who is usually so cool and self-assured. I open my eyes. "Why would you ask me that?"

"Because I don't understand. We're so different."

I reach around the side of his face. Once again, I wipe fresh beads of sweat from his forehead. This time, I don't even bother wiping my hand on my pants. I lace my fingers into his again, and the two of us lie there together, his damp clamminess seeping onto my made-up face and my pretty clothes. Obviously, I couldn't care less.

"But we fit," I whisper. "Like this." And I tighten my grip around him.

"Mmm." He smiles, his eyes still closed. "You're right. We do."

"Richie . . . I'm lying. I don't like you."

"You don't?" His voice cracks.

"No." I bring my lips close to his ear. "I love you, Richie Wilson."

"Elizabeth Valchar. Liz. I love you."

"We fit," I repeat.

"You're right," he whispers. "We fit."

I don't want to watch us anymore. It hurts too badly. I would do anything—*anything*—for one more second with my arms around him, like we were that afternoon.

When I open my eyes to see the present day, when I see my boyfriend kissing my stepsister, moving her toward the same bed where he and I had once lain together and professed our love for the first time, I almost can't look. But what else is there to do? Where else is there to go?

"Wait," Richie says. And he pulls away just before the two of them are about to collapse onto the mattress.

Josie wipes her wet mouth with the back of her hand. "What's the matter?"

Richie stares at the floor. Then he takes a few steps backward, toward his desk. He looks at the pictures of us.

"I can't do this right now."

I feel smacked. "Right *now*? What does he mean, right now?"

"It means he can do it at some point," Alex clarifies.

"Oh no. No, no, no. This cannot be happening."

As Josie sits on the bed, gazing awkwardly at my boyfriend, she twirls a tendril of hair around her index finger, examining the strands for split ends. She seems annoyed by his reluctance. "I know it's hard, Richie. It's hard for all of us. But Liz would have wanted us to be happy."

"Not true," I say to Alex. "Not like this."

Richie stares at her. "What makes you think I'm ever going to be happy again?" he asks. "Just because she's gone . . . it doesn't mean anything. We never told her. It would have broken her heart, Josie."

He crosses the room, where the inside wall is lined with floor-to-ceiling bookshelves. Richie has read more books than anyone I've ever met. He gets straight As in school, and for almost as long as I've known him he's said that he wants to be a writer someday. But that's not why people call him Famous Richie Wilson.

See, he's a drug dealer. A real one. Mostly pot, but other stuff, too—prescription drugs, like Adderall and Percocet, and sometimes a little bit of the harder stuff. He sells it to students in our high school, to people in town, even to his parents' friends. It was the only thing I couldn't stand about him. More than once, I considered breaking up with him because of it. But I didn't. I loved him. And he loved me—at least, I thought so.

He reaches for a copy of *Great Expectations*, a big black hardcover book that I happen to know is hollow. Inside, it's full of measured bags of marijuana.

Josie sits up a little straighter when she sees it. "If you're going to do that, I'm going home." She shakes her head. "I can't handle it."

"Just stick around for a few minutes while I smoke." He shudders to himself, his back still toward her. "I can't deal with reality right now."

"Well, you're gonna have to eventually." Josie sniffles. "We all are. Somehow."

As Richie sits at his desk, carefully rolling a joint, Josie says, "Hey. You want to hear a crazy story? About Liz?"

He doesn't look at her. "I'm betting I've heard it already, but go ahead."

"No," she says, growing excited, "I'll bet you haven't. You know how my mom is really into the paranormal, right?"

"I know how she's a space cadet, sure." He glances at Josie. "Just like you, sweetie."

"*Sweetie?*" I shriek. I cross the room to Richie. I put my arms around his neck. I press my cheek to his. Again, I can't truly feel him, and he gives no sign that he senses me. But I can tell we're connecting. I can feel our breathing, in sync, and I know that a part of me is still with him.

"Well, a few years ago she took me and Liz to the Spiritualist Church in Groton. My mom and I go there all the time. Liz almost never went with us, but that one instance—I don't know, I guess she must have been bored, and it was just something to do on a Saturday. They had psychics there—a whole bunch of them."

I step away from Richie, almost unable to bear the feeling of being so close to him. Richie rolls his eyes. He's never believed in anything like the supernatural. He doesn't believe in ghosts. He doesn't believe in much, really.

"So, you guys talked to the psychics? Or what?"

Josie nods. "We all did, yeah. But here's the interesting part. One of them—this guy—he seemed drawn to Liz. He kept glancing at her from all over the room, while he was giving other people readings. Finally, just as we were leaving, he came up to us and took her by the arm and said something really creepy."

Richie licks the paper on the joint, rolls it shut. "Well? What did he say?"

"He told her to beware of the redhead in disguise. He said the redhead would put her in danger someday. And you know, he was so *insistent* upon it, like it was very serious that she listen to him and take what he was saying to heart."

Richie holds the joint, staring at Josie. "Are you gonna smoke this or what?"

She shakes her head. "I don't want to." There's a pause. "You don't think that's interesting?"

Richie swallows. "No. I think it was a dumb guy trying to get a few extra bucks out of a sweet girl. As far as I know, Liz didn't even know any redheads. Did she?"

Josie gazes at him. "No." She pauses. "Do you really want me to leave?"

"I'm sorry, Josie, it's just really soon." He hesitates. "Come back tomorrow, okay?"

"*Tomorrow*?" I blurt. "Today is too soon, but tomorrow he'll be okay?" I stare hard at Richie. "He's heard that story before. I told him that story right after it happened."

Josie stands up. "Okay," she says. "I'll see you tomorrow." And she leaves without—thank God—so much as a hug good-bye.

Once he's alone in his room, Richie opens his back window. He lights the joint. He stares at the *Elizabeth*, resting so peacefully in the water now, showing no signs of the horror that took place just a few nights ago. As he's exhaling, he says out loud, "I'd heard that story before. Liz told me that story right after it happened."

Seven

Josie hasn't been gone ten seconds when there's a light knock on Richie's door. He doesn't seem happy that, presumably, she's back. For a few seconds, he doesn't say anything; he just sits, staring out his back window, smoking his joint.

Tap, tap, tap.

The joint crackles as a seed pops. Richie is unfazed, holding in a deep inhale, glancing warily at the door.

"Go away!" I shout. "He doesn't want to see you!"

Alex seems uncomfortable, like he doesn't know quite how to handle me. "You're upset," he says. "Try to calm down."

Tap, tap, tap.

But there's no way I can calm down, not right now. "He repeated what I just said, almost verbatim," I tell him. "Do you think he can sense me?"

"I don't know." Alex appears to think about it. "It *was* weird. And you said you could feel him when you touched him?"

"Kind of. Almost. I think that I'll be able to do it—maybe if I concentrate hard enough."

Alex shakes his head. "I don't know, Liz. That's never happened to me before. There are some people who can see me—"

"What do you mean?" I almost scream the words. "Some people who can see you? Like who?"

"Babies," he says. "Babies can see me. I have a cousin. When I died, he was almost two, and he could definitely see me. But when he got older—as soon as he started speaking in really clear sentences—it was obvious he couldn't tell I was there anymore." Alex pauses. "Animals can see me, too. My cat can see me."

I gape at him. "You're kidding. Why didn't you tell me this sooner?"

He shrugs. "I didn't think it was important."

"Maybe not. But it's definitely interesting." I shake my head. "Anyway, you agree that Richie and I are still connected somehow, right?"

Alex nods. "Okay. You might be right about that. So what?"

Before I can answer, we hear the knock at the door again. *Tap, tap, tap.*

Richie sighs. He stares at the joint for a second before

tossing it out the open window. The room is thick with smoke. "Come in," he says, coughing.

I'm fully expecting Josie again. But it's not her; it's the cop, Joe Wright. Any other boy might panic, but Richie isn't any other boy. He's never worried much about getting caught with drugs. He's never worried much about anything. He is cool, calm, and always collected. When I was with Richie, I felt like things were under control. Looking at him now, though, I realize that he's just a kid who didn't have a clue how to keep me safe. After all, I died less than ten feet away from him, while he was sleeping. Why didn't he wake up? Surely there was some kind of noise: a splash, a scream, *something*. But he was drunk. He was stoned. He was in too much of a stupor to wake up, even to save my life.

"Who let you into my house?" Richie asks Joe.

"Your girlfriend." Joe waves a hand back and forth beneath his nose. "You might want to invest in a window fan, kiddo. I can smell that from the stairs." Joe is still wearing his dress shirt and tie from my funeral earlier. Without his policeman's uniform, he looks like any normal guy. He's probably in his late thirties. He's cute and fit, his dark hair short and neat, a sprinkling of freckles spread evenly across his tan face. He looks kind enough, nonthreatening, but I know Richie isn't going to open up to him easily. As a rule, Richie does not trust adults—especially not authority figures.

Richie blinks at him. "Just so you understand, Josie is not my girlfriend. Liz was my girlfriend."

"Okay. Sure." Joe takes two steps closer to Richie and peers at his face. He takes his index finger and brushes it against Richie's cheek. Then he holds up the finger for both of them to see. "Lipstick," Joe says.

"Oh, that's fabulous." I effect a slow clap. "That's some stellar police work right there."

"What's your point?" Richie asks, unfazed.

"My point is that Josie wouldn't look me in the eye when she let me in."

"So what? She's upset. We were just at her sister's funeral." Richie stares at him. "What did you expect her to do? Give you a big smile? A high five?" He shakes his head. "Local cops, man."

Joe ignores his comment. "I know you were at the funeral. I saw you. Did you see me?" He pulls out Richie's desk chair. "Mind if I take a seat?" he asks. Before Richie can answer, Joe sits down.

"I shouldn't be talking to you," Richie says. "You can't come into my house like this. I ought to call a lawyer."

Joe raises an eyebrow. "You think you need a lawyer?"

"No. I didn't do anything wrong."

"Would Liz agree with that? You were just kissing her sister."

"Her *step*sister. Well—that's complicated. Her half sister, maybe."

"Her half sister?" Joe is obviously interested. "Why would you say that?"

"Because some people think Josie and Liz are half sisters. Lots of people think so." He pauses. "But not Liz. She never believed it." Richie pulls a piece of gum from his pocket, puts it into his mouth, and chews slowly, as though he's reluctant to share the information with Joe. "See, there's always been a lot of talk around town that maybe Liz's dad and Josie's mom had a . . . a *thing*, before Liz's mom died. They were high school sweethearts. And some people—my parents, for one—think Josie looks a lot like Mr. Valchar." Richie shakes his head, obviously uncomfortable with the topic. "I don't know if it's true or not. But it doesn't matter. It's totally irrelevant. And we might have been kissing a little bit, but you've gotta understand, it's not like what you're thinking."

"Then what is it like? And you can cut the attitude, by the way. I could arrest you for possession right now, you know."

Richie spreads his hands in a careless gesture. "Do it. I don't care. I don't have anything to lose." I'm surprised he's telling Joe so much about my family history. Maybe he just wants to talk about me.

"I'm sure you don't. Where are your parents right now? I saw them at the funeral earlier."

He nods. "Yeah, they managed to make an appearance."

"But they aren't home now?"

"They're busy people." He snorts. "They're very dedicated to their art."

"I see." Joe takes a moment to look around the room. His gaze falls to all the pictures of me and Richie on his desk.

"Look," he says, "the case is technically closed. But I've got some free time—you know, we local cops always have time on our hands—and I'm gonna ask some questions about this one. The story you kids told me adds up, okay, but it's all so . . . so *circumstantial*. There isn't a lot of hard evidence. I want to find something that makes me certain of what happened. Besides, Liz is the second kid in twelve months to get killed in Noank."

Richie sits down on his bed. "Who was the first?"

"He doesn't even remember me," Alex says. He seems genuinely bothered by the fact.

"Why do you care?" I ask.

He thinks about it for a moment. Then he says, "I don't know. I just do."

"Alex Berg," Joe says. "Come on, you aren't *that* high. He was the same age as you. Hit-and-run last August by the Mystic Market."

"Oh, right." Richie nods in slow recognition. "Sure, I remember. I've seen flyers up in town." He appears to be thinking. "Liz and Caroline went to his funeral. I wouldn't go with them. Funerals creep me out, you know? Anyway, what does that matter? It had nothing to do with any of us."

"It matters," Joe says, "because people are worried. First there's a hit-and-run. Now this. Two healthy kids dying in less than a year. It's a small town. Parents are concerned."

"It was an accident," Richie says. "Nobody killed Liz."

Joe nods in agreement. "Probably not. I hope not. But you see, Richard—"

"Richie," he corrects.

"You see," Joe continues, "here you are, stoned, screwing around with your dead girlfriend's stepsister, or half sister, or whatever she is. On the same day as Liz's funeral. And I don't know how to explain that, from a moral perspective. It seems pretty insensitive, wouldn't you agree?"

Richie stares at the shiny hardwood floor of his bedroom. "Why can't you just arrest me for possession?"

"Why would I want to do that?"

"Because I'm a loser."

"Liz didn't think so."

Richie looks up. "Yes, she did." He swallows. All of his characteristic confidence is gone; I barely recognize him. "She was cheating on me." There are tears in his dark, bloodshot eyes. "It had been going on for months, and I never even realized. Not until Josie told me."

"Ohhh." Alex shakes his head at me. "You *bad* girl."

My mouth falls open. "He's wrong," I say. "I don't know what he's talking about."

"You were cheating on him," Alex explains. "Listen."

So I do.

"It was right after Christmas," Richie says. "I'd been noticing for a while that Liz was disappearing, sometimes for long periods of time. She seemed different. I was worried. She was always skinny, but lately she'd been losing an awful lot of weight. I mean, that's why they think she died, right? The hypoglycemia, combined with all the booze in her system?

We did a body mass index on ourselves in health class last spring, and she was way underweight." He appears to be thinking, remembering. "Anyway, it wasn't just all the weight loss. I don't think the two were connected. It was more than that. She'd become kind of distant with me. And at first I thought, okay, so she's obsessed with running. She was always great at distance, but speed was never her thing. I figured she was trying to get faster. Maybe she was taking it a little bit too far. I mean, it wasn't unusual for her to get up at five in the morning and go for a two-hour run before school." He shakes his head. "Crazy. She was nuts about it."

"What made you think it was something else?" Joe asks. "Something other than just an obsession with running? Josie told you?"

Richie nods. "Yeah, Josie told me. It was a couple of weeks before junior prom. I'd been trying to get in touch with Liz all day, but she wasn't answering her phone. So I walked to her house—you know she's only two doors down—but she wasn't home. I got to talking with Josie. That's when she told me."

"He's wrong," I say firmly. "I never would have cheated on him. Never."

"Think hard," Alex says. "Can you remember anything at all?"

"No, but it doesn't matter! I don't have to remember to be sure. It's impossible."

Alex takes a long moment to study me. "I can't believe you," he says.

"What can't you believe?"

"That you're still like this. Even after everything that's happened to you, you're still a nightmare of a human being. If he says you cheated on him, you probably did. At least, *I* believe him. You're selfish. You're superficial. If someone better than Richie came along and took an interest in you, I bet you'd cheat in a second."

"I didn't cheat on him!" I shout as loud as I possibly can. "I loved him, Alex. I might not have been that nice to you, but with Richie, things were different. And besides, if I had cheated on him—which I *didn't*—why would I deny it now?" I demand. "Why would I possibly lie to you?"

"I don't know. Maybe you don't remember yet. Or maybe you don't want me to think you're a bad person."

My voice is shaky. "Alex, I am telling you the truth. Yes, I don't remember everything from before I died, but there isn't anything else to remember when it comes to this. I've known Richie since we were two years old. Something isn't right. I never would have hurt him."

And then, as if on cue, Richie says, "I don't think she meant to hurt me. We'd been together so long, maybe she felt like she needed to . . . I don't know, to see what else was out there." He swallows. "Anyway, I didn't believe Josie. I called her a liar and everything. But then she said she'd prove it to me. She drove me into Groton, to this apartment complex by the river. We found Liz's car. It was outside the building of this guy I know."

Richie is holding a corner of his bedspread, a maroon-and-navy-blue patchwork quilt, in his left fist. With his right hand, he tugs at the threads in the seam, working them into a fray. His eyes are still watery. As I listen to what he's saying, I realize that I don't remember any of it happening. Not only that, but—despite what Alex might think—it sounds completely unlike anything I would do. I don't even *know* anyone who lives in Groton. It's like someone has taken a cheese grater to my memory. The feeling is beyond frustrating.

But why would Richie lie? Looking at him as he picks nervously at the quilt, I know without a doubt that he believes he's telling the truth.

"A guy you know," Joe echoes. "What was his name? How do you know him?"

"It was this guy named Vince. Vince Aiello." His voice cracks as he says the name out loud. "He was kind of a friend of mine. He's older."

"How much older?"

"I don't know. Twenty-one? Twenty-two? Does it matter?"

"It matters if he was sleeping with Liz."

Richie sucks in a sharp breath of air. For a moment, I expect him to defend me, to explain that I was a virgin, and that I couldn't *possibly* have been sleeping with anyone. But he doesn't.

"How did Liz know Vince?" Joe presses.

"I introduced them."

"And the day you saw her car parked outside his apartment, what happened? Did you confront her?"

"No. Well, sort of. We sat there for almost an hour, until Liz finally came out. I watched her leave his apartment and go to her car, and once she got home I waited a while before I called her. I asked her where she'd been all morning." He looks down at the quilt, still clutched in his fist. Loose threads are scattered on the floor. "She told me she'd been out shopping at the mall. She lied." Richie looks up at Joe again. His gaze is fierce and angry. "I want to kill him," he says.

"Who?" Joe asks.

"Who do you think? Vince." Richie nods, like he's giving the idea some thought. "I really do. I really want to kill him."

"Hey. Be careful what you say to me, buddy," Joe says. He's trying to keep his voice light, but I can tell he's serious. Richie doesn't say anything else; he just stares down at the quilt again, holding it tightly.

For the first time, I notice that Joe is wearing a wedding ring. It's a thin silver band. With the tip of his thumb, he works it back and forth over the middle knuckle of his ring finger as he stares at Richie.

"When did things start to develop between you and Josie?"

"I don't know. A few weeks later." He stares out the

window, at the rows of boats docked along the shore, his gaze narrowing in at the *Elizabeth*, where we'd spent such a happy evening together just a few days ago. Before I died. Back when life was gentle, easy, perfect. At least I thought so.

"What's going on with Josie is nothing," he says. "It's just your normal, sordid teenage drama. I used to think Liz and I were different from all that, but I guess not. Anyway, it just happened with me and Josie. It doesn't mean anything."

"Does Josie know that?" Joe asks.

"I think so." Richie nods, still staring at the *Elizabeth*.

Joe works his wedding ring back into place. He stands up, positions himself behind Richie's shoulder, and follows his gaze.

"What happened that night? Did you and Liz get into a fight? Did you confront her?"

"No. She didn't know that I knew."

"Why wouldn't you tell her? Come on, Richie. You were angry. You were hooking up with her stepsister. I get it; you wanted to hurt her for what she'd done."

Richie turns around. "You're wrong. I was angry, sure. I guess that, on some level, I wanted to get back at her by messing around with Josie. And I knew I'd have to confront her eventually. I knew we'd probably break up because of what she'd done."

Joe looks at him skeptically. "But not yet?"

"No. Not yet."

"And why is that?"

"Because," Richie says, looking at the boat again. He takes his thumb and holds it up in his line of vision, as if to eradicate the *Elizabeth* from his view. "I didn't want to ruin her birthday party. I loved her too much."

Eight

There's so much I can't remember about my life. I can't recall exactly what I was doing the night I died, or a week earlier. Aside from the brief flashback that I experienced, when I saw myself with Richie in his car, I barely remember being at the junior prom at all. I can't recall the last time I spoke to my parents while I was alive. I can't even say for sure whether or not I was cheating on my boyfriend. But I remember running.

The act is worn into my bones; I can remember the cadence of my footsteps against concrete and earth; I remember the gradual process of awakening that took place every morning as I stepped out my front door and worked myself into an easy pace by the time I reached the end of High Street. I remember how it felt to start out cold and dry and tired, then finish sweaty and warm and exhilarated. Running was magic. It was solitary bliss. It was everything, and I miss it more than almost anything.

So there is some fierce irony to the fact that, in my own personal afterlife, I'm wearing ill-fitting cowgirl boots that pinch my already blistered toes. These boots are the only source of pain I can feel, for reasons I don't understand at all. In life, I adored them. I never imagined they'd become a permanent part of my apparition.

Alex and I are sitting on the white linoleum against a wall of lockers on the second floor of Noank High. It's the first day of what would have been our senior year, and there's a palpable sadness in the hallways, thanks to the recent death of everybody's favorite socialite. The students are quieter than usual; it's like nobody wants to seem too happy. Outside, the flag is flying at half-mast. My unofficial parking space in the student lot remains empty. Already this morning I've heard kids talking about the fact that there are grief counselors hanging out in the library, waiting to console anyone who might be overwhelmed by my untimely passing.

"Was it like this after I died?" Alex asks quietly.

As much as I'm glad to have some company, there are times—like right now—when I am *so* annoyed that he's still around. It seems like he's always full of probing questions and biting observations precisely when I'm enjoying the solitude that comes with being a ghost, a silent observer. For a moment I'm tempted to say, "No, of course not. You weren't popular." But I'm not *that* bad of a person—at least not now. If I was as terrible when I was alive as Alex claims, at least I'm trying to do better in the afterlife. Instead I say, "It was kind of like this, yeah."

But it wasn't; not exactly. To my surprise, I find that some memories start to flash of the days following his death. I remember coming back to school last year after Alex was killed. The school did everything that was expected: lowered the flag, supplied a handful of counselors—they even orchestrated a schoolwide moment of silence during morning announcements. But I remember other things, too: the slew of yearbooks being passed around that morning, open to Alex's tenth-grade photo, so that people could accurately remember who they were supposed to be mourning. And the moment of silence in my homeroom was interrupted when one of my friends, Chad Shubuck, let out an obnoxious, very audible fart. Almost everyone laughed.

I blink myself back into reality, beyond relieved that Alex didn't see my memory. I feel a pang of pity for him.

I can see Chad Shubuck now, standing among a group of students in the lobby at the end of the hall, where the administration has displayed a framed, blown-up picture of me, taken from last year's yearbook. He stares quietly at my face—it's a fantastic picture of me—and then he slowly crosses himself, like he's just finished a prayer.

I stare down the hallway to look for my other friends. Not ten feet away, Richie is standing at his open locker, staring at the contents. He seems lost in thought as Topher and Mera approach, their hands in each other's back pockets.

Topher, dewey eyed and almost glistening as an all-American boy, wears a red-and-white football letterman's jacket over his T-shirt and jeans, chews a wad of what's undoubtedly sugarless gum (he is obsessed with oral hygiene—after all, his father *is* Noank's most respected dentist and oral surgeon), and flashes a sympathetic smile to reveal two rows of sparkling white teeth as he leans against an adjacent locker.

"It's crazy, isn't it?" he says, running a hand through his tousled hair. "Being here without Liz?"

"It's horrible." Mera has clearly been up before dawn to work on her hair, which is styled in countless perfect blond ringlets. Her fingernails are smooth acrylic French tips. "Everybody's gonna want to know what happened. And since I'm the one who found her, I'm the one who has to tell them."

I knew it. I *knew* she would milk her discovery of me for every drop of attention that it's worth. It's so typical of her. I'm *dead*, for God's sake. You'd think that, for once, she could restrain herself from seizing an opportunity to be the center of attention.

"Don't tell them anything. There's nothing they need to know." Richie shrugs off his jacket. Underneath, he's wearing an almost threadbare Yale T-shirt and wrinkled jeans that look like they've been rolled in a ball on his floor for weeks.

His hair isn't combed. There are puffy circles of grayish white beneath his big eyes. Richie has never been too fixated on his appearance, but he's definitely far more disheveled than usual. He doesn't seem to care a bit.

"Don't take this the wrong way, Richie," Mera says, frowning at him, "but you look awful."

Inside his locker, there's a picture of the two of us taped to the door. It was taken on my parents' front lawn, before last year's homecoming. The photo only shows our faces and upper bodies, but there's someone just outside the frame whose hand is slung around my shoulders, her fingertips resting on the back of Richie's neck. It's Josie. Richie sees it, too, and I can tell he wants to do something with the picture— maybe take it down? Throw it away?

He doesn't do anything, though. "I have to be somewhere," he tells Mera and Topher. He lets out a long breath; it's like he's trying to summon a semblance of his typically cool, confident self. But there's a weary quality to his voice when he speaks. "What do you need?"

Topher leans in a little closer, lowering his voice. "Hey, buddy. I know it's a rough time for all of us, but can you help a brother out?"

"What's he talking about?" Alex murmurs.

"Shh."

"Is he talking about drugs?"

I look at Alex. "Are you deaf as well as dead? I said *shh*."

"What do you need?" Richie asks again, closing his locker and glancing at the clock hanging in the hallway. "I'm gonna be late, dude."

"You know . . . a quarter?"

Alex shakes his head in disbelief.

"What? What's that look for?" I demand.

"You and your group. You think you can get away with anything. Topher's on the football team. Don't they drug test?"

My gaze drifts to my boots. My feet are positively *throbbing*. Even though I know it won't work, I've tried to take the boots off a few times, but sooner or later I look down and there they are again. It's like magic. They are, at least for now, a permanent part of me. "There are ways around that," I say.

"What do you mean?"

"The drug tests are supposed to be random," I explain, "but Topher was MVP last year. They aren't going to kick him off the team." I pause, trying to explain further without sounding like the entitled snob that I know Alex thinks I am. "I'm just saying, there are things a person can do if he doesn't want to get caught."

"Right. Or he could, you know, just *not do drugs*."

"Come on, he's a good guy." But there's no conviction in my voice; not after witnessing Topher's treatment of poor Frank Wainscott in the cafeteria.

Alex looks at me with what I can only describe as

suppressed horror. "Of all the people to end up dead with," he says, shaking his head, "it had to be you, didn't it?"

"You're kidding me, right? I could say the same thing about you."

"No, you couldn't." His tone is firm. "I'm a nice person. I never did anything to hurt anyone. But you . . . you and your friends." He takes a moment to look up and down the hallway, which is starting to empty as homeroom approaches. "Admit it, Liz. Isn't there a part of you that's embarrassed to be sitting here with me, even though nobody can see us?"

I don't answer him. My silence is enough of a response.

Once Topher and Mera have left, I expect Richie to go to Mr. Franklin's room, which is where he and I have both been in homeroom since the ninth grade. But he doesn't. Instead, Alex and I follow him down to the first floor, through the cafetorium (which is a combination cafeteria/auditorium—Noank High is a small school), and outside to the field house. He stands at a closed office door in a darkened hall and fidgets, waiting to knock.

Richie is no athlete. He's the kind of guy who barely manages a C in gym class—the only mediocre grade on his otherwise impeccable academic record—and is an anomaly among our typically athletic, popular crowd. He has always been far more interested in books and music than in anything physical. Still, as soon as I see him heading toward the field house, I realize exactly who he's looking for.

My cross-country coach, Mr. Riley, sits quietly at his desk in a small, cluttered office. I remember a good bit about him—small factual details about people seem to come pretty easily to me. Aside from being the cross-country and track coach, he teaches the high school boys' gym classes and tenth-grade health, which puts him kind of low on the faculty totem pole. He isn't adorable and witty like our English teacher, Mr. Simon. I've never seen him spontaneously drop to the gym floor and start doing one-armed push-ups, like the football coach, Mr. "Call Me Todd" Buckley. Unlike the cheerleading coach, Mrs. Casey, he never would have dreamed of supplying alcohol to minors. But he was always my favorite teacher. He'd been my coach since I was in the seventh grade, and he was good at it. He understands what it means to love running. Looking at him now, I remember noticing him two weeks earlier at my funeral. It was the only time, I think, that I'd ever seen him wear a tie. And it was certainly the only time I'd ever seen him cry. At least I *think* it was the only time. I'm not sure about anything, not now.

As close as I remember being with Mr. Riley, he never warmed to Richie, even though they were both at every one of my cross-country meets and had plenty of opportunities to get to know each other.

"I'm not surprised," Alex says when I tell him. "Everybody knows Richie's a drug dealer."

"Do they really?"

"Of course." He pauses. "It's a small town, Liz. People

aren't good at keeping secrets." The words feel weighted with significance, somehow. I get the sense that he's alluding to something, but I'm not sure exactly what.

It's funny—I can remember a lot about Mr. Riley, but not everything. I know that he was my coach. I know that he didn't like Richie. But I don't remember many specifics from the time I spent with him.

So I try to bring some of them back. I'm getting more and more used to falling into memories now, and it almost feels gentle and natural when I close my eyes and let myself slip into the past.

I see a slightly younger, very slightly heavier version of myself standing in his office. Judging from my appearance, I'm guessing that it's sometime during my sophomore year— if it's cross-country season, it's the fall. We are alone together. The light in Mr. Riley's windowless office comes from a dim, erratically blinking fluorescent fixture in the ceiling. Dead insects are visible against the translucent sheet of plastic that covers the bulb. The effect is creepy in the otherwise deserted building.

Mr. Riley is in his early thirties. On his desk, there's a photo of what I assume is his wife and baby daughter. I get the feeling I've met them before, maybe multiple times, although I can't remember much of anything about them at the moment.

Mr. Riley is a quiet, kind of nerdy guy with a good tan from so much running outdoors and the wiry build that's so typical in endurance athletes. "Liz," he says to me, gesturing to a chair in front of his desk, "have a seat." He reaches into a minifridge humming on the floor of his office and pulls out a bottled water. "Here," he says, putting it down in front of me, "drink. You just ran six miles. Your body needs hydration."

"I know that." I open the water and take a long drink. It's obviously right after cross-country practice. I'm wearing gray cotton shorts and a pink tank top made of very thin material, so thin that my white sports bra is clearly visible beneath my shirt. Mr. Riley looks at the far wall, at the picture on his desk, anywhere but at my body. I can tell that being alone with me makes him uncomfortable.

"You aren't going out with the rest of the team?" he asks, keeping his tone light.

"What? Where would I go with them?" My tone is flippant and uncaring, and I can guess why. Aside from me, nobody on the cross-country team was what you'd call popular. I wasn't friends with any of them. Thinking about the fact now, it seems like a shame that I was so quick to write them off.

"They're going out for Chinese food together," Mr. Riley says. He meets my gaze. "You didn't know?"

"I knew. Of course I knew." But from my voice, I can tell that I had no idea. They didn't invite me.

"Liz." Mr. Riley hesitates. "I think you should consider being a little bit . . . warmer toward your teammates."

From outside his door, I hear someone clearing his throat. I don't even have to look to know that it's Richie, waiting for me.

"What do you mean, *warmer*? I'm plenty warm. I just don't hang out with them outside practice, that's all." I shrug. "It doesn't bother me. They're losers."

Mr. Riley flinches at the word "losers." As I watch my younger self, so do I.

"That's exactly what I mean," he continues. "Liz, you might want to reconsider your social circle. I've been your coach since seventh grade. I've watched you grow into this . . . this girl who is consumed by the material, by the social ranking of who she surrounds herself with. I know it's not really you."

I place my water gently on his desk. "How do you know that?"

"Because I know you're only trying to protect yourself. You don't want to get hurt again, so you surround yourself with people who would do anything to stay in your good graces. And you push everyone else away."

I lean forward, narrowing my eyes. "What do you mean, I don't want to get hurt again? When did I ever get hurt?"

He hesitates. For a long moment, he doesn't say anything. As I stare at him, my gaze almost challenging him to say whatever he's thinking, I focus on his eyes, which are two different colors: one is light blue, while the other is black, all pupil and no iris.

Finally, he says, "Your mother."

Oh, Mommy. As I watch the two of us, I can tell that the mere mention of my mom hurts; the idea of her is so raw, so fresh, even so many years later. I don't want to talk about it; that much is obvious.

I bite my bottom lip. "Mr. Riley," I say, "can I ask you something?"

He shrugs. "Sure."

"What happened to your eye?"

The question startles him. He looks around the room again. For a second, I'm afraid I've made him angry, that he's going to kick me out of his office.

But he doesn't. Instead, he says, "Okay, Liz. You want to know what happened?"

"Yes." I nod.

"I've never told another student this."

I give him a genuine smile. "I won't tell anyone. Cross my heart."

"I was seven. I was a nerdy kid . . . still am a nerd, I guess." He half smiles. "Anyway, the kids in my neighborhood never invited me out to play with them. Then one day one of the guys—his name was Charlie Sutton—comes to my front door and asks my mom if I can come out to play some baseball. This was back when people still let their kids go outside without a whole lot of supervision. And I was absolutely thrilled. I grabbed my bat and my mitt and went running outside so fast. You can't imagine how excited I was."

He pauses. He closes his eyes.

"So?" I lean forward in my chair. "What happened? Did you get hit by a baseball or something?"

"No." Mr. Riley looks me square in the eye. "When I got outside, to the ballpark behind my house, Charlie Sutton and a few of the other kids were waiting for me. They had a pellet gun. You know—a BB gun. And they shot me." He shrugs. "They hit me a good half a dozen times on my body, you know, just fooling around, not enough to break the skin or anything. I was crying by then. I started to back away, getting ready to run to my house, and one of the BBs hit me in the eye before I had a chance to turn around. It destroyed my iris. I'm legally blind in my left eye now."

Even at sixteen, the story is enough to visibly move me. I put a hand to my mouth. "Oh my God," I tell him. "That's awful. What happened to them? Did they get in trouble?"

Mr. Riley shrugs again. "They probably got hit—this was years ago, when some people would spank their kids, too—but nothing major ever came of it." He leans back in his chair. "We moved away shortly after that. It was hardest on my mom, really. She saw how excited I was that day, how happy I was to finally get to play with the other kids on my street. But it was all just a joke." He stares at his desk. "You know how kids can be. It's all right. I have a good life now. No complaints here."

I take a long drink of water. My hair is pulled into a ponytail that trails down my back. My face is still sweaty. My eyes are wide with pity.

"I'm so sorry that happened to you," I tell him.

"It's okay, Liz. I probably shouldn't have even told you.

But that's the thing—I want you to be careful who you hang out with. Your priorities aren't in the right place. You might regret it someday."

From the hallway, Richie clears his throat again.

I fidget in my seat. "I've gotta go, Mr. Riley."

"I'm sure you do. Your prince awaits." He's being sarcastic.

I watch myself leave his office and go into the hallway, where Richie is leaning against the wall, looking bored. We walk silently out of the building, hand in hand. Once we're in the parking lot, I ask him, "Did you hear what he said in there?"

Richie only nods.

"That's awful, isn't it?"

"Uh-huh."

Caroline, Mera, and Josie are waiting for us. They're in a black Mercedes with the top down. When my friends see us, Mera honks the horn and waves us over.

"What the hell took you so long?" Josie snaps as Richie and I climb into the backseat. There isn't enough room for the three of us to sit side by side, so my younger self curls up on Richie's lap. I can only watch, standing just outside the car.

"Chill out," Richie says to Josie. "We're here now, aren't we?"

"What's the matter, Liz? You'd rather hang out with Crazy-Eyes Riley and the dorks on the cross-country team?" But then she grins at me, and the edge to her voice breaks. "It's okay. I'll still love you."

I wink at her. She winks back. I stick my tongue out at her. She crosses her eyes.

"Seriously," she says, giggling, "what took you so long? You prefer to spend time with your coach? He's so weird looking."

"He's not weird looking. His eyes are just two different colors." I lace my fingers through Richie's.

"Yeah, that's weird." She sniffles. "What a freak."

We're still sitting in the parking lot. The Mercedes is idling.

"He's not a freak," I tell her. "He's nice. And you shouldn't say things like that about him. It isn't his fault that his eyes are different."

As I'm watching myself, witnessing the scene unfold, I notice that Richie squeezes my hand when I don't elaborate.

"Whatever," Josie says, snapping her gum. "It doesn't matter if it's his *fault*, Liz. He's still a freak."

"Shut up," I say to her. "He's a good person."

"All of you, shut up," Mera says, turning up the radio. "Let's go!"

I watch as we all drive away, the music blaring, the tires on the Mercedes squealing as Mera speeds out of the parking lot.

So maybe Alex was right—maybe I wasn't that great of a person. I certainly didn't have any friends on the cross-country team.

But I was friends with Mr. Riley. I cared about him. And,

obviously, he cared about me. So that's something. Right now, in light of all the memories I've seen of myself, I'll take anything to prove that I wasn't—as Alex so clearly articulated—a nightmare of a human being.

And with a blink, I'm back in the present, standing in Mr. Riley's office with Alex and Richie. Right now, Mr. Riley rests his chin against his hands and says, "Well, if it isn't the brilliant Richie Wilson. Looks like you've wandered to the wrong side of the sandbox."

My boyfriend crosses his arms and leans against the doorframe. His posture might be casual, but I can tell from the tension in his clenched jaw that he's nervous. "What's that supposed to mean?"

For a moment, I can tell that Mr. Riley wants to kick him out. Alex is right—he probably did know what Richie was up to recreationally. It's not like Richie ever went to great pains to hide it. Sometimes I thought he wanted to get caught—like it would almost be a relief.

"Look, I know you don't like me," Richie says.

Mr. Riley doesn't argue. But he isn't mean, either. "I won't try to pretend I understand how you're feeling. I know this has got to be awful for you, Richie." He sits up straight, fidgeting nervously with the stopwatch hanging around his neck.

Even though he's only seventeen, I can imagine that Richie would be intimidating to someone like Mr. Riley. They are so different: Richie is thick bodied and confidently slow as he almost strolls wherever he goes, his head full of all the countless books he's read, yet somehow he's so cool, so absolutely *not* nerdy—while Mr. Riley is all fast-twitch muscle fiber, more of a simple, nice guy, single-mindedly passionate about the concept of putting one foot in front of the other, over and over again, until there's nothing but body and road and breath. No way any seven-year-old wielding a BB gun could catch him now.

"I've been going running," Richie blurts. He doesn't look at Mr. Riley. His gaze settles on the bookshelf behind my coach's head, packed with titles like *Changing Bodies, Changing Lives*; *Zen Running*; *Born to Run;* and the embarrassing *Let's Talk about Sex! A Guidebook for Young Bodies on the Verge of Adulthood*.

I'm more surprised than anyone in the room to hear what Richie's been up to in the two weeks that have passed since my death. Alex and I haven't seen him out running at all. I'd assumed he was spending most of his free time looking for comfort in the back of Josie's mouth.

"Running? From whom—the cops?" Mr. Riley stretches his neck, touching his ear to his shoulder.

Richie takes the question seriously. "No, not from the cops. I mean *running* running. Like, recreationally. I don't know why I'm doing it. It's like I woke up one day last week and felt like I needed to *move*." He swallows. "Liz used to talk about that. Sometimes I'd ask her, 'What do you think about when you're out there running for hours on end?' And she'd always say, 'Nothing.'"

I smile. "He's right." I look at Alex. "You don't know how that feels, do you? To think about absolutely nothing for hours at a time? It's like heaven."

He gives me a disappointed half smile. "Like either of us would know what heaven's like."

Mr. Riley is caught off guard; this clearly isn't what he was expecting from Richie. "Well, that's true," he says. "Running is meditation. It clears your mind. It calms you down."

"She was running for hours at a time, like sometimes three or four hours," Richie continues. "Did you know that? Before she died, I mean. Did you notice how much weight she was losing? She was passing out. Shouldn't you have done something? You were her coach."

Alex gazes at my body. "Now that they're mentioning it, Liz, you *are* awfully skinny. I mean, you're *too* skinny."

I frown. "Runners are always skinny. Besides, you said I was hot."

"A hot mess, maybe," he murmurs. I ignore him, choosing instead to pay attention to what's actually going on in the room. Richie. Running. In a million years, I never would have expected it from him. I'd tried to get him to come with me plenty of times, but he was never interested.

"Calm down, Richie," Mr. Riley says. "I know all about that. We'd talked about it, believe me. But I couldn't stop her from running on her own." He pauses. "I didn't realize how dire the situation had become. But I did try to help her. At the end of last year, I told her that if she lost any more weight, I'd keep her off the team."

"You did?" Richie pauses. "She didn't tell me about that."

"You didn't tell him much of anything lately, did you?" Alex says.

I flick his earlobe. "You. Quiet."

"It was right after she got her concussion," Mr. Riley says. "That's when I realized things were going downhill for her."

I press my palm to the side of my head. "Oh . . . that's right. I remember this." And when I close my eyes, I see it; even though I'm outside my body, I'm standing so close to my seventeen-year-old self that I can almost *feel* it happening. I'm at the top of the stairs in my parents' house, stretching, facing the big window at the landing in the upstairs hallway. I'm looking out at the water, the *Elizabeth* tied to the dock behind our house, and the beach stretching in a graceful curve against the horizon. I reach up with the tips of my fingers, stretching onto my tiptoes in my dirty—but very comfortable—running shoes. Then I bend over, letting my fingertips graze the oriental rug I'm standing on. I see shades of maroon, beige, forest green, and crimson in the pattern. But then my balance stutters; my knees buckle, and I take a step back, trying to find my footing on the landing.

I want to reach out to myself, to stop what I know is about to happen. But all I can do is watch.

Just as I think I've found my footing on the landing, I step over the edge of the stairs. Then I'm falling. I watch, helpless, as my body tumbles to the bottom of the steps. When I finally come to a stop, my rail-thin form crumpled on the hardwood floor in the foyer of our house, I'm obviously unconscious.

I open my eyes; I see Mr. Riley sitting at his desk. I blink and blink, trying to go back to the scene. When I find a memory again, I realize that I've gone forward in time to almost two days after the fall. I've just gotten out of the hospital; I can tell because I'm still wearing my plastic ID bracelet. My father has picked me up by himself. I watch the two of us alone in the car together as we drive home in near silence. I don't speak to my dad. I only stare outside, watching the landscape pass by out the window.

Finally, my dad closes his chubby hand over my bicep. His fingers easily go all the way around my arm.

"What are you trying to do, Elizabeth?" he asks. His voice is quiet. My dad has always been this way: calm, mellow, understated, everything kept inside, beneath the surface. Even when my mother died. Even when his own daughter died.

I don't look at him. Instead, I stare out the car window, seeming to concentrate on the trees beginning to bud in the spring air, the blooming flowers, the grass growing in countless determined individual blades against the sharp wind of New England that seems to slice across the landscape. It's *life* that's emerging.

Just from looking at myself, I can sense that I'm starving. All that life, outside, juxtaposed with what I'm sure is a knot of throbbing hunger in my concave belly. My hunger seems to be everywhere. It's in my eyes. It's all over my face. It permeates the space between my father and me in the car.

When he speaks, my dad sounds like he's trying not to cry. "You aren't your mother," he says.

"I know that," I tell him.

"Then what is the matter? Why are you doing this?" He turns the car into our garage, shuts off the engine, and locks the doors.

"You're not getting out until you give me an answer," he says.

But I don't respond. I stare straight ahead, at the wall of the garage, where my stepmom's bicycle hangs from two mounted hooks.

"Therapy," my dad finally says. "You're going to see a doctor. I'm going to make an appointment for you."

I don't say anything.

"You'll go," he continues, "or there will be consequences. Understand?"

But as I watch myself, I know that I had no intention of going to therapy. I certainly don't remember ever seeing any doctors for my eating or exercise habits. And it wasn't like my dad would be able to really force me, anyway. He was too distracted. He worked eighty-hour weeks before I died, sometimes more. It wasn't like we needed the money; he just loved to work. He was almost never around. I'm surprised he was home long enough to pick me up from the hospital.

My father waits for a few moments, looking at me expectantly, before he gets out of the car, slams the door, and leaves me alone in the cool darkness. I press the back of my palm to my forehead. I look like I'm in terrible pain, like I can barely stand to be conscious.

As the memory drifts away, I see Mr. Riley stand up from behind his desk. "If you really want to run," he tells Richie, "you could join the cross-country team."

"Oh no. I couldn't do that," Richie says.

"Why not?"

"Oh, I've got . . . well, you know. I've got other obligations. I'm not exactly a team player."

"Of course you aren't." Mr. Riley glances at his watch. "You'll be late for homeroom."

"I was wondering if you could take a look at my shoes."

Mr. Riley pauses. "What?"

"My shoes. My sneakers." And Richie picks up his foot and rests it on the edge of Mr. Riley's desk.

"What do you want to know?" Mr. Riley only glances at his shoes. "They're fine. You should get new ones every three hundred miles or so. You've got plenty of wear left in them."

"I don't know about that," Richie says. "I've only been running a week and a half, and my feet are in rough shape." He stares at the shoes. "You know, Liz bought these for me over a year ago. She wanted me to come running with her. I never went, though."

Mr. Riley is clearly uncomfortable. "I'm sure she'd be happy you're running now."

"Everybody thinks they know what would make me happy now," I murmur to Alex.

He nods in agreement. "Yeah. People tend to do that after you die."

"I keep thinking," Richie says, "that maybe if I'd spent more time with her, this might not have happened. If I hadn't fallen asleep that night, she would be okay. You know how they say that even the smallest detail can change a person's destiny? Like someone swatting a mosquito over in Africa can cause a tsunami on a different continent? Maybe if I'd gone running with her, or even tried to talk to her more—"

"Hey. Stop it." Mr. Riley studies my boyfriend's expression beneath the ugly glare of the fluorescent light. "Don't do this to yourself. There was no way you could have helped her."

Richie lowers his foot back to the floor. He bites his lip. "People are talking about me," he says. "I know that. People want to turn it into a drama. They're talking about it like maybe it wasn't an accident."

Mr. Riley holds very still. He barely breathes. He doesn't say a word.

"Maybe it wasn't," Richie says. "All I remember is falling asleep that night. Who knows what happened after that? There were six of us on the boat." His eyes are wet. Aside from my funeral, this is the only other time I've ever seen Richie cry. "Somebody must know what happened. Don't you think, Mr. Riley? You knew her. She was special. People like her don't just slip away, do they?"

Mr. Riley shakes his head. "I don't know."

"I feel like I need to listen very carefully," Richie continues. "And something's telling me that I have to run."

I can barely move. "It's me," I whisper. "I'm right here, Richie. I'm with you."

"Okay." Mr. Riley nods. "Then that's what you should do. Find me after school," he says. "I'll be at the track. I'll check your form. We'll see if we can figure out what's hurting your feet."

As they both leave the room, Mr. Riley turns his light out, leaving Alex and me in the dark. I try to wiggle my toes in my boots, but they barely have room to move.

Nine

My friends are stealing my clothes.

"It's not stealing if you can't wear them any-more," Alex points out. We are in my bedroom, which is an absolute mess: my oak canopy bed is unmade, the pink-and-white-striped sheets and comforter in a tangle at the foot of the mattress. The surface of my vanity holds a slew of makeup, everything from bronzer powder to multiple tubes of mascara to body glitter to what must be at least three dozen tubes of lipstick collected in a pricey designer purse that I apparently used exclusively for cosmetic storage. I don't remember being such a slob. I'm almost embarrassed for Alex to see my room in such disarray.

"But this is my stuff." I pout. "It's only been a few weeks. They could wait a little bit longer."

"Yeah, well, they're your friends. I mean, you've gotta

expect them to jump at the opportunity for free clothes. Be reasonable, Liz. To them, this is better than a clearance at JCPenney."

I wince at the suggestion. "Alex. My friends and I do not shop at *JCPenney*."

I feel incredibly sad looking at my old things. There is a history documented in the mess, a genuine illustration of who I was. As I look at everything, fragments of memories surface in my mind, providing small pieces to what seems like an impossibly large—and growing—puzzle. A corkboard hanging above my dresser is crowded with cross-country ribbons. They're mostly for second and third place—like I've said, speed was never my biggest strength—but there are dozens of them. In a corner of my room, beside my dresser, there is a pile of running shoes. I used to go through a new pair every six weeks or so, but I never liked to get rid of the old ones. Instead, I hoarded them. There are probably twenty pairs collecting dust in the corner, their soles worn almost smooth from so many miles against the sandy, salty roads. On the side of the left shoe from each pair, I used to write the purchase date with a permanent black marker, so I'd know roughly when they were kaput.

I have an overwhelming desire to touch everything—to feel the cheap cloth of a hard-won ribbon or the tight threads in the seam of a shoe—just one last time. Knowing that I can't makes me feel so helpless and frustrated, so . . . dead.

My friends—Mera and Caroline, along with Josie—are in

my closet, which is a walk-in nearly half the size of my bedroom.

"Oh, you have got to be *kidding* me," Alex says when he sees them. All three are in bras and underwear, ready to start trying on my clothes. He gives me a wicked smile. "If this is hell, go ahead and chain me to the wall."

I frown at him. "I thought you hated them."

He scratches the side of his head in mock contemplation. "It doesn't mean I don't want to see them half-naked."

Caroline is the only one who seems to have any reservations about what they're doing. She stares at the carefully organized rows of clothing, hung neatly in contrast to my otherwise messy room, and reaches out with a perfectly manicured fingertip, barely touching the sleeve of a red cashmere sweater.

"Are you sure this is okay?" She gives Josie a worried look. "It feels strange. What if your mom finds us in here?"

Josie. My stepsister. My best friend. As soon as I look at her face, I can see that she's upset, too. "It was my mom's idea," she says, tugging a black linen dress from its hanger.

She stares at it for a few seconds. Then she holds the fabric to her face and inhales deeply, smelling it. Searching for me. When she pulls it away, there are tears in her eyes.

"Josie?" Caroline's tone is gentle. "Are you sure you want to do this right now?"

My stepsister takes another deep breath. She has a faraway look on her face. "Every morning when I wake up, I expect her to be home," she murmurs. "I open my eyes and look at my alarm clock and think, 'Liz is probably back from her morning run already.' Then I remember that she's . . . not here." She holds the dress in a crumpled ball, staring at it. "I don't think I'll ever get used to the idea. We knew each other all our lives, you know?"

Mera and Caroline exchange a worried glance. Caroline moves to Josie, puts a hand against her back. "I know, Josie. It's awful. Seriously, let's save this for another time. We can do something else right now. We won't leave you alone today, okay?"

Josie frowns. She shakes out the dress, holds it up to stare at it for a moment before pressing it against her body, almost like she's hugging it. "No. I want to do it now. I want to get it over with. Besides, what else will we do with everything? Give it to the Goodwill? This stuff cost a fortune." With one hand, she wipes at her eyes. She blinks rapidly a few times. Forcing a big smile, she looks at Caroline and Mera. "It's fine. I'm okay."

She's right about my clothes, anyway. Even though it pains me to see my friends going through all of my earthly possessions, I know it's better if they take them. Practically everything looks like it came from high-end boutiques. Even my running gear is top-of-the-line, the latest technology in spandex and microfiber.

"What about Liz's dad?" Caroline asks. "What would he think? I mean, would he be okay with us doing this?"

I already know that my dad probably wouldn't care. Unlike Nicole, he is the complete opposite of a flake: he considers himself a very logical person. He doesn't believe in ghosts or the afterlife or anything like that. So to him, it's likely my clothes don't have any meaning anymore.

It's funny—you'd think he and Nicole would be a poor match. But they're not. My dad is amused by her fascination with spiritualism. He thinks it's cute and harmless; at least, he used to. I don't know what he might think of it now.

Josie gives Caroline a sharp look. "What do you mean, *Liz's dad*? He's my dad, too."

"Oh." Caroline looks like she's swallowed her gum. "Right." I see her exchanging another Look with Mera. But neither one of them says anything.

"She thinks he's her actual dad?" Alex asks.

I try to wave the notion away, like it's nothing more significant than a pesky fly. But it's still here, out in the open now, and I know I don't have a choice but to explain a little further to Alex. "I told you, we didn't talk about it much. She thinks . . . yeah, I guess she thinks he's her dad. She's wrong. But Josie's real dad is a deadbeat. He couldn't hold a job. He never really visited Josie after he and Nicole got divorced."

"But doesn't it bother you that she thinks your dad and her mom were fooling around for all those years?" Alex seems incredulous. I realize that he's kind of right; it's quite an assumption on Josie's part, and it seems strange that I never tried to convince her differently.

I look at my stepsister, who lets her fingers trail over my wardrobe with a bleak, sad expression on her face. She cries every day now. Glancing down the length of her body, I see that she's still wearing her "best friends" anklet.

"It seemed impossible," I tell him. "I never believed it. I don't know, Alex . . . she wanted a dad. I think that, deep down, she knows it can't be true. She *must* know. It was like this ugly rumor that had followed us all our lives. None of us liked to talk about it. We certainly weren't going to ask my dad or Nicole if it was true. It's like there was no point in discussing it."

His tone is doubtful. "I guess so."

"It doesn't matter now," I say. "Pay attention. Let's watch."

Once my friends have each gathered a pile of clothes, they start trying things on, standing in the center of my bedroom, tossing whatever items they reject carelessly onto the floor.

"You're way skinnier than all of them," Alex points out. "I wouldn't think your clothes would fit."

"Richie said I lost a lot of weight quickly," I remind him. "It makes sense that there's plenty of old stuff that's a couple sizes larger."

Josie slips into a pair of jeans and a black one-shoulder top. She gazes at herself in the mirror.

"It doesn't look as good on me as it did on Liz," she says, biting her bottom lip in a half smile. She holds out a piece of her long blond hair and frowns at the ends, which I happen to know are almost always split, no matter how often she gets it trimmed. All those chemicals from the bleach that gets applied every six weeks—plus all the heat she uses to style it—really do a number on her tresses. "Liz looked great in everything. Everything always fit her perfectly."

Mera takes a seat at my vanity and rifles through the drawer. She emerges with an unopened pair of false eyelashes. "Well, what do you expect? She was built like a game show hostess," she says. She digs around in the bag of mascara for a few seconds before turning it over to dump the contents onto the floor. "You can't compare yourself to her."

Josie nods. I notice that she grits her teeth for just a second, her jaw muscles tensing visibly at her cheek, almost like she's chewing on the sentiment. "I know." She turns to the side in front of the mirror, gazing at her profile. "She could have made a paper bag look good."

"Yep." Mera continues to rifle through the makeup. She picks up a tube of lipstick, opens it, and stares at the maroon color absently. "But she was different over the past few months." Her tone is cautious. "You noticed . . . right, Josie?"

Josie nods. "She was wasting away. Everyone knew that." And then she adds, "It's like she couldn't escape her history. She was just like her mom."

I can't *believe* what she just said. The feeling of coldness that is always with me is suddenly sharper somehow.

What is she talking about? I was not just like my mother. I was not anorexic. I just liked to run. All the time. Every day.

Caroline shrugs, unfazed by the comment about my mom. "I didn't think she looked bad, though. You know what they say—you can never be too thin or too rich, right?"

My stepsister seems like she wants to cry again. She stares at my ceiling, which is a light shade of purple. And looking at it, I remember: She and I painted it together, just a few months before I died, on a rainy Saturday afternoon. Before we used rollers on the surface, we took paintbrushes and wrote our names in swirly purple letters. We wrote: JOSIE AND LIZ BFF. I wrote LIZ + RICHIE 4-EVER. Even after two coats of paint, if I squint at the ceiling, I can still see the faint outlines of the letters beneath the color.

"There's something I need to tell you both," Josie says quietly.

"Oh yeah?" Caroline is only mildly interested, choosing instead to study the hand stitching on a houndstooth jacket that I used to *love*.

"Yes." Josie's hair is pulled into a tight, smooth ponytail. As she's gotten older, her hair has grown in darker and darker. As a result, her highlights—which are chunky and so light they're almost platinum—look unnatural and harsh.

Right now, she pulls her ponytail free and shakes her head so that the waves fall over her shoulders. "It's about Richie," she says. She pauses. When she speaks, her voice is shaky, unconfident. "We've been dating."

Mera almost stabs herself in the eye with a mascara wand as she jerks her head in Josie's direction. Caroline—who has put on the houndstooth jacket and is struggling to squeeze her wide foot into one of my narrow shoes—trips and falls in a tan, toned heap onto the floor.

"You and Richie?" Caroline says, sitting upright, tugging the jacket back into place across her chest. "Since when?"

"Since a few months ago." Josie hesitates. "He was going to break up with Liz."

"I've already heard this," I say, covering my ears. "I don't want to hear it again."

Alex pulls my hands away from my head. "You have to listen," he insists. "What else are we here for?"

But I ignore him. I shake myself free from his grasp, go into my bathroom, and sit in the shower. For the moment, it seems I've managed to distance myself from Alex, at least by a few yards. But I've only been in the bathroom for a minute or so when Caroline comes in by herself.

She locks the door behind her. She stares at her reflection in the mirror.

"Hey, Caroline," I say, even though I know she can't hear me. "I'm right here."

She turns on a faucet. Slowly, quietly, she begins to open the drawers on my bathroom vanity and look through their contents.

As I'm watching my friend, a handful of new memories about her seep into my consciousness. This is Caroline Ann Michaels, whom I have known since preschool. She is outgoing, friendly, and sharply smart. Like I said earlier, she's a cheerleader—I remembered that much. But now I recall details of her personality, facts about her family. She expresses her excitement in frequent bursts of clapping and spirit fingers. She smiles so much that it's almost shocking to see her wearing a frown. She is the youngest of four girls in her family, each of whom has been an icon of sorts at Noank High. Her sisters, in order from oldest to youngest: Charlotte, Corrine, and Christy. Her parents are Camille and Colin. The whole family is devoutly Catholic. They are the portrait of the American Dream. Every year, they send out a Christmas card with a photo of their family dressed up like characters from a popular book or movie. Last year, they were all from Harry Potter; the year before that, it was Star Wars. Caroline's mother does a ton of volunteer work, and her dad is some kind of finance wizard who works in Manhattan during the week and is only at home on the weekends.

Caroline is a good person—I'm sure of it. So I'm more than a little surprised to see her rummaging in my drawers like this, so secretly. It doesn't make a lot of sense; Josie has already given them permission to go through all my stuff.

In the top drawer of my vanity, she finds an almost-full bottle of prescription painkillers. They're leftovers from my concussion. She slips them into her purse. She's about to turn off the water when she stops, peering closely into the drawer.

I can tell from the way she's looking that all she wanted were the painkillers; she's obviously stumbled onto something else.

It's money. Cash. She reaches into the drawer and removes a fistful of *hundred-dollar bills.* Her hands are shaking a little bit.

I have no idea what I might have been doing with so much money. I had a bank account and my parents deposited my allowance into it each week. They never gave me cash.

But the money she's holding was obviously for *something*— why else would I have hidden it in a bathroom drawer? Slowly, her eyes glazed in "look what I found" fascination, Caroline begins to count the bills. One . . . two . . . three . . . four . . . it's five hundred dollars.

I gasp. What was I doing with all that cash? I can't imagine. I squeeze my eyes shut and try to focus, struggling to remember something, anything. But nothing appears.

There's a tap at the door. "Caroline? Sweetie, are you okay?" It's Josie.

"Um—yeah, just a second!" She stares at the money. For just a moment, I think she's about to put it back in the drawer.

But she doesn't. Instead, she rolls it into a ball and stuffs it in her bra.

Once she's out of the bathroom, Caroline starts gathering up her stuff. "I didn't realize how late it was getting," she explains, slipping on her shoes. "I have to go home right now."

"But we aren't finished." Mera frowns. "And we were all supposed to get lattes after this and then sleep over."

"I'm sorry, guys, I have to go. We'll do lattes another day, okay?" Caroline grabs her purse. Josie and Mera give each other an unsteady look.

"What's the matter? You're being weird," Josie says. "You're not going to take any clothes? I told you, my parents *want* us to have them."

Caroline inhales a deep breath. She looks around my room for a long moment. Her gaze lingers on my pile of old running shoes. For just a moment, she looks like she might cry.

"I'll keep this jacket," she says, gesturing to what she's already wearing, "but I don't want anything else. Taking one thing is okay, but digging through her stuff like this . . . I don't know, Josie. It feels wrong. It feels like we're stealing from Liz."

Mera looks down at her own hands. She's clutching no fewer than *five* of my old purses. Her grip on them loosens a bit—but she doesn't let go.

Josie stares at Caroline quizzically. "You look great in that jacket," she offers. "Liz would have wanted you to have it."

It's true; she does look great in the jacket. And this time, Josie is right. I want Caroline to have it. I know she'll take good care of it.

"I'll call you later, okay?" Caroline blows my friends a kiss. Then she's gone.

When I tell Alex what I saw in the bathroom, he says, "Well, your boyfriend is a drug dealer. Maybe you were holding some cash for him."

I frown. "I doubt it. I don't remember anything like that."

"Your memory is full of holes, Liz. It seems like a decent explanation."

"No." I shake my head. "It doesn't make sense. Why would he need me to hold money? And I already told you, I hated that he sold drugs. I don't think I would have done anything to help him."

Alex raises his right eyebrow. "But you're not sure. Are you?"

I hesitate. "No," I finally admit, "I'm not sure."

He gives me a satisfied look. "Hey, Liz—if you hated him selling so much, why didn't you do more to stop him? You've told me yourself that you did drugs, too. That's sort of hypo-critical, don't you think?"

I shrug. "Not really. I only did them sometimes. But nothing too bad—nothing heavy." And I take a deep breath. Any memory of Richie—*anything*—is painful to recall. "And Richie didn't like me doing drugs. He was always trying to protect me."

"Huh. He did a great job."

"Shut up. He's just a *boy*, Alex. Just like you. He isn't really famous. He's just Richie. But you're getting off topic. I'm telling you, there's no way I would have had that much cash lying around. For *anything*. I only remember using plastic."

"What other explanation can there be, Liz? People don't walk around with cash like that anymore. Why would you be hiding it in your bathroom?"

"I don't know." I watch Mera getting ready to leave. She carries an armful of my clothing out to her car, then comes back for another pile.

"And you're sure Caroline wasn't specifically looking for the money?" Alex asks.

"Yes." I pause, replaying the scene in my mind. "She was surprised to find it. She was obviously there for the pills. And even that's weird. I don't know what Caroline would possibly want with my old painkillers."

He looks around my room, observing the mess and disarray. "It's funny," he says. "I always thought you guys—everyone in the upper social echelon—I assumed you had such simple, perfect lives. Everything seemed so easy for you."

I gaze out my window. My bedroom is at the back of the house, facing the water. I can see the *Elizabeth* resting alone at the dock, quiet and empty.

The memory begins to slip over me before I can even close my eyes. As it descends upon my consciousness, I feel a sense of calm comfort.

It's the middle of the night; my alarm clock reads 2:14 a.m. For a few seconds, I watch my living self asleep in bed. I'm obviously dreaming, or else having a nightmare. My legs twitch in my sleep; I reach into the darkness with my skinny arms outstretched toward the ceiling, trying to grab on to something, anything. Then I sit up so quickly in bed, gasping for breath, that as a ghost, I'm startled. In the dim room, my wide eyes flash in the moonlight that spills through my windows.

When my younger self turns on my nightstand light, I realize that I'm seeing myself at ten, maybe eleven years old. My bedroom is still decorated the way it was before Nicole redid the whole house: a border of ballet slippers is stenciled along the top edges of my cream-colored walls; my posters are all stills from shows like *The Nutcracker* and *Swan Lake*. This was before I started running; in the corner of my room that is now reserved for sneakers, there are a few scuffed ballet slippers and a pair of shiny black tap shoes. The decor, along with the footwear, are the last remnants of my mother's influence after she died. She loved to watch my recitals. She rarely missed so much as a rehearsal. But I was never that good of a dancer, even though I took lessons from preschool up until the end of sixth grade. I was always forgetting the steps in ballet, and I could never master the complicated tap choreography.

It's incredible to see myself as such a young girl. I wear a fitted white tank top and pink pajama bottoms decorated with—what else?—ballet slippers. There's a softness to my facial features that is long gone now, replaced in my teenage years by an angular jaw and hollowed cheeks. My chest is nonexistent; I probably didn't even own a training bra yet. My long blond hair is all one length, spilling over my shoulders without any hint of layers to frame my face. I watch myself as I look silently around the room before placing my bare feet on the floor, pressing my palms to my flushed cheeks. I can't help but smile when I notice that my toenails are all intact, and painted a deep shade of dainty pink.

As innocent as my younger self appears, it's clear that I was having some kind of a nightmare; my forehead is wrinkled in agitation, and for a minute or two I just look around the room, staring at all of my things, as though I don't know what to do with myself.

Then, walking on tiptoes so as not to make too much noise, my younger self steals out of the bedroom. I follow through the door, down the hallway to the right, where my younger self has come to a stop outside Josie's room.

I don't knock. I simply open the door and go in, pattering softly now to the edge of her bed, where I put a small hand—my fingernails painted the same shade of pink as my toes—on her sleeping form, curled into a ball on her side.

"Josie," I whisper, shaking her a little bit. "Hey, Josie."

"Mmm." She rolls onto her back. She blinks up at me. Her own bedside light is on; Josie has never liked the dark. Even now, at seventeen, she sleeps with a night-light. "Hey, Liz," she smiles, yawning to reveal two rows of metal braces. "What's wrong?"

"I had a bad dream."

She reaches toward me, takes my hand, and squeezes it.

As I watch the two of us together, I feel such a yearning

for those days, for the blissful ignorance of youth. At ten or eleven, we knew we'd be best friends forever. In the light of Josie's room, I see that we're both wearing our half-heart bracelets—this was a few years before we decided they were uncool and needed to be hidden.

"Here," Josie whispers, pulling back her covers, "get in."

My younger self climbs into bed with my stepsister. I put my arms around her waist. I rest my head beside hers, on the same pillow.

For a while we don't say anything—we just lie there together, with our eyes closed—and I'm almost ready to blink myself back to reality, when Josie whispers, "Love you, Liz."

"I love you, too," my young self whispers.

"Sisters," Josie murmurs. "Forever."

"Forever," I echo as we hold each other.

I could watch us together like this all night, but after a few moments, it becomes clear that all we're doing is sleeping. It's time to go back to reality. My heart, which does not beat beneath my chest, aches so badly for those days. At that age, I'd already lost my mother, so my innocence was gone— but life was still full of hope, full of new beginnings. I had a new family. I still had my father. The future was ripe with possibility.

I close my eyes, squeezing them shut as hard as I can, trying to erase the longing that accompanies what I've just witnessed. When I open them, Alex is standing beside me, staring at me with a combination of curiosity and boredom.

"There you are," he says. "Where were you?"

I ignore the question. "I want to get out of here," I tell him. I suddenly can't stand being in my room anymore.

"Where do you want to go?"

"I don't care. Anywhere. Out."

Ten

When I was alive, it was easy to escape reality: I just put on my shoes and went running. But now, it seems, there is nowhere to go that isn't gut wrenching. I am freezing, almost shivering from the feeling of dampness that clings to my bones. My feet ache. I'm tired. Despite Alex's constant company, death is incredibly, immeasurably lonely.

On our way out of my house, we pass my father sitting in the living room alone. He's dressed in his work clothes, but he doesn't look like he's in a hurry to go anywhere. He sits on the sofa, staring at the television mounted on the wall. It's off, the screen black, but my dad doesn't seem to realize that. He's holding a tumbler of what looks like scotch, gripping it so tightly that his knuckles are white.

I remember my dad as such a happy guy. Now he seems hollowed. Despite his dress clothes, there are small clues in his appearance that make it obvious things aren't quite right. Looking him over, I see that he hasn't shaved in at least a few days. His watch—which I don't recall ever seeing him without—is missing from his wrist. And he isn't wearing socks—just a pair of shiny black loafers over his chubby bare feet. It's like he's gone through the motions of getting ready for work, for life, without any real intention of following through.

He looks from the television to his glass. He shakes it a little bit, watching as the ice cubes rearrange themselves with gentle clinking sounds. Then he cocks his head, listening.

Alex and I are quiet as we watch him. I hear sounds of upbeat chatter coming from above, my stepsister's voice lilting down the hallway as she talks to someone on her phone. I hear her laughter.

My dad hears it, too. He closes his eyes and slumps a bit on the sofa.

He takes a sip of his drink. He chews on an ice cube. Then, slowly, he stands up and walks toward the kitchen. Alex and I follow him. My dad puts his glass in the sink. He goes to the cupboard and removes an entire bottle of scotch. He tucks it beneath his arm and heads toward the back door that leads into our yard.

"Where do you think he's going?" Alex whispers.

"I don't know."

"We could follow him."

I watch from the kitchen window as he makes his way through the backyard, heading toward the docks. If any of our neighbors see him this way, they'll think he's come completely undone. Maybe he has.

"I don't want to," I tell Alex.

"Why not?"

I look at him. The question seems ridiculous. "Because it hurts too much. That's why not."

Instead of following my dad, we head in the opposite direction, out the front door. As we're standing on the street in front of my house, I stare down the road, imagining how it would feel if I could go for a run right now. To get away from Alex, from the painful scene of Josie and my friends going through my old stuff, from the sight of my father barely functioning, from death. Even though I know I can probably never go running again, I can't help but imagine how good it would make me feel, how free. As I'm thinking about it, I wander toward the end of the block just in time to see my boyfriend stepping out onto his front porch. Immediately, I hurry toward him. I feel like I need to be with him, to be close to him.

Richie looks startling. In all the time I've known him, I don't think I've ever seen him in workout gear outside of school. But here he is now: standing in a T-shirt—it's actually a white undershirt—and running shorts, tying the laces on his sneakers. Even though they're technically old—I gave them to him over a year ago—they haven't seen much use yet: they're still white, relatively clean, and stiff looking. Richie appears unsteady on his feet. His legs are pale and not toned. It's obvious he hasn't been running for more than a couple of weeks, if that.

As he's getting ready to step off the porch, Josie opens the front door to my house. She waves at Richie.

"Damn it," he murmurs, even as he smiles at her.

"Come here," Josie calls, waving him over.

I follow him as he walks down the street. He looks around self-consciously as though he's afraid someone will see the two of them together.

My stepsister frowns at him. "What the hell are you wearing?" she asks, with a half giggle.

"I'm wearing clothes. I'm going running."

"*You?* Running?"

"Yes." He pauses. "It helps me think."

It occurs to me that it could be more than a coincidence that Richie is setting out on a run just as I was thinking so hard about it myself. But the thought almost makes me feel too hopeful; as quickly as it surfaces, I dismiss it.

Josie twirls a piece of hair around her finger. Compared to Richie, she's meticulously put together: her hair is curled and fluffed into perfect disarray, framing her small face that has been so carefully made up. I've seen her go through the process more times than I can possibly count. She is the kind of girl—I understand now that I was, too—who sets her alarm for the very early morning and gets out of bed to begin the painstaking process of self-care: Velcro hair rollers for volume. Tweezers for stray eyebrow hairs. Foundation. Bronzer. Blush. Eyeliner. Eye shadow. Eyelash curler. Mascara, mascara, mascara. Lip plumper. Lipliner. Lipstick. Lip gloss. Blotting papers to absorb any excess oil. Hairspray. Body lotion. It is amazing how much effort it takes to look just like everyone else—only better.

It's chilly outside by mid-September, the sky blue with a few scattered, perfect clouds. There's a breeze, which is accompanied by the near-constant sound of the brass wind chimes hanging from Richie's front porch colliding in light, pleasant tones.

Josie hugs herself, rubbing her bare, goose-bumped arms. "How are you doing?"

"I'm okay. School's hell, though. Everywhere I look, I'm thinking about her." He stares at the sky. "It feels like she isn't gone, you know? Every morning when I wake up, there's always a moment when I think I'm going to see her again. I'll think something like, 'Well, I'd better hurry up, Liz hates to be late.' And then I remember. It's like she dies all over again, every day."

"I know," Josie says. "I was just saying the same thing to Caroline and Mera." Tentatively, Josie reaches toward Richie. Her fingernails, I notice, are no longer purple, but instead a glossy shade of red. She's had a manicure recently.

"Richie, I've been meaning to tell you something. I shouldn't have told you about her and Vince," she says. "You would have been better off not knowing."

He stares at my house, at my car—a red Mustang, which I got for my seventeenth birthday last year—parked in the driveway. "Maybe. Maybe not." Then he shakes his head, a lock of curly hair falling into his eyes. I want so badly to reach out and brush it away.

"No," he says. "It's better that I knew the truth." He takes her hand, swings her arm back and forth. "We can take care of each other."

Suddenly Josie looks past him. She raises her free arm and waves. "Hey, Mrs. Wilson."

Richie glances over his shoulder. His mother stands on his front porch, watching them.

"Christ," he says, keeping his voice low. "What does she want?"

"Oh, be nice." Josie smiles at him. "She's your mother."

"Barely," he mutters. Like I said before, Mr. and Mrs. Wilson are both successful artists. They are creative, thoughtful people, but somehow they're painfully awful at raising a child. I heard someone say once that there are two kinds of parents: the kind who will do anything for their kid and the kind who will pay someone to do anything for their kid. Richie's parents are the latter. It isn't that they don't care; it's just that they're really quite busy, dear.

"Richard? Can you come here for a minute?" Mrs. Wilson doesn't return Josie's wave. She doesn't even smile.

"What's the matter with her?" Alex asks. "She doesn't like Josie or something?"

I nod. "She doesn't like any of us. Not Josie, not my parents—"

"What about you?"

I flinch. When I look at my house again, Richie and Josie are gone, replaced by another memory. A moving van is parked in the driveway. The front door of the house is propped open with a brick. From inside, two young voices are shrieking at each other, footsteps pounding down the stairs.

"Girls! Calm down!" My father appears in the back of the truck, carrying a pile of boxes.

Nicole steps out the front door. She's wearing a *very* tight T-shirt and jeans, her long hair tied back with a pink bandanna. She's young, in her thirties, her cheeks flushed with hard work and excitement and dewey, newly wedded bliss. And man, is she pretty.

"Let them play, Marshall," she says to my dad. She kisses him on the cheek. "They're excited." She tucks a strand of loose hair behind her ear, revealing a tiny dream catcher for an earring, impossibly small feathers dangling from the circular web.

Josie and I come rushing out behind her, our faces sweaty, both of us giggling. I almost bump into my father as he's carrying the boxes up the walk.

"Watch it!" He jumps out of the way. Sighing, he puts the boxes on the ground and presses a hand to his back. He's only in his midthirties, but my dad is already overweight and out of shape. Beads of sweat shine on his creased forehead. He's out of breath. In four years, he'll have a mild heart attack, over lunch and drinks with a client. His doctor will advise him to lose twenty pounds and stop eating red meat; he'll promptly gain ten pounds and refuse to abandon his love for steak.

He gives the boxes a dirty look. "We should have hired movers."

"Oh, would you relax? You're a big boy. It's not that much stuff," Nicole says, waving a hand carelessly through the air. A big diamond on the ring finger of her left hand gleams in the sunlight. The accessory seems out of place among her other jewelry: the earrings, along with a chunky turquoise necklace and ring, and a wrist of bangle bracelets.

She stares past my father. "Oh—look, Marshall. The Wilsons are home."

Richie and his parents are getting out of the car in front of their house. When Mr. and Mrs. Wilson see my dad and Nicole, they exchange a wary look.

"Hey, Richie!" I call, waving.

He waves back. He has dimples when he smiles. His T-shirt has a Batman cartoon on the front. There is no hint whatsoever of the reluctant delinquent he'll become in a few years. Here, at age ten, he is all curls and sweetness and innocent energy. I adored him then. How could I not? Even as children, whether or not we realized it, we loved each other.

"Richard, get in the house. Now."

"But Mom—"

Mrs. Wilson, smiling, her teeth gritted, says, "*Now*, Richard."

He gives me a disappointed shrug, and I watch as he shuffles toward his house, looking back at me over his shoulder. He points at his mother and draws a circle around his ear with a finger as if to say, *crazy*.

I beam at him. But then I watch as Nicole stands with Mr. and Mrs. Wilson, talking to them as they nod with forced smiles. At such a young age, I didn't understand what was going on, but now, watching the scene play out again, I understand. They don't like her. Not at *all*.

"After my mother died," I explain to Alex, the memory dissolving, "Nicole and my dad started dating right away. Nicole and her first husband were barely separated." I don't know why I'm telling him this. I don't particularly want to talk about it, and like I've said so many times before, I've never believed any of the rumors. Suddenly, though, there is a flicker of doubt, from somewhere deep within my mind. It's just a flicker. But it's enough.

"Her first husband?" he asks. "You mean Josie's dad?"

"Yeah," I say, nodding. "But look at Josie, Alex. She looks

a little bit like my father, don't you think?" I try to remind myself that Josie looked like her *real* dad, too—they both had the same hair and eye color—but still. There's this nagging doubt. People have been talking about this for so long. Could it possibly be true?

Josie is thin enough, and fairly petite, but there's a shadow of thickness to her build. Unlike me—I had my mother's genes, and even before I became rail thin, I was always lanky and slender—Josie struggles to maintain her figure. She doesn't have much of a waistline. There's a fleshiness to her that no high-protein diet or aerobics regime is ever going to change. Her physique fits into my father's side of the family tree like a missing branch.

My dad and Nicole were high school sweethearts. They broke up and went their separate ways after graduation, but both of them eventually settled back in Noank with their respective spouses. It's a small town; they were friends. My mother was sick long before she ever became pregnant with me. Who knows what my parents' marriage was like?

"People think my dad and Nicole had an affair, and Josie was the result," I tell Alex. "Before my mom died. Before Nicole got divorced."

"Uh-huh. And what do *you* think?" Alex asks.

With Richie distracted by his mom, Josie is staring at her phone, busily texting, a half smile playing on her pretty red lips.

"I don't know. Until a few minutes ago, I would have told

you there was no way they ever had an affair. But"—my voice falters for a moment—"they got married so fast after my mom died. They barely even *dated*. I can't imagine that my dad would have cheated on my mother, Alex. I've never thought it was possible, not for a second. It's just that . . ."

"What?" Alex prompts. "It's just that *what?*"

"She does look an awful lot like my dad. I never really noticed until right now."

Alex stares at Josie. "Maybe you didn't want to notice."

Richie follows his mom into their house, leaving Josie alone outside, and I follow Richie, walking effortlessly through the front door after he closes it in my face.

The place has a deceptive sense of warmth. Everywhere you look, there's art: paintings hung on the walls (no prints for the Wilsons—these are all original pastels, protected by museum-quality glass, a collection that could probably pay for Richie's college tuition three times over); sculptures on the floor and on the bookshelves; stained-glass windows; handwoven rugs; plants in every corner of the seemingly casual, loving disarray in what looks to be a real home.

Except I know that it's not. It's just an accumulation of stuff. The paintings are meant to be appreciated, but not necessarily studied. Once, when I was looking at one of them, Richie's dad actually told me to be careful not to *breathe* too close to the glass. The books are all for show, purchased in bulk from an antique auction years earlier. The rugs were imported in bulk from Morocco. They have a maid to water all the plants.

And there's never any real food in the house, just things like wine and ketchup and the occasional container of left-over takeout. Richie's parents spend most weekdays in the city, where they have a gallery—why should they bother to go grocery shopping? It's not like their son needs to eat or anything like that.

Richie and his mother stand in the kitchen together as Mrs. Wilson stares into the massive, almost-empty stainless steel refrigerator. Aside from the shelves on the door, which are fully stocked with condiments, all I can see inside are a two-liter of pop, a pizza box, and a cardboard container of soy milk. The soy milk, I recall as I look at it, has been there for months.

"Richard, I know you won't like hearing this from me, but I don't want you spending time with Josie." The kitchen is modern, sleek, cold: all marble and steel and glass. It screams of hunger by design, coupled with the conspicuous absence of any food whatsoever. A spare set of keys dangles from a hook. The dishwasher, with its transparent glass door, is completely empty. Richie used to eat breakfast at my house most days. I'm not sure what he's doing with his mornings now.

"She just lost her sister," he says. "She's a mess."

"That's exactly the point. She just lost her sister." When she closes the fridge, Mrs. Wilson's face goes dark. The only light in the kitchen comes from the window above the sink and cuts the room in two, dividing Richie and his mom spatially. Mrs. Wilson—thin; in her fifties; no makeup; dark, curly brown hair; wearing a flannel shirt and dirty jeans—presses the heel of her palm to her forehead and leans against the kitchen island. "You aren't old enough to remember what it was like right before Liz's mother died. Lisa was my friend. Richard, she used to cry about Nicole. She used to tell me, 'That woman is trying to steal my husband.' It was horribly sad. The four of them—Josie's parents, Liz's parents—started off as friends. Lisa didn't know that Nicole was obsessed with her husband. Can you imagine?" She scoffs at him a little bit. "Of course you can't. You're a kid."

Richie stares at his white shoes. "What do you want me to do, Mom? I can't ignore Josie. She doesn't deserve it. She didn't do anything."

"She's his daughter. Josie is Marshall's daughter. You know that, don't you? That affair went on for *years* right under everyone's noses. And then his wife died. She *starved* herself to death. She was humiliated and heartsick and broken. You know, I don't think she'd been buried a week when Nicole left her husband for Marshall."

There are some things I don't want to remember, no matter what I might be here to learn. I don't want to listen; I don't want to hear it. But I can't help myself.

"It was years ago," Richie says.

"It was horrifying." Mrs. Wilson stands upright and goes to the only part of the kitchen that is remotely stocked: the wine cabinet. She opens a bottle of red and pours some into a coffee mug with the likeness of Edvard Munch's *The Scream* printed on the side.

Richie bats his long, boyish eyelashes at her. "Mom," he says, "it's barely even noon."

"It's fine." She grips the mug with both hands. Her fingers are dirty with clay. Her nails are short and brittle and unpainted; she seems, for someone so grounded in aesthetics, impossibly plain. She blows into the cup, as though attempting to cool what's inside. "Pretend it's coffee."

"You liked Liz. I know you did." Richie glances out the window, at the sky; it seems he wants to look anywhere but at his mother. She is so concerned about the lives of her neighbors. Meanwhile, it has probably been years since she actually cooked a meal for her only son.

"Yes. Sure, I liked her. She couldn't help any of it, could she? I felt terrible for her."

"How is Josie any different? It isn't her fault what her parents are like."

"She's their daughter, though. At least Liz was Lisa's child." The declaration seems to carry great significance for Mrs. Wilson. "I don't want you going over there anymore. This is your home." And for the first time, she seems to notice his outfit. "Why are you dressed like that?"

"I was about to go running," Richie says. "I need to leave. Right now."

I would do anything to run with him. *Anything.* I would run in these boots, if the pain wouldn't be unbearable. So what if my feet became swollen and bloody? What does it matter? I'm not even a corpse. Amazing how I can still hurt so badly, my toes crowded into the front of my boots, frustration welling into tears as Alex and I watch Richie trotting down our street, turning onto the road leading to Groton Long Point. I know from standing here in these boots, there's no way I can run. The pain would be intolerable. It would kill me all over again. Just being upright feels like torture.

"Why do you think my feet hurt so badly?" I ask Alex. "I can't feel pain anywhere else." It seems odd that we haven't discussed it before now, since the pain is constantly present.

He stares at my boots. "I don't know. What do *you* think?"

The question frustrates me; it's almost like he's trying to get me to realize something, but I don't feel like playing a guessing game right now. "Alex, you've been here a lot longer than me. If you have any answers, just say so."

Alex shrugs. "I really don't, Liz. You're right; it's weird."

I sigh and turn to stare at Richie. "All I want to do is run."

"Yeah?" Alex follows my gaze, then looks down at my boots again. "But you can't. Not now, anyway."

But Richie is free. He can run along the beach, beside

the houses that tower obscenely in their decadence. In Groton Long Point, most of the homes are vacation places, and they're unbelievable. There are homes with elevators. Houses with their own putting courses. In the summer, their driveways are crowded with Mercedes, Ferraris, and even a Bentley or two. These are people who never hear the word "no." They are my neighbors, my parents' friends. In a way—even though I'm a local—I was one of them. Because I wasn't used to hearing the word "no," either—especially after my mom died.

But now everything is no: No, you can't remember. No, you cannot see your mother. No, you cannot run.

Richie, though, can jog on the cool beach; he can breathe the salty air and feel his ankles trembling as he holds his footing in the sand. I've done it hundreds of times myself. It only makes sense that I would not be able to do it now; running made me feel more alive than anything. Of course I can't know it, now that I'm dead.

Richie's mom watches from the front door as her son disappears at the end of the street. Leaving Alex behind, I follow her as she goes upstairs, into his bedroom. For a moment she just stands there. She goes to the bed, takes a corner of the quilt between her thumb and index finger, and studies it. Quietly—as though she knows she shouldn't be in here, as though Richie might come in at any moment and catch her—she crosses the room to his desk. She picks up a photograph of me. She covers my face with her thumb, so all that's visible is my hair and body. I was skin and bones by then, a few months before I died.

"Lisa," she murmurs. And she moves her thumb away to reveal my smiling face. Despite my expression, there is a lackluster quality to my superficial prettiness: my hair, though long and blond, is limp upon closer inspection. There are shadows beneath my eyes, I'm sure, obscured by plenty of thick concealer. And there are my bones, their outlines visible beneath my skin. The leg bone connected to the knee bone, the knee bone connected to the hip bone . . .

"What's she doing?" Alex asks.

I'm startled. I didn't think he was following me, but he's right here.

"I don't know," I say. "She's looking around."

"What's she looking for?"

I shake my head. "I'm not sure. But if she goes snooping, she won't like what she finds."

Mrs. Wilson is inept as a mother, but she isn't a bad person. Watching her now—gazing at the books on Richie's shelves, each one hundreds of pages, their information contained within a son that she knows next to nothing about— I feel almost breathless with pity for her. I knew him better, I realize, than she likely ever will.

Except maybe she knows him better than I thought. Her fingers, tracing the spines of the books, land on the oversized, hardback copy of *Great Expectations*. They stop. She slides it slowly from the shelf and lets it fall open in her hands. Can it be a coincidence that she's chosen *this* book?

The hollow space within is absolutely jam-packed with trouble: bags of weed, several bottles of prescription pills, a knotted plastic bag containing a *serious* amount of white powder, and a wad of money held together with a rubber band. Look, Ma! Your son sells drugs!

I expect her to gasp and cry, to confiscate the whole thing or call her husband or the police or *something*. But she doesn't do any of that. Carefully, with delicate fingers, she closes the book and slides it back into place. She adjusts my photo on the desk until it's exactly where it was before. Then, almost without a sound, she leaves the room, shutting the door behind her.

As ghosts, we can travel so easily. Even if I can't run along-side Richie because of my horrible footwear, all it takes is a series of blinks, the mere *thought* of him—with Alex touch-ing me in order to come along—and we're at his side again.

I try to concentrate as hard as possible on him, to make him realize that I'm here with him. *Richie, it's me,* I think. *It's Liz. Can you feel me? Do you know I'm here?* I try to hone in on our connection, which I know is real. But Alex's pres-ence distracts me from focusing completely on Richie. It is as though the two of them blend together in my mind for a moment, Alex standing beside me and Richie coming to a stop, placing his elbows on his knees.

I'm right here. I'm beside you. Can you feel me? It's your Liz.
Watching him, I become hopeful: he seems transformed,
infused with energy. His face is flushed, cheeks red and
eyes glinting as he stares at the afternoon sun in front of
him. He hasn't been jogging so much as sprinting, it seems;
we're all the way across town from his house.

"He didn't go to the beach." Alex never seems overen-
thused about much of anything, but his tone is flatter than
usual. "Why would he come here?"

He feels a connection. He must. Why else would he have
stopped so suddenly?

I inch closer to Richie, so close that I can reach out and
touch him. Concentrating as hard as I possibly can, trying to
empty my mind of all other thoughts, I do it: I touch him.
And it works. When my hand rests on his sweaty back, I can
feel the life beating beneath my palm: warm, damp, solid. My
arm tingles all over, until my fingertips feel ready to burst,
and in less than a second I go from a feeling of pleasant eupho-
ria to the sense that I'm on fire. I yank my arm away.

"Why not come here? There's a road. He followed it." I
stare at the space between our bodies. The air feels electric,
energy everywhere. Can Richie feel it? When I was alive, I
think I sensed it sometimes, after a long run: the idea that
everything around us is breathing, that there is no such thing
as empty space, that even the air has a presence.

Richie continues to catch his breath. He blots sweat
from his forehead with the bottom of his T-shirt. His pretty

dark curls are matted against his face. He gazes, almost in awe, at the house in front of him.

It's a small white Cape Cod with red shutters. One and a half stories of cramped New England style. Not a terrible place, I guess, if square footage isn't your deal.

It is a dingy corner of town, though: close to the cemetery, far from the beach, and even now, in the bright afternoon with the sun hanging down from above us, the landscape feels like a shadow is cast upon it. There are no clouds, no obvious obstructions to the skyline. But there seems to be a grayish pallor slung across this edge of the universe, like a net that makes the air feel somehow thicker.

My boyfriend looks around, as though he thinks some-one may have followed him. *Me!* I want to shout at him. *It's me!* He walks toward the little white house, around the side, to the detached garage, and stands on tiptoes to look in the window.

"Alex," I say, "I did it. I touched him."

But Alex doesn't seem interested in the breakthrough. "Do you know who lives here?" His voice trembles.

"No. Of course I don't."

"Of course, because it's shitty?" With his foot, he tries to kick at the dirt on the front lawn. Obviously, he can't; his foot goes right through the pile without making so much as a dent.

I'm still reeling from the effect that touching Richie had on my body. I hold on to myself, arms wrapped around my torso, trying to maintain just a trace of the sensation. It slips away like sand through a sieve. I can't stop it. Alex's rotten attitude seems to yank me away from any pleasant feelings I might have managed to make contact with, and I realize that, for a moment, I'd forgotten all about the pain in my feet. But now it's back, so severe that I can barely stand.

"Yes," I say, frustrated that Alex made me lose the feeling, "because it's shitty. Is that what you want to hear? I don't know what he's doing on this street, why he's so interested in this particular house. I've never even *seen* this place before. None of my friends live in this part of town. I wouldn't even want to go trick-or-treating here. I'd probably end up with a bunch of lousy, off-brand candy." Not that it would matter; it isn't like I ever ate candy.

"What is he doing, then?" Alex is almost hysterical. "Why would he come here?"

"I don't know! He's looking around. He's looking . . . in the mailbox." I pause. "What?"

It's true; Richie is going through the mail. He holds each piece up for a moment, taking a hard look before shuffling to the next envelope. Once he's seen everything, he puts it all back. He takes one final, long look at the house. Then he continues on his way, quickly gaining speed as he heads downhill toward town.

"I want to go inside," Alex says.

"Why?" I ask.

The bleak feeling that has stretched so lightly around me

feels thicker, heavier; it has expanded to a sense of genuine dread. Before he speaks, I know what he's going to say. I can't imagine why. I don't fully understand any of it. All I know is that I was thinking about Alex as I watched Richie run. Something beyond my comprehension is happening. Our worlds are intertwined, my thoughts influencing Richie. That much seems clear. I know, even if it doesn't completely make sense to me yet.

"Because it's my house. I want to go home."

Eleven

I guess people deal with death in all kinds of ways. My family, it seems, is trying to let me go without too much messiness: they're giving my things away. My father is drowning his sorrow in liquor. My stepsister, though she's obviously grieving, is still claiming my boyfriend for her own. They don't seem to be embracing the mystery surrounding my untimely passing, or even acknowledging that there *is* any mystery.

But some people don't let go; they cling to the loss of a loved one like a warm blanket. Alex's house is a monument to him, constructed from drywall and linoleum flooring and bad curtains. His photograph hangs in every room, surrounded by religious iconography and dried flowers and—more often than not—a few candles, all of which are burning in the empty house.

"Aren't they afraid they'll start a fire?" I hold my palm over the flame of a bloodred candle, its glass holder painted with a crude approximation of the Virgin Mary, and am enthralled when I realize that I feel nothing. Being a ghost can be fascinating sometimes.

"I don't think they're afraid of anything anymore."

"You said they're religious. Your parents, I mean. They're Catholic?"

The only thing close to religion that I've ever known is Nicole's new age, hipster version of spirituality. In our house, you couldn't get in touch with the other side unless you had the right uniform: fitted tank top, peasant skirt, turquoise jewelry, henna tattoos. Nicole has been quiet and generally uninspired to practice the religion of the month since I died, as far as I've noticed. I'm not surprised. Real loss—the sight of her stepdaughter in a body bag, the vague understanding that my last moments were spent submerged, salt water infiltrating my healthy lungs, certainly an unpleasant death at best—does not lend itself to the casual flip of a tarot card or the absurd ceremony of a séance.

But she had no problem breaking out the Ouija board when my mother died. Why not? Was she only trying to comfort me? If so, the plan seems misguided, insensitive, almost grotesquely inappropriate. What the hell was she thinking?

"Yes, they're Catholic. And I didn't say they were religious," Alex corrects me. "I said they were *very* religious. I mean, have a look around, Liz. Their entire lives revolve around Christianity." He pauses. "Not that it's a bad thing. I think it's brought them some comfort. There's something to be said for the rituals of religion, don't you think?"

I hesitate. To me, the house is just plain creepy. "Sure," I say, "I guess so."

"Like you with running," he adds. "It was a ritual, wasn't it? Something you did over and over again, to keep you feeling sane and in control?"

"Okay. I see what you're saying. But it wasn't a religion exactly. I mean, Alex"—my gaze drifts around the room—"this is taking it to a whole new level of devotion."

"Yeah," he agrees. "My parents are like that."

"So tell me," I ask, "where do your pious parents think you are now? In heaven?"

"Of course. I was baptized." He squints at me; aside from the candlelight, the house is dark. "Don't you know this? Aren't you in the FCA?"

He means the Fellowship of Christian Athletes. "Yes," I say. "In fact, I'm the vice president."

"Then you should know."

I shrug. "I only joined so I could put it on my college applications. I wasn't really a Christian." And I pause. "It's weird that I remember that. Don't you think? Why would it possibly matter?"

"I don't know," he says. "It's sort of telling, though. It says something about who you were." He crosses his arms against his chest. "If you weren't even a Christian, then how did you become an officer?"

I don't answer him at first. Instead, I look around some more. The house is cluttered as hell. Aside from all the religious knickknacks, the candles and figurines and calligraphy prayers hanging from the walls, there is ubiquitous disarray. In the kitchen, I see a sink piled with dishes. Laundry—I can't tell if it's clean or dirty—is heaped into three separate baskets beside the living room sofa. In a corner of the room, a litter box sits in dire need of scooping.

I wrinkle my nose. "I thought cleanliness was next to godliness. And to answer your question, we took a vote. It wasn't like I had to campaign or anything."

"And you just got elected? Even though you're not really a Christian?" His annoyance is obvious. It's like he doesn't have the first clue what it means to be a teenager. Because that's the thing: none of it means anything. We're only kids. What does it matter if I'm not a Christian? Nobody's going to quiz me on the New Testament in order to challenge my authority as the vice president of the FCA, because there *isn't* any authority. I think the most I ever had to do for the position was last spring, when I helped organize a collection for the local food bank. My sole responsibility was to put cardboard boxes in every classroom to hold nonperishable items. Again, the memory seems so random, so meaningless. Why do I know this, yet I can't recall other things that are obviously important? Being dead, it seems, requires a patience that I don't have. Not yet, anyway.

"Big freaking challenge," I say to him. "Let me tell you, I could never have done it without the intervening hand of God." From a young age, religion has seemed ridiculous to me. What kind of God takes a girl's mother away from her at age nine?

Okay, I've pissed him off. He's visibly shaking with anger. "Don't say that. Not in my house. Show some respect."

"For who? For God?"

"Yes."

"Oh." My tone becomes light, almost mocking. I can't help myself. His continued faith seems absurd to me, considering our circumstances. "Let me ask you, Alex, where do you think he is? God?"

"We're here, aren't we? It's not like there's *nothing* after we die."

I gaze at my boots, wiggling my aching toes, each one its own special symphony of pain. "I think this might be hell."

"If that's really what you think," he says, "then you're way more spoiled than I imagined."

At the back of the room, there's a wooden upright piano pressed against the wall. The lid is crowded with photographs. Alex sits down at the bench and stares at the keys.

"Do you play?" I ask him.

He nods. "Since I was four."

Every picture on the piano is of Alex, from the time he was a baby up until what I assume was only a few months—weeks, maybe—before he was killed.

He closes his eyes. His fingers begin to move effortlessly across the keys.

The odd energy—the web of sadness that I first noticed outside, when Richie was looking through the mail—feels even thicker now, as though it is cloaking the entire house, enveloping us so tightly that I feel like it could almost shatter the windows. As I look at the photographs, it's like watching Alex grow up, a display of what seems to be every major event in his life, from his birth up to his school photo from sophomore year. There are pictures of him on Christmas morning, an only child sitting under a tree, smiling beside a small pile of presents. There's a Little League photo: Alex in a baseball uniform, holding a bat, his grin crooked and toothy. Then there's him at a piano recital: he's wearing a coat and tie and has his arm around his mother's waist.

Only now do I realize how bizarre it is that I can hear what he's playing on the piano. I don't understand how it's possible. But the music is so lovely that I don't want to question it.

"What was that?" I ask, once he's finished.

"It doesn't have a name." He shyly lowers his gaze. "I wrote it. When I was fifteen."

"I think I've heard it before." And then I realize where. "I have," I say to him. "At your funeral."

"Oh." He continues to stare at the keys. "You're right."

He seems distracted for a moment as his expression becomes faraway and his hands slip from the keys. Almost as though I'm not here, he shuts his eyes again. But it's different from just a moment ago. This time, his shoulders slump, his normally upright posture going slack. He's slipping away, I realize, into the past. Maybe it's an accident; he's never done this before in front of me, except for the day I died, when he showed me the uncomfortable scene in the cafeteria.

I don't think about what I do next; it just sort of happens. I reach out and grab Alex's wrist tightly. I shut my own eyes.

At first I don't know where I am; all I can tell is that it's some kind of store. I'm standing before a glass display case filled with row upon row of high-calorie foods: pasta salads, breaded chicken breasts, glistening filets of sugar-glazed salmon, charred scallops wrapped in bacon. And the desserts—oh, God, the sight of them alone feels so gluttonous that I actually take a step backward. There's a cheesecake piled with large, glazed strawberries. Beside it, there's some kind of walnut-crusted, butter-and-cinnamon concoction. A silver tray holds piles of brownies, cookies, and thick squares of fudge.

"Oh . . . ," I say, the word catching in my throat. There is genuine yearning in my voice. Now that I'm dead, I assume that I can't gain weight. It would be like heaven if I could eat whatever I wanted without giving any thought to the calorie content. Taste, though, is a foreign feeling now; I don't think a binge on sweets would bring me any pleasure.

"Get out. Now." I've never heard Alex speak so harshly. He's right beside me.

"Where are we? It's your memory, isn't it? This place is from your past."

He doesn't blink as he glares at me. "You know where we are. Now leave."

A brittle-looking middle-aged woman steps between us. "Hello?" she calls. "Does anyone work here?"

She places her hands on the counter and taps her fingernails impatiently against the metal. A tennis bracelet dangles from her slim wrist. She is dressed nearly all in white, except for a red silk scarf knotted around her neck. A marquise diamond the size of a marble adorns her ring finger. Her fine gray hair is pulled into a tight bun. Even here, standing at a deli counter, she exudes class.

"Oh, man . . . ," Alex says, cringing as he looks at her. "Liz, you need to get out of here. I don't want you to see this. None of it."

Then it dawns on me; of *course* I know where we are. I've been here countless times with my friends. Looking around, I recognize the wall lined with racks of freshly baked bread, the charming two-person wrought iron tables at the front of the room, the huge storefront windows that offer a great view of the beach.

And now, stepping out from the back room, wiping his hands on his dirty apron as he hurries to the counter, here's Alex. He's younger, but not by much. We are, of course, at the Mystic Market.

"Mrs. Boyden." He gives the woman at the counter a wide smile. "How are you?"

At the sight of him, her polished, steely demeanor softens a bit. "Alex. So good to see you." She glances around. "I've brought someone with me today, but apparently she's being shy. Chelsea? Where are you hiding?"

I tell Alex, "You never bring me with you when you remember things."

He shrugs, but I can tell he's only trying to be casual; he's obviously nervous. "I don't do it very much. We've been so focused on what happened to you. I had a whole year to go back over things by myself."

I shake my head. "That's not why. You said yourself that you don't know who killed you yet. You must be remembering things. You don't want to let me in, do you? Not even a little bit. We've been together all this time, Alex. I've showed you so much. But you don't want me to see anything from your life. That's not fair."

"Liz," he says, his tone growing impatient, "there's nothing that says I have to show you my life. I don't need your help with anything. This is private, okay? Can't you understand that?"

From between two rows of groceries, a pretty young

girl steps toward the counter. She wears a Catholic school uniform, complete with navy-blue knee socks and loafers. Her brown hair is pulled into a high, simple ponytail. She's wearing makeup, but only a little bit, probably nothing more than some blush and lip gloss. Almost immediately, I notice that her ears aren't pierced. Her fingernails are short and unpainted.

"But all you're doing is working," I say, pouting. "Anybody could walk in here and see you. What could possibly be so private about this?"

"Nothing. It's just—nothing." He sighs. "This is *mine*. I want to keep it that way." And he pauses. "I don't want anything to ruin it."

"You think me being here is going to ruin it?" I frown. "How?"

The other Alex—the one behind the counter—smiles at the girl. Chelsea. "Hey," he says, "how have you been? Long time no see."

There is something odd about Alex's expression, the tone of his voice, even the light in his eyes. And that's not all—he appears taller somehow. He leans his arms against the countertop and rests his chin casually in his hands.

Mrs. Boyden looks back and forth between the two of them. "I picked Chelsea up from school today," she says. "She's spending the weekend with me."

"I don't know her," I tell Alex. "Should I? Why is she wearing a uniform?"

"She goes to a Catholic school in Groton," he mutters, clearly unhappy to be clarifying anything for me.

"Oh, yeah?" The Alex behind the counter nods with interest. "Any big plans for this weekend?"

Then it occurs to me what's so different about him in this memory. He is happy. Calm. Relaxed. More than anything, though, he's confident.

"Look at you," I say, grinning at him. "Flirting like a pro."

"Stop it." He almost looks ready to cry.

"Alex, what's the matter? It's okay. We're in this together, you know? We're both dead. I'm not going to make fun of you, I promise."

"Whatever." He stares at the floor. "It's not that."

"Then tell me," I demand. "What is it?"

But he ignores the question, choosing instead to focus on his former self with Mrs. Boyden and Chelsea. "Oh, I don't try to fool myself into thinking that Chelsea wants to spend her evenings with me anymore," Mrs. Boyden says. "She's almost fifteen. She wants to go out and have fun with kids her own age, not stay home with her grandmother. Right, dear?"

Chelsea blushes. She shrugs. "I don't know many people here, Nana."

"She likes to go for walks," Mrs. Boyden continues. "We live right along the beach. Did you know that, Alex?"

Alex shakes his head. "No, I didn't. That's great."

Mrs. Boyden beams. "It's a lovely property. Mr. Boyden and I had it built shortly after he retired. Of course, we're

only here from April to August—it's too cold for u
the rest of the year. Chelsea will be done with s
week, and I'm trying to talk her into staying witl
summer." She winks at Alex. "What do you think?"

"I think it's a great idea," Alex says. "You'd meet lots of people, Chelsea."

She brightens a bit. "Could you introduce me to some of your friends?"

"Sure. I know tons of people." He pauses. "I'm older than you, though. Most of my friends will be juniors next year."

"Alex," I say, "this is only a few months before you died. Isn't it?"

"Yes." He nods.

"So you never got to take her out?"

He frowns. He doesn't answer.

"What do you like to do when you're not working?" Chelsea asks. Nervously, she begins to wind a thick strand of hair around her index finger. She's so cute.

Alex stands up straighter. "Go to parties, mostly," he says. Then, with incredible nonchalance, he adds, "And I spend a lot of time with my girlfriend."

I stare at Alex. He won't look at me.

"Oh. You, um, you have a girlfriend?" Chelsea asks. The poor girl looks like someone has just stolen her ice-cream cone.

Alex nods. "Yeah. We've been together almost a year."

By the look on Alex's face, I can tell this wasn't true.

"Why did you lie?" I ask him. "She liked you, Alex. I don't understand."

He continues to look at the floor. "You wouldn't."

"Well, I mean, of course I wouldn't! It doesn't make any sense. Here's a perfectly nice girl who obviously has an interest in you, and you're totally pushing her away. Why would you do that?"

He gives me a sudden, fierce look. "Because I *didn't* have a ton of friends. I *didn't* get invited to parties. And if she knew all that—if she knew the truth—she never would have liked me in the first place. She didn't really like me. She liked who she thought I was."

I shake my head. "You don't know that."

"You heard her grandmother. They live along the beach. They're rich."

I can't believe what I'm hearing. "Alex," I ask, "don't you get it? You could have taken her out, let her get to know you. At least you could have gone on one date, and probably more than one. But you decided to lie to her instead. You didn't even want to try." I shake my head. "And you call me and my friends fake."

"I want to go back now," he says.

"Of course you do." But I don't move; I just continue to stare at him.

My gaze is obviously making him uncomfortable. "I don't want to talk about this, Liz."

"Did you remember this before now? Did you remember lying to her?" I ask.

He shakes his head.

"Don't you see? You told me yourself—all these memories we're reliving, that we're seeing for the first time, it's like we need to realize something about ourselves. What are you supposed to understand, Alex? Think about it."

"I have thought about it. And in the future, I'd like to think about it alone." To drive the point home, he adds, "By myself. Without your help."

"Okay. Fine, then." I sniffle. "Whatever."

"Thank you." He reaches toward me, putting his hand on my wrist. "Ready?"

I take one last look at the old Alex as he stands behind the counter. Mrs. Boyden and Chelsea are leaving now. As soon as they're gone, Alex turns around. He takes a few deep breaths. He shuts his eyes and tilts his head back. Then he walks toward the back room. As he steps through the doorway, he kicks the wall hard with a sneakered foot.

"I'm ready," I say, nodding. A part of me wants to hug him after what I've just seen. But I know that even my grip on his arm is bad enough. Everything I was, and everything I represented—it wasn't just that he disliked me and my friends, I realize. It was so much more complicated than that.

. . .

Once we're back, it seems that there is nowhere comfortable: not here at Alex's house, not anywhere. Aside from my dad's obvious grief, my house is too full of life and energy, my stepsister and friends so clearly moving on. But I'm beginning to think that any place is better than here, the atmosphere absolutely suffocating, the grief so palpable it almost seems to breathe around us.

"Can I ask you something?" Alex looks up at me, leans against the piano. His forearm resting against the keys produces a crush of sound that makes me wince. "Sure," I say, positive he won't ask me anything about what we've just seen together. He undoubtedly wants to change the subject. "Did you ever think this would happen?" he asks. "That you'd die while you were still young?"

There's a sound from the stairwell. A cat, a fat calico with long, thick whiskers and a puffy tail that sweeps the air as though cutting through invisible netting, struts into the room. Alex was right about animals; there is no doubt it can see us: it strolls directly to Alex and weaves in and out of his legs, purring, arching its back, and finally settling at his feet. I'm not sure why—it isn't like we can really communicate with it—but knowing the cat can see us, like being able to hear Alex playing piano, makes me feel reassured somehow, certain that our ties to the living world have not yet been entirely cut.

And I feel such sympathy for Alex all of a sudden. It's not only because of what I've just seen. Maybe it's also because we're in his home, which is cloaked in such sorrow in the wake of his passing.

"Death was familiar to me, in life," I tell him.

He blinks at me. "Because of your mom?"

I nod. "Yes. It's hard to explain. It's like . . . it's like it had a place in my heart. When I was nine . . ." Just saying the words out loud hurts so badly. But suddenly I want him to know the whole story, the one I've been holding back on telling him since we ended up together. I want him to see that I was a little girl once—that, like him in the photographs on the piano, there was a time when I was innocent and kind and knew very little of the social echelons that would come to dictate my life as a teenager. I want him to know what happened to me, to understand that it changed everything.

"I want to show you something," I tell him.

He blinks a few more times. "What?"

"Put your hand on my shoulder."

He's hesitant. "Why?"

"Alex . . . come on." My tone is gentle. "It's okay. There's something I want you to see."

So he does. As soon as I feel his touch, I close my eyes. And we're there.

It's a summer day in the middle of the afternoon. I am nine years old, and my dad is at work. It's a Tuesday. I'll never forget this day.

"Look at you, all dressed up," Alex remarks, not unkindly. We're standing in my parents' bedroom. There I am, just a kid, walking back and forth across the room in a pair of my mother's strappy high heels. I'm wearing a floor-length fur coat and dainty pillbox hat—both my mother's—and striking poses in front of the mirror, hands on my hips, sashaying like a pro while I bat my eyelashes and kiss the air. My lips are a shade of red called—I'll never forget, *never*—crimson heat. I'm wearing mascara and eyeliner and big pink circles of blush, and as I watch myself, I remember so clearly how I could barely believe how lovely I looked. My fingernails are press-ons. I hold a pen between my index and middle finger and bring it to my mouth with a deep inhale, pretending to smoke. Just like my mom.

As I begin to shakily execute a spin before the mirror, this amazing sound rips through the house, the kind of sound that is undoubtedly accompanied by a huge mess. I stare across the room, at the closed door to my parents' bathroom, where my mom is taking a shower. It takes my nine-year-old self a few seconds to realize what I'm looking at.

"What is that?" Alex asks.

I can barely talk. All I can do is stare. I thought it would be different now, but I'm quickly realizing that seeing it happen all over again is no less horrifying than it was the very first time, nine years ago. "Just wait," I manage to whisper.

From the crack beneath the door, water starts to trickle into the room, slowly at first, then in quiet, horrible gushes that absorb immediately into the white carpet. It's like watching a magic trick: as quickly as the carpet grows wet, it turns red.

"Let's go, okay?" I say to Alex, glancing frantically at my younger self, aware of what's about to happen and suddenly sorry that I've brought him here. I thought I could handle this, but I can't. I don't want to see it, not again. Once—when I was only nine!—was enough.

But he shakes his head. "I want to know, Liz."

"Then you stay. I'm going."

"No." He tightens his grip on my shoulder. "I can't stay without you. Liz—please?"

"Why are you making me watch this?" I plead.

"It was your idea to show me! Why did you bring me here?"

I stare at him. "Because I want you to understand me. I want you to see that I was like you. I wasn't always a bad person."

He stares back. "Then let me see."

I cover my eyes while he watches. I don't need to look. I already know what's going to happen.

At nine years old, I run into the bathroom, and there she is: oh, Mommy. Her fall has broken the glass shower door, slicing her to ribbons.

I do everything you'd expect a little girl to do. I try to wake her up, to help her in some way, cutting my own hands and knees on all the broken glass in the process. I scream at her to get up. I shake her. There is nothing in the world worse than her absolute stillness.

Then I watch as she takes her last breath. Even as a child, I understand that she's gone. There, in that moment, I think my heart breaks. Forever.

"I want to go," I repeat, my voice near tears. "Please, can we go? Alex, *please?*"

He lets go of my shoulder. We are back in his house. But it's too late; the memory is back, front and center. I can't escape it.

For other people my age, death doesn't seem like a possibility. Teenagers, as everyone knows, tend to believe they are immortal. But I'm not sure I ever felt that way. See, I knew death so well. I watched it take my mother; a girl doesn't forget something like that.

Alex looks away from me. He doesn't seem to know what to say.

I put my hands against my face and shake my head, trying to forget what I've just seen for the second time in my life. Even though the memory has always been with me, ever since it happened, witnessing it firsthand all over again makes me feel shaky, heartsick, and very small. I feel like a little girl, all alone in the world. But I don't think I can explain all of that to Alex. I already regret showing him my mother's death; I can't stand him seeing me so shook up now, so vulnerable.

I stare past him, at a print of *The Last Supper* that hangs on the wall. "So to answer your question, maybe there was an inkling," I tell him, trying to keep a casual tone. "I don't know. I can't remember. Neither can you, right?"

"No." He taps out a sleepy version of "Heart and Soul," looking down at the piano keys. "Before you died, I spent so much time sitting along the road, just watching the cars go by. My parents nailed a wreath to the tree, close to where they found my body. They used to visit every day, and then it became once a week." He places his hands an octave lower, begins to play the song again. "I kept waiting for someone else. I thought that the person who hit me would have to show up eventually. I waited and waited." He shakes his head. "Nothing."

There is a long pause. Finally, he says, "You were just a little girl. I'm sorry that happened to you."

I stare at the floor. "Thank you."

The cat at his feet has been lazily cleaning its paws, until now, when it stops to look suddenly at me. Its pupils dilate as it stares. It reaches toward me, stretching its front leg, claws out.

Alex's hands go still against the piano keys. He tilts his head at me, his eyes glassy in the dark room. His teeth, I realize, are still as crooked as they were in the Little League photograph. I'm guessing he never had braces; it occurs to me that his parents probably couldn't afford them. "None of this makes sense, Liz. Do you realize that?"

A car turns into the driveway. We hear the garage door open.

I feel anxious, like we're trespassing, like Alex's parents will come in and we'll be caught. "What do you mean?"

Alex is thinking hard now, suddenly excited. His breath quickens. He claps a hand to my wrist. His touch feels cold and limp; it feels *dead*. "I mean what I said. Things aren't making sense. Think about it. Don't you have questions, Liz? Like why would Richie come to my house? I don't understand. Do you?"

I shake my head. "No. You know more than I do."

"It can't be a coincidence," he says. "And you and me together now. We're ghosts. Why? We weren't friends." He glances at the door, a key jiggling in the lock. "I hated you," he says.

"I know. I'm sorry. You have to believe me, Alex—I didn't realize how terrible I was. I used to be different. Everything changed after my mom died."

"All you cared about were things," he says simply. "Clothes and cars and parties. Cell phones and purses and . . . shoes." He stares at my boots. "Lots of good it did you. Here you are, with me."

We look at each other. The front door opens.

"Please," I beg, "let's go now."

"Why, Liz? What's the matter?"

I can barely coax my voice above a whisper. "I can't breathe."

"What do you know? Why are we here?"

"I don't know. I can't remember."

"What was all the money in your room for? Why were you keeping secrets from everyone?"

"I don't *know*!" The cat hurries away. I close my eyes, pressing my palms to my lids. There is a flurry of memories, stacked almost violently in succession: my mother on the bathroom floor. My first cross-country meet, complete with remnants of the butterflies in my stomach. My own body as I first saw it the night I died, lodged helplessly between the boat and the dock. Lying on the beach with Caroline, Mera, and Josie, listening to Top 40 music and working on our tans. And air, crisp and fresh and filling my lungs as I recall running through town, my feet hitting the ground with a *slap-slap-slap* rhythm that feels like a heartbeat, life-affirming and strong. The sweat used to drip down my forehead, stinging my eyes. I could taste salt: from the air around me and dried on my lips, which were always open slightly when I ran.

I wanted to keep running forever. *Slap-slap-slap-slap*. I realize now that I wanted to disappear. To get so lost that nobody ever found me. To go so far away that I'd never be able to make my way home again. But I have no idea why.

Twelve

We go back to my house, both of us quiet and solemn after the memories we've shared and the conversation we've just had. It's evening, the streetlights glowing, illuminating the haze from the cool night air as we make our way up the steps of my front porch. The pain in my toes is so intense that I can barely walk. I didn't walk home; Alex and I just blinked ourselves here magically, but now with every step I feel a fierce stabbing sensation in my feet, so unbearable that I'm almost out of breath, tears in my eyes by the time we get to my bedroom door.

The door is closed, but I can hear voices on the other side before we walk through. Immediately, I recognize the noises as my friends: Mera, Caroline, and Josie.

"Think they're back for more clothes?" Alex asks. I can tell he's trying to be casual, but the remark stings. After witnessing the incredible display of mourning at his house, I can't help but feel a little bit miffed that my friends seem to have moved on from my death so quickly.

"I don't know. Probably." I stare at the door to my room. "Let's see."

I gasp as we step inside. In the space of a couple of hours, my room has been almost entirely cleared out. The bed has been stripped of its dainty, pink-and-white-striped sheets; all that's left behind is the bare mattress and box spring on the frame. There is no makeup strewn on the vanity, and the closet—its door hanging open—is practically empty. My ribbons and plaques from cross-country have been packed away somewhere, and are probably collecting dust in the basement—or worse, I think, in a landfill. The only thing that's left from my life is the pile of old running shoes. It's funny— you'd think they'd be the first things to go. They probably seem like garbage to everyone else in my family. I wonder why they're still here.

My closest friends are back here, too. The three of them are in a semicircle on my floor, sitting around a Ouija board. And right away, just from looking at them, I can tell that they're drunk. Even before I hear Caroline hiccup. Even before I see the almost-empty bottle of red wine sitting beside Josie.

"Josie . . . ," Mera murmurs, obviously reluctant. Her cheeks are flushed from the booze. Her lips are stained a deep red. "This is weird."

"It's okay," Josie says, putting a hand on Mera's arm. I notice right away that Josie is wearing one of my favorite outfits: black skinny jeans and a tight red sweater. "My mom took me to church this morning. I know how to do this. They have séances there all the time."

"With a Ouija board?" Mera is doubtful.

"No, but I've seen them contact people from the other side. Don't worry."

"I thought you weren't religious," Alex says, staring at them, his eyes wide with fascination.

"I'm not. I mean, we aren't. She means the Spiritualist Church. It's nondenominational." And I roll my eyes. "It's real hippy-dippy kind of shit. They're into trances, auras, tapping into the collective subconscious—that kind of mumbo jumbo."

"So what happened at church?" Caroline asks. "They told you to have a séance to try and contact your . . . sister?" She clears her throat. I can tell she's working up the drunken courage to speak her mind. "Because I find that hard to believe, Josie. I think this is a bad idea."

Josie's eyes flicker in the almost darkness; the only light in the room comes from a lamp on my nightstand and a single candle burning on my dresser. "Actually, they told me *not* to have a séance. There was a psychic there this morning. He's there a lot."

For a moment, I wonder if it's the same psychic who told me to beware of the redhead in disguise. But like Richie said,

I don't even know any redheads. The guy was obviously way off in his warning.

"He said that under no circumstances should we use any tools of the occult to contact Liz."

"Then why did you break out the Ouija board?" Mera practically shrieks.

"Shhh," Josie says. "You'll wake up my dad. He'll freak if he sees what we're doing." She pauses. She stares at the ceiling for a moment, and when I follow her gaze, I can see that she's focusing on the faint but still-visible brush strokes. *BFF.* "I want to know that she's safe," Josie says. "I have to know that she's okay, wherever she is."

"Let's stop, Josie," Caroline pleads. "She's not here. She's gone."

Josie looks at Caroline. She narrows her eyes. "You don't know that. There's so much about life that none of us understands." She attempts a smile; it's shaky. "Have another drink." Josie picks up the bottle of wine and hands it to Caroline, who stares at it for a minute, then reluctantly takes a swig.

Good old Caroline, I think to myself. *She always wants to fit in.*

"Don't you feel like you have to know?" Josie implores. From her tone, I can tell she's being sincere. She's truly worried about my place in the hereafter. "Don't you want to know that she's at peace now?"

Mera and Caroline nod.

"Well, this is how we'll do it. It's going to work." Josie is breathing heavily, her face flushed with wine and anticipation. "But we all have to concentrate. We have to want it."

Alex shudders. "Nice friends you've got."

"They don't want to," I murmur, staring at them. "It's just Josie."

"Do you think it will work?" Alex asks.

"I don't know. I'm standing right here. Maybe."

"You could go over to them. You could put your hands on the pointer and try to make it move."

For a second, I consider it. With the exception of Richie, I can't make real contact with physical objects. But it *is* a Ouija board; I suppose I could give it a try. I know that it's just a cheap board game—Josie probably got it at a toy store—but she's right about one thing: obviously, there's a lot that none of us understands about life—and death. If I can connect with Richie just by being in the same room with him, like I did when he was talking to Joe Wright after my funeral, then what might happen if I put my hands on the pointer? Could it possibly work?

Something stops me, though, just as I'm about to walk over to them. I'm here; I know I'm safe. I want to see if the Ouija board tells me anything I don't already know. Even if it is just a toy, I'm willing to give it a shot.

"Let's watch," I tell Alex. "I want to see what happens."

All three of my friends place their index fingers slightly

above the pointer, which is positioned in the center of the board.

"We are trying to contact Elizabeth Valchar," Josie intones, her voice low but firm. "Liz, are you there?"

After a few moments of stillness, slowly, the pointer glides across the board to *yes*.

"Oh my God," Caroline whispers. "I didn't do that. Are you moving it, Mera? Josie, is it you?"

"It's not me." Mera swallows. "I want to go home."

"Shhh." Josie's eyes are positively ablaze with excitement. "Liz, are you safe?"

The pointer swings to *no*.

"That's not moving all by itself," I tell Alex. "Somebody's doing it. One of *them* is moving it."

"You think?" he murmurs.

"Alex, yes. Who's doing it, though?"

He takes a few steps closer. He kneels down, trying to get a better look at the board and the fingers hovering above the pointer, barely even making contact. "I can't tell. All three of them are kind of touching it. They're all shaking, Liz."

"Liz, why aren't you safe?" Josie asks.

After a brief pause, the pointer starts to move again. It begins to spell. *L-I-E-S*.

"Lies?" Josie repeats. "What kind of lies?

It continues to move, spelling clearly, pausing for just a moment on each letter before moving on. *C-H-E-A-T-E-R*.

"What does that even mean?" Caroline asks. "It doesn't mean anything. This is creeping me out. Josie, I want to stop."

"Me, too." Mera reaches past Caroline, picks up the wine bottle, and takes a long drink.

"She was cheating on Richie," Josie whispers, her eyes wide, pupils dilated. "And now she's sorry."

Above Josie's lowered head, Mera and Caroline exchange a glance.

"Liz, are you at peace?" Josie asks.

The pointer swings quickly to *no*.

"Why not?" Her breath is almost fevered.

I stare as the pointer spells its final word. *H-E-L-L*.

"She's moving it, Liz," Alex whispers. He's still peering at the pointer.

"Who is? Who's moving it?"

"Josie."

He and I stare at each other.

"But this isn't hell," I say to him.

There is a long pause.

"Are you sure?" he asks.

"Of course I'm sure." And I stare at my stepsister, who is so focused, her expression practically electric. Then I understand: she wants my friends to know that I cheated on Richie. She wants to feel absolved for having a relationship with him now, and she's using the Ouija board to convince them that I didn't deserve him.

She is my best friend. She's obviously not thinking straight.

I just died a few weeks ago, and she's still upset—that much is clear. This is exactly the kind of thing Nicole would do.

In fact, it *is* what Nicole did. Right after my mom died. Like mother, like daughter.

"I'm done with this," Caroline says, yanking her hands away. "This is weird, Josie. These things are junk. I'm not doing this anymore."

"What's the matter?" Josie blinks at her innocently, as though nothing all that interesting has just happened. "We all knew Liz was acting differently over the past few months. She was keeping secrets, even from me. Maybe now she's trying to tell us the truth—"

"This doesn't prove anything," Caroline interrupts. She stands up, rubbing her hands against her shoulders. She's shaking all over.

Josie blinks calmly. "There are things in this world we don't understand."

"Yeah, Josie, but a twenty-dollar board game from Target doesn't hold the key to unlocking the secrets of the universe." Mera stands up quickly, but she's unsteady on her feet. She's already in her pajamas—I can't believe my friends are having a sleepover, in my house, practically in my *room*—and she paces to my window, yanks it open, and starts rifling through her purse for a cigarette. She lights one up, leaning almost her entire body out the front window.

"Hey," she says, exhaling, turning her head to look down the street. "Richie's leaving his house."

Josie is putting the Ouija board back in its box. She seems uninterested in Richie's whereabouts. But I know Josie better than anybody. I can tell she's only pretending not to care. "He's probably going running again. He's been running like a fiend lately."

"Richie?" Mera's tone is doubtful.

"Mera? Can you not smoke in here?" Caroline sniffles. "Liz hated smoke. It seems disrespectful to her."

I glance at Alex, who's still on the floor. "This from the girl who stole five hundred dollars from me not two weeks ago," I say.

He nods slowly with understanding. "You're right."

The expression is startling. It occurs to me that it might be the first time since we've been together that Alex has smiled at me with anything other than detached disdain.

Then I remember something. "Richie already went running once today."

"Yeah? Maybe he's going out again," Alex offers.

As soon as the words leave his mouth, Mera says, "I don't think he's going running, Josie. He's wearing jeans and a sweatshirt . . . and flip-flops." She pauses. She exhales a ribbon of smoke. Then she says, "It's past ten. You don't know what your own *boyfriend* is up to?" Again, she and Caroline exchange looks. It's clear they're skeptical of the idea of Richie and Josie dating.

"I thought you were going to go out with Jason," Mera says. "He wants to ask you. You know that." She's talking about Jason Harvatt, who is only a junior but very popular. He's on the basketball team. He's cute. And he's had a crush on Josie forever, but she's never shown any interest in him.

"He's not my type." Josie shrugs.

"Where do you think Richie's going?" I ask Alex.

"I don't know. Probably on a drug run."

But I don't think so. I'm not sure why. It's like I've said from the beginning—Richie and I are still connected. It's almost like there is an invisible thread between us, binding us together somehow, and I can feel its tug as he makes his way down the street.

"I want to follow him," I say.

Alex hesitates. He gives me a mock pout. "Can't we stay? I was kind of hoping your friends would change into negligees and have a pillow fight."

I walk over to him and grab him by the arm. "Yes, because that's what we do at *every* slumber party. Come on. We're leaving."

But just as we're heading toward the door, it swings open.

"Oh no," I say, stopping dead in my tracks. "This is going to be bad."

It's my dad. He's standing in the doorway in red pajamas—a Christmas gift last year from Nicole. His reading glasses are perched on top of his messy brown hair—exactly the same shade as Josie's natural color.

He turns on the lights, looks at the floor, at the Ouija box. He sucks in a sharp breath. "What's going on in here?"

Mera, stunned into stillness, is frozen at the window, her lit cigarette burning between her fingers.

In a swift motion, Josie slides the Ouija box under my bed. "Nothing, Dad," she says. "We were just playing a game."

"A game?" His eyes are wide with disbelief. "Is that a Ouija board? Where did you get that?"

Josie glances first at Caroline, then at Mera. Both of them are staring at the floor, unwilling to make eye contact with my dad. I don't blame them.

"Did your mother give it to you?" my dad demands.

Josie doesn't say anything.

"And what's this?" He strolls into the room. There is an edge in his voice unlike anything I've ever heard before. He isn't just angry. He's *furious*. "Wine? Where did you kids get wine?" He raises his voice and, before Josie has any time to protest, booms, "Nicole!"

There's a thick, awkward silence in the room as my friends continue to avert their eyes. Only Josie will look at my dad, and she does so with a fierce gaze; she seems almost angry with him.

"My mom said it was okay." Her tone is calm.

"Marshall?" Nicole appears in the doorway. "What's the matter?" She stares at my sister, at my friends. "What are you girls doing in Liz's room?"

"I smelled smoke," my dad tells her. "I was afraid the damn house was on fire. But no. It's just your daughter in here"—Josie winces visibly when he says "your daughter"—"having a damn *séance*. And they're drunk." My dad's voice is steadily rising. "Whose idea was this, Nicole? You two went to church today, didn't you?"

Nicole presses her lips together in a tight smile. "Marshall," she says, her voice so calm and kind that it seems patronizing, "your heart."

"I don't give a damn about my heart. Your child is in here trying to contact the dead." He stares at my friends. "You girls. You think this is okay? Elizabeth was your best friend. She's dead now."

He chokes up. He begins to sob. It hurts so badly to look at him as he's falling apart.

"She was my daughter," he says, his voice wavering with sorrow and tears. "My daughter is dead. You think there's anything okay about that? You think it's okay to come into her room, to conduct a séance? What did you learn? That she's never coming back? She was just a baby. You girls are just babies, do you know that?"

My dad cannot stop crying. He's breathing hard.

"Marshall," Nicole soothes, rubbing his back, "come back to bed." She glances at Josie. "The girls are just having a slumber party. It's what they do."

"It is not *what they do*. It is not okay, Nicole." He stares at the floor. His cheeks are flushed with anger.

"Oh, Dad," I whisper. "I'm right here."

Alex stares at me. "I wish he could hear you," he offers.

"Me, too," I murmur.

"Think about him," he suggests. "Remember something happy."

Reality slips away almost effortlessly as I close my eyes. When I open them, trying to remember my father, I see that I've settled on a memory of the two of us. We are alone, and right away I realize that I'm revisiting the short period of time in between my mother's death and my dad's marriage to Nicole. He was only single for a few months before she and Josie moved in with us.

We are standing outside my dad's car; back then he drove a silver Porsche. He has pulled over to the side of the road, where a large cardboard box rests in the sandy brush a few feet away. On the box, in black permanent marker, somebody has written: FREE KITTENS!

I am nine. It's summertime. The sun shines brightly overhead in midafternoon, and from the looks of it, I've obviously just come from swimming somewhere. I'm wearing a pair of denim shorts over a one-piece red bathing suit. My long hair hangs in thick wet strands down my back. My shoulders are tan, my face slightly sunburned. My dad, I realize, probably had no idea how to raise a little girl by himself. I'm guessing he didn't think to put sunscreen on me before I went swimming.

"Stay there, honey," my dad says, taking a step forward by himself to peer into the box. "Let me see." He stops, staring downward. "Oh my . . . would you look at that?" he breathes.

"What is it? Dad, are there really kittens?" I stand on tiptoe in my jelly sandals, trying to catch a glimpse.

"Come here, Liz. It's okay." He smiles at me over his shoulder. "There's a whole litter, I think." His forehead wrinkles in mild concern. "Who would leave them out here alone? How awful."

Standing beside my younger self and my father, I look inside the box, already knowing what I'm about to see. Inside are seven tiny kittens, bright orange balls of almost unbearably adorable fluff and paws and sweet pink noses, their small mouths open, all of them mewing in a high tinny cacophony. There is barely enough room for them to move around in the box; they almost pile on top of one another, stumbling as they struggle to claw at the cardboard walls. Their tails are short and pointy, eyes glassy and bright blue, and as we gaze down at them, they tremble a bit, undoubtedly frightened, all alone in the world, beside the road, with no food or water. Whoever left them here didn't care a bit what happened to them.

At age nine, I kneel beside the box and pick up a few, one by one. My dad watches as I hold their furry bodies against my chest, pressing them to my cheek, grinning wildly. "Daddy? Can we take them home? Please?"

Watching us now, the request strikes me as absurd. There are *seven* of them. But I remember this: I know how it works out. I realize that Alex is right about me, at least in one way: I was incredibly spoiled.

My dad shades his eyes, staring at the cloudless sky.

"Kittens grow up, Liz. They won't be little and cute forever. We should take them to the humane society." He pauses. "I'll let you keep one of them, if you'd like. But just one."

"But Daddy, they're brothers and sisters! They'll miss each other!" And I pick up two more—they're really tiny—so that I'm clutching five of them against my body. "Please? Please can we take them home? Just for a few days—then you can give them to the humane society. Daddy, they're hungry. They're lonely." I gaze at my father with wide, pleading eyes.

My father: recently widowed, living with his young daughter, wanting more than anything in the world to make her happy. Wanting more than anything to make her smile. For her to not be alone. He would have done whatever I wanted. He *did* do whatever I wanted.

I didn't have to pout or cry. I barely even had to beg.

"All right," he says, smiling, "you can keep them for a few days. Maybe a week."

I watch as my younger self—so overjoyed, so giddy with happiness that I practically seem drunk at nine years old—places the kittens back inside the box. My dad carries it to the car. Since the Porsche doesn't have a backseat, he rests it on my lap for the ride home.

I watch the two of us drive away. I don't have to follow to remember the rest of what happened with the kittens.

A week went by, and they were still so small—so cute!— that I couldn't bear to part with any of them. I named each one after a day of the week. Sunday used to crawl into my dad's dress shoes and fall asleep. Thursday never quite grasped the idea of a litter box. I remember it all so vividly.

I loved them for the next two months, for the rest of the summer. Then they started to grow into cats; eventually, they weren't as cute anymore. I lost interest. I stopped playing with them. And one day, when I came home after school, they were gone. My dad had realized I didn't want them anymore, so he took them to the humane society. He traded those seven cats in for a new, tiny kitten. I named her Little Fluff. And when she started getting big, he took *her* to the humane society and returned with another kitten—Mister Whiskers, who used to curl up in bed with me at night and purr away. I decided to keep Mister Whiskers.

I realize now that, if I'd let him—and if the humane society had tolerated it, which they probably wouldn't have after a while—my dad might have continued trading cats for kittens, over and over again, so that I would never have to experience them growing up, so that, to me, they would be tiny and cute forever.

After my mother died, he did everything in his power to make me happy. Everything. He gave me whatever I wanted: the most expensive name-brand clothes, front-row concert tickets, designer handbags and shoes and makeup, and all the things my heart could possibly desire. He bought me a brand-new car when I turned seventeen.

He let me have a party on our boat for my eighteenth birthday. Anything and everything I wanted. No matter what the cost.

Back in the present, I watch my father as he stands in my old bedroom, crying. We don't have Mister Whiskers anymore. One snowy day a few years ago, he went outside and simply never returned.

"Looks like the rest of your family isn't holding up as well as you thought," Alex says quietly.

"Yeah," I say, nodding, "it looks that way."

"Girls," Nicole tells Josie and my friends, still keeping her tone light, "why don't you all go down to the living room and . . . I don't know, drink some cocoa or something?" To my father she says, "Marshall, let's go. Let them be."

Before they leave the room, he turns to Mera, who is still frozen, holding her cigarette. By now, it has burned down so far that it's mostly ash, dangling at an angle from her limp hand. "Put that damn cigarette out right now," he says, his teeth gritted.

Mera flicks the cigarette out the window.

"Good." My father takes a deep breath. "That's better." He looks at Caroline—who seems to be near tears—at Josie, and finally at Nicole. "Let's go back to bed," he tells her.

"Sure, honey. Let's go."

They leave, closing the door behind them. My friends don't say anything for a long time.

Finally, Mera says, "Wow, Josie. Liz's dad is in rough shape, isn't he?"

Josie stares at her. She narrows her eyes. "*My* dad," she corrects Mera. "He's my dad, too. You know that." When I was alive, she was never this forceful about the idea that we might have the same father. Now that I'm gone, though, she is adamant.

"She really believes it," I say. "Listen to her, Alex." I look at him. "She's convinced we have the same father. I never thought it was possible, never once."

"But now?" He lets the words dangle with possibility in the air.

I shake my head. "Now I don't know. I feel like I don't know anything."

Alex nods. Then he asks, "Do you still want to follow Richie?"

I'd almost forgotten. But I'm grateful for the interruption. Seeing my father so upset is heartbreaking. My poor dad. He seems so alone now. I feel an incredible sense of guilt for having left him. Even if I didn't do it on purpose, it doesn't change the fact that I'm gone.

"Yeah," I say, my voice cracking, "let's go."

There is almost no moon, just a tiny slice of silver crescent hanging in the sky as if by magic as we follow Richie through town.

"I wish we knew where he was going," I say, wincing

with every step. I can feel the blisters on my toes. I can feel nerves being pinched with every motion. "You don't know how badly this hurts. If we knew where he was headed, we could just *go*."

"I have an idea about that," Alex says.

"You do? Where do you think he's going?"

"It's pretty obvious, isn't it? We're almost there." And he nods at the wide iron gates ahead of us in the distance. "He's going to the cemetery."

It's a cool night; Richie's feet must be freezing in his flip-flops. For a minute, I imagine how my toes would feel in a pair of sandals—so free, finally.

Almost immediately, it becomes clear where he's headed. It should have been obvious right away. He walks past several rows of tombstones until he reaches a fresh plot that is cluttered with flowers and teddy bears. It's my grave.

Alex and I are close together, watching him. For a long time Richie doesn't say or do anything: he only stands there in the dim moonlight, staring at the earth. My tombstone is not up yet; according to Alex, it takes at least a few weeks for them to carve the stone—sometimes more, depending on how elaborate the marker is.

Slowly, Richie kneels, brushing his fingers against the dirt. He puts his head down. He starts to cry.

"I would have forgiven you, Liz," he says out loud. "I don't care what you did. I don't know why you would have . . . I don't know anything. But I would have forgiven you. I promise."

I have tears in my eyes. "I'm so sorry, Richie," I whisper. "I don't know what happened. I love you."

Alex is staring at me. "You really do," he says.

"I really do what?"

"You really do love him."

I nod. "Yes. I've loved him forever. Alex, I don't know what's going on, or why you and I are here together. But when I saw my dad back there, in my old room, I remembered something . . . Alex, I used to be different. You don't have to believe me, but it's true. I was just a normal little girl, and then my mom died, and everything was different after that. It's almost like . . . like I thought that if I were pretty and thin and popular, if I surrounded myself with people who liked me, if I could control everything that went on in my world, then what happened to my mom wouldn't hurt so much anymore. And my dad was willing to do anything to keep me from suffering. It made me shallow. I get that now. Alex, you have to under-stand, I'm sorry for how we all treated you . . . for how I ignored you. And for how we treated other people, too, people like Frank Wainscott. I'm sorry things were so hard for you in school. If I could go back and change the way it all happened—"

"You can't," he says simply. He doesn't sound angry or compassionate. Maybe just a bit regretful, but mostly, his tone is matter-of-fact. "It's over for us."

I look at Richie. "It's not over for him."

My boyfriend kneels for a long time. Then, in a deliberate motion, he lies down on my grave. The grass beneath him is young and thin; it has barely begun to sprout over my freshly dug plot.

Richie lies on his side. He lies on top of my body, down there in the earth, and he closes his eyes.

I go to him. I lie beside him and put my arms around his body. As my sea legs make themselves known again, the ground seems to rock gently. Like last time, when I concentrate hard, I can feel Richie. But it's also different from before, outside Alex's house. Instead of our contact growing unbearably hot, forcing me to pull away after a few seconds, I'm thrilled to find that, this time, I can really hold Richie. The feeling is beyond wonderful. It is the most alive I've felt since my death. As we lie there, it occurs to me that I held him almost exactly the same way over a year ago, when he was sick in bed. And even though Richie doesn't give any sign that he can sense me, I am almost giddy from the feel of his curly hair against my face, his clothing beneath my hands. I can feel his breath. I can hear his heart beating, feel the coolness of the damp earth beneath us.

He lies like that until he falls asleep, his breath eventually growing deep and even. He stays there all night, until the first rays of sun begin to break at the horizon. And I stay there with him—Alex watching both of us wordlessly, watching and understanding that I might not have always been the nightmare of an individual that he thought. Maybe not.

Richie sleeps, but I don't. I stay awake, my arms around him, wishing that he could feel me just one more time. Wondering what the hell happened to put me in the ground. And fearing, more than anything in the world, that I might never find out.

Thirteen

The following Monday at school, it's almost like none of the bizarre events from the weekend—the séance in my old bedroom, my boyfriend sleeping on my grave—ever happened. It's high school; the popular kids are clustered together as usual at their lockers in between homeroom and first period, taking their time getting to class. For years, my friends and I have coordinated our schedules as much as possible. So it doesn't surprise me a bit when I see that Richie has first-period English with Caroline and Josie.

Still, when I see my stepsister taking her seat next to *my* boyfriend in the back of the class, edging her desk so close to his that they're almost touching, I can't help but scowl.

"It's like she's stepping right into my place," I complain to Alex.

He shrugs. "You guys were like sisters. She's dating Richie now. I'm sure it comforts him, in a way. What's the big deal?"

I stare at him. "What's the big deal? Richie slept on my *grave* just two nights ago, Alex. He is obviously not over me. And Josie is just moving on like . . . like it's a natural progression." I shake my head, staring at her from across the room. "I never had any idea that she liked him. Not a clue." I pause. "Not that I remember, anyway."

"Well . . ." Alex hesitates.

"Well, what?"

"She thinks you two are half sisters. Right?"

I nod.

"Does it really surprise you that she'd want to step into your shoes, Liz? I mean, isn't that what sisters do?"

I stare at the dry-erase board on the front wall of the classroom. Somebody—probably not our teacher—has written DIAGRAMMING SENTENCES IS AWESOME! in big block letters. The sarcasm is obvious. "But it's not fair," I tell him, pouting. "Lots of guys like Josie. Jason Harvatt is practically obsessed with her. She should date somebody else. I should be with Richie."

"But you're dead. And you aren't with Richie anymore. You're with me." As quickly as the words come out of his mouth, he stumbles over them, clearly embarrassed. "I mean, you're not *with me* with me, but we're together in the—"

"Alex." I give him a half smile. "It's okay. I know what you meant."

The seniors are reading *For Whom the Bell Tolls*, and for a few minutes Alex and I listen to a boring discussion on symbolism, which seems to drag on forever. When I look at the clock, I see that it's only been five minutes.

"I always hated English class," I remark. We're sitting on the floor at the front of the room.

"Really? You don't like books at all? And yet you said Richie wanted to be a writer."

"He does. But that's his thing. I never liked to read much. Just, you know, magazines and stuff." I pause. "Well, that's not entirely true. Sometimes if Richie read a book he thought was really great, he'd give it to me to read. There were a few I liked a lot."

"Like what?" Alex seems genuinely interested.

"Um, let me think . . . well, I loved *Catcher in the Rye*. That's Richie's favorite book. We read it sophomore year, I think."

"Yeah, it was sophomore year. I read it, too." He pauses. "I loved it."

There's an odd moment of awkwardness. We're both quiet. Then Alex says, shyly smiling, "Well. That's one thing we've got in common."

"Yeah." I smile back. "It's something."

The awkwardness lingers. It's clear that neither of us knows where to go from here.

"I'm bored," I say, trying to change the subject.

"Okay. What do you want to do?"

"I don't know." I look around. "We could remember something together." I pause. "I mean something about me," I add. We have yet to discuss further the memory from Alex's life that we shared the other day. I can tell it's not a topic that either one of us feels comfortable approaching, and I'm in no hurry to force the issue. It's obvious he doesn't want me in his head.

There's a part of me that feels like it's unfair—after all, I've shown him so much from my life—but I'm mostly okay with letting him keep his memories to himself. After all, it's not like our lives intersected much while we were alive, and more than anything, I'm interested in figuring out how and why I died. What could I possibly learn from watching Alex's memories? They have nothing to do with me.

He's quiet.

"Or I could do it alone," I offer. "I don't know if I want you to come with me."

"Why not?"

"Because I don't want to give you more evidence of what a terrible person I was."

He studies me. "You're more complicated than I thought, Liz. You aren't just a superficial, spoiled brat."

"You think I'm complicated?"

"Yes." He puts a hand on my shoulder. "Let me come with you. Let's remember something together."

I nudge his hand away. "I kind of want to go alone."

"Then what am I supposed to do, sit here while you space out?" Our teacher, Mrs. Davis, has transitioned from talking about symbolism to a discussion of the Spanish-American war, which I've gathered is the subject of the book. Oh God. I could die again, just from boredom.

"Okay," I say, "we'll play a game to decide."

"We'll what? Liz, just let me come."

"No, I want to play a game. Let's do rock, paper, scissors, okay?"

Alex rolls his eyes. "Fine."

I hold out a fist. He does the same. "Ready?" I ask. "One, two, three . . . oh no."

Alex is paper; I'm rock. He wins.

"Best out of five," I plead, unable to suppress a giggle. "Best out of five."

"No, no, no. You said you wanted to play, and we played. I won." He clamps his hand on my shoulder again. "Now let's go. Where are we headed?"

I shrug. "Let's not decide. Let's see where we end up."

When I open my eyes, I'm still in high school. I look up and see myself standing in the doorway of my junior year English class. I can tell right away that it's junior year because I'm limping as I walk through the doorway, and I have a bruise on the side of my face that looks *awful*.

"Oh my God," I say to Alex, staring at myself. "This is the

day I came back to school after I fell down the stairs." I look at him. "You were already gone. Do you want to try again? We could try to go back farther—"

"No," he says. "I want to see what happens."

"It's just going to be me sitting in English class—"

"No it's not, Liz. It might be important. You can barely remember anything from last year, you've said so yourself. Aren't you curious? Don't you want to know how you ended up in the water?"

"Yes," I admit. But what I *don't* want to see is more of me acting like a total bitch. And when I let my gaze drift across the room, toward the back, I can tell immediately what kind of display we're in for, even if I don't remember specifically what's about to happen.

"Just watch," Alex says calmly. "It's okay." The corners of his eyes wrinkle in a half smile. "I won't be too hard on you."

Richie is sitting in the back of the room. He always sits in the back; he's just that kind of guy. Normally I'd be right beside him, but as I walk in, I stop dead in my tracks: sitting next to Richie, her desk against my boyfriend's, is Beth Follet.

Beth is on the cross-country team with me. Her parents are divorced. She lives alone with her mom, who is a dental hygienist at Topher's dad's office. Beth and I don't get along. Like so many of the other girls in school, she's always had a thing for Richie—she even went so far as to ask him to dance with her at sophomore year homecoming, while I was in the bathroom. The *nerve*. Of course, Richie said no. But now, here she is, sitting beside him like it's the most natural thing in the world.

I walk to the back of the room, a smile plastered onto my face. "Hey," I ask, "what's going on here?" I stare pointedly at Beth, still smiling. "You're in my seat."

"No, I'm not," she says, smiling right back at me. "You've been absent for three days. We're working in groups. Richie and I are partners."

"What?" My voice is flat. "Richie, is this true? You're partners with her?"

He nods. When Beth isn't looking, he gives me an apologetic shrug and mouths, "Sorry."

I turn on the ball of my foot—despite my injuries, I'm still wearing three-inch heels that undoubtedly pinch the hell out of my toes—and walk to the front of the room, where our teacher, Mrs. Cunningham, is sitting at her desk, paging calmly through a copy of the *New Yorker*, paying absolutely no attention to her class.

"Mrs. Cunningham," I say, "I know I've been absent for a few days, but I don't have a partner for the assignment now—I mean, I don't even know what the assignment *is*—and I was really hoping I could work with Richie." My voice is confident, head held high. "We're always partners."

Mrs. Cunningham barely looks up from her magazine. "Yes, Liz, I'm aware of who your partner usually is. But we paired off on Monday, and today is Thursday, so I'm afraid you'll just have to do the assignment by yourself." And she looks at me with a wide smile. "Once you read your syllabus and figure out what the assignment *is*. Which," she adds, "you would have known already, had you taken the time to look over the syllabus before today." Then her tone softens just a bit. "I know you've been sick, Liz. But you have to do the project like everybody else. Okay?"

"You're saying I'll have to work all by myself, when everyone else is working in pairs?" I ask.

She nods. "That's exactly what I'm saying. I'm sorry, but there isn't anybody left for you to be partners with."

I spend the rest of the period sitting alone at a desk near the front, first reading the syllabus, and then getting started on a sheet of questions about Shakespeare's *Titus Andronicus*— which I obviously haven't read, even though I was supposed to have finished it over a week ago. When I'm not pretending to do work, I spend most of my time glowering in my seat, staring at the blank paper, doodling in the margins. I can guess exactly what I was thinking: it doesn't matter if we're not partners in class. Richie will help me do all the work later.

When the bell rings, I gather my things quickly. I wait just outside the door, in the hallway, until Beth leaves the room.

Alex and I follow her to the girls' bathroom.

I wait for her to finish up in the stall. Aside from the four of us, the bathroom is empty.

"This is nothing special." Alex sounds disappointed, looking around the bathroom.

"What do you mean?"

"I don't know. I always thought there were, like . . . sofas in here, or something like that."

I roll my eyes. "Right. Wait—watch."

"What's going to happen?"

"I don't remember, Alex. That's why I want to watch."

When Beth comes out, before she even has a chance to turn the corner and face the sink, I reach out with a swift arm and grab her *by the hair*, yanking her close to me.

"Oh my God," I gasp, staring at myself. "What the hell am I doing?"

Alex is wide eyed, obviously stunned. He doesn't respond.

"Listen to me, you little brat," I say to Beth, my voice low and threatening. "Maybe you're partners with Richie today, but you aren't going to be his partner tomorrow. Got it?"

"Ow!" Beth is almost crying—panicked, genuinely afraid of me. "Liz, you're hurting me! Let go!"

But I only yank her closer. I seem absolutely livid. "When you get to class tomorrow, tell Mrs. Cunningham that you changed your mind. Tell her you don't want to be partners with him anymore. And if I ever see you so much as glance in his direction—let alone ask him to dance or try to get close to him—I swear to God, you'll be sorry." And I let go of her hair.

She stands there, trying to blink away her tears, rubbing her head, shocked by my display of anger. "I'm sorry," she says. "I didn't even pick him. We were assigned to each other."

"Don't lie," I say, taking a step closer to her.

She steps back, shrinking against the wall. Her gaze darts to the door. I can tell she's desperate to get away from me. "I'm not lying. I'm sorry. But Liz, the project is over. It's done. I'm not his partner anymore, okay?"

"Okay." I nod. My breath is heavy; my hands are shaking with anger. "Good. Then we don't have anything else to say to each other."

Beth hurries toward the door. But just as she's about to leave the bathroom, she stops. For a moment, she is completely still. Then, slowly, she turns to face me. Her gaze is steady and suddenly unafraid.

"I remember eating dinner one night at Pasqualino's with my parents when I was a little girl," she says calmly. Pasqualino's is an Italian restaurant in Noank.

"So?" And I smirk. "You had enough money to eat out?"

"Your father was there with your stepmother." She swallows. "I remember my parents talking about what a shame it was, the way the two of them were so obviously running around together. See, Liz, your mom wasn't dead yet. Your dad was just out with his girlfriend, having a good old time, letting the whole town see what was going on." She takes a step backward. "My family might not have a lot of money, and my parents might not be together anymore, but at least I have a mother. Your mother starved herself to death. Your dad had an affair while she was dying. Everyone knows that."

"Shut up," I say. "You're poor. You're poor and you're ugly."

"You're ugly, too." Beth smiles at me. "You're so ugly

inside, and you don't even know it." She's practically beaming. "And you're starving yourself. Just like your mother. But you know what? I'm glad." She puts her hand back on the door, preparing to leave the room. "The world would be better off without you, Liz."

And she's gone.

For a moment, I just stand there, staring after her.

"Wow," Alex breathes. "That was really . . . something."

I can't even find my voice to respond; that's how horrified I am by what we've just seen. I almost can't process how cruel I was to Beth. Beyond that, I am humiliated by the idea that *everyone* in our town seemed to believe, without a doubt, that my dad and Nicole were having an affair. Everyone. Even Beth Follet's parents.

As I continue to watch my younger self, I manage to speak up. "Wait," I tell Alex. "Look. What am I doing?"

For the last few seconds, I've been staring at myself in the mirror. Now I'm touching the bruises on my face, wincing when I make contact. I turn on the water in the sink and watch as it swirls down the drain. I lean over and take a few deep breaths, and then I turn off the water. When I straighten up, there is a fierce, intense look in my eyes.

"She's right. You're ugly," I say to my own reflection. "Everybody knows."

I begin to cry. The tears trickle down my cheeks, smearing my makeup, destroying my mascara.

"Ugly," I repeat, almost as though I'm embracing the word, trying to convince myself that it's true.

I follow my younger self around the corner as I lock myself in a stall and sit on the closed toilet, pulling my knees to my chest. I sit there, sobbing without making much sound at all, until the bell rings, signaling the beginning of second period. But I don't get up. I continue to cry.

And then, just when it looks like I'm never going to stop, I suddenly stand up. I smooth the wrinkles from my outfit. I take a deep breath. I step out of the stall, open my bookbag, and stand in front of the mirror. Carefully, calmly, I reapply mascara, lipstick, and loose powder.

I smile at my reflection. "Okay," I say, under my breath. "Let's go, Liz."

There are still a few stragglers in the hall, students dawdling in between classes, and almost immediately I spot Josie and Richie next to his locker, talking. Richie has his back to me and is leaning against his closed locker, cool as usual. When Josie sees me, she raises her arm in a wave.

"Hi there," I say, beaming at them breathlessly. There is no trace of the Liz I just saw in the bathroom; in almost an instant, I've gone from a sobbing mess to calm, collected, and smiling. "We should get to class, guys." I look at Josie. "What are you doing down here? Don't you have Spanish upstairs second period?"

"Do you think she and Richie were fooling around

already?" I ask Alex. I can feel the jealousy welling up inside of me, uncontrollable. "Right under my nose like that?"

He shakes his head. "Didn't she say it only started a few months before you died?"

"Yeah," I agree, "and this was the fall . . . it was a long time before I died. So what were they talking about?"

Alex can only shrug. "Beats me. Let's watch."

"We just saw Beth crying," Josie says to me with a giggle. "Did you have something to do with that? Richie told me about the scene you made in English."

The hall is empty now except for the three of us, lingering like we don't have any place else in the world to be, even though we're officially late for class.

I widen my smile. "That would be correct." And I place my arm on Richie's, squeezing it possessively. "She was trying to weasel in on my turf."

"Oh God, Liz. As *if*," Richie says, sighing. "You didn't go all psycho on her, did you? It was just a class project. It's over."

Josie narrows her eyes. "Liz is right, Richie. Beth should know her place. She has a lot of nerve even talking to you."

I smile at Josie, but when I speak I can detect the slightest hint of shakiness to my voice. "That's right," I tell Richie firmly. "You're mine. She should have known better."

My boyfriend seems to be used to our attitude. He gives me a lopsided grin. "I'm yours, okay?" He rests his forehead against mine, gives me a kiss on the nose. "How are you feeling, anyway?" With the back of his hand, he lets his fingers graze the bruise on my face. I wince.

"Still swollen?" he asks.

"Yeah. A little bit."

Josie bites her lip, tilting her head in concern. "She has a concussion, you know." To me, she says, "You're lucky you didn't break your neck falling down those steps. We could be at your funeral right now." Her gaze drifts down the length of my body. I can tell she's concerned about how thin I'm becoming.

As I stand with my stepsister, I ignore her comment—but Alex and I, watching, exchange a wide-eyed glance.

"Creepy," Alex says. "Don't you think?"

I shudder a little bit. "Yes. Very creepy."

My younger self stands up a little straighter, as if I'm gathering my confidence for something. Glancing around the hallway to make sure there's nobody coming, I lower my voice. "Richie?" I ask tentatively. "I was wondering—I have all this homework to catch up on, and I just can't focus."

"Yeah?" He's hesitant, like he knows what I'm about to ask.

"Do you have anything? Like . . . anything to help me get my work done?"

Richie tilts his head back and stares at the ceiling. He doesn't answer me at first.

"Richie?" I ask again. "Seriously. I can't think straight. It would really help me out."

"Why can't you think straight? Because of the concussion?"

My gaze flickers to Josie—for just a second, but it's enough. There's more going on here, and she knows it. I can tell that much just from watching us together. But I have no idea what it is.

"Yeah," I say, "because of the concussion."

"And you're on painkillers?" he continues.

I nod.

"What kind?"

"Um . . . Percocet."

"How many milligrams? How many times per day?" He's like a walking reference book on prescription drugs.

I shrug. "I don't know how many milligrams they are, Richie. They're big and white. I can show you the bottle after school today."

"And you want me to give you—what? Something to help you concentrate? Like Adderall?"

I nod. "Yes. Would you?"

"Liz, no." He shakes his head firmly. "No way. I'm not hooking you up with prescription drugs just so you can catch up on homework. You can't mix painkillers and stimulants like that. It's not a good idea."

"What's Adderall?" Alex murmurs.

"It's for ADD," I tell him. "But it's an amphetamine. People use it to help them concentrate." I pause. "They use it to control their appetites, too. It keeps you from getting hungry."

"Uh-huh." He nods. "And how do you know all this? Do you have ADD?"

"No." I look at the floor. I'm so embarrassed that he's seen me act this way—toward Beth in the restroom, and now here, with Richie, asking him for drugs. Why would I want Adderall? Aside from a little pot from time to time, I do *not* do drugs—not powders, not pills, nothing. "I must know what Adderall is because Richie sells it. To students, you know—he used to get like twenty bucks for a single pill. I have no idea where he got them."

But there's something else, too. There's another reason why I know about drugs for ADD. And as much as I hate admitting it to Alex, I believe that he wants to help me figure out my past, which for the most part is still such a blank slate, only now being peppered with memories that are illustrating so clearly what a reprehensible person I was capable of being when I was alive.

"My mother used to go to all these different doctors," I explain, still staring at the linoleum tile in the hallway. "She was what they call a drug seeker. Aside from the cold medicine, she'd take just about anything to keep herself from getting hungry." I swallow. "Including Adderall, when she could get her hands on a prescription for it."

Alex doesn't respond. He just listens. I'm grateful for the momentary silence.

Then Josie says, "Richie? Do you *have* any Adderall?"

Richie grins again. "Who are you talking to, Josie? Do I have any Adderall?" He winks. "Of course I've got some stashed away. Why?"

"I'm really stressed, too," Josie tells him. "We've got midterms coming up, and I have like three projects that are due. Plus, I have to build a freaking *diorama* for history class." She lets the sentence dangle with possibility for a moment. Then she scoffs and says, "I bet you won't let *me* have any either, will you?"

Richie and I are holding hands now, standing close together, swinging our arms back and forth as we get ready to head into class. "Sure," he says, "why not?"

Josie seems almost disappointed. "Oh. Okay. Well, can you give it to me after school?"

"Come on," I tell Richie, tugging his arm as I start to walk away, "we're already late." To my stepsister, I say, "Josie, you've got to get to Spanish."

"Hold on, Josie. Let's get something straight." Richie grins at her as the three of us walk down the hallway together. "I'm not *giving* you anything. You're a paying customer. Twenty bucks a pop. Okay?"

Josie's trying to seem unfazed, but I can tell that she's agitated. "Sure," she says. "Of course."

"He doesn't care about her," I tell Alex. "Not like he cared about me. You see? He wouldn't give me any pills, but he'll *sell* them to her. He doesn't care and she knows it damn well."

"Yeah," Alex agrees, "you're right." He meets my gaze. "So what changed? Why does he care about her now?"

I narrow my eyes. I stare as my former self, along with my boyfriend and stepsister, stroll casually toward our classrooms, Josie's and my heels clicking in a faint rhythm against the linoleum as we walk. "I don't know," I tell him, "but I think it must have been something big."

Fourteen

There is no sleep for the dead; at least, not for Alex and me. We spend our nights in quiet loneliness, lost in our own memories—mostly we travel into mine together, but sometimes I go alone, and on occasion Alex will slip into his past, though I haven't asked to go with him again. Aside from that, there isn't much else to do except wait for the sun to come up, so we can watch our living friends and relatives as they go about life without us. I dread the end of every day, the inevitable quiet darkness, the lost feeling of seclusion that makes me ache for sleep that I know isn't coming anytime soon.

It's late September now, two weeks after we witnessed my scene with Beth in the girls' bathroom. It's the middle of the night, probably close to dawn. There's no clock in my room anymore, but after so many nights spent here, gazing out the window, I've gotten good at reading the sky, at being able to tell where we are in the night based on the position of the moon.

"Someone's outside," Alex says. He's standing at my window, staring at the street below.

"So?" I'm on the floor, beside my pile of old running shoes. In the dark, they look almost alive: tongues like mouths, laces pulled like expectant facial features through multiple sets of eyes. We watch each other.

"It's your boyfriend." Alex's face is pressed against the window as he peers down the street. But there is no circle of breath on the glass from his mouth. "Maybe he's going to sleep on your grave again."

I sit up straighter. "Do you think so?"

Alex stares for a moment longer. "No," he says. "He's going somewhere in his car."

It's true: once Alex and I are outside, we watch as Richie works quickly, loading a small suitcase and duffel bag into his backseat. He's about to climb into the driver's side when a car turns down our street and its lights shine directly onto him, stopping him in his tracks.

"Shit," he murmurs, closing the driver's-side door, shoving his keys into his pocket. He stands beside the car, trying to look nonchalant. I almost expect him to start whistling.

Joe Wright, off-duty, in a maroon sedan with two car seats secured in the back, puts his car in Park and lets it idle in the middle of the street.

Richie puts his hands up. "I'm not doing anything wrong. I was out for a run, that's all."

"At four in the morning?" Joe looks around innocently. "It's dark, you know." He stares at my boyfriend, who is wearing a T-shirt, gray sweatpants, and the same flip-flops he wore to the cemetery a few weeks earlier, their soles still caked with mud from my grave. "You're a lousy liar."

"I'll be eighteen in a month. I can do what I want."

Joe cups his hands to peer into Richie's backseat. "Your parents know you're going on a road trip?"

Richie glances at his house. All the lights are on inside. "Hell if I know. They aren't here."

Joe nods. "What about school? It's your senior year. You aren't just going to disappear, are you?" His gaze drifts to my house. "Your new girlfriend sure would miss you."

Richie stares at the bright moon dangling in the sky. He doesn't say anything.

"Don't you think people will find it strange? You disappearing in the middle of the night?"

"Maybe." He shrugs. "They'll get over it."

Without any warning, Joe opens Richie's car door and reaches across the backseat. He emerges clutching a bouquet of flowers. White lilies.

"My favorite," I murmur. "He's going to put them on my grave."

"What are these?" Joe asks, frowning. He rests them on the hood of the car.

Richie is not intimidated. "They're none of your business. Hey, you don't have a warrant. You can't just go through my stuff."

"Who are these flowers for?"

Richie crosses his arms. He stares at Joe, silently defiant.

"You know," Joe continues, "when I saw you on the boat, I knew I remembered you from somewhere. It took me a while to figure it out." Then he taps his nose with an index finger, pointing at Richie. "Prom night, last spring. Right? I even wrote up an incident report. You and Liz sure were steaming up those windows."

Richie puts a hand on the driver's-side door. "Can I leave? I've got somewhere to be." He reaches for the flowers; in a swift motion, Joe closes a hand over Richie's wrist.

"I'll go with you. We need to have a talk."

"We've talked plenty."

"What am I gonna find if I look through those bags you've got in the backseat?"

"Nothing." Richie tries to wriggle his arm away.

"Nothing? Then you don't mind if I take a look."

"You don't have a warrant."

Joe levels his gaze. "Don't need one, buddy. It's called probable cause."

Richie glowers at him in the moonlight. Finally, he says, "Whatever you want. Go right ahead."

With great interest, Joe unpacks both the duffel bag and the suitcase. Initially, there doesn't seem to be much out of the ordinary: in the suitcase, there are clothes, books (*The Great Gatsby*, *Slaughterhouse-Five*, and *Gravity's Rainbow*), and a map of New England. The duffel bag holds more clothes, a few unopened packs of cigarettes (which Joe confiscates, to Richie's obvious annoyance), and the same framed picture of the two of us—the one from a track meet—that used to sit on Richie's desk.

Once he's gone through everything, Joe stands back, frowning in dissatisfaction, tapping a finger to his lips.

"See? There's nothing." Richie seems smug, wiggling his toes in the cool night air. "Can I go?"

Joe takes a long moment to stare at him. He looks around: at Richie's house, at my house, and then at the car again. Without a word, he strolls to the back of the car and opens the trunk. My boyfriend's mouth drops. Joe tugs at the floor of the trunk until he pulls it free, exposing the space where the spare tire should be. But it's not there; instead, there's the all-too-familiar *Great Expectations*, along with a brown paper bag.

My boyfriend is clearly trying to play it cool, but I notice that he is visibly sweating now. He opens his mouth to speak, closes it, opens it again. He stares at his feet in what seems like regret. I can guess what he's thinking: if he were wearing running shoes, he'd be able to sprint away.

It's no surprise to me when Joe opens *Great Expectations* and finds it full of drugs and money. But I'm completely unprepared for what he discovers in the paper bag when he tugs it free of its contents.

"Holy crap," Alex says, taking a big step backward—as though anything could possibly hurt him.

But Joe steps back, too. His eyes are wide open, a grown man—and a policeman, at that—suddenly nervous to be alone on the street, in the dark, without so much as a pair of hand-cuffs to subdue my boyfriend.

Richie is frozen for a moment. His gaze flickers from the trunk, to Joe, then back to the trunk. In a single, swift motion, he leaps forward and closes his hand around the object that came from the paper bag.

It's a gun.

Joe rushes toward Richie, but he's too slow. With the gun pressed to his chest, almost in an embrace, my boyfriend turns on his heel and begins running down the empty road, his flip-flops beating in frantic rhythm, his getaway via car gone suddenly awry.

Richie is fast; Joe doesn't even try to chase him beyond a few feet. He stands on my street, stunned—this is obviously more trouble than he'd anticipated on this early morning in our otherwise sleepy town.

Aside from the drugs that Richie has left behind, there's something else: as Joe picks up the paper bag again, a mem-ory card, so benign looking, so tiny that it could almost go unnoticed, slips from the bag and bounces onto the ground, falling underneath the car. Out of the corner of his eye, Joe sees the memory card as it lands.

He bends over and picks it up carefully, holding it between

his thumb and index finger. Then he raises his arm, bringing the card into the moonlight. The three of us all stare at it.

"Well, what do we have here?" Joe says out loud.

Alex looks at me. "Do you know what's on it?"

I search my mind for an inkling or recognition, anything at all that would give me the slightest clue as to what kind of information might be stored in the tiny card. But I have no idea.

It could be anything, I guess. It could be private information about me or Richie, or maybe something I can't even imagine. But there will be no opportunity for me to protect the contents, to keep them from the rest of the world. Richie can't do it, either—not now. All he can do is run away from the heap of trouble he's gotten himself into. And all I can do is wait.

Fifteen

There are cops everywhere. It's a scene that I've grown way too familiar with over the past month: chaos caused by something gone terribly wrong. There are throngs of my neighbors huddled on their front porches, most of them still wearing pajamas or bathrobes, watching with tired but wide eyes, captivated by the unfolding drama.

"It's like entertainment to them," I tell Alex, disgusted. "Like a soap opera or something."

He presses his lips together in thought. "They're just curious."

"Yeah, well, I wish they'd mind their own business. Like my family hasn't been through enough. Like they need everyone gawking at them."

The police are searching Richie's house. His parents—called home from their Manhattan apartment in the middle of the night—stand on the sidewalk, watching as uniformed officers emerge from their home carrying bags of evidence—evidence of what, though?—from my boyfriend's room.

When Mera and Topher show up at my house—they've been giving Josie a ride to school lately—Josie ushers them inside, where my family is sitting at the kitchen table, my stepsister intermittently crying and sending frantic text messages to Richie, who's nowhere to be found.

Joe is with them, leaning against my parents' fridge, drinking a cup of coffee.

"What can we do?" my dad asks. He appears to have lost maybe twenty pounds in the past few weeks. His face is ashen, eyes glassy and somber. "I don't believe Richie could have had anything to do with . . . with what happened to Liz." My dad has always liked Richie. And of course, he's right—Richie never would have hurt me. I feel pleased that my father is so convinced that, deep down, Richie is a good kid who really loved me. But there's still obviously something very wrong.

"We don't know that he did." Joe blows on his hot coffee. "We have to find him before we can jump to conclusions." He stares at my stepsister. "Josie? Any ideas?"

She looks at Topher and Mera. It seems ridiculous that they're even here. They're both shrinking into a corner of the room, hands in each other's back pockets, as usual. It's like they don't even know how to stand beside each other without one groping the other. Their clinginess has always annoyed me. Today I notice that they're wearing matching outfits: jeans, red sweaters with a gray argyle stripe going down the front, white dress-shirt collars peeking out from their necklines, and identical gold bracelets around their wrists. *Puke.*

Almost imperceptibly, Mera nudges Topher. He glances at her. "What?"

"Tell them."

"Oh." Topher stares at the ceiling, his mouth slightly agape. "Right."

"What's that on his teeth?" Alex asks.

I roll my eyes. "It's a whitening strip." Topher, like all of my friends, is fully dedicated to his personal appearance. But he's also a smoker. To combat the inevitable yellow teeth that accompany the habit, he uses whitening strips twice a day, every day. Right now, he reaches into his mouth, plucks the plastic strip away, and takes a long moment to run his tongue over his teeth as everybody else stares at him, anxious, waiting.

He rolls the plastic into a tight ball and hands it to Mera, who holds out an open palm. I know for a fact that he's got a tiny bottle of mouthwash and a roll of dental tape in his book-bag, and that he's dying to rinse and floss before he has to—God forbid—interact with anyone besides Mera. But it's clear that nobody's willing to wait.

Lowering his head, awkwardly covering his mouth with a

hand as he speaks, Topher says, "Richie came by my house early this morning. He wanted to know if I could lend him some money."

"I was there," Mera adds. "He was pretty upset."

"There she goes again," I tell Alex. "Always has to be the center of attention."

Joe leans forward with interest. "Did he say what it was for? Did he tell you he was leaving?"

Topher shrugs. "Not really. He just said he needed it."

Immediately, I think of Caroline and the money she stole from my bathroom.

"How much did you give him?" Joe asks.

"Um, not very much."

"How much is 'not very much'?"

Topher clears his throat. He refuses to look at anyone. "I went to the ATM. I took out as much as I could. Seven hundred dollars." He pauses. "Richie wanted more."

Nicole presses a hand to her forehead. She clutches my father's arm. "My God," she murmurs. "We saw him all the time. We know his family. He's like a son." She stares at Joe. "It is not possible that he hurt Liz. I've known that boy since he was a toddler. He's been in our house almost every day."

Nicole is right. I close my eyes, trying to remember. I don't touch Alex. I want to be in this kitchen alone with my family, with Richie—who *was* like family—to witness a time when we were all happy. I'm starting to feel like that's impossible.

·   ·   ·

When I open my eyes, I see snow falling heavily outside the kitchen window. From the doorway into the living room, I notice a big tree adorned with twinkling white lights and dozens of ornaments. My family might not be Christian, but Christmas was always a big deal in our household. Josie and I used to get piles of presents; we'd make a list of the things we wanted, and it was rare that we didn't get all of it. Like I said, my father refused us nothing, and Nicole never seemed to have a problem with his desire to spoil me and Josie—but especially me.

I am seventeen, a junior in high school. I can tell because there's a book of CliffsNotes for *Othello* resting in front of me at the kitchen table; we studied Shakespeare my junior year.

Even though it's so early in the morning—the clock on the stove reads 7:48—my cheeks are naturally flushed beneath my makeup, eyes wide and alert. I probably got up at five a.m. to go running. I always enjoyed running in the snow, feeling my breath leave my body in puffs of moisture, finding the balance between body heat and cold air that cloaked me in a sweaty blanket of warmth.

Josie stands at the stove, her back to me. She's busy cooking; there are cast-iron pans on two of the burners, both of them sizzling as she stirs. She's always liked to cook.

The kitchen door opens without so much as a knock, and Richie steps into the room. Even though he lives only a few doors down, he's bundled up in a heavy winter coat. A black-and-gray argyle scarf is wound around his neck, gloves on his hands. The only thing missing is a hat; his curls are full of still-frozen snowflakes. He is adorable.

"Good morning," he says, grinning at me as I sit at the table. He kicks his winter boots off on the small oriental rug just inside the doorway. He walks over to me, leans down, and kisses the top of my head.

I beam up at him. "Morning."

Nicole stands at the fridge, its door open, staring at the contents. She's still in her pajamas, which aren't much: a short white nightgown peeks out from beneath a cream-colored satin robe that falls to her midthigh. Her legs are toned and deeply tanned, even though it's winter; when she can't lie out in the sun, she uses an expensive bronzer that gives her entire body a natural-looking glow.

Richie takes a seat beside me at the table. I watch us with longing and deep regret as my living self leans toward him and kisses him full on the lips.

"You're so cold," I giggle, pulling away. "How much snow is out there now?"

Before he can answer, my father walks into the room. He's wearing a suit, complete with black-and-red-striped suspenders that stretch against his big belly, his jacket slung over his shoulder. "It's cold enough that school is canceled," my dad says. He walks to Nicole, puts an arm around her waist, and kisses her cheek.

Things might not have been perfect, but we *seemed* so happy. I would give anything, I think, to go back to this moment, to be living it for real instead of watching as an outsider.

"School's closed? Really?" Josie turns away from the stove, grinning. "They *never* cancel school."

She's right; everybody is used to snow in Connecticut. It practically takes a blizzard for the administration to cancel classes.

"I just saw it on the news upstairs," my dad says. "A frozen pipe burst. You kids got lucky."

As I'm watching all of us, I notice that Richie and I aren't paying any attention to my dad. Beneath the table, I can see his hand resting on my knee; I'm wearing a black pencil skirt and dark stockings. My shoes are shiny red high-heeled boots. How the hell was I expecting to walk through the snow in that outfit?

Sitting close to each other, Richie and I have locked gazes. With his free hand—the one that isn't on my knee—he reaches toward my face, tucks a stray blond hair behind my ear.

We are in our own world, oblivious to my family around us. It occurs to me that this was after my fall down the stairs, after I started losing weight and acting distant. Still, he and I were in love. That much is obvious. We can barely take our eyes off each other.

"What *will* we do with our day?" Richie murmurs to me.

A tiny smile plays on my lips, which are carefully lined, filled in with crimson lip stain, finished off with a coat of gloss. "We'll think of something," I almost whisper.

"All right, you two." Josie stands above us, holding a plate of scrambled eggs. "That's enough already. You're going to make me vomit."

I glance up at her. I'm still smiling. "Sorry."

"Don't say 'sorry.' Just cut it out." She sets the plate in front of Richie. "Here you go. Eggs with bacon, onion, tomato, and smoked mozzarella." She pauses. "You like it. Right?"

"Oh, yeah. Thanks, Josie." Richie grins at her. "You're the best."

For a moment, she seems at a loss.

She liked him already, I realize, watching her. *She was cooking him breakfast. She was trying to take care of him.*

"It's no problem," she finally says. "I like to cook." She turns around, picks up another plate from the counter, and places it in front of me. "For you, Liz. Egg whites. Plain."

"Thank you." I wink at her.

Josie smiles, but it's almost a smirk. "We wouldn't want you to balloon to a size zero, would we?"

"Marshall," Nicole says, frowning at my dad. "You're not seriously going into work today, are you? There's almost a foot of snow on the ground. The roads won't be cleared yet."

My dad takes a long sip from the mug of coffee that he's holding. "Don't worry about me. I'm only driving to the train station."

Nicole shakes her head. "They can manage without you for a day. It's not worth risking your safety."

He takes another sip of coffee, puts the mug on the countertop, and shrugs himself into his jacket. "I'll be fine." Looking from me and Richie to Josie, he asks, "What are you kids going to do with yourselves?"

"We can watch a movie at my place," Richie says to me.

I give him another tiny smile, like we're sharing a secret. "Okay. Sure."

"Josie?" my dad asks. "What about you?"

There's a silence as Richie and I look first at each other, then at my stepsister. It's awkward; that much is obvious.

She liked him already, I think again. *She wanted him.*

Finally, from the table, I say, "Josie? You can come, too, if you want."

Josie glances at her mother. Nicole, I can tell, understands what's going on. She half frowns at her daughter. Then she shakes her head, almost imperceptibly—I don't think Richie or I notice, but as a ghost, *I* do.

"No," Josie says. "I have homework." She looks at Richie. "I'm actually going to read *Othello*." And she smiles at him. "Not just the CliffsNotes."

"Good for you." Richie takes a big bite of his eggs. "Mmm, these are great. Liz, you could learn a thing or two from your sister."

Another silence. Josie looks at me, I look at her; Richie stares at his eggs.

As I stand in the corner, watching the three of us, I take

my index finger and draw a triangle, its invisible lines connecting our bodies. There it is.

"Liz?"

The voice is coming from somewhere far away. I feel disoriented, a little dizzy.

"Liz? Hey. Are you there?"

It's Alex. He's shaking me, tugging me away from the memory.

I blink and blink. Then I'm back, standing with him in the kitchen, still surrounded by my dad, Nicole, Josie, Mera, and Topher—and Joe Wright.

Josie is staring at her cell phone, as though she's willing a message to appear.

"Tell Mr. Wright," Nicole implores Josie. "Tell him Richie would never hurt anybody. You know him almost as well as Liz did. Right, honey?"

Josie wipes her eyes. Her fingernails are a freshly painted hot pink, perfectly matched to the ribbon in her hair. "There's something you should know." She looks from my dad to Nicole to Joe. "Richie and I started seeing each other," she says, "a couple of months before Liz died." She pauses. "She didn't know about it. Liz. We were going to tell her eventually."

Mera stiffens but doesn't say anything. She catches Topher's gaze, and as they're looking at each other, I see them communicating in such a familiar, easy way. Richie and I used to do it, too: it's the kind of look that only two people who've been together for a long time can share, a look that says volumes without either person having to speak at all. Richie, I know, could not look at Josie that way. Never had. Never would.

Topher tugs himself away from Mera. "I'm sorry," he says, "I can't stand it. I've gotta use the restroom." He picks up his bookbag.

"He's flossing," I say to Alex. "Let's follow him."

"Really?" Alex is surprised. "You don't want to stay in here and listen?"

I shake my head. "No. It's too much." What I really mean is that it's too painful to watch my stepsister explaining her new relationship with Richie to our parents. But I don't have to tell Alex all of that; he understands.

In the bathroom, the first thing Topher does is dig his dental tape and mouthwash out of his bookbag. Carefully, he flosses in between every single tooth. *Twice.* He rinses with the mouthwash. Then he unzips the main compartment of his backpack and roots around until he emerges with a small bag of weed. He flushes it down the toilet. He takes a deep breath, leaning his fists against the bathroom sink and staring at his reflection in the mirror.

Topher pulls his lips back with his fingers to expose the tops of his teeth, studying them. When he's finished— apparently dissatisfied with what he sees—he shakes his head, muttering, "Fucking cigarettes." He takes a long, shaky breath. He's sweating, clearly nervous, his usual nonchalance nowhere to be found. "Fucking Richie," he whispers. "Couldn't let it go."

Topher comes out of the bathroom just as Joe is walking to my front door. He stares at Joe for a second, his stride frozen, and glances over Joe's shoulder at the kitchen. My family can't see him—my parents are out of sight and Josie, still seated at the kitchen table, has her back to him. But Mera is standing in the corner, watching Topher. She widens her eyes, shifts her gaze past Topher, toward Joe.

Topher holds a finger to his lips. Almost silently, he and Joe leave my house.

"Hey. I need to talk to you," he says to Joe, fidgeting a little bit, staring at the bright blue sky.

"Okay." Joe folds his arms across his chest, looking around. My neighbors are still on their porches or looking out their front windows. There are three police cars, lights silently flashing, parked on my street. Richie's mother is sitting down on the sidewalk, legs crossed. She looks small and defeated. She looks like a child.

"God, she's falling apart," Alex says.

I think of the empty kitchen. The stash in Richie's room that Mrs. Wilson saw and did nothing about. "She had it coming," I murmur.

"How was the flossing?" Joe asks Topher.

"It was great. You shouldn't neglect your gums." Topher

puts a cigarette between his lips. "Don't lecture me. I'm eighteen."

"All right, no lecture. So what do you want? It's been a busy morning."

"How come you just happened to come across Richie as he was packing up to leave? That seems awfully lucky."

"I'm the law, kiddo. It's my job to keep an eye on things." Joe begins to crack his knuckles, one by one. With each distinct *pop*, Topher winces.

"Aren't you kids shook up?" Joe asks. "Two of your classmates have died in the past year. One of them was your close friend. How many kids are in your grade? A hundred? Ninety?"

"Something like that." Topher shoots a nervous glance at my house, blowing a ribbon of smoke into the air. "You're right, it sucks." He pauses. "If you find Richie, are you going to arrest him?"

"Yes."

"For what? I guarantee you he didn't kill Liz."

"Possession of a firearm, for starters. And he's got other problems, too, believe me."

"I know that. He's my friend. I know all about Richie's problems, okay? Listen, Josie's lying to you. She wasn't hooking up with Richie before Liz died. There's no way."

Joe shakes his head, clearly annoyed by Topher's supposed insight. "That's not what I understand."

"Well, then you're misunderstanding. He wouldn't have

done that." Topher rubs a hand nervously across his mouth and lowers his voice, even though there's nobody else around. "If you want to find Richie, you need to go into Groton. There's an apartment complex by the river called Covington Arms. Apartment nine. You need to find a guy named Vince Aiello."

At the mention of the name, Joe's attention snaps into focus.

My vision tunnels. My stomach turns. When I look at Alex, he's staring at me with obvious doubt. For weeks, I've been maintaining that I've never heard of Vince Aiello. It's clear Alex thinks I'm lying, that I must remember *something* about a man who obviously played a prominent role in my past.

"I must be forgetting," I say weakly. "I swear, Alex, I don't know who he is."

"Richie's been weird lately," Topher continues. "He's been parking outside the guy's building, following him, things like that." He tosses his cigarette butt onto the street. Joe stares at it but doesn't say anything. "He was a mess when he came to my place this morning. Mera was there, she saw how he was acting. He's going crazy about Liz. That's why I know he didn't kill her. He's losing his mind without her. He thinks she was cheating on him, but the thing is, the guy—Vince— he's a total loser. He works in an auto shop. He's a greaseball, you know?"

"Maybe Liz liked greaseballs. Lots of girls like bad boys." Joe glances over his shoulder at Richie's house. "Richie sells drugs. I know it. You know it. Maybe Liz wanted to step it up a notch."

"No." Topher shakes his head. "No way. You didn't know Elizabeth Valchar, sir. I did. I've known her since kindergarten. Let me tell you something about that girl. She was my friend and everything, but sir, with all due respect, you're wrong. I'll give you an example, okay? One time Mera and I picked her up for school in the morning, and the night before we'd been at the drive-in movies. We were eating popcorn in the back of my car, and there were all these little kernels stuck in the seams of the leather, you know? And there were greasy napkins on the floor. Not a big deal, right? You push it aside, you sit down. But not Liz. No, sir. That girl refused to get into my car. There were too many crumbs to just brush them onto the floor, and even then, they still would have gotten her dress dirty. That's what she told me. She said she'd get in my car again after I went to the car wash and vacuumed it out."

"I remember that day," I say. When I look at Alex, he's staring down at his shirt. It was his uniform from the Mystic Market. It's smeared with food stains and grease.

"I'm sorry if my appearance is disgusting to you," he says, his stance self-conscious.

When Topher tells the story, it seems absurd. Was I really that prissy? I must have been. I frown. "I was wearing white linen. It was dry-clean only." Even as I speak them, the words sound weak. Why didn't I just get in the car? It was only a *dress*.

"Your entire life," Alex says, "was dry-clean only."

"I was with Richie once or twice when he drove by Vince's apartment," Topher continues. "I saw Vince myself." He wrinkles his nose, remembering. "Even from across the street I could see that he had these long, dirty fingernails. His hands were all beaten up. They were weathered, you know? I mean, he was filthy—you could tell from a mile away. He was wearing a T-shirt with holes in the armpits. He's not a bad boy, or a gangster, or anything cool like that. He's a freaking slob. A real loser."

Topher hesitates for a moment. He fishes a piece of gum from his pocket and begins to chew. Shading his eyes with a hand, he peers at the sky again—it's a clear, pretty day, the sun just starting to really blaze overhead. "Elizabeth Valchar would have jumped into the Sound herself before she let a guy like that lay a finger on her. If Richie says he saw her coming out of Vince's apartment, you've gotta find out why, because believe me, there is something funny going on."

"All right," Joe says. "I believe you. Anything else?"

"Yes." Topher shivers. "Richie said he was going to kill Vince. He has a gun. So you might want to look for him at the Covington Arms"—he blows a bubble—"like, soon."

Sixteen

The Covington Arms is a big, three-story brick building that has clearly seen better days: the sidewalks are cracked, the parking lot is littered with deep potholes. Even though I've sworn up and down to Alex that I've never heard of Vince Aiello and that I've never been there before, when we approach apartment number nine I feel a shiver of recognition that starts in my spine and tingles outward into my fingertips and face. I feel a churning sense of nausea, the intense desire to leave before we even go inside. The physical feeling is identical to the way I felt the first—and only—time I ever smoked a cigarette. I feel like I've ingested poison.

We've gotten here by riding in the backseat of Joe's sedan, sitting on the floor so as not to crowd ourselves between the car seats tethered in the back. It's ironic, considering the story Topher told Joe about my disdain for dirt: the floor of

Joe's car is littered with empty juice boxes, ratty coloring books, and general messiness. But that's nothing—and I mean *nothing*—compared to what we find inside number nine.

The apartment consists of a living room, a kitchenette, and a door leading to what I assume is a bedroom and a bath. There's only one window, in the front of the living room, closed and covered with cracked plastic venetian blinds. There aren't any curtains. This guy Vince obviously doesn't have a decorator. The apartment floor is covered in filthy-looking beige shag carpeting, except for the kitchenette, which has peel-and-stick linoleum. The kitchen sink overflows with dirty dishes. There's no dishwasher. No microwave. Just a small oven with dirty electric burners, and a narrow beige refrigerator. All the walls are white with fingerprint smudges around the doorways. In the living room, there's a threadbare orange sofa, a wooden coffee table littered with three ashtrays (each of which is stuffed with cigarette butts) and empty beer cans. The only thing in the apartment that could remotely be considered nice (and I'm using the word generously) is a big flat-screen TV mounted to the wall in front of the sofa.

Since Alex and I have the luxury of not having to knock, we're already in the apartment by the time Joe starts banging on the door.

"Nice company you've been keeping," Alex observes, looking around. "And all those years, you and your friends made fun of people for being poor." He gives me a broad smile. "Quite a secret you were hiding, wasn't it?"

I frown at him. "I never made fun of *you* for being poor. Did I?" My gaze drifts to the far corner of the living room. Oddly, there's a stack of *National Geographic* magazines that's almost as tall as the TV. Maybe Vince is a nature lover.

"You certainly did."

"Name one time." But even as I'm saying the words, I know he probably has more than a single example in mind.

"Okay. I was working at the Mystic Market a couple of years ago. You and your . . . your *ilk* came in to get lunch. I remember because all we serve are wraps and sandwiches and pasta salad, and your friend Mera was horrified by the fact that everything on the menu had carbs. After I rang you up, you took a ten-dollar bill and stuffed it into the tip jar. Do you remember what you said?"

I shake my head.

"You looked at your friends and asked, 'Do you think this counts as a charitable donation?'"

Joe's banging is more persistent. From the bedroom, we hear rustling. A man's voice shouts, "I'm fucking coming! Jesus, let me put some pants on. It's like the middle of the goddamn night." It's eight in the morning.

"I'm sorry, Alex," I say. And I mean it.

He gives me a doubtful look.

"Hey." I steady my gaze at him. "I'm sorry. It's true, Alex. If I could go back and change things now, I would. You have to believe me." I should leave it at that, I know. But I can't help myself. "Alex . . . people grow up," I continue. "Didn't you say your friends at the Mystic Market told you that the real world isn't like high school? That it would get better when you got older?"

The air reeks of stale cigarette smoke. I can hardly breathe—not that it matters. I might not remember exactly what Alex is talking about, but I believe he's telling the truth. Now, more than ever, it seems obvious that I was a rotten person. Especially in the months leading up to my death, it's clear that I was nothing but a jumble of nerves and angry energy. I meant it when I said that I wish I could take it all back. I just wish I knew why I'd acted so terribly in the first place.

"My friends did tell me that," he says. "They told me all the time. Both times my bike got stolen from work, they told me that, in the adult world, people are different. All those times I ate alone to avoid your crowd, they told me 'real life' would be better."

I fan the air with my hand. Of course, it does nothing. But for once, I'm grateful to be wearing my boots; no way would I want to be standing on this carpet in bare feet. "Well, maybe they were right," I say. "We were just being kids. It would have gotten better." But there's no conviction in my voice as I speak. It was hard for Alex—partly because of people like me and my friends—and I know it.

"Right," he says. "Except, instead, I died. And here I am,

stuck with you for the foreseeable future. Things didn't get better."

I stare at him. "They could have been a lot worse. You could have been treated like Frank Wainscott."

He stares back. "You're right. I know that."

Before I can say anything else, the bedroom door swings open. Despite his insistence that he needed to get dressed before opening the door, Vince has not taken the time to put on pants.

Immediately, I recognize him with such aching certainty that I can feel my whole body go limp. My knees buckle. If my heart were beating at all, it would be racing. Vince Aiello. How could I have forgotten this man? And why can I not remember what he did to me?

He's a big guy, built like a lumberjack, fat around the middle with an otherwise stocky frame and arms sleeved in tattoos. He's wearing stained white boxer shorts and nothing else. He's already got a lit cigarette between his teeth as he answers the door.

Joe takes a long moment to look him up and down. "I thought you were going to put on some pants."

Vince shrugs. "My house, my rules."

"Vince Aiello?"

Vince runs a hand through his thick, greasy black hair. "Yup."

"Can I come in?"

He crosses his arms, narrows his gaze. "You're a cop?"

"Yes." Joe shows him a badge.

"I didn't do anything."

"Then you don't mind if—"

"Yeah, yeah, yeah. Sure. Come on in."

Vince goes into the kitchen, scratching his butt as he walks away from Joe. He opens the fridge and rifles around inside. I feel a pang of heartache as I realize that this man's refrigerator is better stocked than Richie's. Then it occurs to me that my boyfriend could show up here at any second. Where else would he go? He has no car, but he does have a gun, and Topher said he wanted to kill Vince. All our friends are at school, so he can't go to their houses. All I want is for him to be safe, for him to disentangle himself from the mess that was my life.

Cracking open an energy drink, Vince takes a seat on the couch. "Let me guess," he says. "You're here about Elizabeth Valchar."

Joe seems startled. "Then you knew her?"

"Sure, I did. She was my girlfriend. Been together almost a year." He takes a long slurp of his drink. "I've been real broken up about what happened to her. She was a beauty, you know. A real class act."

Joe clears his throat, looking around the apartment. "I don't mean to be rude," he says, "but I have a hard time believing the two of you were a couple."

"So do I." Alex shakes his head, smiling at me. "And you

came here all the time, right? You? *Here?* What would your friends have said?"

I close my eyes. "I can't imagine."

"Neither can I." And before I have a chance to say anything else, he adds, "By the way, don't even think of leaving yet. We are definitely staying for this."

The memory sucks me into it like goo falling through a sieve; I can't stop it, I can't avoid it. All I can do is feel momentarily grateful that Alex hasn't come with me. I can see every crevice of the back bedroom, with its peeling lime-green paint and windowless walls. I see my body against the mattress, the springs pressing into my spine. There are no sheets, just a pilly, navy-blue bedspread dirtied with white stains. I'm in my bra and underpants. It's a matching set: light pink with tiny red bows at the edges of my bra straps and the fabric gathered at my hipbones. Vince rests on his side, shirtless, leaning over my body. With a dirty index finger, he draws a slow line from my collarbone to the space between my breasts, all the way down to my belly button. He slides his hand to my hip.

"You're too effing skinny," he growls. "You gotta put some meat on your bones."

He tries to kiss me. I turn my head away from his face, wincing like I'm in physical pain. As I watch the scene play out in front of me, I almost gag.

.   .   .

"Liz." Alex is squeezing my arm. "Hey. Snap out of it." He nods at Vince and Joe. "Listen."

"We met last fall," Vince says, "when she came to my shop with this other guy. She needed some work done on her car. We had, like, an instant connection. She was tired of all the white-glove treatment, you know?" He shakes his head, coughs a few times, then continues. "She could relax around me. I let her be herself. I guess you could say we had a perfect arrangement."

Joe fidgets in his seat. "And what kind of arrangement did you have, exactly?"

"When she got sick of her life as a princess, she came over here. We had some fun together. You know what I mean?" He raises his eyebrows. "But when it was all done, she'd go back to her life, with her rich friends and her boyfriend and high school, all that bullshit. It was casual. But believe me, she enjoyed it every bit as much as I did. She was a tiger."

"I was a virgin," I say weakly. "I wouldn't have slept with him. I was saving myself for Richie. I only wanted to be with Richie."

Alex is looking at me intently. "You know what? I think I might actually believe you."

For the first time since we've entered Vince's apartment, I feel a rush of relief. "You do?"

"Yes. But then what were you doing here, Liz? There has to be an explanation. I know it's not that you actually *liked* this guy."

I stare at my boots. My toes are in so much pain that they're almost completely numb, except for the persistent stabbing sensation. It hurts so badly, I almost wish I could just cut my feet off and get it over with. I give Alex a pleading look.

"Let me guess," he says, "you *really* want to leave."

I nod.

"Where do you think we should go? We don't know where Richie is."

"I don't care." The smell in the apartment is beginning to overwhelm me. I'll do anything to avoid confronting another memory with Vince Aiello. I close my eyes and think to myself, *Take me anywhere.*

Maybe I need the catharsis. The memory that I slip into, alone, feels as good as a long soak in a warm tub. It's prom night, junior year—the same night, I realize, when Richie and I ran into Joe Wright while our car was parked at the beach. I wore a pink halter gown with a trumpet skirt. As I look at myself, I remember that I had to have the dress taken in twice before the big night; that's how much weight I'd been losing.

Richie has never been much of a dancer. I love to dance, but he's always acted like he's too cool for it. I know the truth, though: he's shy, too afraid of looking anything but fully composed in front of our friends and classmates; he'll usually stay near me, kind of swaying, moving just enough so that he doesn't stand any chance of embarrassing himself. That night, my girlfriends and I all gather together, dancing

in a group while our dates sit at a table watching. The room
is dark, lit with floating tea candles that sit in glass bowls.
The tables are covered with them, casting shadows all over the
room, and there's glitter and confetti on their surfaces, too,
along with fat arrangements of flowers, three or four bouquets
each. It's magic. We'll only be this young once. Even as I'm
standing on the dance floor with Mera and Caroline and Josie,
the four of us grinning so hard that our cheeks probably hurt,
my shoes stowed under the table hours ago so that I could
dance without my feet aching, I recall thinking to myself:
remember this forever.

The dance is supposed to last until midnight, but Richie
and I slip out a little after eleven.

We took a limo to the dance. All our friends chipped in,
$17.65 per person—it's amazing how these tiny details are all
coming back to me now—and the car was supposed to take
us wherever we wanted all night, but Richie and I aren't just
going to run off with it, leaving everyone else behind. It's a
warm night, and it's less than a mile walk back to Richie's
house. We can't go up to his room; his parents are actually
home for once. So we take his mom's SUV and drive down
the shore, along the winding rows of empty vacation homes,
until we find a long driveway leading to a clearly vacant house.
We park at the very end, close to the garage, and pretend that
it all belongs to us.

Richie and I have been together for so long, we almost

don't have to say anything to each other. I loved being alone with him; I loved the deep, comfortable silence between us that was woven by so many years of conversation, of learning to read the nuances in each other's expressions, in our body language, in our breath.

I watch from the front as we climb into the back, put the seats down. Carefully, so gently, with fingers that I imagine are soft and cool, his breath calm, Richie unzips my dress. I feel so close to him that I can almost sense his touch, even though I'm not in my living body. I watch myself slip out of my gown and fold it across the back of the front seat. I'm not wearing a bra, just a simple white thong, so thin and light that it's almost like nothing.

As he kneels above me, I lie flat on my back. I stare up at Richie, who's watching me, tugging his bowtie loose almost without any awareness of what he's doing. He presses a palm against my stomach, which appears to be nothing but skin over muscle. He leans over to kiss me.

"I love you," I tell him. I've said it a million times before over the years, but this time, it seems different somehow. There's something odd about my tone.

He pulls away. It's dark in the car; I can see his eyes flashing in the moonlight spilling through the windows, but I can't read his expression. "Do you?" There's doubt in his voice.

"Richie. Of course. I've loved you forever."

He takes a fingertip, traces it along the outline of my rib, which is fully visible beneath my skin. "It's like you're disappearing," he murmurs.

"I'm not disappearing. I'm right here."

"Where do you go when you're out running?"

I laugh, but the effort seems hollow. "You know where I go."

He opens his mouth. He tightens his grip around my rib cage, pressing so hard that it looks like it might hurt. "I want to be your first." He swallows. "I want to be the only one. Forever."

"You will be."

"Promise?"

He already knew about Vince; I understand that now. And as I stare at the two of us together, I realize that I *knew* he didn't believe anything I was telling him.

Then why doesn't he confront me? Why does he kiss me, and continue to love me, when everything we have built together over all these years is dissolving into lie upon lie?

"I promise," I whisper. Maybe he doesn't want to know the whole truth. Whatever it is, it was too terrible for me to share with Richie.

And if I'd told him, would things have been different? Could I have lived? Or were the events that led to my death already in full swing, too far along to be prevented, no matter what I might have done to stop them?

.   .   .

As soon as the memory drifts away, Alex grabs my arm to take me somewhere else. "We're here," he says.

I can tell from looking around that we're in the present; Alex and I are nowhere to be seen. And if I didn't know any better, I'd think it was just a normal day at a normal high school. We're in the cafeteria.

"It's pizza day," he says.

Right away, I spot my friends sitting at their usual table. It's our premium spot in the lunchroom: a big, circular table in the far right corner of the room, next to the potato bar, closest to the double doors leading to the parking lot.

"I thought you hated lunch," I tell Alex.

"Well, I thought you might like to see some familiar faces." He half smiles. "Did I say that I hated lunch?"

"Yes. Because of me and my friends. You told me you ate lunch in the library sometimes to avoid us." I stare at him. "I remember. I'm sorry."

"You can stop saying that you're sorry."

"I can't help it." It's true; I can't.

We position ourselves beside my friends. It might be pizza day for the other students, but for all of my girlfriends, every day is salad day.

Josie is picking at her Caprese salad, nibbling the edge of a basil leaf.

"You okay?" Mera sips a Diet Coke. "Worried about Richie?"

Josie nods. "They're going to arrest him."

"Josie, would you relax?" Topher stretches lazily, slings

an arm around Mera. "So they'll arrest him. His parents will bail him out. He'll end up with, like, probation. It's not a big deal. He's still a minor."

"Leave her alone," Caroline says. "He's her boyfriend. She's concerned about him."

"Oh, he is not her boyfriend," Mera says, shooting a glance at Topher, who remains casually uninterested, a far cry from the chatty informant he played earlier with Joe. "Richie's freaking out. You should have seen him this morning at Topher's house. He wants to figure out who killed Liz."

When she says the words out loud—*who killed Liz*—a silence falls across the table. Josie's gaze shifts downward. Caroline bites her lip so hard that I almost think it's going to start bleeding.

Then, as though she's summoning all of her confidence at once, Josie sits up straight in her chair. In a gesture that seems almost defiant, she flips her hair over her shoulder. She gazes at each of our friends, one at a time, giving them a stony look of authority. "Nobody killed my sister," Josie pronounces. "She fell. It was an accident. Everybody knows that."

"Do they?" Mera pauses. "Look at us. We're sitting here all by ourselves. Even my teachers are treating me differently. And I don't just mean they feel sorry for me because my friend died. People are talking about us. Don't you know that?" She turns to Josie. "It doesn't help that we're wearing her clothes to school practically every day. Or that you're going after her boyfriend."

Josie narrows her eyes. She seems to be completely in control of her emotions, totally unfazed by Mera's comments. "I told you, Richie and I started seeing each other before . . . well, you know." Josie pushes her salad away. "And I was her sister. It's fine for me to wear her clothes." For just a second, her confidence falters. "It makes me feel close to her."

Cool silence. Looking around, I realize that half the room is stealing glances at my friends. My friends, in turn, are all staring at the table's vacant chairs. Richie's empty seat. *My* empty seat.

"Mera, don't you dare tell me how I should act right now. Don't tell me how I'm supposed to be feeling. You don't know what it's been like at my house," Josie says. "My dad is barely functioning." She takes a strand of her long hair and winds it around her index finger. "He's been sleeping on the boat. He thinks I don't know. He waits until my mom and I are in bed, and then he walks down there and . . ." She shudders. "It's so morbid."

It's true, too. In the past week or so, I've seen my father, late at night, walking to the *Elizabeth* all by himself. Sometimes he's already in his pajamas. More than once, I've seen him walk down the street in his bathrobe. I don't think he does much sleeping, though; mostly he sits on the deck, smoking cigars, staring at the water. It seems incredible to me that he can spend so much time in the places where he lost both his wife and his daughter: his house and his boat. After my mom died, it isn't like we moved or anything. We didn't even redo the bathroom right away. My dad just had the shower door replaced, as well as the bedroom carpet.

"I don't know about the rest of you, but I'm dying for a smoke." Topher stands up so quickly that he almost knocks over his chair. "I'm not gonna sit here for the next twenty minutes feeling like an outcast." He looks at my friends, who stare blankly at him. Even Mera is frowning at her boyfriend.

"Come on!" he says. "We are better than this. We all know that none of us did anything to hurt Liz. This is a disgrace to all of our good names." He thumps the varsity *N* sewn to his jacket. "I am Christopher Allen freaking Paul the Third. My father is this town's most respected dentist and oral surgeon. My mother was Miss Connecticut 1978! Mera, get up. You're coming with me." He stares at everyone. "All of you. Now."

Obviously, nobody is allowed to smoke on our school's campus. But my friends and I were always different; faculty has a tendency to look the other way for us. Athletes, pretty girls, children of the town's most respected professionals (despite the fact that Topher's dad happens to be Noank's *only* dentist, and thus the most respected by default) get a frequent pass for their indiscretions.

My friends gather beside Mera's car in the student parking lot. Topher lights a cigarette, takes a few long drags, and passes it to Mera. She sticks her neck out, leaning as far away from her body as possible while she inhales, her hair stuffed under a pink corduroy hat to avoid smelling like smoke.

"There's something I need to tell you guys," Caroline says. She wrinkles her nose at the cloud of smoke hanging in the air. "My dad lost his job a few weeks ago."

Josie, who has been chomping on a piece of gum, blowing, and then snapping her bubbles so that tiny shreds of pink are collecting at the corners of her mouth, freezes. "But he works on Wall Street."

"I know that." Even though the sun is shining, Caroline hugs herself, rubbing her shoulders like she's cold. "It happens, Josie."

"But . . . but he's a *stockbroker.* How can he just lose his job? It's not like he's expendable, is it? I mean, people are always going to need brokers." Josie is clearly confused. "How else will they handle their investments?"

"We might have to sell our house." Caroline blinks rapidly, trying not to cry. "We almost couldn't make my car payment last month."

I remember the money she stole from my bathroom and feel a surge of pity for her. Whatever *I* was planning to do with it, I have no doubt Caroline put it to better use. Maybe she made her car payment. Maybe she gave it to her parents.

"See?" I nudge Alex. "My friends have problems, too. It's not like we're all a bunch of spoiled brats."

Mera, finished smoking, tugs off her hat and takes a long

moment to shake her blond tresses free so they spill over her shoulders. "Don't freak out. You won't have to move." She sniffles. "I guess you could always . . . you know . . . get a job."

Caroline's face turns a deep shade of red. "I am not getting a job. I'll forfeit my allowance before I do that."

"Oh, right," Alex observes. He seems almost amused by my assertion. "You're nothing like spoiled brats. You've all got your priorities fully in order, obviously. Caroline would steal money from her dead friend before she'd go out and get a job."

"Please don't tell anyone," Caroline begs my friends, her voice barely breaking above a whisper. "I'd be so embarrassed. My parents are freaking out. My sister might have to take a semester off from college if my dad doesn't find work soon."

Leaning against Mera's car, Topher lights another cigarette. "Relax, Caroline. Everything will be fine."

Mera gazes up at her boyfriend, hooks her arm around his waist. "You're so levelheaded. I love you."

He winks. "Love you, too, babe. You got any gum?"

"Put that out." Josie means the cigarette. She shades her eyes, peering at the end of the parking lot. "Somebody's coming." Then, continuing to squint, she says, "Oh. Never mind." She giggles. "It's just Crazy-Eyes Riley."

Mr. Riley teaches something like four classes a day. When he's not teaching or in his office, he's told me that he takes the opportunity to go running on the trails that wind through the woods behind campus. As he approaches now, his run slowing to a jog, my friends make no effort to hide what they're doing. They're outside when they should be inside, eating lunch. They're loitering in the parking lot, which is definitely not allowed during school hours. And they're smoking. But they all know that Mr. Riley doesn't have the nerve to do anything to them; he is a nerd at heart, and my friends' experiences with him over the years have proven that he's just as afraid of them as he likely was of the popular kids at his own high school.

His face is red and sweaty. He leans over, palms on his knees, and tries to give them his most intimidating stare. If I were alive, standing there with them, I know I wouldn't have let this happen. I would have told Topher to put out the cigarette. I would have made everyone go inside. At least, I'd like to think so.

"I ought to send you all to the principal's office," he says, standing upright, stretching his arms overhead. "You're supposed to be setting an example. You're athletes."

Almost instantly, like magic, Josie turns on the waterworks. "We've had a horrible morning. Our friend is missing. We shouldn't even be at school." She wipes her eyes with the back of her hand. Her cheeks glisten with glitter blush. When she tucks a lock of hair behind her ear, I notice that she's wearing a pair of my chandelier earrings. They belonged to my mother before they became mine. I realize that it doesn't bother me that she's taken them; I'd rather she wear them than let them collect dust somewhere. But I wonder if my father knows that she has the earrings, or if he would notice. If he did, would he care? It isn't noon yet, but I have no doubt that he's already down at the *Elizabeth*, gazing at the water, waiting for something, for anything, to make sense.

Mr. Riley stares at Josie. "I'm sorry about your sister. I haven't had a chance to tell you that yet."

"Thank you." Josie stares him straight in the eyes. I know it makes him feel uncomfortable; how could it not? Imagine having to face the world with mismatched pupils every day. He averts his gaze after a few seconds.

"She liked you," Josie says to him.

"I liked her, too."

"So . . . don't tell on us, okay? We aren't doing anything wrong."

Mr. Riley stares at all of them, his mouth slightly agape. He seems small and self-conscious, the difference in his eyes so awkwardly noticeable. Even as an adult—as a teacher, an authority figure—he's unable to stand up to a group of teen-agers. "You really don't think so, do you?"

They don't answer him.

"Look at you," he says, with a sudden burst of unchar-acteristic confidence. "First there were six of you . . . then five . . . and now there's four. You're not invincible, kids. I would think you'd realize that by now."

"Alex." I put a hand on his arm. I feel restless, agitated, and excited all at once. "I have an idea."

Topher flicks his cigarette on the ground in Mr. Riley's direction. "You can't talk to us that way."

Mr. Riley only stands there, red faced and glowering. He begins to back away.

"Isn't he going to do something?" Alex nearly shrieks. "He's just going to let him get away with that?"

"Hey." I squeeze him. "Come with me. I think I know where Richie went."

Seventeen

The memories are coming more quickly now, with less warning or time for me to prepare. I don't have to seek them out as much as I simply fall into them accidentally, as though I'm getting better at accessing them. As I remember more and more, it's like pieces of the puzzle are getting filled in, one by one. I don't necessarily like the picture of my life that they're creating, but I'm grateful to have something other than a blank slate peppered with a few random details.

In one memory, I'm riding my bike—with training wheels—down the sidewalk as my parents stand behind me, watching nervously. In another, I'm at a slumber party with Josie at Mera's house. We're maybe eleven years old. It's the middle of the night, and we're drinking diet soda straight from a two-liter bottle, passing it around like booze while we play Truth or Dare. A few seconds later, I see myself in high school—probably

ninth or tenth grade, from the looks of my hair and outfit—
sitting in the back of study hall, my desk pulled close to
Richie's as we doodle on each other's history notebooks.

Almost as quickly as it appears, the memory dissolves,
replaced by another. This time, it is an early winter morning.
I'm at home. My house still has its original antique windows.
When it gets below a certain temperature, frost will form on
the insides of the glass. I watch myself standing in my messy
room, doing stretches in thermal running pants and a top,
and lean over for a moment to scratch my initials into the
frost on my window with an acrylic fingertip: *E.V.* ♥ *R.W.* I'm
older now, a bit thinner. I'm guessing I'm seventeen.

The clock on my nightstand says 5:02 a.m. It's so thickly
dark, the moon obscured by clouds, barely a star to be seen,
that it might as well be midnight outside. I own reflective
gear to keep me safe from traffic, but I'm not wearing it today.
Even the streetlights are out this early. In the dark, alone, with
nobody to see me, it seems almost like I'm not even there.

The only light from my room is the glow of the computer
monitor on my desk. I check to make sure my door is locked.
Then I sit before my computer and open the Internet, find a
bunch of e-mails from lovemycar@gmail.com. The first message reads:

For youre entertainment, baby.

Xoxo

Vinny

There are attachments. It's photograph after photograph, each one worse than the next. There must be close to
a hundred in total. In some of them I'm wearing a bra and
underpants. There are a few of me on the filthy mattress in
Vince's apartment, posing in trashy lingerie that I could not
possibly have purchased myself. The poses are so unlike
anything I would ever think of doing that, even as I'm staring at them, even though I *know* it's me, there is a part of me
that thinks: this could not have happened. I can't remember
ever sending so much as a racy picture of myself to Richie. I
am a virgin. This is practically pornography. It makes no
sense. Yet it's here, not Photoshopped: me, degraded, smiling with teeth gritted so tightly that my cheek muscles are
visible beneath the skin. My only small comfort is the fact
that, behind my forced smile, it's obvious I'm not enjoying
myself.

I notice that my eyes are wide as I stare at the pictures,
scrolling down to look at all of them, clearly horrified by
what I'm seeing. Once I reach the bottom of the last e-mail,
I close the files, shut off my computer, and leave the room.
Outside, the air is so cold that I'm sure my face goes hotly
numb almost immediately. I'm wearing a hat and gloves, but
my cheeks are undoubtedly on fire as I run, breathing in
and out, finding a rhythm, burning through mile after mile
until the sun begins to rise, cracking against the horizon.

It is torture that all I can do is watch and follow, my

motions automatic and ghostly, literally hovering behind myself, unable to run. Unable to free myself from these damn boots.

I run all the way to his house. The kitchen light is on. He's waiting for me; it seems like he's expecting my arrival any time now. I tap lightly at the door before letting myself in, and I stand in the warm room, catching my breath, watching Mr. Riley as he spoon-feeds a tiny baby girl who sits in a high chair at the table.

He barely glances at me. "How long have you been out so far?"

The clock on the stove says 6:54.

"A couple hours." I stretch my arms overhead. The ceiling is so low that my fingertips graze the pale yellow spackling. "Where's your wife?"

"She's asleep. I took the morning shift with the baby. Get yourself a glass of water, Liz." Finally, his glaze flickers in my direction. "You'll dehydrate. You won't make it home."

The baby—her name is Hope, I remember—has applesauce smeared all over her fat, red cheeks. She coos with delight and smiles adoringly at her father, who is wearing a white T-shirt and pajama pants.

"Did you eat breakfast?" he asks.

When I don't answer, he says, "I'll take that as a no. You've gotta eat, Liz. You want to pass out along the road? You want another concussion?"

"I'm in trouble, Mr. Riley."

He nods, feeds Hope another spoonful. "You look like shit."

It occurs to me how totally inappropriate this could seem to any other onlooker: me, standing in my coach's kitchen at seven in the morning, listening as he tells me I look like shit. Me, watching him feed his baby, his wife asleep down the hall, while her husband shares the intimate quiet of early morning with a breathless teenage girl.

But there's nothing sleazy about it. I know that for sure. I don't think I ever realized the fact while I was alive, but it seems obvious now: since my real dad was almost never around after my mom died—and when he was around, he let me do pretty much whatever I wanted—Mr. Riley wasn't just my coach and friend; he was also a sort of authority figure to me. What did he know? Did I tell him what was the matter before I died? I keep watching, hoping to learn more.

"I mean it. I'm in a lot of trouble. Can't you help me?"

Mr. Riley pauses, puts down the spoon, and looks around the kitchen for a moment. It's a small room, but lovely, bright and warm, messy with dishes and coffee stains on the countertop, the refrigerator covered in family photos. Even if I leave before Mr. Riley's wife gets up, I'm guessing she knows that I come here. He doesn't seem like the kind of guy to keep secrets from the people he loves.

"You could talk to Mrs. Anderson. Have you considered that?"

I almost choke on my sip of water. "The school guidance counselor? Are you kidding me? She goes to yoga with my stepmom." I shake my head. "No freaking way."

"How about a psychologist? I know someone in town. He's a PhD. Very good."

"Why can't I tell you? Why can't you just sit here and listen, and I'll tell you everything." I swallow a mouthful of water. "I want to tell you. I want someone else to know."

Mr. Riley looks at me, glances at Hope—who is still smiling, highly entertained by my interaction with her father—and closes his eyes. "You shouldn't be coming here. If somebody sees you, coming into my house this early in the morning . . . I could lose my job, Liz. Anybody could get the wrong idea." He stares down at his outfit, which is sparse enough to be construed as inappropriate: the thin undershirt, bare feet, his face unshaven. He's just rolled out of bed.

"I don't have anywhere else to go. I run and run, and it never gets any better." My tone is desperate, pleading. "I can't think about anything else. I can't live like this."

"I told you, there's a psychologist—"

"Let me tell you about psychologists. You know my boyfriend, Richie?"

He rolls his eyes. "Famous Richie Wilson, dealer to the high school stars."

"You can think what you want about him. His parents sent him to a shrink last year. He had like three sessions with the guy, and he *confided* in him that he sometimes . . . well, you know. He sells a little pot. It wasn't more than a month and the good doctor was hitting up my boyfriend for drugs. His *psychologist*." I sit down at the table and push my water glass away. "I'm not talking to any shrink."

Then, as I'm watching the two of us, Mr. Riley does something I'm not expecting. He leans across the table and closes his hand over mine. Just from looking, I can tell that he's holding on tight. I don't try to pull away.

"Liz. Elizabeth. I care about you, but I can't do this. You can't come here anymore. I can't risk my career." He shakes his head firmly. "You need to talk to a trained professional. Someone who can really help you. I'm only your track coach, Liz."

I blink at him through teary eyes. "But you're the only person I have to talk to. You're not doing anything wrong."

"I know that. You know that. But other people might not see it that way." He pauses. "What if I set up an appointment for you? I could ask around. What if I do some research and find a therapist who has experience with teenagers? I can find you someone good, I promise."

I stare at my hands. I don't say anything. I just shake my head.

We both stand up. Mr. Riley hands Hope the plastic spoon, and she bangs it against the high chair with glee. He puts his hand on my back and nudges me toward the door.

I look around the kitchen again. It's so warm, so calm,

so safe. I put my head down, resting it on his shoulder. "I don't want to leave." And I start to cry hard. My nose runs onto his shirt. He's right; I look like shit. I don't think that I care.

He folds his arms around me in a hug. I imagine his wife walking into the room right now, and what she might think if she saw us this way. But despite how it might look, I know for a fact that it's nothing; there's no reason for her to be upset with either of us. It's just warmth and comfort. It's innocent. After seeing the pictures of myself earlier, it occurs to me that this might have been the only innocent thing I had left.

He pulls back slightly, brushes a strand of hair from my sweaty forehead. "You're miles from home. Do you want a ride? I could put Hope in her car seat. It's no problem."

"I'll be fine." He is pulling away, nervously glancing out the window, probably terrified that a neighbor will see me in his arms.

As I'm walking through his kitchen door, gearing up to start running again, he says, "I don't care what you say. I'm going to find you someone to talk to."

I don't answer; I act like I didn't even hear him.

Mr. Riley stares at his daughter. He shakes his head. Under his breath, he murmurs, "All right, then. I'll see you at school, Liz."

.   .   .

My family is awake when I arrive at home. My parents are used to my early-morning runs; they wave to me from the kitchen as I make my way upstairs.

Josie is in my bedroom. She's at my computer. She's looking at the pictures. Specifically, she's staring at a shot of me and Vince, lying in bed together. Vince is winking at the camera, grinning widely. His teeth are yellow and crooked. No plans to visit Topher's dad and get them fixed anytime soon, I'm sure.

Josie and I stare at each other.

"You've been gone for hours," she says. Her tone is almost accusing. "I heard you leave. It was barely five in the morning."

"And you came into my room? You thought it was just fine to go through my computer?" There's an edge of irritation to my voice that strikes me as unusual. I don't remember Josie and me ever fighting.

She shrugs. "Yes, I came into your room. What does it matter, Liz? Who is this guy?"

"Take a guess."

She lets out a long, shaky sigh. "The mechanic."

"He knows everything, Josie. He's an asshole, but he's not stupid." I tug my hair free from its ponytail. "I had to do what he wanted."

All the color drains from her face. "So you went along with it?"

"Yes. He told me he'd go to the police if I didn't mess around with him. The pictures are just insurance."

"So . . . he's blackmailing you."

I nod. I start to cry again.

But the information almost seems to reassure Josie. "So that's it? You did what he asked?"

"I didn't sleep with him. I'd rather go to jail than have sex with someone like that."

"He didn't try to force you?"

I shake my head. "Not yet. He said . . . he said it turns him on to know that I'm a virgin." I swallow hard. "But it's only a matter of time, Josie. He's going to want sex. Then what will I do?"

Again, she seems oddly unconcerned. "He can't force you to do anything. It would be rape."

"It already feels like rape."

She takes another deep breath. A corner of one of her false eyelashes has come loose; it dangles awkwardly in her line of vision. Her hair is in a set of Velcro rollers. She is calm, face perfectly made up aside from the crooked eyelash, the portrait of relief. "So you did it. You let him take the pictures. It's over. Just ignore him from now on. We don't have to worry anymore."

I reach past her to switch off the monitor. "It isn't over, Josie. It's never going to be over. He'll want more and more from me."

My stepsister closes her hand over my wrist. She doesn't blink as she speaks. "Liz. Listen to me right now. We aren't going to tell anyone. You understand that, don't you?"

Watching us, I would do anything—*anything*—to know exactly what she's talking about. What am I not going to tell anyone? What do we know that's such a secret?

She and I stare at each other in a silence that seems to go on forever. It's the first time I've ever seen myself at a total loss for words around Josie.

Once I return to the present, I fill Alex in on everything I've seen.

"What do you think it means?" he asks, interested.

"I don't know." I close my eyes. "I wish I did."

When I look at him again, his gaze is serious. "I think you will. I think it's just going to take some time. Be patient, Liz." And then he looks around, staring at the clear, sunny sky. "It's a beautiful day," he says, obviously trying to change the subject.

He's right; it *is* a beautiful day. It's late afternoon. We could go wherever we want with as little as a blink and a thought, but instead Alex and I walk through town together, taking in the sights, trying to enjoy ourselves even as we're looking for Richie. If we didn't have more pressing matters to attend to, I almost feel like we could have just been two ordinary people, relaxing and appreciating the fall. Alex and I have seemed to get more comfortable around each other in the past week or so, despite the fact that so many unanswered questions about my life have started to surface.

I feel certain now that I know where Richie is, and I'm also sure he'll still be there when we arrive. He doesn't have anyplace else to go. Still, walking along with Alex is almost nice; we're moving slowly enough that my feet aren't in intolerable pain.

We pass the Noank Creamery, where they sell homemade ice cream and fudge. Tourists love the place. It isn't even a weekend, and there's a line going all the way out the door.

Alex closes his eyes, smiling. "I wish I could eat," he says. "I used to love ice cream."

I stare in the window. There are families gathered around the small metal tables, children with ice cream smeared on their faces, parents clutching piles of napkins to clean up messes. Everybody looks so happy to be eating what's obviously terrible for them.

"It's poison," I tell him. "I never ate there."

He stops in his tracks. "Shut up. You lived here your whole life, and you never ate at the Creamery?"

"Well, my mom didn't eat dairy, so that pretty much meant I didn't eat it, either. And I didn't eat sweets. They aren't good for you. They make you fat."

"Liz, come on. The way you used to run, you could eat a gallon of cookie dough and not gain weight."

"It's not about that, exactly."

"Then what is it about?"

I press my lips together. I can feel my spine stiffen, my

quads engaging as I stand completely still, gazing at the smiling customers inside. "It's about being in control."

He shakes his head. "That's silly. You're so skinny." And he pauses. "You ate birthday cake the night you died, didn't you?"

"One bite." As the words leave my mouth, I can almost taste it: the moist vanilla cake and creamy chocolate icing. I can feel a long-lost sense of power, of discipline, snap into place from somewhere within me. "Just a taste."

He reaches toward me. He presses his palm against my flat belly, pinching the flesh. There's no fat to grasp, only muscle and organs and skin. "A lot of good all that working out did you, dead girl."

I close my hand over his arm. He barely flinches. "You want to know why I'm like this?" Even as I'm saying the words, it's like I'm realizing their truth for the first time. *Aha. Of course.*

"Sure," he says. "Why are you like this, Liz?"

I squeeze his arm more tightly. I don't have to say anything; he knows the drill by now.

We both close our eyes.

We're standing in the kitchen at my house. Everything is the same—the layout, the view of the Sound from the back window, the black-and-white-checkered porcelain tile—but everything is different. My mother stands in front of the open fridge in workout shorts and a sports bra. I can see all of her ribs. Her skin is pasty and white. She is in her bare feet, tapping her manicured fingernails against the fridge door.

"I forgot how this kitchen used to look," I tell Alex. "It's so different now."

He looks around. "You aren't kidding. Your mom and Nicole—they're not very alike, are they? Nicole is—what? A flaky bombshell? And your mom"—his gaze flickers to her back, her torso, the visible outline of her spine—"what was she like?"

I think about it for a minute. Even when I was alive, sometimes it was hard to remember the good things about my mother; she was sick for so much of my childhood. But I hate admitting to Alex that I don't have an abundance of happy memories of her. It doesn't change the fact that I miss her. It doesn't make me want to see her any less now. She's my *mother*.

"Well," I begin, "she was different, that's for sure. She kept the house very neat, and everything was sleek and modern and clean all the time." And I look around the kitchen. The walls are a pale, clean beige. All of the appliances are stainless steel: dishwasher, wine cooler, refrigerator, oven, microwave. There isn't a dish in sight. There is no food on the countertops; no open cereal boxes, no bananas resting gently in a basket, no tortilla chips or soda bottles.

Now there's always food strewn everywhere in the kitchen; Nicole likes to *eat*. And she redecorated after my mother died, too. Almost as soon as she moved in, the old appliances were gone, replaced by white ones. Nicole repainted the walls a light green and stenciled them herself with clusters of yellow lilies, their fragile green leaves and stems drawn so carefully by hand that they almost looked real. She hung photos on the fridge. I hate to admit it—it feels like a betrayal of my mother—but in plenty of ways, Nicole made it feel more like a home.

Except that it *was* a home when my mom was alive. It was just a different kind of home.

I'm sitting at the kitchen table. There's a big, frosted glass bowl in the center. It is filled with shiny, lovely, artificial fruit: plastic apples, oranges, pears, and nectarines. Look—but don't taste.

"I'm nine," I murmur, staring at myself. I look so much like my mother: we are both wearing our long blond hair in two braids that fall almost to our waists; we are both thin, although my mother is frightfully so, whereas I'm just a skinny kid. We have the same eyes, the same nose, the same small ears, the same tiny attached earlobes. There's no mistaking that I belong to her.

"How do you know how old you are?"

I don't want to say it out loud. But I do. "Because my mother is going to die in a few weeks. I can tell."

"Oh." He swallows. "I'm sorry."

I shake my head. "It's all right. Just—let's watch, okay?"

My mother reaches into the produce drawer of the fridge and emerges holding a big yellow apple in her bony hand. She stares at it for a moment, considering it.

"I'm hungry, Mommy," I say to her.

"You just ate an hour and a half ago at Richie's house," she murmurs. "Your tummy is still full, honey."

"But I'm *hungry*."

She turns to me, apple in hand. "Okay. You want a snack?"

I nod.

She holds out the apple. "We can share. How about that?"

"Can I have mine with peanut butter?"

My mom's eyes are a deep blue, the exact same shade as mine. Even in workout clothes—she probably just finished exercising—she's wearing a full face of makeup. Her lipstick has been freshly applied.

I'm in a yellow-and-white plaid outfit, a matching top and skirt that seem overdressed for a playdate with Richie. And I notice that *I'm* wearing a little bit of makeup, too. It's subtle, but it's there: some blush, a little bit of silver eyeshadow, and lip gloss the same shade as my mom's. It has all been applied carefully, with a deft, expert hand. It's undoubtedly my mother's work. She never saw anything wrong with letting me wear makeup, even at age nine.

"Are you sure you want peanut butter?" she asks quietly.

"Yes. Why not?"

"Peanut butter has a hundred calories per tablespoon. Eight grams of fat," she says. "Now, Liz"—she leans toward me—"do you know how many calories there are in a gram of fat?"

I nod. "Nine calories in every gram," I say. I'm reciting the fact from memory. Even at age nine, my mother is training me. Does she realize how sick she is? Does she even care? I want to scream at her, to shout for her to eat, to live, but I know it won't make any difference. In a handful of weeks, she'll be gone.

"So if there are eight grams of fat, and nine calories in every gram," she prods, "how many calories are from fat?"

I bite my glossy lip as I'm thinking about it. "I don't know."

My mother's face is solemn. "You don't know how to multiply eight times nine, Elizabeth?"

I shake my head no.

"Seventy-two," she pronounces. "That's almost seventy-five percent fat. And how much of our diets should be made up from fat?"

I bite my bottom lip harder and stare at the tabletop. I look deeply embarrassed. "I don't remember."

"You do remember," she says gently. "What did I teach you?"

"Thirty percent," I say to Alex.

At almost the same time, my younger self whispers, "Thirty percent."

"That's right." My mother smiles. "So do you still want peanut butter?"

I shake my head. I don't look at her.

"I hate peanut butter," I tell Alex.

"No wonder," he says. "God, this is awful."

"That's my mom. She was always like this."

We watch as my mother reaches, on her tiptoes, into the

upper corner of a cabinet. She removes a small digital food scale. She weighs the apple. Then she takes it off the scale, cuts it in half, and weighs each half individually.

Before she sits down at the table, she reaches into another cabinet—this one full of prescription bottles and over-the-counter pill packets—and takes out a box of non-drowsy cold medicine. She presses eight tablets from their blistered pouches. She stares at them in her hand. They are small and red. There are so many of them; it seems like an impossibly large number of pills for someone her size to take. But she does it anyway, putting all of them in her mouth at once, swallowing them with a single gulp of water.

My nine-year-old self watches her do all of this as I wait, patiently, for her to hand over my half of the apple. When she finally sits down across from me at the table, she gives me a big smile. "Here you go," she says, handing it to me.

"Thank you." I stare at it. But I don't take a bite.

"Mommy?"

"Yes?"

"Why do you weigh all your food?"

My mom stares at her own half of the apple. She takes the question seriously. She appears to think about it for a long time.

Finally, she says, "Liz, when you become a grown-up, life can get very complicated. Things happen all around you that you have no control over. You can't control what happens to the people you love. You can't control every part of your life.

But you can control *pieces* of it. Tiny pieces. And sometimes, when everything else feels like it's so much bigger than you, so much more than you could possibly manage on your own, it feels good to know that there's something—even if it's very small—that you can control completely." She peers at me. "Do you understand what I mean?"

I nod. "I think so, yes."

"Good. It's a good lesson to know." And she smiles again.

"She's sick," I murmur. "I knew she was sick, but my God. This is . . ."

"It's terrible," Alex finishes.

I look at him. I attempt a smile. "Control," I say. "It's like I was just telling you."

We both stare at my mother and me, eating our apple in silence, the only sound coming from our jaws working the flesh of the fruit.

"Want to go?" he offers.

I nod. "Okay."

Alex squeezes my shoulder with his cool hand, closing his eyes.

Back in the present, we keep walking. We're quiet, the silence a tad awkward; I know we're both thinking about what we've just seen together. We were strolling before, but now I walk with a purpose, more quickly, every step in my boots a tiny hell, to the end of the main drag and past all of the tourist traps—people *love* kitschy stuff from quaint New England towns—until we reach a cluster of newer, smaller homes behind the Baptist Church.

School is out for the day. Mr. Riley's car is in his driveway. The lights are on in his house. And Richie is in his living room, rolling a ball back and forth across the hardwood floor with Hope.

"How did you know he'd be here?" Alex sits on the floor beside Richie.

"Because he didn't have anywhere else to go. No car, and no adults he can trust. Aside from that cop, Mr. Riley is the first grown-up I've seen Richie have a serious conversation with in ages. He doesn't like adults."

"But they barely know each other. And Mr. Riley doesn't like him."

"They both knew me," I tell Alex. "And Richie knew I trusted Mr. Riley."

I sit on the other side of Richie. Alex, I realize, was right about animals *and* babies: Hope can obviously see us.

"Why do you think she sees?" I ask Alex.

"I don't know," he says. "I've thought about it a lot, and my best guess is that babies just don't know any better."

Hope is so much bigger than I remember; she must be almost two years old by now. She giggles, pointing at me, and says, "Lady!" I smile. I hold a finger to my lips.

In the kitchen, Mr. Riley and his wife, whose name is Karen, are arguing, their voices hushed, the disagreement punctuated

by Karen's downright aggressive preparation of macaroni
and cheese.

"I want him out of this house, Tim. You'll get fired. It's—
what do you call it?—harboring a fugitive. He brought a gun
into this house. A *gun*. How do you know he didn't kill Elizabeth Valchar? Isn't that what everyone thinks?"

"Karen, he gave the gun to me. It wasn't loaded. He's not
going to hurt us. I'll talk to him. I'll convince him to let me
drive him to the police station." Mr. Riley flinches as Karen
whips a wooden spoon into the sink. "He's in trouble. It's my
job to help."

"Your job to help?" She crosses her arms and presses her
lips together, cheeks flushed with anger. Karen is short and
slim and could be pretty if she weren't so ordinary. She
doesn't wear makeup or do anything in particular with her
hair. She's always pale, even in the summer. She wears clothes
that look like they came from a thrift store. For the life of me,
I could never understand why a woman would treat herself
with such indifference. To me, it always seemed there was
nothing worse in the whole world than being ordinary.

"He was Elizabeth's boyfriend, wasn't he?"

Mr. Riley nods.

"Does he know about your little early-morning meetings
with her? Your quiet talks in our kitchen while I was asleep?"

"Karen, get a grip. You knew about that. She was in trouble. It was my *job* to look out for her."

Karen is positively glowering. "Your job. Where in your

job description does it require you to invite a teenage bomb-shell into your home? To comfort her. To hold her."

Mr. Riley glances toward the living room, where Richie and Hope are still rolling the ball back and forth. Richie seems calm, which doesn't surprise me. By now, I'm sure he realizes he'll have to face the police sooner rather than later. Knowing him, he's probably relieved that things will be over soon. For now, though, he's got a break. Playing a sweet game of catch with a toddler: what could be more comforting?

"I don't want him alone in there with Hope." Karen runs a hand through her dull brown hair. Her fingernails, I notice, are unpolished, her cuticles ragged, knuckles dry and cracked. For a moment, I find myself wondering why she doesn't get a manicure.

"Okay. I'll go tell him he has to leave. Will that make you happy?"

"Yes. That will make me happy." She takes a long, deep breath. "This is crazy."

Mr. Riley steps close to his wife, presses his cheek against hers. "I never did anything with Liz that I wouldn't have done right in front of you."

He's telling the truth. He was the only comfort I had. He didn't feel like there was any choice but to hug me, to try and make me feel better.

"She was a very pretty girl. Girls like that . . . the girls in this town, at that school . . . you know I'm not like that. I never was."

"She was a very sick girl. That's all. Sickness and sadness dressed up in expensive clothes and covered with makeup. It doesn't change who she was." He swallows. "It probably got her killed, Karen."

Her eyes flash with accusation. "What do you know that you're not telling me?"

"Nothing." His tone is firm. "She begged me to let her tell me what was the matter. I wouldn't let her. I didn't want to invite it into our lives."

The pot on the stove begins to smoke. The heat is turned up too high. Dinner is going to burn.

Karen turns down the electric stove. She stares at the gooey mess inside the pot. "It's in our lives now."

"Then let me help Richie," Mr. Riley says. "Please. You know, I can't stop thinking that if I'd done more for Liz . . . if I'd talked to her parents or gotten her an appointment or let her tell me what was the matter . . . maybe she'd still be alive. Do you know how that feels, Karen?"

She shakes her head. "No. I can't imagine."

"I can't do *nothing*. Not now." He swallows. "I have to help Richie. I owe it to Liz."

Standing in the living room above Richie and Hope, Mr. Riley claps his hands together. "Okay, bud. Time to go."

Richie looks up with an expression of bewildered innocence. "Where are we going?"

"The police station. You have to turn yourself in. Every

cop in town is looking for you. You know they almost canceled school?"

Karen makes a final appearance to scoop Hope into her arms before retreating to the kitchen again. She doesn't say good-bye to Richie or her husband.

Once they're in the car together, Richie says, "I've been running every morning."

"Well, that's great. If you don't end up in jail, you might consider going out for track this spring."

"I keep running to the same place. It's like a compulsion . . . like some kind of force is urging me to go. It's the weirdest thing, Mr. Riley. I can't go any other direction. It's this dumpy house at the edge of town, but I'd never been there before. None of my friends live around there. They all live in nice places, you know?" He pauses. "I come from a good family, Mr. Riley. I'm a good kid."

"You're a drug dealer, Richie."

"Okay, aside from that. You're not listening, though. Every time I run, I end up at this house. For a while, the first few times, I just stared at it. I didn't know why I was there. But a couple of weeks ago, I started looking around. I did some investigating."

They're almost to the police station.

"Oh, yeah?" Mr. Riley seems like he couldn't care less. "What did you do? Break into the place?"

"No. I looked in the windows. I looked in the mailbox. You know whose house it is?" He doesn't wait for a response. "It's that kid's house—the one who died last year. Alex Berg. All this time I've been running, like someone was leading me right to the place, and it turns out to be another dead kid's house. What do you think that means? It doesn't make any sense, does it?" He hesitates. Then he says, "Mr. Riley, I know it sounds crazy, but . . . do you think it could be Liz? Maybe she's still here. Maybe she wants me to go there for some reason, to show me something."

"It's me," I whisper. I'm shivering, staring at Richie with nothing but love and a pure yearning to be closer to him. "I was thinking about Alex, and you felt it. You still feel it."

Mr. Riley pulls into the gravel parking lot outside the police station. "I'll tell you what I think, Richie. I think you kids need to focus on living. What does it matter if it was Alex's house? He's gone."

"He was killed," Richie says. "They never arrested anyone. There's still a reward."

Mr. Riley shifts the car into park. "Time to get out. I'll walk you in, if that will make you feel better."

"Mr. Riley?"

My coach stares at the roof of his car. "What, Richie?"

"You didn't really answer my question. About Liz."

"You think Liz is somehow compelling you to run to Alex's house? You think there's a grand conspiracy taking place in Noank?" Mr. Riley shakes his head. "No. I don't believe that. Neither should you. It's a coincidence, that's all. I don't believe in conspiracies, and I don't believe in ghosts, either."

From the backseat, I lean forward and press my hands against Mr. Riley's shoulders. I hold on tight. I concentrate. The effort doesn't work nearly as well as it does with Richie. I can almost sense the blood running through the veins beneath his skin—but not quite. He doesn't even flinch.

"Wait a minute. Before I go in, can I ask you something else?"

"Sure."

"I was going to ask . . . do you think that, if I get back to school, they'll still let me go to homecoming? It's just that I already promised Josie we'd go together. She bought a dress and everything."

Mr. Riley stares at him. "You're about to get arrested, and you're worried about homecoming?" He shakes his head with wonder. "You're one hell of a lousy criminal, you know that?"

"I know." Richie nods. "You're right."

"Then why don't you give it up? Stop selling. You have more to offer the world. You're an honor student." Mr. Riley pauses, studying my boyfriend. My coach's eyes twinkle with a combination of amusement, pity, and—what else? It almost seems like fascination. There's so much more to Richie than he's thought for all these years. He seems like he's realizing that now.

Richie smiles. "It's what I do. Too late to change."

"No, it isn't. It's never too late."

My boyfriend doesn't say anything. He's clearly not up for an argument about his future at the moment.

Mr. Riley clears his throat. "So you're telling me you're worried about Josie's feelings? About whether or not she'll have to return her homecoming dress?"

"Not return it. She'd find someone else to go with, I'm sure." Richie reaches for the door handle. "I feel so bad for Josie. I feel bad for the whole family. But I guess you don't care, right? I mean, why would you?"

Before Mr. Riley has a chance to answer, Richie steps out of the car. "Thanks for giving me a place to hide out today. Wish me luck."

Eighteen

After Richie turns himself in, he's subjected to an hours-long interrogation that seems to lead nowhere. It's true: rich people are treated differently, especially in our town. Richie's father brings their attorney to the police station, and after a meeting with the magistrate, Richie gets off with two years' probation. Luckily for him, Mr. Wilson made a sizable donation to the community a few years ago, and his generosity allowed the town to build a new police barracks. As a result, he has quite a bit of pull with the local law enforcement. Since this is Richie's first offense—and since the gun wasn't loaded, and he handed it over to Mr. Riley willingly, who then turned it over to the cops—everybody agrees that it's best not to blow the situation too far out of proportion. The drugs are kept in evidence, the gun is returned to Richie's father (who is its rightful owner), and the memory card remains in Joe Wright's possession.

Shut in a room at the station after his interview with Richie, venetian blinds on the windows closed tightly, Joe looks over those photos with obvious reluctance at seeing me in such compromised positions. They're the same pictures from my computer: Vince and me. Staring at them, I realize with disgust that Josie must have given the memory card to Richie in order to secure him for herself.

"Please," I beg Alex as we stand behind Joe, "please don't look."

He doesn't say anything; he just nods and turns around.

My heart breaks at the thought of Richie seeing me this way. How long has he had the pictures? For weeks before I died? Months? How did he ever look me in the eye, knowing what I'd been up to? How could he possibly still have loved me? The only answer I can come up with is that he's *Richie*. He's known me forever. Just like I can't stop loving him because he might have been fooling around with Josie behind my back, I don't expect he could simply turn off his feelings for me either.

Days turn into weeks without much excitement after Richie's arrest. September rolls into October; the leaves change, the weather grows even cooler, and life goes on—sort of—for my friends and family. Richie still runs every morning. He still goes to Alex's house, stares at it for long stretches of time without any hint of understanding.

He visits my grave. He doesn't say much, but sometimes he'll sit down on the earth, bringing himself up against my tombstone—which was finally put into place a good six weeks after my death—and hold on to it like he's folding me into an embrace. He thinks I'm in the ground, beneath him, when I'm right there beside him.

I get lots of visitors; my father comes now and then, when he isn't spending long stretches of time at the boat. My grave is beside my mother's. Her stone is large, with elaborate carving around the edges, and reads:

Analisa Ann Valchar

Beloved Mother and Wife

1968–2001

My father stopped putting flowers on her grave years ago. After he married Nicole, it seemed to me like he wanted to move on in every way; the only remnants of her that he kept were the house and the boat.

My tombstone, now that it has been put up, is covered with sentimental offerings. The stone itself is huge, bigger than my mom's, and carved with an ornate ivy border, my name etched in delicate cursive writing. The grave site is still a mess of flowers, even so many weeks after my funeral. It would almost be embarrassing, if I weren't so shockingly pleased with the display. Even in death, it seems, I'm incredibly popular.

With the amount of time we spend hanging out in the cemetery—it seems a fitting enough place for us—Alex and I see plenty of mourners come and go. His parents visit his grave once a week, every Sunday after church. And I get an almost steady stream of visitors: kids from school I was barely even friends with show up to lay flowers at my grave. Some of them bring stupid things like teddy bears or balloons. On the day of the season's first cross-country meet, my team-mates (who didn't like me in life, but seem more than happy to flex their grief muscles now that I'm gone) leave a pair of shoelaces tied in a bow. Mr. Riley comes by every couple of weeks and says a prayer. Mera and Topher always come together, and Mera always leaves a blubbering mess.

Just once, in mid-October, Karen Riley visits. She brings Hope. It seems so morbid to me—who brings a toddler to a cemetery? But the little girl occupies herself by running around the graves while her mother stands at my plot and stares wordlessly at the ground. She doesn't bring flowers. She doesn't stay long. As usual, she isn't wearing makeup; her hair is pulled into a loose ponytail. Her jeans are stone-washed, a few inches too short, revealing plain white socks peeking out from her flat sneakers. She kneels for a moment at my tombstone, touching it, running her fingers across the let-ters, almost like she wants to make sure it's really me down there.

Then, still kneeling, she presses her palms flat against the earth. "I should have been kinder to you," she whispers.

She glances at her daughter, who is chasing a moth in circles around a fresh grave site. Hope is long and lanky, just like her father. She already has silken blond hair and perfect blue eyes. She'll be a knockout someday. I'm guessing Karen Riley already knows that.

Karen is crying a little bit. "You were just a little girl," she says. "I'm sorry for hating you."

After she leaves, Alex and I are quiet for a long time. This used to be my favorite time of the year. It was always perfect running weather: just cold enough, the air thin and brisk, and I used to love the way my feet crunched against the leaves as I ran along the road. But now I am constantly chilled, more so than ever. At least I can still lie on the grass, staring up at the stars. I can still keep watch over my own grave.

There is always a small part of me that hopes I will catch a glimpse of my mother: her apparition, her ghost, whatever. But she's nowhere. We were so similar in life; in death, we are in entirely different places. The fact that, even now, she is not here to offer me any comfort makes me feel incredibly alone. The more time passes, the more I feel that I might never see her again. I am so afraid that I'll be stuck here on Earth forever, with Alex, the two of us left to haunt Noank while everyone else moves on and forgets that we ever existed.

On a particularly cold evening in mid-October, after we've passed the whole day in the cemetery watching a funeral for an old woman who died peacefully (her relatives barely cry, and comment more than once that it was her time), Caroline arrives at dusk and comes quietly to my grave.

She's wearing her cheerleading uniform; there must have been an evening football game, and she probably walked here straight from school. She looks ridiculously out of place in the otherwise somber graveyard: her hair is pulled into two high ponytails, cheeks painted with NH for "Noank High." Her pom-poms dangle at her sides. She puts them on the ground at my grave site and gives them a wary look, like she expects me to reach out from the earth and grab them.

Like so many other people who come to see me at the cemetery, she kneels at my tombstone and takes a moment to trace the letters on my stone.

Alex watches Caroline. "It seems like she really misses you. You said she was one of your best friends?"

"Yeah, she was." I stare at Caroline and wish that I could hug her. She is obviously still upset about my death. "She was more than just a good friend," I tell Alex. "She's a good person, too, whether you want to believe me or not."

I expect him to reply with some kind of witty comeback, but he doesn't say anything.

Caroline stands up, smoothes the nonexistent wrinkles from her perfectly pressed skirt, and pulls her letterman jacket tightly around her body. "Hi, Liz," she says. She kicks at the earth with her toe. "I'm sorry I haven't come to see you yet. I don't really like graveyards." She looks around. "When I was a little girl, my dad would tell my sisters and me that we had to hold our breath whenever we passed a cemetery, or else we might inhale the souls of dead people and get possessed. I know it's stupid, but it always kind of scared me." She pauses. "You'd think it's dumb, I know. But I figure you wouldn't want to possess me, even if you're around here somewhere." And she looks down at her legs. "You'd never be caught dead in a body with such thick ankles.

"I just wanted to tell you a few things, though," she continues. "They're things I never would have told you when you were alive. Because, Liz, you must have known . . . it was hard to be your friend. You wanted to be nice, I know that. You weren't trying to be a bad person. But sometimes I used to wonder why I even hung out with you so much. Do you remember the parties I had last year? My parents were in Egypt. Remember that? They were gone for a whole month, and you and Josie convinced me that I should have a party every single weekend while they were gone. You promised you'd help me clean up after all of them, but you only did it once, the very first weekend. After that, you'd just get up and leave in the morning.

"I never told you this," she goes on, "but remember the very last weekend, when you got drunk and threw up in my living room? You puked all over the oriental rug. You didn't offer to clean up the mess, either. You just left. I was so worried that you wouldn't get home okay because you'd been drinking, but you promised you'd text me once you got there, and of course you never did. I couldn't get ahold of you until the next night. I was scared out of my mind. But you know all that, I guess. The thing I never told you is . . . the rug you threw up on, it was an antique. My parents bought it at an auction in Beijing. It was worth tens of thousands of dollars, and you ruined it. You were drinking vodka and cranberry juice all night, before you switched to beer, and that's when you got sick. Anyway—the stain was bright red. I couldn't get it out. And when my parents came home and saw what happened, I took all the blame."

She blows out a deep breath, a cloud of fog forming in front of her face. "I didn't tell them what really happened because I knew they'd tell your parents. I knew they'd want your parents to pay for the damage, and I was so afraid"—she starts to cry—"I was so afraid that you wouldn't be my friend anymore, that you and Josie would turn on me if I got you in trouble. So instead I got grounded for a month. And now my dad doesn't have a job, and my parents are starting to sell all their antiques just to pay our mortgage. The other day, my mom told me that if they still had the rug to sell, it would keep us in our house for another three months. Can you believe that?"

I feel bad for Caroline, obviously. I feel worse about how I acted, and that she didn't have the courage to tell me what happened with her parents and the rug. "She should have saved herself all that trouble. I still would have been her friend," I tell Alex. "She ought to know that. My parents would have paid for the rug."

"Are you sure?" He's staring at me intently. "What about Josie? She said she was afraid you and Josie would turn on her."

"I don't know what she means. Josie's a good person. She just likes being popular, that's all."

"She sure does," Alex agrees. He doesn't elaborate.

"Anyway," Caroline says, wiping her eyes, "it's not like any of it matters now. You're gone, and my parents are still probably going to lose their house, and Josie told *everyone* at school that my dad lost his job. I don't even have a date for homecoming. Josie's going with *Richie*. You died a few months ago, and he just got arrested a few weeks ago, and your parents are letting her go with him like it's nothing." She shudders. "It's horrible. Everything's terrible without you." She pauses. "But it was terrible even when you were around. I know it sounds crazy, but for months before you died, it's almost like there was this . . . this sense that something bad was going to happen."

She picks up her pom-poms, gives them a shake to get rid of the leaves that have gotten caught in the plastic. "I don't know why, but when I heard Mera scream that morning, I knew something terrible had happened to you. I just knew."

Then she bows her head, says a quick, quiet prayer, and crosses herself with a pom-pom. "You were falling apart before you died, Liz. Everybody could tell. I hope things are better for you now. They sure are awful around here."

Caroline takes a few steps backward, like she's about to

walk away. But then she stops. She stares up at the dark sky and takes a long, deep breath, looking around to make sure she's alone. Then, instead of turning to walk on the path that will take her out of the cemetery, she cuts diagonally across the grass and heads uphill, toward the edge of the graveyard that is closest to a dense patch of woods. "Where is she going?" I ask.

Alex is suddenly tense as he crosses his arms against his chest. "She's probably going home."

"No, she's heading the wrong way." I begin to follow her, but Alex doesn't move. "Hey," I tell him, "come on."

He hugs himself more tightly. He shakes his head. "That's okay."

I stop to stare at him. "Alex, come on! What's wrong?"

He looks at the ground. "Nothing."

Caroline is almost at the top of the hill. She turns left onto one of the cemetery's narrow gravel roads and walks toward a small cluster of tombstones situated just before the woods. In an instant, it becomes clear: she's going to Alex's grave.

But why? She didn't know him. She went to his funeral, just like me, but so did plenty of kids who didn't know him. I don't remember her being overly upset at it, either. They weren't friends; they obviously didn't run in the same circles. I just can't imagine that they might have known each other for any reason at all.

Yet here she is, kneeling at his grave more than a year after his death. I stand beside her, watching in confusion and fascination as she leans forward and places both of her hands against the top of his tombstone. Coming to rest on her knees in the grass, she tilts her head down until her forehead touches the side of the grave marker.

She stays that way, keeping her body almost completely still, for a long time. As I'm watching her, Alex approaches behind me. For a while, neither of us says anything.

When Caroline finally raises her head, I see that her eyes are red. The letters painted on each of her cheeks are smeared with tears. She looks around again, double-checking to be sure that she's alone.

"Hi, Alex," she whispers. Her voice is so soft that I almost can't hear her.

Standing beside me, Alex smiles at her. His expression is kind. He seems more relaxed than he was just a few minutes ago. "Hey, Caroline," he replies.

I gape at him. "Alex," I demand, "what is going on? Tell me."

Caroline stands up. She wipes her eyes and cheeks with the back of her hand, smearing the painted letters into unrecognizable blobs of red and white.

Alex holds a finger to his lips. "Shh." He continues to smile at her.

"I'm so sorry," she says out loud. And as she squeezes her eyes shut, she looks ready to cry again. "I'm so sorry, Alex," she repeats.

"What is she sorry for?" I ask. "How do you two know each other?"

Alex glances at me. "It's nothing."

"It's obviously *something*. Alex, come on. This isn't fair. Please tell me."

He ignores me and continues to watch her. Caroline bows her head, closes her eyes, and begins to speak again. Her voice is sweet and soft, her words haunting as she pronounces them in the silent, empty cemetery.

"Hail Mary, full of grace, the Lord is with thee. Blessed art thou among women, and blessed is the fruit of thy womb, Jesus. Holy Mary, Mother of God, pray for us sinners. Now and in the hour of our deaths . . ." And she pauses. "Now and in the hour of our deaths," she repeats. "Now and in the hour of our deaths. Now and in the hour of our deaths . . . Amen."

She opens her eyes. "You rest now," she says, staring at his tombstone. "Find some peace."

She leans over to pick up her pom-poms. Then she walks away, down the hill toward the cemetery's exit. We both watch as her form grows smaller against the backdrop of the evening, her steps unhurried as she moves between row after row of tombstones. She was uncomfortable when she visited my grave, but not so much at Alex's. And now, even from far away, she seems calm.

"Okay," I say once she's gone, "what was that all about? What is she sorry for?"

Alex tilts his head to one side. "I think she's sorry for what happened to me, that's all."

But his explanation doesn't satisfy me; it still doesn't

explain why she would visit his grave or the odd way she recited the Hail Mary.

"Alex," I repeat, trying to sound stern, "what aren't you telling me?"

He sighs, running a hand through his hair. "It's hard to explain. But I could show you, if you want."

"Show me? You mean like—"

"Yes." He nods. "I'll take you. You can see for yourself."

"But I thought you didn't want me to see anything from your life."

He's still wearing a dreamy smile. "I'll make an exception."

Before I can accept the offer, something occurs to me. "This isn't the first time she's been to your grave, is it?"

He shakes his head. "No."

I almost can't believe it. Caroline. Here. Visiting Alex. Praying for him, and telling him she's sorry—but for what? As stunned as I am, I find that I'm also so happy for Alex, that he has at least one visitor aside from his parents. He deserves at least that much. "How often does she come?"

"Not often. Every few weeks." If he were alive, I'm sure he'd be blushing. "The first time she came, I was so surprised," he says. "It's amazing that she even remembers." And he gives me an expectant look. "Do you want to know? I'll show you, but that's it. Nothing else."

"Okay." I reach toward him and grasp his wrist. "Let's go."

. . .

Once we slip into Alex's past, I open my eyes to see that we are standing in the middle of a big room filled with long wooden tables. I think we're in a basement of some kind; there are no windows in the room, and at the far end, past a set of double doors, I can see a staircase.

"Where are we?" I ask.

"You don't know?" Alex seems amused.

"No." On the wall with the double doors, I notice a life-sized color drawing of Jesus. His arms are spread wide. He gazes downward, where a group of children is drawn at his feet. There's a chalkboard on the same wall with several Bible verses written in neat cursive handwriting.

"It's some kind of church," I say. "Is this Sunday school?"

"It's CCD," Alex tells me.

I give him a blank look.

"Confirmation classes," he explains.

"Confirmation," I repeat. "What's that?"

"It's something Catholic kids do. You have to go to confirmation classes for a year, and then you get to take your First Communion." He pauses. "You know what that is, don't you?"

I nod. "Sure. Wine and wafer, right?"

For a second, Alex looks like he's going to launch into a full explanation of communion—obviously there's more to it than what I understand—but he stops himself with a smirk and a shake of his head. "I'm in first grade," he says, nodding at the room. There are about eight kids seated at each of the tables. He points to one of them. "Right over there."

I spot him immediately. I clap a hand to my mouth. "Alex," I say, "you're adorable!" It's true, too; Alex looks like such a sweet child. His cheeks are full and pink. He wears a T-shirt with Spider-Man on the front underneath a pair of denim overalls. His hair is straight and a little too long; his bowl cut hangs into his eyes. "Aww," I say, nudging him. "What a cutie you were."

"Stop it," he says, embarrassed. But he's smiling, too.

"Everyone's so quiet," I observe. In a room full of kids, you'd think there would be some noise. But they all sit with their mouths closed and their eyes cast downward, like they're waiting for something to happen. As I'm looking at them, I hear a soft noise behind me and I turn around. There is a door at the back of the room; it hangs open just a crack. That's where the sound is coming from.

Together, Alex and I go to the doorway and look inside. The room is small, barely bigger than a closet. It's empty except for a few shelves stacked with video cassettes, an old television and VCR on a portable stand, and a metal folding chair. A middle-aged nun sits on the chair. Her expression is bored; she listens as a little girl dressed in a plaid jumper stands before her, reciting the Hail Mary prayer.

"We had to memorize it," Alex explains. "Then Sister Barbara—that's her right there—would take us into this room, one at a time, and we'd recite it for her."

"Oh. Okay." I watch as the little girl leaves the room and is replaced a few seconds later by a chubby boy with curly black hair. "What does this have to do with Caroline?" We're back among the tables of children as they silently wait their turns, though the younger Alex is now nowhere to be seen.

"In the hallway," Alex says. He points at the double doors leading to the stairwell.

Before the landing to the stairs, there is a dark, narrow hallway with three doors: one to a men's restroom, another to the women's room, and a third one, which is shut and unmarked.

As we're standing there, little Alex comes out of the bathroom, wiping his hands on his overalls. He looks down, notices that his shoelace has come undone, and bends over to tie it.

That's when I hear something. "Listen," I say.

Little Alex hears it, too, and pauses mid-tie. He looks up toward the unmarked door. And there it is again: a tinny, clanging sound.

I look at Alex beside me. He's smiling; I can tell he knows exactly what's about to happen.

His younger self takes a few steps forward, until he's close enough to touch the door. Tentatively, he turns the handle and pushes it open.

It's a coat closet. And inside, standing on her tiptoes, trying to reach high enough to hang up her jacket, is first grader Caroline Michaels.

The younger Alex stares at her. "I thought you weren't here today," he says.

Caroline doesn't reply. She takes a quick step backward and almost falls into a rack full of choir robes. Already, at age six or seven, she is beautiful. She's small and wiry, her skinny arms and legs sticking out from a pink collared shirt and stone-washed denim skirt. Her long hair is wound into two braids, their ends neatly curled and tied with pale pink ribbons. She stares at Alex, clearly surprised to see him.

"Caroline?" little Alex says. "What are you doing in the closet?"

She still doesn't say anything. At her feet, there is evidence that she's been here for a while. There's an open backpack, its contents arranged in a semicircle on the floor: Barbie thermos. Coloring book. Almost empty plastic bag of cheese and crackers. Bottle of glitter nail polish. Half-completed math worksheet.

"Are you hiding in here?" Alex presses. "Why?"

Caroline seems terrified. "I-I-I . . ." Her bottom lip trembles. "Don't tell."

Alex glances behind him. He pulls the door shut. "What's wrong?" he asks, genuinely interested. "Don't worry. I won't tell."

Caroline bows her head. "I can't go to class." She begins to nibble at the edge of a painted fingernail. "I don't know the prayer."

Alex looks like he doesn't know what to do. He glances around helplessly, as if he's searching for an answer.

"She was hiding in here the whole time?" I ask Alex.

He nods. "We would all come straight from school every Friday. It's less than a block. She must have kept her distance from everyone on the way here, and then she hid in the closet so her parents wouldn't know she missed class."

The two of them are sitting on the floor now, their heads close together. "Hail Mary, full of grace," Alex whispers.

"Hail Mary, full of grace," Caroline repeats, but her face still looks panicked. "I know most of it, Alex. It's just the end. I always forget how the last part goes. And now it's too late."

"No, it's not," Alex says. "I'll help you. Say it again."

Caroline nods. "Hail Mary, full of grace," she begins, "blessed art . . . blessed art thou among women, and blessed is the fruit of thy womb, Jesus. Holy Mary, mother of God . . . pray for us . . . pray for us . . ." She squeezes her eyes shut. "I don't know the rest."

"Pray for us sinners," Alex finishes.

"Pray for us sinners," Caroline echoes.

"Now and at the hour of our deaths," Alex pronounces.

"Now and at the hour of our deaths."

"Now and at the hour of our deaths," he repeats.

"Now and at the hour of our deaths."

"Now and at the hour of our deaths," he says again.

Caroline opens her eyes to look at him. "Now and at the hour of our deaths."

Alex smiles at her. "Amen."

We watch as they sit in the closet for a few more minutes

while Caroline practices the prayer. Finally, they both get up and go back into the classroom.

Alex and I stand in the coat closet, alone. "Caroline remembers this day," he says, "after all those years. Can you believe that? We were never friends, not even as kids. I don't think we ever talked to each other again after this happened. It was just a few moments in our lives, but it mattered." He pauses. "It mattered to both of us."

"She never told me," I say, "not even when we went to your funeral. You'd think she would have said something."

He shrugs. "What was there to tell?" He looks around the room for a moment, then back at me. "So now you know," he says.

I smile. "Thank you for showing me."

Above us, the fluorescent ceiling light buzzes. Without another word, we reach for each other and let the past slip away.

Back at the cemetery, we both agree that we're ready for a real-life change of scenery. As we walk, I can't stop thinking about Caroline at Alex's grave and how sweet their shared experience was. I want to talk about it some more, to get a better glimpse at Alex's past, but I don't want to push the issue. He's already shown me more than I expected to get from him.

Alex seems to be thinking about something, too. He's

quiet for a long time as we walk. Then, out of nowhere, he says, "Hey, Liz? When we were talking earlier, at my house, I thought you said you didn't sense that something bad was going to happen to you."

"That's right," I say.

"But how could that be?" he asks. "I mean, even Caroline knew. How could you not have had any clue?"

"I didn't say that, not exactly. I said I was familiar with death. But I was telling you the truth, Alex. I mean, I don't remember feeling like anything bad was going to happen."

"Think," he says. "Try."

"How am I supposed to do that? How am I supposed to try?"

"You know how. Close your eyes. What do you see?"

Nineteen

I am seventeen years old, a junior in high school. I can tell because there's a copy of *Cliffs Complete Macbeth* on my nightstand, undoubtedly for English class. The CliffsNotes are untouched. My face looks like I haven't slept all night; my skin is blotchy, my eyes bloodshot and shaky in their sockets. I look awful. I've been lying in bed with the covers pulled up to my chin, staring at my ceiling, waiting for the sun to come up. When I finally put my feet on the floor, I take a long moment to press a hand to my stomach, another hand to my forehead. Obviously, I'm not feeling so hot.

Normally, I'd get up early and go for a run, but not today. Today, I get up and take a shower. I get dressed. I'm wearing new jeans; the tags are still attached to the waistband. They're skinny jeans, which are *so* in right now, with rhinestone detailing on the back pockets and a low-rise waistline that shows off my flat stomach. I pair them with a short, flowy pink halter top that Nicole bought me at a high-end consignment shop in Manhattan and a pair of patent leather kitten heels (the rhinestones on the heels are a nice touch combined with the detailing on the jeans); I look *great*. I'm sure that I know it, too. I remember standing in front of my full-length mirror and just staring at myself. Sometimes it would occur to me that I might not have this body forever. But it's here now: toned, lean, lovely. I use my measurements as my locker combination at school: 34-23-32.

Hair and makeup takes a good forty-five minutes every day, and even though it seems that I feel terrible now, I go through my routine as usual: a four-step skincare regime that was customized for me by a dermatologist, even though I've never had a problem with acne. My pores are almost invisible. There's cleanser, toner, moisturizer, and under-eye cream. My mom, I remember, used to spend plenty of time staring in the mirror, lamenting the dark circles under her eyes. Not me. From a very young age, I was well versed in the concept of preventative maintenance.

Then there's foundation, bronzer, blush, and a dusting of loose powder to set everything in place. Again, the shades are all custom: three times a year, Nicole takes Josie and me into New York City to visit a makeup artist whose clients are by appointment only. We have the best of the best. My father rolls his eyes at the tediousness of our routine, but he always shrugs eventually, saying, "Girls will be girls."

There's eye shadow, three shades of it: a neutral base for the entire lid, a lowlight that runs close to the eyelashes, and a highlight across the browbone. Then there's blending and eyeliner. False eyelashes with pre-applied glue that stick so well they feel like a quick attack of bee stings when you peel them off. One coat of mascara; wait a few seconds, comb it out, then another coat. There's a careful application of lip liner, matte lipstick, and gloss. Finally, I put on a pair of half-carat diamond studs that belonged to my mother. Unless I'm wearing another pair of earrings that belonged to her—her silver-and-diamond chandelier pair is a favorite of mine—I almost never go anywhere without them. They were a gift from my father for their first wedding anniversary. In a year, I'll be buried with them.

My hair is a whole different story. Unlike Josie, who has been cursed with limp, dull locks, I've got this amazing blond hair that only needs a good blowout and some brushing in order to fall perfectly into place. My hair was always my best feature, I think. It definitely wasn't my feet.

My parents aren't home, so it's just Josie and me at the breakfast table. It must be Saturday or Sunday; we don't look in any hurry to get to school. Josie's drinking orange juice, eating an English muffin smeared with peanut butter, and paging through a copy of *People* magazine.

"That's garbage. That crap goes straight to your ass, you know." I must mean the peanut butter. Of *course* I mean the peanut butter.

"Shut up. It's protein."

"It's all fat. You glob it on like it's nothing."

She pauses in midchew. She's still wearing her pajamas. "What are you all sexed up for? Aren't you going running?"

I lean against the granite countertop. I cross my arms and stare at her. "I'm going to see Richie. I need to get the car fixed."

Silence. With a tight expression, Josie stares at what's left of her English muffin before pushing the plate away. She drums her acrylic fingertips against the table.

"How is Richie going to help you with the car?"

"I talked to him last night. He knows a mechanic who does body work."

"Liz. Are you sure it was a good idea to involve Richie? We have to be careful."

"I am being careful."

She studies her manicure like she's examining the polish for chips. "I don't know about that. If you screw this up—"

"I'm not going to screw it up! Nobody's even going to know where we went. I mean, except for you. I'll have the car back before Nicole and Dad ever know it was gone."

She raises a plucked eyebrow. "Really? You're certain you'll have it back within two days?"

Two days until my parents get home. They must be out of town.

"Yes," I say, "I'll have it back before then."

"And what happened to your car, Liz?"

I bat my eyelashes. "You know what happened. When we were at the outlets last week, I hit a parking meter. Richie already saw it at school. It's just a small dent."

"But Dad would kill you if he knew you damaged the Mustang."

I nod slowly. "That's right. He'd be furious."

"So you have to get it fixed right away without anybody knowing."

"Yes."

She glances at the kitchen clock. "What time is he expecting you?"

"The shop opens at nine. The guy is a client of his."

"A client. You mean like . . ."

"A customer, yeah." What I know I mean is that Richie supplies the guy with drugs. Maybe weed. I probably didn't ask specifically, because I don't want to know. All I can tell is that this guy's doing us a favor: fixing the car quickly, taking product instead of money, and keeping everything hush-hush.

Richie must understand the predicament. The Mustang was my seventeenth birthday present. I didn't even have my driver's license yet—just my permit—but my father had it waiting in the driveway on the morning of my birthday, a huge red ribbon tied around the body. I've only owned it for a few weeks. Technically, according to Connecticut law, I'm still not supposed to drive with passengers, even though my friends and I do it all the time. My dad trusts me; he expects me to be safe. He'd go berserk if he knew I already smashed the car.

"Wait a minute," Josie says, standing up. She goes to the cupboard in the far corner of the kitchen, peers into it for a few seconds, and emerges holding a giant blueberry muffin in plastic wrap. "Here," she says, holding it toward me.

I make a disgusted face. "Ew. You expect me to eat that?"

Muffins, I think, as I'm watching the two of us, *are notorious for their high fat and calorie content. It's smart to avoid them.*

Josie rolls her eyes. She shoves the muffin into my hand. "Obviously not," she says. "It's for *Richie*."

"Oh." I stare at it. "Okay. Thanks."

On my way out the door, I glance over my shoulder to see Josie still in the kitchen. She's slumped in her chair again, eating peanut butter straight from the jar with a spoon.

"Boys don't make passes at girls with big asses!" I shout. I remember I used to tell her that all the time.

"Screw you, Barbie!" she shouts back.

I must know Richie's parents aren't home, even though it's the weekend, so I don't bother knocking on his front door. He's still in bed. I take a minute to stare at him, peacefully asleep, hair messy and face shiny with oil, hands pressed together in an almost prayerful gesture between his cheek and the pillow. I love him so much that, even as a ghost, it sometimes still hurts me inside. Watching myself as I watch Richie, I want to crawl into bed with him and stay there forever, wrap my arms around his warm sleeping body for a hundred years, until everything occurring in the time surrounding us has slipped into distant memory.

Instead, the alive me slips off my heels and tiptoes to his side. I brush the hair from his forehead, and when my fingertips touch him, his eyelids flutter open.

"Hey, beautiful." He yawns. "It's morning already?"

"Mm-hmm. We have to go."

He gets up, plucks a pair of wrinkled jeans from his bedroom floor, and pulls them on. A T-shirt, a sweatshirt, a quick run of his hand through his hair, and he's ready.

"What's that?" he asks, nodding at the muffin, which is still in my hand.

"Oh, right." I toss it to him. He catches it with one hand. "For you. Breakfast."

He grins at me. "You're so thoughtful. You take good care of me." He puts the muffin on his nightstand. "I'm not hungry yet; I'll eat it later. You want to get going?"

I wrinkle my nose at him. "Aren't you even going to brush your teeth?"

He shrugs. "You got any gum?"

"We're a terrible match, you know." But I dig through my purse, toss him a stick of spearmint gum.

"You ought to dump me then," he says, chewing. "Go out with a polo player." He blows a bubble. "You'd have fun with a guy like that. You could go shopping together, get facials, manicures . . ."

"I already have enough girlfriends. Besides, your good

looks make up for your lack of grooming." I kiss the tip of his shiny nose. "Love you."

Richie sighs. "I know. I'm irresistible. It's a curse . . . and a blessing."

As we're walking out the door, I stop. "Wait a minute. Deodorant?"

"I thought I'd let you fully enjoy the allure of my natural pheromones."

I frown. "Richie. Please. For me?"

He laughs. "Wait till you see who's going to fix your car. Then you can lecture me about personal hygiene."

I drive the Mustang to the garage, following Richie as he leads the way in his car. On the outskirts of Groton, in a section of town I know I normally wouldn't have been caught dead in, there's an auto body shop called Fender Benders. The place seems empty at first; it's nothing more than a huge cinderblock building with a bunch of garage doors, tools lining three of the four walls, and a few glaring fluorescent lights overhead. A radio in the corner of the room plays a fuzzy broadcast of the news from NPR. The whole room reeks of smoke, and there's a lit cigarette burning in an unmanned ashtray beside the radio. A fat, drooling bulldog who obviously needs a bath is chained to a support beam in the center of the room. There aren't any people around, let alone cars.

My heels click against the cement floor, creating an eerie

echo. "Richie." I giggle, clearly nervous. "Where the hell did you bring me? This is like a circle of hell."

"It's my family's business. But thanks, sweetie. Appreciate the compliment."

I turn around to see a tall, chubby man standing in coveralls and work boots. His hands are filthy, several of his fingernails bruised black. A pair of safety goggles is perched atop his very greasy dark hair. An unlit cigarette is tucked behind his right ear; a lit cigarette dangles from his lips, and I can't even imagine who the one burning in the ashtray might be for. His name—VINCE—is embroidered on his coveralls.

Standing beside Richie, alive, it is impossible for me to hide my disgust. And I don't blame myself—Vince isn't a man; he's a *specimen*. I take a step closer to Richie, hooking my arm tightly around his waist, and pinch his side. He winces; I must have pinched him hard, to make sure he knows I'm not happy.

I stand on my tiptoes and press my mouth to Richie's ear. "I want to leave," I whisper. It's clear I don't care that Vince can see everything I'm doing, and that he might even be able to hear me.

"You want your car fixed or not, Liz?" Richie murmurs. "Calm down. Be cool."

"What's the matter, sweetie?" Vince keeps the cigarette between his lips while he talks, exhaling through his nose. "You ain't used to hanging out in this neighborhood?"

The dog sits up like it's been startled and barks loudly. It rushes toward us, but gets yanked back by the chain. It stands on its hind legs, panting, drool hanging in thick foamy strands from its black gums. Watching the scene play out, I almost gag. I'm surprised to realize that I wish Alex were with me. His presence would be comforting—or at the very least, distracting—right now.

"That's just Rocky," Vince says, grinning at my apparent disgust. "He's a good dog, ain'tcha, Rocky?" To Richie, he says, "This is really your girlfriend?"

Richie shoves his hands into his pockets. "Yeah, she's really my girlfriend." He flashes an apologetic smile. Watching myself, observing my dull expression, I can guess what I'm thinking: I always knew that Richie's extracurricular activities meant he spent time around some unseemly people, but I never imagined anything like this. I'm probably going to take a shower as soon as I get home, trying to wash the stench of the place away.

"Well. Let's take a look at this car. You need it fixed quick, right?"

"I need it fixed, like, yesterday," I clarify. "It was a birthday present. I hit a parking meter. There's just a tiny dent in the front fender, so I'm sure it will be easy to repair." I look around the empty garage. "You don't seem all that busy."

"Huh." Vince narrows his eyes at me. "What's the matter? Don't want Daddy to find out you wrecked the car? Afraid he'll take away your platinum card for the weekend?"

I glare right back at him. "I go to high school. I need a mode of transportation."

Vince licks his lips, slowly, and curls his mouth into a sick-looking grin. "Can't you just ride your broomstick?"

We leave my car with Vince and his promise that it'll be done within twenty-four hours. Once Richie and I are in his car, he sits quietly for a minute, his eyes closed. The stereo plays "Scarborough Fair" by Simon and Garfunkel, which is Richie's favorite band. The CD is part of a mix that I made him a few months ago. Small details like these, which materialize in my mind seemingly out of nowhere, always bring pangs of sadness that border on desperation. If only I had known how little time we had left together. Things would have been different, I'm certain of that. I would have held his hand more tightly. I would have listened more closely to the song lyrics; I would have tried to appreciate their meaning and significance. After this track, I know there's a Radiohead cover of Carly Simon's "Nobody Does it Better," which is our song. Every word of it is honest-to-goodness truth between us; I understand that now. But back then, I was so distracted—because of what? My car? My preoccupation seems so painfully absurd.

"What's the matter?" I ask him, digging through my purse, emerging with a tiny bottle of hand sanitizer. "You're so quiet."

"Liz." He stares ahead at the Fender Benders parking lot, where Vince is leisurely strolling around my car, taking a good long look at the very minimal damage. "You didn't have to be so rude. You were being a prissy bitch."

"Don't call me a bitch. You didn't tell me we were going to the asshole of the universe." I offer him some hand sanitizer. When he declines, I grab his hand and squeeze some of the clear goo into his palm. "Now rub your hands together," I order him. "Richie, I can't believe you actually do business with that guy. He's trash."

"Then why didn't you just tell your dad about the car? So what if he was upset. What's the worst that could have happened? You get grounded for a few weeks? Besides, you hit a parking meter. It isn't a big deal."

I notice that my hands are shaking slightly. "I don't want to have to deal with my father. You know he spent a lot of money on the car. He would have insisted we file a claim. This is way less trouble, trust me."

Richie shrugs. "Whatever. I'm just saying, you could have at least been polite to the guy. He's doing you a huge favor, and you treated him like dirt."

"I treated him like dirt because he's dirty!"

"He's a *human being*, Liz."

I cross my arms. "Take me home."

We drive back to Noank in silence. But once we reach our street, Richie pulls his car into his driveway, shuts off the engine, and reaches over to touch my cheek.

"You were right," he says. "We are a terrible match."

I frown, but there is a hint of a smile on my face, in my eyes. "What do you plan to do about it? Break up with me? I'll date a polo player, and you can date . . . I don't know. Who *would* you date?"

He smiles. "Nobody. If I couldn't have you, I wouldn't want anybody."

I take his hand in mine. "Really?"

"Really." And he kisses me on the forehead. "Remember? We fit."

"That's right." I rest my cheek against his. "We do fit," I whisper, my lips close to his ear.

We sit quietly for a few minutes, enjoying the feel of each other's skin, before I pull away and ask him, "You're sure? Even though I'm high maintenance? Even though I'm a prissy bitch?"

He doesn't answer. He says, "How did you hit a parking meter, anyway? You're usually a pretty good driver."

"I wasn't paying attention. I was talking to Josie." With my thumb and index finger, I take my gum out of my mouth. I stare at it. "It was like it came out of nowhere."

Coming in and out of memories is always a bit draining, but when I snap back into the present, I feel more exhausted than usual. Quickly, I fill Alex in.

"I should have just taken you with me," I said. "It would be easier than having to explain everything."

He shrugs. "It's okay. It's your memory."

"I'll bring you next time," I say. I can't help but feel excited by what I've seen. More and more pieces of the puzzle are beginning to fall into place, and the new information I'm recalling seems more and more significant. Finally, I know how I met Vince. Now I just have to figure out how I ended up in his bed, being blackmailed.

"So you must have gotten your car back in time," Alex says. "You didn't get in any trouble, did you?"

"Not that I remember."

"Why don't you try—"

"I'm not going to try and remember anything else. Not now. I'm exhausted." I pause. "Do you think it was more draining to see this memory because it matters so much? Because it's more important than other things I'm remembering?" The thought is exciting. "I'm getting closer, Alex. I'm going to figure it out."

He nods. "Yeah. I think you are."

"And then what?" I blink at him. "What happens once I know everything?"

He thinks about the question. "I don't know. Maybe we go somewhere else."

"Hmm. Okay." We both know that I don't want to ask the most obvious question: where else is there for us to go?

"I can't believe you don't want to try and remember more right away," Alex says, shifting the conversation. "Aren't you curious? Don't you want to know how you went from hating Vince to . . . well, to those pictures?"

We're walking back through town together—slowly, to keep the pain in my feet from becoming unbearable—and headed nowhere in particular.

"Of course I want to know. I need to recover for a while, that's all." And then something occurs to me. "I know you don't want me to see your memories," I tell Alex. "But will you at least tell me if you've learned anything important?" And just as I'm saying the words, I glance up to see a telephone pole with Alex's picture on it. They've been all over town for more than a year. It's his sophomore yearbook photo, blown up and printed in color. Beneath it, it says, KILLED BY A HIT-AND-RUN DRIVER. $10,000 REWARD FOR INFORMATION LEADING TO ARREST.

On this particular poster, someone—undoubtedly one of the less-sensitive jocks from our school—has taken a pen and drawn a pair of wings on Alex's shoulders. His eyes are blacked out for no good reason. The act is incredibly cruel; what seems even worse, though, is that nobody has bothered to replace the poster with a new one.

"You know what your parents should do," I say, trying to be helpful, "they should rent a billboard. Maybe along the highway. Someone must have seen *something* from that night, don't you think?"

"It's been over a year, Liz. They aren't going to catch anyone." He pauses. "Even if somebody did know something, ten thousand dollars isn't exactly a lot of money around here."

"Then they should offer more."

"They don't *have* more. It's not like they own a house full of antiques they can sell for cash." He's talking faster, obviously getting upset. "Caroline sounded like a spoiled brat. So her daddy lost his job on Wall Street. There are worse things."

I press my lips together for a moment. "Alex. You don't know what her life is like."

"You don't know what *my* life was like."

"Good. I'm glad. I wouldn't have traded places with you for anything." I don't know why I'm reacting this way; Alex's confrontational attitude is making me defensive.

We're near my house, close to the docks. "This might surprise you, Liz," he says, "but I wouldn't have traded places with you, either. I mean, it would be nice to be rich, and to have all those friends . . . but I wouldn't actually take it. You might have had everything material that you could have wanted, but it sure seems like you were a miserable person. And all your money didn't buy you another second of life, did it?"

I glare at him. It's amazing how quickly I can go from enjoying myself with Alex to wishing I were anywhere but with him. I know he's angry because I suggested that his parents offer a larger reward, because I assumed it would be easy for them, when in reality I'm guessing their offer is already stretching them thin. It was insensitive, I know. But I also feel like he's overreacting. It was an honest mistake.

He hesitates. "Look . . . I'm sorry. We've been getting along so well."

"Me, too." I pause. I know he has a point about my friends, too—or at least some of them. "But you shouldn't have said that about Caroline. She's a good person. You know that."

"Okay. You're right." I can tell he's trying to keep his tone light. "Hey. Look who it is."

My father sits alone on the deck of the *Elizabeth*. It's the middle of the afternoon. There's a sizable number of people in our town who are rich enough that they don't have to work, so plenty of people are out, going about their day, relaxing on their boats and doing their best to pretend they don't see my father staring at the water, an open beer dangling from his hand, a lit cigar in his mouth. My dad, though, should be at work; he was always at work when I was alive. I imagine he's getting pretty close to using up all his unused vacation days by now. But then, it's not exactly like he's got a big trip to Disney World coming up anytime soon.

Nicole saunters out the back door of our house. She's wearing a flowing white skirt that grazes her ankles, a yellow halter top that exposes her belly—which is just a *tad* pudgy—and a light jacket. Her long hair is pulled into a messy ponytail that hangs down her back. With every step, her signature turquoise jewelry clinks around her wrists, ankles, and neck. As she strolls down the street and toward the dock, she is the portrait of serenity. *My God*, I think, *what the neighbors must be saying about my family*.

She lets herself onto the boat, takes a seat beside my

father, and rests her head on his shoulder. For a long time they sit together without speaking, the boat rocking gently on the water, my father staring intently at the sea, barely acknowledging Nicole's presence.

"Marshall," she says, "this isn't living. You can't sit here day after day." She rubs his grizzled cheek with the back of her hand. "When was the last time you shaved? When was the last time you took a shower? I wake up in the morning alone. I miss you." She hesitates. "No matter how miserable you are, it isn't going to bring her back. I know you're heartbroken, honey, we all are. But we're a family, and we should get through this together. I need a husband. Josie needs a father."

He doesn't look at her. When he speaks, his voice barely breaks above a whisper. "We could have prevented this. That's what everybody is saying. If we'd gotten Liz some help before she got so frail, or if we'd told her she couldn't have her party on the boat—"

"You tried, Marshall. She refused. She was adamant. Short of putting her in the hospital against her will, what could you have done?"

"That *is* what I should have done, Nicole. I should have put her in the hospital. But I didn't. I let her down. I didn't pay enough attention. If I hadn't been at work all the time, I would have noticed things were getting really bad. If I had forced her to see a therapist, maybe driven her there myself—"

"If, if, if . . . Marshall, there's no *if*. There's only what *is*. You think I don't know what people are saying about us? You think I'm not sorry every day that we didn't do more to help Liz? We had no way of predicting the future. She was spending time with her friends. She wanted to have a birthday party. They're good kids. We've known them all their lives. How could we have possibly known something like this would happen?"

"We shouldn't let Josie go to homecoming with Richie. It looks terrible. He's on probation, for Christ's sake. And he was *Liz's* boyfriend." He takes a long sip of his beer. "You know, I'm surprised the Wilsons are letting him anywhere near Josie. My God, they hate both of us so much."

"He and Josie are taking comfort in each other. They both lost their closest friend." Gently, she takes the beer from his hand and places it off to the side. "You and I both know how that works. When you lost Lisa—"

"When I lost Lisa and then I married you, everyone in this town assumed that you and I had been having an affair before she died. And Josie says she and Richie were seeing each other when Liz was still alive. Don't you understand how damn screwed up that is? Can't you imagine what people are saying?"

It pains me to know how right he is. Everyone's talking about it. Everyone has been talking about our family for years.

Nicole only shrugs. "It's a small town. People are going

to say things. Do you want to move away? Take Josie out
of school in the middle of her senior year, go someplace
where nobody knows anything about us? We can't do that
to her. She's been through enough already."

My father reaches past Nicole, reclaims his beer. He
slumps in his seat. "Have you ever thought it's possible that
someone did something to Liz that night? The whole thing
with Richie . . . and now him and Josie?"

"We've known Richie almost his entire life. He did not
hurt Liz," Nicole says firmly. "If you start believing that,
you're just like everyone else in this town."

"Maybe they're right."

"They are not right." Nicole hesitates. She rubs the larg-
est stone in her turquoise necklace, thinking. "Marshall, I
know you don't want to hear this, but I've been going to the
Spiritualist Church more often than you realize. They have
people there who are connected to the other side. I've talked
to them about Liz."

"You're right. I don't want to hear this."

"Would you listen? Just for me?" Nicole smiles. "She's at
peace, Marshall. She's in a better place now. Instead of sitting
here, day after day, imagining your daughter in the water, I
want you to try—just *try*—imagining her somewhere peaceful, where there isn't any darkness or sadness. Imagine that
she isn't running for hours anymore, doing everything she
can to stay thin. Imagine that she's with her mother, and

they're together, maybe even looking down on us. I'm sure they'd want you to be happy. I really believe that."

I snort. "I can't believe she buys into that crap," I say to Alex.

He laughs. "Well, how would she know any different?"

"I know, but it's all so . . . so *hokey*. Like my mom and I are up in heaven together. I mean, Nicole couldn't be further from the truth."

Alex nods. "But don't you hope she'll be right someday?"

I don't answer him. It's not like I haven't thought about it. For right now, though, it seems like too much to wish for.

My father's eyes are glassy and damp. He tosses his cigar into the water. "She was barely eighteen. She was only a baby. It was our job to protect her, and we failed. *I* failed. Just like I failed with Lisa. I promised to stand by her in sickness and in health, and she got sick, and I *let her die.*"

"How could you have helped her? You did everything you could. You took her to doctors. You tried to get her to eat. You loved her. You stayed with her."

He looks sharply at Nicole. "You and I were spending plenty of time with each other while she was wasting away."

Nicole presses her lips together. I wait, anxious to hear whether or not she'll say anything to confirm that she and my dad were having an affair before my mom died. But all she says is, "Marshall, I loved Lisa, too." She stands up. "The universe works in mysterious ways. You didn't know I would come back into your life after so many years apart. We became friends. What happened after that was organic. It was natural. Do you think that, if I could go back in time and change the way things happened, I wouldn't rather have Lisa stay alive, healthy, married to you, even if it meant you and I never got to be together again?"

My father doesn't answer. He wipes his eyes with a chubby hand. He takes one last sip of his beer, tilting it all the way back until it empties. "Fuck the universe," he says, standing up. He heads inside the boat, probably to get another beer. "And I don't want to hear another word about that church, you understand? Not one goddamned word."

Twenty

It's homecoming night, the first weekend in November. True to form, extenuating circumstances notwithstanding, my friends have pooled their money for a limo. There are Mera and Topher, of course. Mera's red dress matches Topher's tie *exactly*, and her earrings are identical to his cufflinks. Caroline has found a date with the obnoxious but passably popular Chad Shubuck—the same Chad who so memorably farted during our school's moment of silence for Alex. And then there's Richie and Josie. The limo driver picks them up last. There's no celebration in the yard in front of my house like there have been in past years, no parents taking pictures of our giggling crowd, no mothers fussing over boutonnieres or making last-minute adjustments to dress straps. Instead, Josie and Richie leave separately from their houses and hurry to the limo, where the driver is waiting for them with the door open.

As Richie gets inside, his parents watch from behind their front door, keeping their distance while still paying attention. Since their son's arrest and probation, they've been spending significantly more time at home, which definitely isn't a bad thing.

"His parents are talking," Alex says as we're waiting for everyone to get situated in the limo. "What are they saying?"

I blink; in a flash, I'm standing beside Richie's mother.

"I swear on Lisa Valchar's grave, may she rest in peace, that after tonight, I never want my son around Josie again," Richie's mom says to his dad.

"He likes her," Richie's dad replies. "Dr. Andrews said it's important for him to maintain his friendships." Dr. Andrews is Richie's shrink. The same shrink who buys weed from him on a regular basis. Now that Richie's on probation—and presumably not selling drugs—I wonder if the good doctor will increase his hourly rate.

"I don't care if he likes her." Mrs. Wilson shudders. "If we're lucky, they'll move away soon. I don't know how the hell they're still living in that house after everything that's happened. The place is probably crawling with angry spirits. I can't believe those people even have the nerve to show their faces in town."

"Okay. I get it. Enough already." Richie's dad pauses. "What do you want to do for dinner? Sushi?"

.   .   .

In the back of the limo, my friends pass around a bottle of peach schnapps that Chad has produced from the inner pocket of his suit jacket.

"Hey Richie," Chad says, taking a long swig from the bottle, cringing as the liquor burns his throat, "you got any weed on you?"

"I'm on probation." Richie shakes his head. "I'm done with all that." He gives a wry grin. "I'm clean as soap now."

"Come on." Chad frowns. "You don't have anything? Not even a joint?"

Richie is always a nice guy, difficult to upset, and he typically has a high tolerance for the jock set in our school, but I know he can't stand Chad. "Nothing means 'nothing,'" he clarifies, enunciating the words like Chad is some kind of idiot—which he pretty much is. "Not even an aspirin." But when the bottle of schnapps comes Richie's way, he takes a sip with only the slightest hesitation.

All of my girlfriends look gorgeous. Josie is in a strapless pink gown, her hair piled into a tedious updo that took three hours to pin into place at the salon. She and Richie sit beside each other, but they don't hold hands or show any other signs of affection. I'm sure my boyfriend feels self-conscious being out with my stepsister, but like everyone keeps saying, apparently she's bringing him some comfort.

Mera is, as usual, a knockout with her D-cups on prominent display in a low-cut red halter dress. She looks like a blond Jessica Rabbit. She rests her head against Topher's shoulder, their fingers woven together in casual solidarity. I remember how it felt to be like that with someone, with Richie. It was so easy, so comforting, to have a partner no matter what.

Caroline is wearing a one-shoulder black-and-silver cocktail dress that looks *expensive*.

"Where did you get this?" Josie asks, rubbing the material between her fingers. "It's silky." Her eyes flash with admiration. "Nice."

"At a boutique." Caroline seems intentionally evasive.

Josie raises a perfectly plucked eyebrow. "How's your dad? Did he find a new job yet? This dress couldn't have been cheap."

"My dad is fine." Caroline pushes Josie's hand away. "And the dress was four hundred dollars."

Alex, sprawled like a king in the farthest backseat of the limo, looking incredibly out of place in his filthy Mystic Market T-shirt and jeans, says, "Four hundred dollars. Wonder where she got that kind of cash?"

I stare at the dress, at Caroline's shaky expression, her vulnerable confidence. Maybe she planned to use the money she stole from me to help her family, but it wouldn't surprise me one bit if she kept it for herself to buy a new dress. What other option would she have? It's not like she could go to the mall and buy something from a department store. My friends, I know, do *not* buy formal dresses at the *mall*.

. . .

I used to love school dances. I loved everything about them: shopping for just the right gown for weeks beforehand; the way it took all day to get ready, from getting my hair done to doing my makeup; posing for pictures with Richie in front of a cheesy backdrop while a professional photographer told us we make a really great-looking couple; it was all like magic.

Tonight, the school gymnasium has been transformed into an explosion of glitter, balloons, and crepe paper. A huge disco ball hangs from the ceiling, turning slowly to create shadows across the thick crowd of students. There's a long table covered with cookies and finger sandwiches and punch. There isn't a trace of death or sadness anywhere. It's happy. It's normal. It's high school, exactly the way it should be.

By the time they get out of the limo, my friends have polished off the bottle of schnapps and are all adequately tipsy.

"I want to dance," Mera tells Topher, tugging at his sleeve. "Come on."

"Hey, Richie," Chad says. His arm is around Caroline, who seems uncomfortable despite how pretty she looks. "I'm not much of a dancer. How about you?"

"Huh?" Richie barely seems to notice that Josie is standing close to his side, holding his hand. Instead, he's scanning the crowd, looking for—for what? I have no idea.

"I said, I was never much of a dancer. Always thought dancing was for fags." Chad elbows Caroline. "This guy's supposed to be a dealer, and he doesn't bring any weed. You believe that?"

Caroline stares at the crowded dance floor. She and I took all kinds of lessons together when we were little girls: ballet, tap, jazz, gymnastics. She's a *cheerleader*, for God's sake; of course she wants to dance. "My favorite uncle is gay," she says, "and he doesn't like to dance, either." She looks at Chad. "I don't like that word. *Fag*. Don't use it, okay?"

Chad stares at her dumbly. "What are you saying? You saying you really want me to dance with you? To get out there and shake your ass?" He shrugs. "Fine. If that's what it takes for you to loosen up."

And then it's just Richie and Josie, standing alone near the bleachers, Richie still looking at everything, distracted.

"What's the matter?" Josie nudges him. She looks like she wants to wrap herself around him, to show everyone that he's with *her* now.

He knows what she wants. He stares down at their interlaced fingers, looks at the rest of the room, and asks, "Do you think people are talking about us?"

"What do you mean? Because we're here together?"

"Yes."

"Maybe." She takes a small step closer to him. Their navels are almost touching. She stands on her tiptoes and whispers in his ear, "Let them talk, Richie. We're good together. You make me happy." She pulls away slightly, frowns at him. "Don't I make you happy?"

"Yes." There's no conviction in his voice, though. He

breathes a long sigh, gazes at the ceiling. "I shouldn't have drank. I could get into a lot of trouble."

"Would you relax?" She giggles. "Since when are you concerned about getting into trouble? Just stay with me. Nobody's going to know anything. Let's go dance."

He shakes his head. "Nuh-uh. I don't like to dance. I'm no good."

"Oh, come on. You need to loosen up. Have some fun for once." She pauses. "Liz would want you to have fun. She'd want you to be happy, Richie."

I'm starting to get very annoyed by everyone talking about what I would want. How do they know? Josie's wrong; I want Richie to be happy—just not with her. In this moment, more than ever, I cannot *stand* the sight of them together.

But why shouldn't they be happy? She's my sister. I love her. And if they care about each other, why does it bother me so much?

"I never even danced with Liz." Richie pauses. "Well, only sometimes. Just for slow songs."

"Is that true?" Alex has been hanging back since we got here; he seems almost paralyzed by the crowd, even though they obviously can't see him.

I smile. "Yeah, it's true. He wouldn't dance fast. He would never admit it, but I always knew he was too self-conscious." I close my eyes. "But he'd dance slow. He was a great slow dancer." I can almost sense his hands on my waist. I can remember the way it felt to rest my chin on his shoulder. We've been to so many of these together, ever since our first school dance in the seventh grade: homecomings, winter formals, spring flings, Sadie Hawkins, and prom. It was always Richie and me.

Now he's here with my stepsister, and she's tugging him toward the floor. "Come on! I love this song."

"Go dance with Caroline. She looks like she could use a friend." It's true; Chad is like an octopus, hands all over her in the middle of the floor, his grip *very* low on her waist, hips grinding against her body. She looks embarrassed and obviously tipsy, trying to keep her balance while simultaneously preventing him from putting his tongue down her throat.

"All right." Josie pouts. "But I'm coming back for you."

Richie strolls alone to the refreshment table, gets a plate full of cookies and a big cup of punch, and sits by himself on one of the bleachers.

Alex and I perch a few feet away from him, just watching the crowd for a while, not saying much.

"I know you didn't . . . uh, you couldn't make it to prom last year," I finally say, "but what about other dances? Who'd you go with? Did you ever have a girlfriend or anything?" As soon as the words leave my mouth, I'm reminded of Alex's memory from the Mystic Market, and the lie he told about having a girlfriend. I still don't understand why he did it. I would never bring it up again, but I wonder if he's thinking about the same thing.

If he is, he doesn't show it. Alex shakes his head. "This is the first dance I've ever been to." He gives me a shy smile. "Ironically, I've come with someone who's way out of my league."

"You mean you never—not even *one* dance? Not in junior high or anything?"

"Nope." He stares at the crowd. "Even if I'd wanted to, I wouldn't have been allowed. My parents. You know—religion and all that."

"But you're Catholic. Catholics are allowed to dance."

"Liz, I don't think you quite understand. My parents are *super* religious. I wasn't allowed to go to dances or date girls . . . nothing like that. My mom found a *Playboy* in my room once. Know what she did?"

"Oh, please tell me."

He won't—or can't—look at me. "She tore out a few of the pages. The worst ones. You know, *Playboy* has all these pictures of women who are—"

"Alex, I've seen *Playboy*."

"Okay, then you know what it's like. Anyway, she tore out a few of the photos and she put them up on the fridge. You've been in my house. You know we don't have a dining room. The table is in the kitchen. So that night, while we ate dinner, I had to sit there with my parents and look at those pictures with them. My mom said, 'If there's nothing wrong with what you were looking at, then you shouldn't be ashamed to have them right out in the open for everyone to see.'"

My mouth drops. "That's awful. I mean, *Playboy*'s pretty bad, but . . . God, Alex. Talk about repressed."

He nods. "I know. And you want to know the grossest part?"

"Oh, it gets worse? Fabulous."

"The *Playboy*? I found it in my dad's dresser. He never even owned up to the fact that it was his. He acted completely shocked."

I don't know what to say. I almost can't imagine anything more humiliating. I look around at my classmates—at Richie by himself, sipping punch and staring at his shiny brown loafers, at Caroline and Josie waving their hands in the air, shaking their hips with the easy carelessness of pretty, popular girls, at Topher and Mera dancing cheek to cheek, even though it's a fast song. Are any of them even thinking about me tonight? Richie is, I'm pretty sure. He looks like he'd rather be anywhere but here. But if I were still alive, would we even still be together, knowing what I'd done with Vince?

"I guess everybody has their secrets," I say.

"Yeah." Alex squints at me through the dimness. "I guess so."

The music shifts; the DJ starts to play a slow song. Almost without thinking, I grab Alex by the hand. "Come on," I say, "stand up."

He flinches at my touch. "What? Why?"

"Because." I smile. "It's homecoming. We're here together. And I want to dance with you."

He shakes his head. "Liz, no. I can't. I've never—"

"You can, and you will. Alex Berg, Elizabeth Valchar wants to dance with you. Now get up and show her a good time."

Still holding him by the hand, I lead Alex to the middle of the floor. "Put your hands on my waist," I say, positioning his arms, "like this."

"Liz . . ."

"No arguments." I put my arms around his neck. "It's easy," I whisper. "Just . . . sway."

My friends are all around us. Josie has dragged Richie onto the floor, and they're barely ten feet away.

"See?" My mouth is close to his ear. "There's nothing to it."

Alex is very tense at first. But after a few moments, I feel him relax a little bit. It's peaceful. It feels right, and good, and so ridiculous that, in life, I know I never would have considered sharing space on a dance floor with someone like him.

He steps on my feet. "I'm sorry. I'm not good at this."

"You're doing fine. Trust me, it would be much worse if I were wearing open-toed shoes." I try not to wince. I don't want him to know how much it really hurts.

Above us, the silver disco ball rotates, casting shadows all over the room. I rest my head on Alex's shoulder and close my eyes, but not before I notice Mera and Topher by themselves in a corner, barely moving, holding on to each other tightly. Topher kisses Mera on her forehead. She beams at him. I feel happy for them.

"My mother would be praying for my soul if she could see me here," Alex murmurs.

I smile. "How's your soul doing right now?"

"It's doing good." He pulls me a little bit closer. "It's doing pretty great, actually."

The song doesn't last long enough. The music ends, followed almost immediately by a synthesized drum roll. Our principal, Dr. Harville, steps onto the platform at the front of the room. As soon as the students notice her, people begin to cheer.

"What's going on?" Alex asks.

I grin. "It's homecoming. Time to crown the queen."

Noank High doesn't have a homecoming king. There's only a queen, selected every year from the pool of senior girls. In early October, there's a voting process where all the seniors decide who will be on court. Every year they elect ten girls. At the homecoming dance, every girl on court picks a random rose from a pile of boxed flowers. Of those ten, only one of the roses is red; the rest are white. Whoever gets the red rose gets the crown. The idea of the random rose drawing is supposedly to prevent the whole process from being nothing more than a popularity contest. Even though, when you think about it, it's still nothing more than a popularity contest—it's just that everyone's voting for their top ten. In

past years, I know, the list of girls has been unofficially organized by the senior boys into rankings for best face, best ass,
best whatever. What can you do? It's high school.

Dressed in a strappy black cocktail dress and high heels
that make her look *very* unlike a principal, Dr. Harville takes
the microphone from the DJ.

"Good evening, ladies and gentlemen," she coos, beaming
at the crowd. "I think we all know what it's time for. Could
I have the ladies of the court assemble onstage, please?"

I'm not surprised to see that all of my close friends—
Caroline, Mera, and Josie—are on the court. Then there's Grace
Harvey, Kelly Zisman, Alexis Fatalsky, Anna and Mary Ste-
vens (who are twins), Julia Wells . . . and that's it.

"There are only nine of them," Alex says. "Who's number
ten?"

"As we all know, our community lost someone very special this year," Dr. Harville says, her tone becoming solemn.
"As your principal, I was incredibly moved when Elizabeth
Valchar's name was written in on so many ballots that it
became clear to me we needed to include her on court this
year, even if she cannot be with us tonight."

The crowd of students is silent. The girls onstage stand
with their heads bowed, holding hands, already looking
defeated. It doesn't take a genius to understand what's going
to happen next. I realize there are no roses anywhere onstage;
there isn't going to be a selection process this year.

"After a great deal of consideration, since it has become

abundantly clear what the loss of Elizabeth has meant to our student body, the faculty and I have decided to posthumously honor her as this year's homecoming queen."

Everyone cheers. The other members of the court applaud politely, even though I can all but guarantee there will be plenty of bitching afterward about how unfair my honor was. Even Josie doesn't look thrilled by the turn of events; she has a tight smile plastered to her face, but her eyes are stony as she stares straight ahead. I don't know that I blame her. No matter how special I might have been, I'm sure every girl onstage wanted to be queen—especially Josie.

But they're not the queen. I am. And I'm here.

"Come on," I say to Alex, grabbing his hand again. This time he doesn't flinch.

"Why?" He follows me as we weave through the crowd. "Are you kidding me?"

"No, I'm not kidding." I pull him onstage. We stand beside Dr. Harville together, staring out at the sea of students. "I'm the queen," I say, still holding his hand, enjoying the long moment of applause. "And I'm crowning you the king."

After the ceremony, there's still a good hour left of the dance. Once she's offstage, Caroline manages to lose Chad in the crowd. He looks for her for a few minutes, then gives up and gets himself a plate of cookies and sits down on the bleachers to ogle all the girls in tight dresses.

Caroline finds Richie in the hallway outside the

gymnasium. He's by himself, sitting on the ground beside a vending machine, his back against the wall, head down.

"Hey, you," Caroline says, nudging his foot. "Cheer up. It's a dance, not a funeral."

"Might as well be," he says, looking at her. "I knew it was going to happen, though. When I found out Liz got voted onto the court, I knew the faculty would do something like that." He half smiles. "If she's around, I'm sure she's on cloud nine. Leave it to Liz to get elected homecoming queen after she's dead, right?"

"Huh." Caroline kicks off her shoes to reveal swollen, red feet. "These heels are killing me." She slides onto the ground next to Richie. "You have no idea what girls go through to look pretty, Richie. I should have just stayed home. Chad's a jackass."

"I could have told you that."

"I know." She gives my boyfriend a sideways smile. "You doing okay? Must be tough getting arrested."

Richie doesn't say anything, not even when Caroline rests her head on his shoulder. It is a sweet, innocent gesture that doesn't make me feel the slightest bit jealous.

"I can't believe you had a gun, Richie," she says. "I mean, were you really going to kill someone? That guy you think Liz was seeing?"

"Vince," he murmurs.

"Right." She wiggles her toes, staring at their shimmering pink polish. "Vince."

Richie stares at the ceiling. "I wouldn't have used the gun. I wanted to, but I couldn't have gone through with it. But I'll be honest, Caroline. I liked having it. Just to be able to hold it, to *imagine* doing something with it. It made me feel . . . I don't know, like I was finally in control of something for once. Everything has been so crazy lately."

"I know," she says. "It sure has." Then she asks, "Did you have those pills when the cop busted you?"

"The pills you gave me to sell? Yeah, I did. They're in evidence now." He pauses. "Sorry."

"It's okay. I could have used the money, though." She's chewing a piece of gum. She snaps it nervously, each crack breaking the eerie quiet in the hallway.

"How much do you need?" He starts to fiddle with his boutonniere, unpinning it from his jacket, then removing the petals from the red rose, one at a time, and letting them drift onto the floor.

"Why?" She half smiles. "You want to loan me some money?"

"I would if I could."

"I stole the pills from Liz's bathroom, Richie." She pauses. "That's not all. I stole some money from her, too."

My boyfriend drops his boutonniere. It falls among a mess of petals between his legs. "You what?"

"I stole money from her. It was in her bathroom with the pills." Caroline closes her eyes as she continues her confession. "Five hundred dollars. Do you know what she would have been doing with that kind of cash?"

Richie scratches his head. I can't help but smile at the fact that he's done next to nothing with his hair; it's the same pile of messy curls that he usually has, only tonight it looks like he took a moment to run a comb through them. "I have no idea," he says. He hangs his head again. "But she was keeping lots of secrets. From me. From everyone."

"Right." Caroline nods. "She'd been different for a while." She bites her lip. I can tell she's thinking hard about something. "Hey, Richie?" she says. "Do you remember the party I had last year, when my parents were out of town?"

He nods slowly. "Maybe. Which one? You have a lot of parties . . . they all start to blend together after a while."

"Yeah," Caroline agrees, "I know. But this one . . . oh, never mind." She shakes her head. "It doesn't matter anymore. Forget I mentioned it, okay?"

"Okay," Richie agrees, without much interest. "Sure."

Caroline stands up. She smoothes her dress and shoots a wary glance at her shoes, which are still on the floor. "Richie, she wasn't a bad person. Everybody knows about her and that other guy, but I just keep thinking there has to be some kind of an explanation. Don't you?"

He looks up at Caroline. He shakes his head. "I don't know. I've been over it a thousand times."

"Did you really start seeing Josie before Liz died?"

Richie shrugs. "Kind of. Not really. Josie was the one who told me about Vince. She thought I had a right to know. She was looking out for me. I guess I was so angry with Liz, and Josie was just kind of there . . . and now we're together, I guess. She reminds me of Liz, you know? They're sisters. Sometimes, if I really pretend, it's almost like being with Liz."

Caroline blows a tiny bubble. It pops, leaving shreds of pink gum on her glossy lips. "I guess that makes sense."

He smiles. "It drives my parents crazy, too. My mom *hates* Nicole. She calls her a home wrecker, which I guess she kind of is. But that's history. It wasn't Josie's fault." He peers up at Caroline again. "It's not awful, is it? My being with Josie, I mean? It feels okay. Josie's nice enough. It almost feels natural."

Caroline leans over, scoops her shoes off of the floor, and lets them dangle from her hand. She doesn't answer Richie's question about Josie. "It's only a rumor that they're sisters. Nobody knows for sure. And you know Liz didn't think it was true."

"My parents believe it. And Josie and Mr. Valchar sure do look alike."

Caroline starts to walk away. "I'll see you in there, okay? The dance is almost over. I'm sure Josie's looking for you." She pauses. "And, Richie? Parents don't know every-thing."

He lets out a deep breath. "Ain't that the truth," he murmurs.

I watch my friend stroll toward the double doors to the gymnasium. She and Richie are still alone in the hallway. Just before she reaches out to open the door, Caroline pauses. She looks over her shoulder at my boyfriend. He's picking up the pieces of his shredded boutonniere, collecting the wilted rose petals in his cupped hand.

"Hey," Caroline says, "can I ask you something?"

"Sure." Richie looks like he has no plans to get up and rejoin the dance anytime soon. He opens and closes his hand around the petals, watching as they shrivel from the heat of his palm.

"When you voted for homecoming court, did you write in Liz's name?"

He leans his head against the wall. He closes his eyes. For just a second, I almost think he's going to cry.

But he doesn't. Instead, he keeps his eyes shut. He tilts his head toward the ceiling. He smiles. I know he's thinking about me.

"Yeah," he says, "I did."

Caroline's hand is on the door. She pulls it open a few inches. Noise from the gymnasium spills into the hallway, a din of teenage voices and a loud Black Eyed Peas song blaring, the poor acoustics in the room making everything sound a little bit fuzzy.

"Me, too," she admits.

Richie opens his eyes. He looks at Caroline. The two of them are almost grinning at each other.

"She was something," my boyfriend finally says. "Wasn't she?"

Caroline keeps smiling. But she doesn't say anything. She kneels down and slips on her shoes. She stands in the open doorway, visibly adjusting her posture, smoothing her dress, patting her updo to make sure everything is in place. Then she steps into the dance, leaving Richie alone in the hallway.

Only then, once there is nobody else around, does he allow himself to cry. He doesn't make a sound.

When the dance is over, my friends make their way back to the limo waiting outside. As soon as the driver sees them, he quickly tucks a bottle of liquor—poorly concealed in a paper bag—into his jacket pocket.

"All riiiight," Chad says, smirking. "Been having some fun while you're waiting for us?"

The driver leans against the limo, crosses his arms. "What else am I supposed to do?" He snorts. "Read a damn book?"

"We're ready to go," Caroline says. She has taken off her shoes again, and has given them to Chad to hold. "Can you drive us to a party without wrecking the car?"

"You want to go to a party?" The driver looks at his watch. "It's eleven already. You're only paid up until midnight."

"So we'll pay you a little extra," Topher says. "It's not a problem."

"Wait." Josie grabs Richie's arm. "I'm not getting into that limo if he's been drinking."

Richie looks bored and tired, his buzz from the schnapps long gone. "It's like two miles to Chad's house," he says. I assume that's where the party is. "It's nothing. We'll be fine."

Josie shakes her head. "No. I'm not doing it. I'll walk before I get into a car with him."

"Josie, you're overreacting." Topher lights a cigarette, completely unfazed by the fact that there are faculty chaperones milling around in the parking lot. "He'll go slow. It's fine."

"It will take forever if we walk," Richie tells her. "Besides, you're in heels. Come on, Josie. Just get in the car."

"No!" She steps away from the group and looks around the parking lot, which is full of students getting ready to leave, most of them probably heading to after parties. "I'll get a ride from someone else. I don't care. I'm not riding with him. Richie, please. Stay with me?"

Caroline stares at her. "It's not like you've never been in a car with a drunk driver, Josie."

"Whoa, whoa, whoa," the driver interrupts. "Let's get something straight. I'm not *drunk*. I'm *buzzed*. I had a few nips to keep myself from dying of boredom out here. This isn't exactly the greatest gig in the world, kids." But his words kind of slur together as he protests, which seems to make Josie even more determined to go nowhere near the limo.

She looks at Richie. When she speaks, her voice is firm. "Are you staying? I see Shannon and James right over there." She points across the parking lot. "They'll give us a ride to Chad's, I'm sure of it."

Richie looks from the limo to Josie. He seems puzzled by her adamant refusal to get into the car. Everyone does.

Finally, he shrugs. "Okay. Let's go ask Shannon."

Alex and I watch my friends pile into the limo and drive away. We watch Josie and Richie climb into the backseat of Shannon's car. We stand together in the cool night air as the parking lot slowly empties, the party over, until we're alone outside the school. The lights are now on in the gymnasium, the metal double doors leading to the outside are propped open, and I can see the school janitor beginning to clean up the mess from the evening.

I look at Alex. "Well? What do you want to do? We could go to the party and watch everyone get sloppy drunk."

He doesn't smile. "No. I have a different idea."

"What's that?" The temperature must have dropped twenty degrees since the beginning of the evening. I'm beyond freezing.

"There's someplace I want to take you."

"Okay," I say, smiling. "Let's go."

But he only stands there, staring at me. His gaze is so steady and lasts for so long that I begin to feel uncomfortable, and my smile slips away. "Alex, what is it? Why are you looking at me like that?"

"I just want to tell you," he says, "that I had a really great time with you."

"Thanks." I flash another, more tentative smile. "You're a good dancer."

He shakes his head. "I wasn't just talking about tonight. I was talking about everything. All of this." He swallows. "And there's something else I've been meaning to tell you. It's about the memory we saw together, the one of me at work."

I can't believe he's bringing it up. "Yeah?" I ask.

"I've been thinking about it a lot," he says, "and I think I made a mistake. I shouldn't have said those things to Chelsea. I should have taken her out. But it's just—I just couldn't. I was scared." Suddenly, he seems embarrassed. He puts his head down. "I'm being dumb. I'm sorry."

"You're not being dumb. I think you're right about Chelsea. You probably would have had a good time." I pause. "Anyway, I'm glad we've had fun together. You deserve it." I stare at the sky. It's a cloudless night, the stars bright and fat. The moon is almost full. "Where are we going?"

"You'll know when we get there." He puts a hand on my arm. "Ready?"

I close my eyes. When I open them, there is an immediate sense of disorientation. I am surrounded by dirt, in the woods somewhere.

"Alex?" I can't feel his hand anymore; I don't see him anywhere. "Where are we?" I start to feel sick to my stomach.

When he speaks, he sounds far away. "I want you to find

a memory," he says. "Whatever comes to you. Just close your eyes and let it in."

"Where are we?"

"This is where I died." It feels cold and desolate, the earth around me damp and littered with dead leaves and broken sticks. The tree branches all hang low. I have a horrible feeling in my gut. I'm afraid of what I might see.

"Close your eyes," he says, still sounding far away. "I'll be right here, Liz. I'll wait for you. Go."

Twenty-one

I'm alone in the memory; Alex is nowhere to be seen. Immediately, I recognize that I look different. I'm younger, sure, but that isn't all: I'm at least fifteen pounds heavier than I was in the weeks leading up to my death. My long blond hair is full of life and bounce. My cheeks are flushed.

And I'm drunk. I'm standing in Caroline's foyer with my palm pressed to my forehead, staring at the ceiling. When I follow my gaze, I see that I'm staring at an enormous, twinkling crystal chandelier. My eyes are tight; I'm trying to focus on the light despite the chaos surrounding me. The house is packed with bodies in motion, teenagers dancing and bumping against each other, everybody holding big red plastic cups with their names written on them in black ink.

"Oh God," I mouth, swaying slightly as I stand there, holding my cup so crookedly that it's threatening to spill its contents. Nobody can hear me; nobody notices that I'm distressed. Sublime's "40 Ounces to Freedom" blares from speakers in the living room, the sound infiltrating the entire downstairs. The music, which is upbeat rock, is such a contrast to Caroline's otherwise stately house. The foyer's wallpaper is patterned with dark green ivy. The floors are a deep, rich hardwood, covered with antique oriental rugs. On the wall next to the front door, there's an actual fountain, a stone angel poised in silent watch over the party's happenings, water flowing in a pool that surrounds her dainty bare feet.

"There you are! Liz, I've been looking everywhere—oh no. What's wrong?" It's Josie. My stepsister is positively giddy, holding her own cup, looking at me with wide, curious eyes that have the glazed look of somebody who's under the influence.

"I don't know. I feel sick," I tell her, taking a step to my left, toward the dining room. We have to shout just to hear each other.

"Liz, is the room spinning? Pick something to focus on. Don't close your eyes."

She's trying to be helpful, but I wave her away in annoyance as I take another step into the room. "The whole house is spinning," I yell.

"What?" she shouts back.

"I said the whole house . . . never mind."

"Where are you going?" Josie is close behind me, her hand at my waist. "Do you need to throw up?"

I nod. It's much quieter in the dining room. There's obvious relief in my expression as our surroundings shift, becoming palpably calmer.

"Go to the bathroom." And she points. "Down the hall."

"I know where the bathroom is," I say, putting my hands on my knees. My cup tilts to the side, spilling foamy beer onto the oriental rug beneath me. "Why is it so far away? Where's Richie? Josie, will you go get—"

I'm wearing four-inch heels that make it almost impossible to walk straight. I take another staggered step, and then I throw up with *force* onto the rug.

"Damn! Liz blew chunks!" It's Chad Shubuck. Of course.

I'm bent over, elbows on my knees now, and from the looks of it, I'm doing my absolute best not to collapse.

Chad thumps me on the back. "Keep it coming, honey. Get it all out. I always feel better after I puke."

"Richie," I mutter, wiping my mouth, my eyes bloodshot and watery. "Please find Richie."

"Oh my God. Liz, what the hell is the matter with you?" It's Caroline. She rushes to my side, staring at the mess on the rug. "My parents are going to murder me," she whispers, with genuine fear in her voice. "They're really going to kill me. For God's sake, couldn't you make it to the bathroom?"

I regain my footing, find a chair, and sit down. "I'm so sorry," I tell her, wiping my mouth. But the words sound empty somehow; I'm obviously distracted by the puke on the floor, and the fact that I've just embarrassed myself in front of all my friends. "Oh my God. This is so humiliating."

Richie hurries into the room. "Liz, what happened?" He looks at the rug. "Oh. I see."

"Did I get any on my outfit?" I stare down at my clothes. With shaking hands, I touch the layers that I'm wearing: a white babydoll dress with pink detailing over pink leggings.

"Was I right, or was I right?" Chad asks, edging his way between Richie and Josie. "You feel better, don't you?"

I smile at him. "Yeah, I do. I feel good." And I grin at my friends. "Plus, I didn't get anything on my clothes."

Josie beams. "Yeah, Liz! Give it up for projectile vomiting."

I beam back at her. She and I give each other a high five.

Richie hands me a glass of water, which he seems to have produced from thin air. He's like that, though: always looking out for me. "You feel better now?" He's worried, but he's also wasted. Like me, his eyes are fully bloodshot. But he also reeks of weed and cigarettes.

I nod, wrinkling my nose at his smell. "Yes. What time is it?"

"It's time to go home." Josie bites her lip, her gaze lingering on the grandfather clock that sits against the far wall of the dining room. "It's almost ten. We have to get home, Liz." To Richie, she says, "Our parents are leaving for Dad's conference early tomorrow morning. They want to see us before they go."

My boyfriend narrows his eyes at her. "She shouldn't drive, Josie. You two should spend the night here."

I stand up. I finish my water, shake my head, and pronounce, "I'm fine." I take a deep breath. "I think I got all the alcohol out of my system," I tell my friends. "I'm good."

Richie crosses his arms, frowning in disagreement. "No, Liz. You can't drive. You'd still blow drunk on a Breathalyzer. You shouldn't try to go home like this."

"Richie, it's like three miles." I give him my best, most reassuring smile. "What am I supposed to do? Call my parents and tell them I'm too drunk to drive home? We'll go. Everything will be fine."

He glances at Josie. "Can you drive her car?"

Josie shakes her head. "The Mustang's a stick shift. I haven't learned to drive it yet. Didn't you know that?"

"No, I didn't. Then you should take my car." He rubs his forehead with worry. "Jesus. I shouldn't have let you drink so much. I should have been watching you closer. This is a bad idea."

Josie smirks. "Richie, don't be such a mom. Liz, you're good, right?"

I nod. "Yes."

"But what about the rug?" Caroline pleads, looking frantic. "You promised me you'd help clean up in the morning! You didn't tell me you had to go home!"

"I'm really sorry. Look—just tell your parents the dog did it."

Josie hands me my keys. With Richie at our heels, we walk toward the front door. Just as I'm taking steps to follow us, I hear Caroline murmur under her breath—out of earshot of my alive self—"We don't *have* a fucking dog, Elizabeth."

As the Mustang makes its way down Caroline's long driveway, rain begins to hit the windshield, the droplets growing heavier by the second. But I don't switch the wipers on. As I watch my living self, my hands gripping the wheel tightly, body leaning forward slightly to get a better view of the road (*why* don't I turn on the wipers?), it is obvious to me that I should not have gotten behind the wheel. As soon as we're on the main road, I can see that I'm having trouble staying to the right of the double yellow lines. I've only had my license for a little over a month and I've only had the Mustang for a few weeks; I'm not that great at driving in general, and I'm definitely not very good at driving a stick yet. Twice, I almost stall out. Luckily, there's next to no traffic. Noank is a sleepy town; not much happens after nine p.m.

"Put your wipers on, Liz," Josie instructs.

"Ohhh . . . where *are* they? I can't find them."

"To your right. Try to stay focused."

Finally, I find them. "Wow, that's much better," I tell her, giggling.

She turns the radio up. "Good. You feel okay?"

I nod. "Yes. I feel fine."

But I can tell that I'm lying. I'm not fine; I'm clearly still drunk.

Regardless, with the music blaring, Josie and I start singing along with R.E.M.'s "Losing My Religion." The speed limit is twenty-five. I look past my living self at the dials on the Mustang's dashboard, and am shocked to see that I'm going over fifty miles per hour. The rain grows steadily heavier. It's becoming a downpour.

"Slow down, Liz," I murmur to my living self. Even though I know it's only a memory, I feel a growing sense of dread. We're going too fast, and there's nothing I can do about it.

It comes out of nowhere. My focus is shaky, and at first, watching the scene unfold, I think I've hit a small animal, or maybe a rock, but I realize almost immediately that it was something else. Something bigger. As quickly as it appears in my line of vision, there's a thick-sounding *thump*—and then it's gone.

"Shit," I say, pulling over, looking around. There's no other traffic in sight. "Shit. What was that? I think I hit something."

Josie turns the music down, but not off. "What did you say?"

The sound of the rain falling all around us creates a thick din of noise. "I said, I think I hit something." I pause. "It was probably a deer. Should we get out and look?"

Josie stares out her window. "It's pouring."

"I know."

And we both sit there, looking at each other. Watching us, I feel a heavy sense of disappointment that blossoms into disgust. We don't want to get out of the car because we don't want to get *wet*.

Finally, I say, "Josie . . . we really ought to check."

She glances into the backseat. "Do you have an umbrella?"

I shake my head. "No. We'll shower later anyway. Come on."

She presses her lips together, wrinkles her nose. "Why don't you go?"

"No. I'm not getting out by myself. Josie, please?"

She switches the music off altogether. She looks around, peering at the road through the wet windshield. "You really think it was a deer?"

"It was *something* big. Come on. We have to check."

My stepsister gives me a long sigh. Taking her time, she reaches into the center console and fishes out a ponytail holder. She pulls her hair back tightly so it won't get completely soaked. Once she's finished, she rolls her eyes at me a little bit and says, "Fine. Come on, then."

We get out of the car. We're about a quarter of a mile down the road from the Mystic Market, which is closed for the night. There's nothing else around us but woods, a windy two-lane road, and the rain.

"Turn off the car," Josie instructs. The rain is coming down so heavy now that there's no point in trying to stay even remotely dry; we're both immediately drenched. "Turn off your headlights."

I reach into the car and do what she says. Then I find a flashlight in the glove box.

I gesture toward the woods. "I can't go out there in these heels. They were three hundred dollars." I frown. "The mud will ruin them."

"Take them off," Josie says.

I pout. "But then my feet will get all muddy."

She stares at the dark sky in frustration, rain pouring down her cheeks. "What are we doing, Liz? You're the one who wanted to get out. Now do you want to look, or do you want to look? Make up your mind. I'm cold."

I shine the flashlight into the woods. Its beam of light is weak; I can't see anything but barely illuminated trees.

"If I hit a deer," I say to her, "there's probably nothing I can do about it now. Right?"

"Wait," she says, looking at my car. "Oh, wow. Check it out."

I've hit *something*, all right. There's a dent on the right side of my front fender.

"No blood," Josie says. "That's a good sign, right?" She peers at me in the darkness. "Maybe the rain washed it off, though."

"I feel like I have to throw up again," I tell her.

"No, you don't." She's curious now. She wants to know what happened. "Come on, Liz. We should find out what it was."

With clear reluctance, I take off my heels, placing them on the floor of the front seat, and the two of us begin walking toward the woods. We haven't taken more than ten steps when we both stop cold. Standing beside my living self, I come to a halt.

"Oh my God," I say. "Josie. Where's your cell phone?"

In the slim beam from my flashlight, a bicycle wheel spins on its rear axis in the pouring rain. All three of us hurry toward it. I imagine that, in my bare feet, I can feel the stones and sticks in the dirt cutting my feet, but I obviously don't care. My breath, audible despite the downpour, sounds sharp and panicked. I don't seem the slightest bit drunk anymore.

The bike is a mangled mess, lying upside down on the ground, its front smashed up against a tree. But there is no rider. Whoever was on the bike is not in my range of vision.

Out of nowhere, the rain slows to a light drizzle.

"Be quiet," Josie orders. "Listen."

What I hear next, I know, has stayed with me ever since this night, except that I'm only realizing it now. Even before I see him, I understand what has happened. I know. It is not the sound of breathing so much as it is a liquid gasping, the noise of a horrible struggle. I watch as we follow the sound and find him on the ground, his limbs bent at cruelly awkward angles. His face is so bloody that at first I don't recognize him. I can see his skull beneath his hair. I can see his brain.

"Josie, he's breathing."

He's *barely* breathing. His eyes are open. They stare up at us—at me—pleading for help, for life, for something that I cannot possibly give him.

"Go get your phone, Josie," I whisper, my voice cracking. "Call 911."

He takes another labored breath. Josie waits. She does nothing.

"Josie, what are you doing? Go get your phone!"

"Liz, we're drunk." Her tone is flat.

"So what?" My voice trembles with panic. "Call someone! He's going to die!"

I stare at him. It's the most curious thing, watching someone slip away. Our gazes are locked together, and in that moment I know that he sees me, he recognizes me.

"We know him," I say, unable to stop staring. "Josie, I recognize him. We go to school with him."

"What's his name?" she whispers.

As a ghost, the frustration is overwhelming. "Do something!" I scream at myself, at Josie. "He's going to die! Help him!"

But we don't do anything.

"I don't know his name," I tell my stepsister.

He takes another breath. It's his last one. And then— nothing. He becomes completely still. Drops of water roll from his cheeks, falling like countless silent tears.

"Jesus Christ, we're in trouble," I say. I take a big step backward. I almost fall over.

"No. We're not." Josie looks at me. She reaches over, turns off the flashlight, and we are instantly surrounded by darkness. "Let's go back to the car," she says. "Let's go home."

I stare at her. "What do you mean?"

"Liz." Her tone is calm and steady. "You just got your license. You still aren't allowed to drive with passengers. We're both drunk. If anybody finds out what happened here, it will ruin our lives. Do you understand?"

I shake my head. "Josie, we can't just go home. We can't leave him here all alone. Besides, it was an accident. He came out of nowhere. People will have to understand—"

"No, they won't." She reaches for my hand. "I'm not kidding, Liz. We don't have a choice. We have to go, *now*, before somebody gets here."

My dead heart breaks for Alex, lying there in the dirt. How could we just leave him? This act, I realize, will destroy me from the inside out. It will consume me in the months that follow.

Josie tugs my hand. "Let's go. Let's go home."

So we do. We pull my car into the garage, parking it close enough to the wall that my dad likely won't notice the small dent. I'll worry about getting it fixed later. For now, we both agree, the most important thing is to act normal.

That night, clearly unable to sleep, I sit on my bed and pore through my yearbook, searching for the face that I could not match to a name. After pages and pages of looking, I finally find him, staring up at me with a shy smile, a quiet, unpopular boy who I barely knew existed when he was alive: Alexander Berg.

"Alex Berg," I whisper to my empty room.

We are together in the same spot where, a little over a year ago, we locked gazes as Alex took his last breath. Of course, he's no longer bloody and broken. He's no longer wet from the rain. He's calm now, almost smiling at me as it becomes clear what I have recalled.

"I killed you," I tell him.

He nods. "I know."

"Did you always know? The whole time we've been together?"

He only hesitates for a second. "Yes."

"Why didn't you tell me? When we were in your house together, I asked you, 'What did I ever do to you?' You could have told me then. You could have told me a thousand times."

He is sitting cross-legged on the ground. "It doesn't work that way. If you had known the whole time, you would have acted differently toward me."

"So?"

"So, I think this is a process. I think it's supposed to work a specific way. The way you remembered things, little by little—you weren't ready to face what you'd done, not right away. You had to understand certain things first. And I helped you, Liz. Maybe you couldn't have done it without me. Maybe we were brought together for a reason."

"For what reason?"

His gaze is steady and calm. "For me to forgive you. See, Liz, I thought that I already had done that, but I was wrong. I had a year to think about it. I've gone over that night a thousand times in my mind. I thought I'd let it go. But then, when I was able to talk to you again, the day you died—all the anger came rushing back. I realized that, even though I might have tried to forgive you, it didn't work. I still hated you. Not just for . . . for hitting me that night, but also for the way you treated me when I was alive . . . like I didn't even exist. Because you didn't even know my name." He shrugs. "So there we were, together, and it was obvious you didn't remember anything about what had happened. I went along with it."

As he's speaking, something becomes clear. "This is why you didn't want me to touch you at first," I say, "isn't it? This is why you didn't want me to go into your memories. You were afraid I would see something that would make me realize what had happened before it was time."

He nods. "Yes."

"When did you know?" I press him. "How long after you died did you realize I was the one who hit you?"

"I always knew," he admits. "There was plenty I couldn't remember, the same as it was for you, but right from the beginning, that night was clear in my mind. I remember staring up at you and Josie in the rain. I remember looking into your eyes. Your face was the last thing I saw before I died."

"And after that," I ask, "did you watch me? While I was still alive?"

He nods. "Yes. I watched you all the time. It was like I was obsessed. I needed to know that you felt something about what you'd done to me. I saw you running every day—it was like you were trying to escape what had happened, like if you just went far enough, you could put it behind you somehow. I saw you with Mr. Riley at his house all those mornings. I was there, Liz. I was watching everything. I know how guilty you felt." He swallows. "It was killing you. In a way." He gives me a weak smile. "And then you died. But Liz, I think there's something else. I don't think it's just about me forgiving *you*. I think it's also about . . . about you. Forgiving yourself." He hesitates. "Do you forgive yourself for what you did to me?"

"I don't know." But it's not true, I realize immediately; I *do* know. "No. I don't forgive myself at all. Alex, you have to understand—how could I possibly forgive myself? I drove drunk. I drove too fast. And after it happened, I could have helped you. I could have called 911, I could have gone to the police—"

"But you didn't. Things happened the way they happened." He looks at me sadly. "You tried so hard to forget. Even after you died, you tried to tell yourself a different story. You tried to tell *me* a different story. Remember? At your funeral, you told me you changed your cross-country route after they found my body. But that's not true, Liz. You changed it *before* they found me."

I close my eyes for a second. He's right. Of course I changed it beforehand—how could I possibly have continued to run past him, knowing he was still in those woods? Knowing that I was responsible for putting him there? The truth was so awful that I couldn't bring myself to face it. I wanted to believe the lie so badly. And for a while, it worked. Almost.

When I look at Alex again, his gaze is steady. "And now we're here," he says. "And you still can't remember what happened the night you died."

"So you've been watching me for the past year," I say slowly.

He smiles at my realization. "Yes."

"You saw what happened after you died? You saw me running, going to Mr. Riley's house, meeting up with Vince."

"Yes."

"Then what else did you see, Alex? Did you see what happened that night on the boat?"

Something is changing. He begins to appear wispy, almost translucent.

"What's happening to you? Alex?"

"I was worried about my parents for a long time," he says, ignoring my question. "Especially my mom. You know, she used to visit my grave all the time. She lit candles for me all over our house. But it's getting better. My parents don't go to the cemetery as much. They're going to find out what happened to me that night. It will be okay. They'll finally know the whole truth, and then their lives will go on without me. I feel all right about it. Nothing will ever be the same, Liz— you know that as well as I do—but it will be okay. Doesn't that make you feel better? Aren't you happy that everyone will finally know the truth, about everything?"

"When will they know? Alex, why won't you tell me what happened? When will everyone know the truth?"

He continues to fade.

"Soon," he says. "You have to be patient. Remember, it's like a puzzle. You have all the pieces now. It won't be much longer, and then you'll understand everything. You'll be fine without me, Liz."

"Where are you going?" I'm completely panicked. "Alex, you can't leave. Tell me what you saw the night I died!"

"It's not my mystery to solve, Liz." He smiles again. "I really did have a great time with you. You aren't a horrible person like I thought you were. I forgive you, I really do. For everything."

"What did you see? Did somebody kill me? Alex, please wait—"

"It's so warm, Liz." He's fading faster now. "I think I'm finally going to get some rest. You'll like it, once it's your turn." He gives me one last lovely smile. "It's been fun hanging out with the homecoming queen. But every party's gotta end sometime."

"Alex—"

"See you later," he says.

And like *that*—he's gone.

I sit alone in the woods, feeling cold and damp. I cry. I miss Alex. I am overwhelmed with regret. If only I hadn't driven home that night. If only I'd taken a ride from someone else. But I was seventeen, I was full of life, and I didn't think anything bad could possibly happen—not to me, the rich and popular Elizabeth Valchar. How could my life cross paths in such a significant way with the so *insignificant* Alex Berg? How could I possibly have the power to take his life away with one momentary collision?

Where is there to go from here? I wait around for a while, hoping that Alex might reappear, but in my heart I know that he's gone forever now, undoubtedly to a better place.

All alone for the first time since my death, I get up. I go home. I climb onto my bed and stare at the ceiling, waiting for the morning to come, hoping the daylight brings something more than another piece of an endless stretch of time.

Twenty-two

There isn't anything to do but watch. On a Saturday morning in early November, a few days after Alex disappears, I observe as Josie walks down the street to Richie's house and knocks on his front door.

Mrs. Wilson answers. She stands behind the screen door, making no gesture to open it. She doesn't smile at Josie.

"Hi, Mrs. Wilson. Is Richie home?"

Mrs. Wilson glances over her shoulder, toward the stairs. "Actually, Josie, he's not."

Josie frowns. "But your cars are all here. And he told me he'd be around."

"Josie . . ." Mrs. Wilson appears to be summoning her nerve. "How is Liz's dad doing?"

Josie stares at her for a long minute. Then, in a defiant tone, she says, "My dad is okay. He'll be all right." She swallows. She continues to stare. "We all will, Mrs. Wilson. Richie, too."

Mrs. Wilson begins to close the heavy front door. "I think you need to go home, Josie."

"But when is—"

My stepsister stands on the front porch, stunned, as the door closes in her face.

The memory sucks me in like I'm made of liquid. All of a sudden, it's everywhere around me, and I can't do a thing to stop it.

I am five, maybe six years old. Josie, Richie, and I are on the floor of my parents' living room. Josie and I are playing with Barbie dolls, but Richie is trying to coax us into battle with a handful of plastic toy soldiers.

"We can fight each other!" he urges, lining them up in a row. "Liz, you and Josie can be on one team. I'll be the enemy. You can be the good guys. Or we can all play together and break into Fort Knox and steal all the gold! My dad says that's where the government keeps all the money." When it becomes clear we aren't paying any attention to him, he gives up on the idea of toy soldiers. "I've got Hungry Hungry Hippos at my house," he offers. "I could go get it. You guys want to play that? We could play cards, too. Liz, want to play Uno?"

"She's playing Barbie," Josie says, without looking at him. "Leave us alone."

But my young self glances shyly from Josie to Richie,

considering. When he and I make eye contact, I blush. I say, "We could all play beauty salon. Richie, you need a haircut. Me and Josie can be your hairdressers."

He brightens. "Okay. Where do you want me to sit?"

Our parents are having a dinner party in the dining room, which is adjacent to the living room. They are drinking wine and eating brie on crackers. My dad sits at the head of the table. To his right, there's my mom. To his left, there's Nicole. Mr. and Mrs. Wilson sit across from each other. Josie's dad, Mr. Caruso, is at the opposite end of the table.

The adults are loud and probably all a little drunk. It's past our bedtime, but they always let us stay up late when they get together like this, which is often. The only quiet one at the table is Josie's dad. He never talked much, not that I can remember.

Richie's mom stands up. "How about another bottle of wine?" she asks. She looks at my mom. "Lisa? I'm going into the kitchen. Want to come?" And she puts two fingers to her lips in a silent puffing gesture. She means *cigarette*.

"I'll be in. Just a minute," my mom says. Her elbows are on the table and she's leaning forward, her gaze interested even though her eyes are dull, listening to my father as he tells a story about something that happened at work. She hasn't touched her plate of cheese and crackers. She's so skinny that she's hard to look at.

Richie's mom stops in the living room on her way to the

kitchen. She smiles down at us. "You kids having fun in here?"

"Yeah, we are." Richie sits completely still in a chair, a kitchen towel draped over his shoulders like a barber's cape, as Josie and I pretend that our fingers are scissors. We're so busy "cutting" his hair, we barely glance at her.

"That's good," she murmurs. She sighs. "Oh, to be young and careless again. You kids don't know how nice you have it."

She strolls into the kitchen by herself. She opens a bottle of wine and refills her glass all the way to the top. Then she cracks open the side door leading to the patio, lights a cigarette, and leans against the doorway, clearly enjoying her moment alone.

But only for a moment. As she's standing there, watching the conversation in the dining room, her body stiffens. She leans forward just a little bit. Her eyes narrow. I follow her gaze and am immediately thankful that what's going on under the table is out of the line of vision for my much younger self.

Mrs. Wilson is staring at a spot beneath the table: it's my father's feet. My mother is so skinny that she can sit with her legs crisscrossed in her chair, lotus style, so her feet don't even touch the floor. But Josie's mom has slid *her* feet right next to my father's. Under the table, she's using her toes to rub his calf.

Right there in the dining room. Anyone could glance

under the table and see what was happening: my mother, Josie's dad, anyone in the room. And I'm certain that Richie's mom notices. She takes a long sip of her wine and continues to puff on her cigarette, but she isn't smiling anymore, and she doesn't look at all relaxed.

My father keeps telling his story like nothing's going on at all. Only once, just for a moment, does his gaze flicker to Josie's mom. He flashes her a brief, knowing smile. Just for a second. But it's enough. I feel sick with understanding. All the rumors are true.

When my mom gets up to go into the kitchen, Josie's mom pulls her feet away from my dad's and tucks them underneath her chair. She hands her empty wineglass to my mom. "Lisa? Do you mind getting me a refill?"

"Sure thing." My mom takes Nicole's glass into the kitchen, along with her own.

"All right," she says to Richie's mom, "give me one of those cigarettes." She lights it quickly, takes a long, dramatic inhale. "Ahhh. That's the stuff." She's careful to blow the smoke out the cracked door, fanning the air with her free hand. "I don't know why Marshall gets so uptight about me smoking," she says. "He's got his precious cigars, and I don't hassle him about those."

"Speaking of Marshall," Richie's mom says, taking another gulp of wine, "how are you two doing?"

"Oh, you know. Fine, I guess. Why?"

"No reason. Nicole's up to her old tricks, that's all."

My mom closes her eyes. She takes another drag from her cigarette. "Is that so?"

"I'm sorry, Lisa. She's got some goddamned nerve, though, playing footsie with him right under your nose—"

"They're playing footsie?" my mom whispers.

Richie's mom nods. "You should do something. Get your claws out. He's your husband."

My mom stares at the floor. "That bitch."

"Why did you invite her? Why not stop spending time with them altogether? She's got her own marriage. She and Marshall dated for three years in high school, they broke up, he married you. End of story. If she wanted him so badly, she should have held on to him when she had the chance."

"Oh . . . I don't know. I almost feel like she can't help it. She gets drunk and then it's like she thinks it's okay to flirt." My mom glances over her shoulder, into the dining room. "Marshall would never do anything to hurt us. He's a good man."

"If you say so." Richie's mom flicks her cigarette into the yard. "But I'll tell you, Lisa . . ." Her stern expression fades. "I just want you to be happy. You look too thin. You're obviously stressed. You don't need someone flirting with your husband on top of everything else you're going through."

My mom flashes a weak smile. "It's only flirting. He's mine. And I was just at the doctor last week. I'm up almost two pounds!"

Richie's mom seems uncertain how to take the comment. "Is that a good thing, to you?"

My mom's smile wavers. "Yes." And she picks up a bottle of wine, heading back to the dining room. "Come on, now. Let's go play nice."

I've spent a lot of time at home since Alex left. My dad is rarely here—usually he's at the boat—and Nicole stays busy volunteering at the Spiritualist Church, doing whatever it is she does. Reading auras. Participating in séances. Keeping tabs on other women's husbands, just in case one of their wives might happen to die.

Like I've said before, the matter of Josie's paternity was never talked about in our house, even though I realize now it was always present, just beneath the surface. I was so young when I lost my mother, and I have always loved Josie. Nicole was never anything but kind to me. I might have grown up hearing rumors that she and my father had an affair, but I thought I knew better; I thought it was impossible. I never believed my father was capable of cheating on my mother.

Obviously, though, he was.

Seeing Nicole rubbing my father's foot under the table at the dinner party, right under my mother's nose, was sickening. Especially now that I know what stress can do to somebody who is already prone to an eating disorder. After all, when I became consumed with guilt over Alex's death, I stopped eating and threw myself into running. Everybody assumed I was just taking after my poor dead mother. Nobody put two and two together. If they had, everything might be different now. Well, not everything—Alex would still be dead. And it would still be all my fault.

With Alex gone, I feel desperate to find some closure to my wandering in this town. I keep expecting him to reappear, to offer a snarky comment about me or my friends, but after several days spent alone, watching, drifting in and out of memories from my childhood, it becomes clear that he's not coming back. Wherever he is, I hope it's beautiful. I hope it's peaceful. I hope it's kind.

It is a sunny afternoon. Josie and Nicole are in the kitchen, making egg frittatas. With *real* eggs. Even as a ghost, I cringe. The fat content (seven grams). The calorie count (seventy calories per egg). I don't think I'd eaten a whole egg since I was ten years old. Some things we learn from our parents simply become ingrained within us. My mother—my *real* mother—was horrified by fat. And so was I. Even before I killed Alex. There was a problem; I see it now. Nine-year-olds should not be counting fat grams. Nine-year-olds should be able to eat eggs. They should be allowed to like peanut butter.

Nicole gives her daughter a furtive smile. "This is nice. We haven't relaxed like this since . . . well, in ages." She winks. "Do you want a mimosa?"

"Mom!" Josie's cheeks flush. "Dad will be pissed."

"Dad isn't here, is he?" Nicole opens the fridge, removes

a carton of orange juice. She's popping a bottle of Moet when—as if on cue—my father walks in the front door.

"Shit!" Nicole murmurs. But she's giggling. The champagne bubbles over the side of the bottle, making puddles on the floor. She mixes two mimosas in champagne glasses (heavy on the champagne, light on the orange juice) and turns her attention back to the frittata, sipping her drink, pretending not to notice when my father shuffles into the kitchen.

He's wearing a button-down flannel shirt and gray sweatpants. His beard is thick and bushy enough for a family of squirrels to take up residence inside. He hasn't bothered with his contacts in months, not since I died, so he's wearing his glasses instead. He stands in the doorway to the kitchen, watching as my seventeen-year-old stepsister sips her mimosa and flicks through a copy of *Self* magazine.

Nicole has her back to my father. She sways lightly back and forth at the stove, her flowing, white cotton skirt swishing around her ankles. Her bare feet are smooth and tanned. She's wearing no fewer than three toe rings, and her toenails are bright blue. It's a ridiculous color for a grown woman.

"What are we cooking?" My father, I can tell, is making an attempt at normalcy. It's not working so great. He looks like he hasn't showered in days, if not weeks. He doesn't look like he should even be in the same *house* as Nicole and Josie, let alone the same room.

"A frittata." Nicole looks over her shoulder and smiles at him. "You should have some, honey. You've lost too much weight."

"Josie." My father's attention snaps to my stepsister. "What are you drinking?"

"It's just a mimosa." She takes a gulp. "There's almost no alcohol."

"I don't care. Throw it out."

"Marshall—" Nicole begins to protest, but before she can get a sentence out, my dad swoops toward Josie, picks up the glass, and tosses it into the sink.

When I say "tosses it into the sink," I don't mean that he dumps out the mimosa and places the glass gently aside. I mean he tosses the whole glass. Actually, he kind of throws it. The champagne flute shatters. A thick, angry silence permeates the entire room.

Finally, Nicole says, "I don't know what you did that for. It was one drink. It's not like I'm getting her plastered."

"In case you've forgotten," my dad says, his tone conversational but sarcastic, "just a few months ago, we agreed it was no big deal to allow a boat full of teenagers to have a few drinks to celebrate Elizabeth's birthday. And that didn't end so well."

Nicole stares at the floor. Josie pretends to study her magazine. The frittata begins to burn.

"Marshall." Nicole's voice is barely above a whisper. She starts to gather pieces of broken glass from the sink. "Things have to go back to normal sometime. We've talked about this. You have to work. We have to be a family. You can't sit on that boat, day after day, staring at the water—"

"I'm selling the house," my father announces.

Nicole's fingers slip. A shard of glass cuts deep into her index finger. Blood appears, bright and fast, dripping into the sink.

"Mom, are you okay?" Josie rushes toward Nicole to help her. She shoots a glare at my dad.

"I've already talked to a real estate agent. She'll be here later this afternoon to put up a sign."

"You're selling the house?" Nicole retorts, her finger wrapped in a paper towel. "Were you planning on discussing this with me? What about Josie? What about school? It's her senior year."

"Josie can finish out the school year. Then she'll be in college."

Nicole—whose glass is still intact, still almost full—finishes her drink in one long gulp.

Then she throws it into the sink. *Throws.* It breaks, just like Josie's.

"Where are we going to live, Marshall? What are we going to do?"

My dad removes his glasses. Beneath the frames, his eyes are shockingly tired: deep, dark circles; heavy lids; no shine at all to his once sparkly gaze.

He rubs his eyes. "I don't know. I don't know what will

happen to you and me, Nicole. I just know I can't live in this house anymore."

"That's just great." Nicole begins to cry. "Josie, go to your room."

"But Mom—"

"Go!"

Josie scurries down the hall and up the stairs, but she stops on the landing and sits quietly at the top of the steps, listening.

"I have done everything in my power to make you happy. I'm every bit as heartbroken as you are about Liz. You know that. Marshall, she was like a daughter to me. I loved her. I would do anything to bring her back."

"It isn't about that." My dad shakes his head. He crosses the room to Nicole, holds her injured hand in his own, applying pressure to the paper towel, where a bright spot of red is appearing against the white as it bleeds through. "Lately I've been feeling like this has all been a mistake."

Nicole breathes a sharp inhale. "What do you mean?"

"I mean all of it. You. Me. This family we've tried to create. It feels . . . it feels like some kind of Greek tragedy. I feel like we're being punished."

"We fell in love. We didn't do anything wrong."

"Do you know what this whole town is saying?" my dad asks. "What they've been saying for years? The Wilsons will barely look at us. If they were ever home, they would never have let Richie get within ten feet of Liz or Josie."

"I love you." Nicole looks desperately at my father. "You're the love of my life."

"I know." He pauses. "I know you think that."

She rests her head on his shoulder. She sobs quietly.

"I'm sorry," my dad says. "I don't think I can do it anymore. It's killing me, Nicole. Can you understand? Can't you see? It's killing me."

With Alex gone, I've found that the memories come more quickly, with less warning. It's like they're gaining momentum somehow. One minute I'm standing in my parents' kitchen, watching my dad and Nicole's marriage fall apart, and the next moment I'm standing in the kitchen at age seventeen, very much alive, picking at a bowl full of plain brown rice while the rest of my family stuffs their faces with Chinese takeout.

I stand up, pushing the bowl away. "I think I'll go for a run."

My dad and Nicole look at me, surprised. Josie continues to eat. I realize that I'm watching us shortly after Alex died, just when I started to go downhill. The guilt was already making me sick.

"It's nearly seven o'clock. It's dark," my dad says.

"I'll wear my reflective gear. You know I run at night sometimes."

"Yes, but Liz, you ran this morning before school. You ran after school for cross-country. Why do you need to go again?" My father's gaze drifts down my body. "You aren't trying to lose weight, are you? Because you don't need to. You're thin as a rail."

Josie pauses in midchew. She swallows. She still doesn't look up from her food.

"That isn't it. I'm just stressed. I won't be too long. See you soon, okay?" And I'm off, hurrying upstairs to change into my running clothes. As I watch myself heading down the hallway, I hear Nicole say, "She's probably going to meet Richie somewhere, Marshall. Don't worry about it."

My dad's voice is laced with concern. "If she wanted to meet Richie, she could go meet him. She wouldn't have to hide it from us. I think maybe she should see a counselor."

Knowing what I know now—the truth about why I was going running so much—I feel almost angry at my dad, at Nicole. Why *didn't* they make me see a counselor? Why didn't anyone try to help me?

Well—that's not entirely true. In his own way, my dad did try to help. It's just that I refused to be helped. I wanted to suffer. I wanted to be punished for what I did to Alex. I understand that now.

I've got a reflective vest that I'm supposed to wear anytime I run at dusk or later—or even during the day, if I'm running alongside the road—but as soon as I leave the house, I take it off and leave it beside the front porch. I can guess now what

I was thinking. Who cares if someone hits me? It would be karma, right?

First I run through town, weaving in and out of the streets lined with gorgeous old houses. Then I make my way down the beach, all the way to the tip of the shoreline, turning around to run back down the road, crossing the tiny bridge and making the right that begins the five-mile trek into Mystic. As usual, I feel pained that I can't follow by actually running alongside the memory of myself; I can only watch it unfold like a vivid dream as my feet throb in their boots. If I go the whole way to Mystic and back, it'll be past nine p.m. by the time I get home. I'll have run over ten miles today, which is a lot, probably too much. It's obvious that I don't care.

I'm about a third of the way into Mystic when a car approaches behind me, slows to a crawl, and finally comes to a stop. The driver winds down his passenger-side window.

"Liz," he says, keeping his voice low. "Liz Valchar. Get your butt in the car."

It's Mr. Riley.

But I don't stop. Clearly I don't want to. The thing about running is that it empties your head. I don't want to think about anything—not all the signs I'll pass in Mystic, posters of Alex Berg offering a reward for any information leading to the arrest of whoever killed him. Not the fact that even Richie—who I am closer to in this world than *anyone*—doesn't know what happened, and never can. I don't want to think about whether or not what I've done makes me a murderer. I don't want to think, period.

So I just shake my head at Mr. Riley and keep running. He lets his car roll along beside me, following, the window still down.

"Where are your reflectors? Are you trying to get yourself killed? Did you run this morning, too? What are you doing, Liz?"

"Leave me alone." Still running, I glance over at him. He continues to follow me.

"What are you doing out here, anyway?" I ask.

"Trying to get Hope to fall asleep. And if you don't get in, I'll have to yell at you, and it'll wake her up." He smiles. "You want that on your conscience?"

Watching us together, the irony of his joke makes me feel a little bit sick to my stomach. But I've known him for years. He's persistent; it's one of the things that makes him a great coach. And since I'm not wearing anything reflective, there's no way he'll let me keep running out here in the dark. I understand all of that. So I get in.

For a brief moment, Hope stirs in her car seat. Then, before she even cracks her eyes open to see what the noise is about, she's asleep again.

"So . . . you're just driving around with your baby?" I ask.

He half smiles. "If you were a parent, you'd understand. Kids—well, babies—you put them in motion, they're out cold in like ten seconds. But otherwise, she doesn't sleep well. My wife is about to lose her mind. Hope is up at all hours of the night and then she's awake almost all day. I'm doing my best to help. But then I find you out here. What are you thinking? I could barely see you. You know better than to go running at night like that."

Even though his car isn't very warm, I'm sweaty as hell. Once my body begins to cool off, I start to visibly shiver. It's clear that I do *not* want to have this conversation with him right now.

"You couldn't see me?" I ask.

"Barely. I could see someone. The first thing I thought is, 'Who the hell is that jackass running at night without anything reflective?'"

"So how did you even know it was me?"

He reaches over to tug my long blond ponytail. He smiles. "Do you have to ask? The hair."

"Oh." I pull my knees close to my chest. "Can you take me home?"

"Why? So you can turn around and head out again?"

I hesitate. For a second, it seems like I'm considering lying to him, just to get him to leave me alone. But I can tell from my thoughtful, serious expression that there's a small part of me that wants him to know something is not right. There's a small part of me that needs to tell someone *something*, to reveal even the smallest hint that my world has been knocked off its axis.

"Yes," I say to Mr. Riley. "If you take me home, I'm just going to turn around and start running again."

"Why?" He squints at my body in the darkness of the car. We're driving slowly toward Mystic. Even though it's dark, the road is still thick with tourist traffic from the fall foliage. "Are you trying to lose weight? Because if you are—"

"I'm not starving myself," I say. "I eat." I pause. "It's important to stay in control, that's all."

"There's control and there's starvation. And there are different kinds of starvation, Liz. There's food starvation and there's exercise starvation. Some people are better at one or the other." He glances at me again. "And some people are good at both."

I lean back in my seat. I turn my head to look at him. "I'm not trying to lose weight. Don't worry about me."

"I am worried about you." He makes a left, into the hills of Mystic, as though he's going to turn the car around. "I'm taking you home. And if you try to go out running again, I'll knock on your door and have a talk with your parents."

My voice is small. "Can you drop me off at Richie's house? He's two doors down. I'll feel better if I can just talk to him for a while tonight." I know now that I'm not going to tell Richie anything, but I understand that I just want to see him, to hear his voice, to feel his arms around me. Richie has always brought me so much comfort. Even now, in death.

"Richie Wilson is no good for you, Liz. Anybody could tell you that." Mr. Riley shakes his head. "I ought to have a talk with your parents about *him*. Do they know what he does . . . recreationally?"

I feign innocence. "What? You mean, do they know he's at the top of his class? That he wants to be a writer someday? That his favorite poet is John Keats and his favorite book is *Catcher in the Rye*? Yes, they know how amazing Richie is."

"Okay. I get it. Liz Valchar, popular girl. No time for a heart-to-heart with her coach. You want to break all the rules? Go running at night without the right gear, date a drug dealer— fine. You won't get away with whatever you want forever." He stares at me as he turns onto the main street in Mystic, heading back toward Noank. "You know that, right?"

He's so insightful that, if I could touch him now, I'd almost want to slap him. Instead, my living self has to blink, fast, again and again, to keep from crying.

We drive almost the rest of the way in silence. As we're turning onto High Street, Mr. Riley says, "Liz, are you sure there isn't anything you want to talk about?"

This was before I started running to his house, I realize. Before he decided that, whatever was wrong, it was too huge for him to let into his life.

I take a deep breath. I wipe my eyes. "It's this one, on the right," I say. "Two houses before mine."

He pulls to a stop in front of Richie's house. The only light is coming from my boyfriend's bedroom. Richie's front window is open. He's sitting in the frame, one leg perched against the side, smoking a cigarette.

"What a class act. Quite a catch you've got yourself there." Mr. Riley pauses. "So we're here. I guess I'll see you tomorrow."

"I guess so."

"You're sure there isn't anything—"

"There is," I say. "But not yet. Okay?"

He nods. "Okay."

I open the door to get out, but before I've even got a foot out the door, Mr. Riley puts a hand on my shoulder. "Liz, my God."

"What?" The light is on in the car, since I've opened the door, and he's peering at me with disbelief. "What is it? Why are you looking at me like that?"

He reaches toward me, takes a lock of my hair between his fingers. "I'll be damned," he murmurs. He holds up the strand from my ponytail to show me. "You're going gray."

Twenty-three

Periodically—every few days or so—Joe Wright makes a visit to Vince Aiello's apartment, ostensibly to check up on him and make sure Richie has been leaving him alone. It's a condition of Richie's probation that he can't get within five hundred feet of Vince, but Vince doesn't exactly seem like the type to go calling the cops over a breach in proximity.

I've never believed, not for a moment, that I was legitimately seeing Vince. Now that I know I was the one who killed Alex, it seems clear enough what must have happened. Somehow, Vince figured out that my car was involved in the accident that night, and that's why he was blackmailing me. Knowing what I know now, the explanation seems obvious enough. But as far as I can tell, Joe doesn't know any of that— how could he? And even though I can put the pieces together well enough, I still don't have any solid memories to confirm everything I suspect.

Even when the memories come—if they come at all—what will I do with them? There's not much I can prove from beyond the grave. There's nobody to tell. Not even Alex.

It's a rainy Tuesday evening in mid-November when Joe pops in on Vince at his apartment. I saw him leaving the police station, and I had a gut feeling that I should follow him. I was right—he went directly to the Covington Arms.

It's been about a week since my dad announced that he was putting the house up for sale, and since then things at home have been grim, to say the least. My dad is living on the boat pretty much full-time. He still isn't working. Josie is going to school, and Nicole is packing boxes—but to go where? I don't know if they'll get a divorce or if they'll all simply move away together—I don't know anything. I feel lost. I *am* lost.

Vince is watching the Nature Channel, engrossed in some kind of documentary on elephants. He's by himself, except for his dog, Rocky, who sits at Vince's feet, head on his paws, asleep. Apparently, the guy's a real animal lover. It occurs to me that knowing the difference between good and evil is tricky this way: it isn't nearly as obvious as I'd like to believe. Here is Vince, who I know is a bad guy, watching elephants as they play in puddles of water, a small grin of appreciation on his face. He isn't doing anything overtly distasteful: he isn't looking at a *Playboy* or getting high. A person's character, I realize, is never black-and-white. There is so much gray.

When Joe knocks at the door, Vince glances toward the sound, clearly annoyed at being interrupted. Even though he isn't doing anything awful, I hate being in this place; I'd rather be pretty much anywhere else. But I don't feel like I have much of a choice. I have to hear what they say. I have to remember. Even if it doesn't make any difference, I have to know exactly what happened. It's the only way I can possibly imagine that I'll ever get out of here, beyond this life, to wherever Alex is—and maybe to my mother.

Vince is practically hacking up a lung as he opens the door, a freshly lit cigarette dangling from between his lips.

"Oh, it's you." His sarcasm is obvious. "What a pleasant surprise."

"Well, I figured you'd be missing me by now." Joe leans in the doorway. Cops, I've learned, are like vampires; they can't come in unless you invite them. I guess if they have good enough reason they can barge on in without permission, but so far Vince has been cool as a cucumber with Joe.

Vince glances at the television. "I'm kind of in the middle of something." He coughs again. "I'm taking it easy today. Think I might be getting the flu."

"Well, I hear chain-smoking's good for that," Joe says.

"Uh-huh. Look, Richie Wilson ain't here. He hasn't been bothering me. You don't have to keep coming over like this. I can take care of myself."

"Yeah, I'm sure you can." Joe glances past Vince into the disgusting apartment. His gaze lingers on the elephants, who are now charging through a barren landscape on the TV screen. "Can I come in?"

Vince narrows his eyes. "Why?"

"I have a few questions."

"About what?"

"About Liz Valchar." Joe crosses his arms. "She was special to you, wasn't she? Don't you want to do all you can to help with her case?" I notice he doesn't use the words "close" or "solve" or "murder."

Vince wipes his runny nose with the back of his sleeve. " 'Course I do. Sure. Come on in."

They sit down on the sofa. Joe settles in, makes himself comfortable, and waits for Vince to give him his full attention before he begins the conversation.

But before Joe has a chance to say anything, Vince starts. "I was under the impression that her case was, you know, already closed. She fell, right? I mean, that's what you told me."

"Sure, that's what we think happened. But it's my job to be thorough."

"Well, I got an alibi if you need one. I mean, I loved her. I wouldn't have killed her. You looking at Richie Wilson at all for this? You think maybe he pushed her?"

Joe peers at him. "You loved her?"

"Well . . . yeah."

"I thought Richie loved her. He says she was the love of his life. Isn't that why he wanted to kill you? For having an affair with her?"

"Aw, I don't know, man. The kid's obviously all screwed up. You're asking the wrong guy. His girl messes around with someone else—someone like me—he's bound to go off the deep end." Vince nods to himself, his head bobbing up and down in a furious motion. "Yeah, it makes sense. It all makes sense now that you mention it. I mean, the guy's a fucking drug dealer. He's nuts."

"He's *your* drug dealer," Joe says.

Vince hesitates. "Well. Yeah." Then his lips curl into a small, slow grin. "But not anymore."

Vince isn't even making any sense. He's so obviously lying that I can't believe Joe doesn't arrest him right now, or at least call him out. He might have been messing around with me, but he definitely didn't *love* me. That much is clear.

But all Joe does is open his trusty wire-bound notebook and start looking over his notes.

"You said you started dating Liz about a year ago?"

"Ummm . . . yeah, that's right."

"And you were still seeing her up until the time she died?"

"Yeah. Yes. I already told you all this, man."

"Okay, that's fine. It's just—well, I'm just wondering what the two of you did for fun."

Vince's eyes flash in defiance. "You can imagine, I'm sure."

"All right. You had sex?"

"Sure did."

We *didn't*. I'm certain of it.

"And she . . . enjoyed herself."

"Obviously." Vince flashes his creepy smile again.

"Why do you think that is, Vince? I don't mean to be rude, but a guy like you, a girl like Elizabeth Valchar . . . you know, it doesn't quite add up."

Vince shrugs. "They call it slumming. You ever hear of it? You ever hear that Billy Joel song 'Uptown Girl'?" And he starts snapping his fingers, humming the melody.

"Here's the thing, Vince. Did you and Liz ever go to the movies? To a restaurant? What I mean is, did you two go on any real dates?"

Vince shakes his head. "She liked to stay in. If you get my drift."

"Right. So nobody ever saw you two together."

"That's the way she wanted it. I told you, I was her dirty little secret."

Joe sighs. For the first time, I notice he has a manila envelope tucked underneath his right arm. He takes it out, lays it on the coffee table. "I think you're lying to me, Vince. Want to know why?"

Vince frowns. "Why?"

"Because I've spent a lot of time talking to Richie. He's told me things about Liz. I've talked to her family. I've talked to her friends. Did you ever meet any of her friends?"

Vince shakes his head. "I told you, it wasn't that kind of a relationship."

"I understand. Liz had her secrets." Joe is almost smiling—but not quite. "You know what's funny about secrets, Vince? They don't keep very well. No matter how hard a person tries, somebody always gets a clue." He takes a long, even breath. "Liz had a friend named Caroline. I talked to her for a long time yesterday."

"Oh yeah?" Vince stares straight ahead. "Must have been some good conversation."

"Yes, it was. This friend, Caroline, she'd been worried about Liz for a while before she died. Caroline knew something was wrong, but she didn't know exactly what it was." He nods to himself. "She had quite a guess, though."

The two of them are silent for a moment as Joe waits for any response from Vince. But he just sits there, unmoving, unwilling to break even as the truth is unraveling.

"Anyway," Joe continues, "I've been learning everything possible about Liz for months, and I just don't buy the idea that she would want anything to do with a guy like you. I think she was seeing you against her will. I think you had information about her that she would have done anything to keep secret." He pauses. "Does the name Alex Berg mean anything to you?"

Vince nibbles a hangnail. "Nope."

"Really? That's odd. Because when I was interviewing Richie over at the station, he mentioned something to me.

He told me he'd been going for runs around Noank, thinking about Liz. And he told me that almost every time he went running he ended up at the same place. Alex Berg's house."

"So?" Vince demands, a tad defensive. "What does any of that have to do with me?"

"I didn't think it had anything to do with you, not at first. But it kept bothering me. I felt like it all had to fit together somehow—you, Liz, Alex, Richie, Caroline—I just didn't know how, not exactly." Joe nods at the coffee table. "I want you to look in that envelope now."

I literally *clap my hands*. "Yes!" I shout, standing on tiptoe despite the searing pain in my toes. "Yes! You've got it! You did it!"

With shaky hands, Vince opens the manila envelope. Inside, I'm expecting to see the same photographs of myself that have turned my stomach so many times already.

Except that's not what we're looking at.

Alex stares up at us. He is just as I remember seeing him that night: wet, bloody, broken, dead. Seeing him now isn't any easier.

Vince is silent as he shuffles through the photos. After Alex, there are five different shots of his bicycle: mangled, twisted, thrown far from his body.

"What are these?" Vince asks. His voice trembles—just a smidge, but it's enough.

"Keep looking." Joe's tone is light, almost conversational. "The next one is the one you'll really want to pay attention to."

It's a shot of Alex's bike, close up. Immediately, I know what Joe is referring to. On the back pedal, so small that it's almost invisible, there's a smear of red.

"See that?" Joe asks.

Vince nods. "Blood. So what?"

"It's not blood. It's paint."

Vince lets the photos drop into his lap. "It's like I told you already. I don't know what any of this has to do with me."

"According to you—to *you*, Vince—one week after this boy, Alex Berg, was killed by a hit-and-run driver, you fixed Elizabeth's car for her. You told me yourself that's how you met her. Remember? She didn't want to file a claim. She wanted it done quick. And she wanted to keep it quiet. Is that right?"

Vince only nods.

"I think you noticed something while you were fixing her car. I think you figured out—just like I did—that she was the one who killed this boy. It was raining the night he got hit. Liz probably checked out her car, looking for blood, looking for some indication that she'd been a part of the accident. But she didn't check the *underside* of her front fender, did she?"

Vince bites his lip hard. He doesn't say anything.

"I think you found paint from Alex Berg's bicycle underneath her bumper. You knew she was responsible for his death. I think you were blackmailing her. What did you do? Threaten to go to the cops if she didn't sleep with you?"

Vince sniffles. He looks like a caged animal. "That little

bitch," he says, "treated me like I wasn't even as good as the dirt on the bottom of her goddamn shoe."

"Tell me what happened," Joe says. "Come on. Ease your conscience."

Vince licks his lips. He *smiles.* "Sorry to say," he tells Joe, "I ain't got a fucking conscience."

"I'm sure you don't." Joe stands, reaches for his cuffs. "Get up. You're under arrest."

I realize what the memory is almost as soon as it appears before me: I'm standing in Richie's room, asking him to come with me while I pick up my car from Fender Benders.

But Richie is unavailable to drive me to Vince's repair shop.

"I have homework," he tells me apologetically as I stand in his room, pouting.

"What kind of homework? Richie, it will take an hour, there and back. Come *on*." I've got his keys dangling in my hand. I'm all dolled up, ready to go. But I can't take his car, not unless he comes with me. I won't have a way to get it back.

"I'm writing a paper for lit class. It's on *Macbeth*. Want to read what I have so far? It was only supposed to be ten pages, and I've already got an outline for twelve pages. It's going to be really good, Liz."

I frown. I look like I'm about to cry. Obviously, he doesn't understand the gravity of the situation. "Richie. Who cares about *Macbeth*?"

"I do. I care." Richie pauses. "Have you even read the play yet?"

I actually stomp my foot in agitation. "You know I'm more of a CliffsNotes kind of girl, Richie. It's just a stupid play."

"Liz, I'm sorry. The paper's due tomorrow. You haven't started yours yet, have you?"

What I understand now—and what Richie didn't know then, and still doesn't know—is that I have much, *much* bigger things to worry about. I have to get my car back before my parents ever notice it was gone. Besides, I can probably talk my way into getting an extension on the paper.

Richie runs a hand through his messy hair. "Can't we pick the car up tomorrow? I'll give you a ride after school, I promise."

"It has to be today!" I'm almost shrieking, clearly frantic to get my car back. "Richie, I know you think I'm being prissy and ridiculous, but I need your help. Please."

"Liz, I don't *think* you're being prissy and ridiculous. I *know* you're being prissy and ridiculous. Here." He puts his hand into his pocket, pulls out a fistful of change and dollar bills. "This is more than enough. Take the bus. It'll be like a ten-minute ride."

My mouth falls open. "Take the bus?" I repeat. "Who the hell do I look like to you? Do I look like a homeless person? What if someone tries to accost me? What if we get held up? Haven't you ever seen that movie with the woman on the bus where there's a bomb?"

"You mean *Speed?*" He snorts. "Yes. Liz, there won't be a bomb." He takes a step closer to me. He touches my hair. He kisses me on the lips. "I think it will be good for you. It will be broadening. You go ahead and take the bus, honey, and when you get back, you can come tell me all about how horrible it was."

I don't have a choice, do I? I take the money from his outstretched hand. "Oh, trust me. I'll tell you all about it." As I start to leave the room, I call over my shoulder, "If I make it back alive!"

So here I am: alone on a Sunday afternoon in the still-deserted Fender Benders garage. Just before I left, I tried to talk Josie into coming with me, but there was no way she would take the bus. Surprisingly, it wasn't that bad. Almost everyone looked normal. Relatively normal. You know—for the bus.

My car is parked outside the garage. It appears good as new. As I'm looking it over, Vince strolls up to me with Rocky the bulldog in tow. Rocky, I notice, is not on a chain or a leash.

"I just want my keys," I tell him. "I have to get home."

Vince nods. Rocky stares at me, threads of slobber hanging from his gums. I try smiling at the dog, but it only makes him bark loudly.

"So . . . my keys. Where are they?"

Vince leans against my car, his filthy coveralls pressing

right up against the shiny red paint. Even though I know I didn't have much of a choice, I still can't believe I came here alone. I can't believe *Richie* let me come here alone. On a bus. Knowing myself, I'm certain that he is so going to hear about this later, whether he has a paper to finish or not.

"This might surprise you," Vince begins, wiggling his pinky finger in his ear, "but I'm a big fan of the local news."

I cross my arms. "So? What, do you read the papers, too? Good for you. Give me my keys."

"Matter of fact, I do read the paper. That surprises you, don't it? Bet you thought I was illiterate."

I swallow the gum I've been chewing. Even though I've got a full face of makeup, even though my hair is perfectly styled, there's an ashen look to my face, and my eyes are bloodshot. I wouldn't be surprised if I'd barely slept at all the night before. I imagine I might have stayed up, scanning old yearbooks for more photos of Alex Berg. I picture myself poring over them, studying his face, trying to replace the image of him that had already been burned into my brain: bloody face, desperate eyes, trembling mouth gasping for that final, horrible breath.

"I didn't assume you were illiterate." Why am I even having this conversation with him? I should snatch the keys from his filthy hand—they're right there, less than an arm's reach away—and get out of here.

"Anyway, it's the funniest damn thing. You know, last

week, a kid in your town got killed riding his bike home
from work. They just found his body a couple of days ago.
You hear about that?"

I put a hand on my stomach. I'm probably nauseated;
watching myself interact with Vince, I'd be surprised if I
weren't sick to my stomach. I probably should have eaten
that morning, but I'm guessing I didn't.

Control. It's all about control. Or—I realize now—the illusion of being in control. I probably won't let myself eat lunch
after I get home from this encounter with Vince, either.
Instead, maybe I'll go for a long run. That is, after I finish
chewing out Richie.

"I heard all about it," I say, doing my best to keep my
tone light. "It was a hit-and-run. It was terrible. What does
that have to do with anything?"

"Well, it has to do with a lot, Liz. Or is it Elizabeth? Can
I call you Elizabeth?"

"No."

"All right, Elizabeth. Let me cut to the chase." His lips
curl into a satisfied grin. "You hit that boy, didn't you? I knew
you were lying about hitting a parking meter, that's for damn
sure. Didn't make any sense at all." He scoffs. "What kind of
idiot hits a parking meter? And with their right front fender?"
Vince shakes his head. "Nope. Didn't make sense."

My whole body is shaking. Gum, bile, whatever's in my
stomach—I'm sure it's all churning now. "You're wrong. I
didn't hit him."

"Well, whoever was driving your car is the one who hit him. I'm damn sure of that. See, Elizabeth, even though this was under-the-table work, I'm in the habit of taking pictures of my repairs. It's become automatic over the years. And while I was taking photos, I noticed *this*." He pulls a printed photograph from his back pocket and hands it to me. It's a picture of the underside of my front fender. There, in a spot I didn't notice when I inspected the car myself, is a spot of blue paint, surrounded by several small scratches on the Mustang.

"Blue," Vince says, as though any explanation is necessary. "Blue like the kid's bike. Am I right?"

We stare at each other. I can actually see myself shaking, my bottom lip trembling. None of this would be happening if Richie were here—would it? Wouldn't he protect me? But he's not here, and I'm all alone with Vince and his ugly dog, and he can do anything he wants to me. Anything. This is worse than a bomb on a bus. This is a nightmare. And there's a part of me that knows I deserve it. I killed someone. People don't just get away with a thing like that. Not even people like me.

"What do you want?" I ask.

Vince smiles again. "Lots of things. We'll start with five hundred bucks. You can bring it to my apartment later this week." His eyes graze my body. "No. Not later this week. Make it tomorrow. Maybe you and I can have some fun, too. What do you think?"

"Five hundred dollars," I say. "That's all. Nothing else."

Vince raises a single eyebrow. "I don't think you get to

make the rules anymore, Elizabeth. Five hundred bucks. You and that hot little body of yours, at my place, alone. Tomorrow. Or else I go to the cops and show them this picture. You don't want that, do you?"

I shake my head. I'm crying.

Vince hands me my keys. "I'm at the Covington Arms. Apartment number nine. I'll see you tomorrow, you beautiful bitch."

I pull over twice on the highway back to Noank, veering right off the road to an onslaught of car horns and lovely gestures from my fellow drivers. I am crying so hard, shaking so violently, that I have to pull over for a third time before I reach my street in order to compose myself. What choice did I have? Aside from doing what Vince wanted—which is what I know I ended up doing anyway—the only other option is to confess that I'm responsible for Alex's death. I know I can come up with the money easily enough, but I can tell I'm terrified by the idea of what he might want from me physically. At the very least, I know I won't have sex with him. I'm a virgin, for God's sake. I'm saving myself for Richie. I will not sleep with Vince Aiello. I did not sleep with Vince Aiello.

I manage to collect myself well enough that, when I pull into my driveway and see Richie smoking out his window, I wave at him and force a weak smile.

"You made it," he calls. "You're alive." He grins. "I take it there was no bomber on the bus?"

I shake my head.

"Want to come over? I'm almost done with my first draft. I'd love for you to read it." He tosses his cigarette butt onto the lawn. "You might learn something about *Macbeth*. It's a really great story. You'd actually like it, I think."

I shade my eyes, staring at him. "I'm going to go for a run," I call.

"Again?" He frowns. "Weren't you already out this morning?"

"It's cross-country season." I shrug. It's a flimsy explanation.

"Oh. Well, you'll come over later, then?" He looks at the Mustang. "The car looks great, by the way."

"Yeah, it does. And sure, I'll stop by later. Tonight. Okay?"

"All right." He stands up, moves to close the window. As an afterthought, he says, "Hey, I'm sorry I didn't go with you. But it was all right, wasn't it? Vince doesn't bite."

I close my eyes. I look like I might start crying again. "You were right," I say. "It was fine."

"Good. Love you, Liz."

"I love you, too."

Inside the house, Josie is half-asleep on the living room sofa. An open can of diet soda rests on the coffee table, along with a half-eaten bowl of popcorn. She's watching some stupid reality TV show while simultaneously attempting to read *Macbeth*. I notice she's barely past the first few pages. Looking at her now, it doesn't surprise me. Richie is the only person I know who loves Shakespeare. I remember that, before I died, it always put me to sleep. Apparently, it has the same effect on Josie.

"Hey." I shake her awake, hard. "We have to talk. Now."

"What?" She sits up, groggy. "Did you get the car? Is it fixed?"

"Come up to my room."

"Mom and Dad aren't back yet. We can talk here."

"No," I say, insistent. "My room. Now."

Once I finish telling her everything, she sits cross-legged on my bed, her eyes wide. "Christ," she murmurs. "What are you going to do, Liz?"

"I don't know. What choice do I have? I'm going to pay him."

"And you're going to do . . . whatever else he wants?"

I don't say anything.

"What about Richie?" she prompts. "If you do anything with Vince, that'll be like cheating on him."

I cringe at the word "cheating." "It won't be like that. I don't have a choice. Josie . . . you were in the car, too." I close my eyes for a minute. "It doesn't seem fair."

She takes a deep breath. She nods. "I guess it's not. But Liz . . . you were driving."

My mouth drops open. "That's not fair, Josie. You were the one who didn't want to call for help."

Josie shakes her head. "It wouldn't have mattered. He would have died anyway."

"Maybe." I pause. "But I still can't stop thinking about it. I'd do anything to take it back."

"But you can't take it back. It happened, and now you have to do this, or else we're both in deep shit. Just—just go over there tomorrow and give him the money, and that will be the end of it. Okay? Then we can put it all behind us."

I stare at her. "What about Alex? What about his family? They aren't going to put it behind them. Josie, we ruined their lives. We killed him."

She bites her lip. She's quiet for a long time. Finally, she says, "Liz, we didn't kill him. You did. All I did was get into the car with you."

"I'm so sorry," I say, beginning to cry again. "I'm sorry I got you into this mess, I'm sorry about Alex . . . maybe I should just go to the cops, you know? Maybe I should turn myself in. I don't know if I can do this, Josie. I don't think I can do what Vince wants. I don't know what he expects, but whatever it is—"

"No! You have to do what he wants. Liz, just get it over with." She reaches toward me, strokes my blond locks with her small hand. One of her fingernails catches in my hair, and I wince as she tugs it free. "You have to do it, Liz. You can't tell anyone what happened. Nobody. Not the police, not Richie, nobody. Understand?"

I nod.

"We would be in so much trouble. It would ruin our lives, too, and what's the point in that?" She's almost breathless. "I'm looking out for you," she says. "I'm your best friend." Josie smiles weakly. "We're sisters. I promise, nothing bad is going to happen to you. I won't let it. This will all be over soon."

Twenty-four

The news of Vince's arrest—for blackmail, extortion, and sexual exploitation of a minor—spreads almost instantaneously. It is on the morning news. I see it at Richie's house, where he and his parents watch in amazement, all three of them silent and stunned as they stare at the television.

"That poor boy's family," Mrs. Wilson says. She's talking about Alex.

Mr. Wilson is putting on his coat. On the news, there's no mention of anything specific about the night Alex was killed—like the fact that I wasn't alone. And, at least according to the morning anchor, my death is still accidental. It was a terrible end to a horrible tragedy that stretched over the course of an entire year.

"I assumed Liz had some issues with food," Mrs. Wilson says. "I guess I just thought, with her mother's history . . ."

"It made sense." Mr. Wilson is ready to head out the door. "She was wasting away." He tugs at his wife's elbow. "Now we know, don't we? See what a guilty conscience can do to you?" he says to Richie. Richie doesn't nod. He doesn't move. He just stares at the television. In his head, I can tell, the pieces are all falling together. Just like they've been coming together for me all night, ever since I watched Joe Wright take Vince Aiello off to jail.

"Your father and I are going into the city. Just for the morning," Mrs. Wilson says. She peers at her son. "Richard? Are you okay?"

He nods slowly.

"Say something," she demands.

He clears his throat. "I'm okay. I mean . . . yeah. I'm just shocked, that's all."

"I know. It's horrible." She shudders. "But the Valchars are moving away now. That's good. So. Your father and I will be home later today, and there's grocery money for you in the kitchen. Will you be all right by yourself?"

Richie nods again.

In a gentler tone, Mrs. Wilson says, "Please call if you need anything. We're only a phone call away. We love you." She musses his hair. I close my eyes, imagining how it feels to run my fingers through those curls.

"And whatever you do," Mrs. Wilson says as she and her husband are heading out the door, "do not go over to the Valchar house. You are not to see Josie under any circumstances. Do you understand me?"

Richie doesn't say anything.

"Richard. I want an answer from you."

"Yes, Mom. I understand."

He waits until his parents have pulled out of their driveway. He watches from the window as their car makes a left off of High Street. Then he walks right out the front door, down the sidewalk, and straight to my old house.

Josie is sitting among boxes. The television is off. It's a Saturday, so there's no school, and I can only imagine how my classmates will be buzzing on Monday morning. I wonder if they'll rescind my homecoming crown. The notion makes me think of Alex, of our dance together, and our time onstage. In spite of everything, I smile. They can take the crown. I never deserved it in the first place.

Richie walks in without knocking. Josie is home alone. My father is at the boat, of course, and Nicole is nowhere to be found.

He stands in the doorway to the living room. Josie is sitting on the floor, her back against the sofa, looking through an old photo album.

"Did you hear the news?" Richie asks.

"No news in this house. I'm cut off from the world. We've got no Internet, and Dad canceled my cell plan. Cable's off, too. Why?"

"They arrested Vince Aiello for blackmail. A bunch of other stuff, too. They know Liz is the one who hit Alex Berg."

I can actually see the color fading as it drains from Josie's face. "What?" she asks, her voice laced with a hint of panic.

"Yeah." Richie nods. "It's all over the news. The cops are probably talking to all our friends right now. Josie," he says, "that was the night you two drove home from Caroline's, wasn't it? I remember it happening. It was just a few days later when Liz came to me about her car. The cops are going to figure it out, Josie. They're going to find out you were in the car with her that night. You're going to be in some kind of trouble."

Josie puts her head down. Her hands clench the corners of the photo album. "I wasn't driving, though," she says. "I didn't do anything wrong."

"You knew what happened and you didn't tell anyone. It's a crime."

"I was a minor," she protests. "I still *am* a minor. What are they going to do, throw me in prison? I didn't know how to fix things. What was I supposed to do, Richie? Turn in my own sister? It was horrible enough when—" She stops. She shuts her mouth.

"When what?" Richie takes a step into the room.

"Nothing." Josie shakes her head. "It was just horrible, that's all. It's all so horrible."

"You were her best friend," Richie says. "She told you what Vince was doing, didn't she?"

Josie doesn't say anything.

"You showed me those pictures. You let me believe she was cheating on me. You knew I would break up with her eventually. You knew I would confront her. And when I did, what would she say? She wasn't going to tell me what happened. You did it all on purpose, just to . . . to what, Josie? To steal me from her? I loved her. I still love her."

Josie's look is pained. "You love *me*," she whispers. "And I love you. We have a love story. It's like my mom and dad. We're supposed to be together. She didn't deserve you."

"What she *didn't* deserve was to die. She didn't deserve what Vince did to her. But if you think she didn't deserve me, then you didn't really know her at all." Richie shakes his head. "Josie, there's no love story here. I care about you. I don't want to see you get into any more trouble, but it's unavoidable at this point. I wouldn't be surprised if the cops are on their way over here right now. You're gonna have to face up to what happened."

My sister wipes her eyes. "You're right. I guess I will."

"I just wish . . . God, I just wish so badly that Liz had confessed. I wish she'd gone straight to the cops that night, you know? Maybe she'd still be alive. Maybe everything would be different."

Josie gets a faraway look in her eyes. "Maybe."

I begin to feel dizzy. So dizzy, in fact, that without thinking about it, I reach toward Richie for balance.

As soon as we make contact, his entire frame stiffens. For the first time since I've touched him after my death, I'm certain that he can feel it, too. He might not know that it's me, but he knows that it's *something*.

"Richie?" Josie asks, sniffling, still crying. "What's wrong? You seem weird."

He shakes his head. I pull away from him. I still feel dizzy, but I've managed to right myself in my boots—these *damn* boots—and slide to the floor beside Josie. The room is almost spinning. I feel like I could pass out. I take deep breaths, struggling to regain my bearings.

"What are you looking at?" Richie asks. He still seems rattled from my touch.

"Nothing. An old photo album. It's from way before my mom got divorced. It's my baby album."

"Baby pictures, huh? Can I see?" I can tell that he's only making conversation. He wants to get out of my house. He wants to get away from Josie. But Richie is a nice guy—he isn't just going to up and leave her alone, not like this.

"Sure. Sit down."

The three of us are on the floor together, Josie seated in the middle. She's looking at photos of herself as a newborn, in her mother's arms. Nicole and her first husband look so thrilled to be with their baby daughter. There are no hints of discontent in their eyes, no outward signs that they are anything but a happy family.

Even as a newborn, Josie was wide eyed. She gazes at the camera. A shock of red hair covers her head.

In an instant, I remember. I understand. Here it is: the last piece of the puzzle.

"That's weird," Richie says.

"What?" Josie rests her hand on his leg like it's the most natural thing in the world.

It is like someone has flipped a switch and turned on the lights. Everything is clear now. Everything makes sense. Of course. This is the truth. It's always been here, waiting for me to remember.

Get out! I want to scream. But instead, almost instinctively, I reach across Josie's body and grab Richie's arm. I'm doubtful that it will work, but I have to try. I want him to know. I want him to realize. I need him to understand what I know I am about to see.

"Beware of the redhead in disguise," Richie says. "Isn't that what you told me the psychic said to Liz? At the Spiritualist Church you guys went to?"

"Oh. Yeah, I guess so." Josie takes her hand off of Richie's leg. "But I only had red hair until I was like four. As I got older, it turned into . . . well, this." She tugs at her dirty-blond locks. "I've been dyeing it for years."

"But you had it once," Richie says. He's staring at her.

I hold on to him as tightly as possible. Focusing. Concentrating. *Please,* I think, *please remember. We're connected. Show me. Show him.*

It's after midnight. Almost everybody else on the *Elizabeth* is asleep. Everyone except Josie and me.

"Our friends are lightweights," she complains, taking a long swig from an almost-empty beer bottle. "Can you believe they didn't even stay awake for your real birthday? What do we have, less than two hours to go?"

I stand up. I'm clearly dizzy, unsteady on my feet. "I need air," I tell her, stepping onto the deck of the boat. "Come out with me."

We climb down the steps linking the boat to the dock and stand on the rickety wooden surface together. The night is silent, all of our friends sleeping inside. I'm almost eighteen years old, and I am in the biggest mess of trouble.

"We need to talk, Josie," I tell her.

She gives me a doubtful look. "About what?"

"You know what. Alex. What we did. I can't do it anymore," I say. "Not for one more day."

My stepsister's expression shifts to alarm. "What did you say?"

My speech is a little bit slurred. "I'm going to tell Mr. Riley what happened, Josie. I don't know what I'll do after that. Probably go to the police."

She shakes her head. "No way. Liz, be serious. You aren't

going to tell him anything. You're done with Vince. It was just some pictures and some money."

"He's never going to stop, Josie. No matter how much I give him, he wants more. Every time he contacts me, he wants more money, and now he wants sex." I laugh out loud. "Can you believe he expects me to have *sex* with him? I'm not doing it." I shake my head hard. The docks rock gently against the water. For a moment, it appears that I almost lose my footing. The boots look great, though. I know there's no way I'd be willing to take them off—not simply for the sake of balance. They complete the whole outfit.

I can tell Josie is doing her best to remain calm. "Liz, listen to me. You're drunk. We'll figure something out. But you can't tell anyone. We talked about this. We'll both be in serious trouble. It's been over a year. Just . . . just sleep with him. How bad could it possibly be?"

"I don't know," I tell her, "I'm a virgin. You know that."

"Well, you've gotta lose it somehow."

"I want to lose it to Richie."

She snorts. She doesn't say anything.

I put my hands on my knees. "I'm so dizzy," I breathe. "I feel like I'm going to pass out, Josie."

"Put your head between your knees," she instructs me. "Take deep breaths."

"Josie," I mutter, "I need juice. Can you get me some juice? I'm gonna faint."

"Yeah. Hold on." She climbs onto the boat. She goes

inside. For a long moment, my stepsister looks around. She observes my sleeping friends: Topher and Mera, their arms locked around each other, sharing the same sleeping bag. Richie, asleep on a sofa. Caroline, curled in a ball on the floor. Everybody is out for the night. Nobody knows we're still awake, alone together on the docks. Nobody can see a thing.

Josie doesn't go to the fridge to get me any juice. Instead, she comes back outside, steps gently onto the dock, and stares at me.

I'm drunk. I'm exhausted; I've probably run a good ten miles today—maybe more—and aside from a small bite of birthday cake, it's likely that I've barely eaten. Plus there was that joint we smoked. I remember it all so clearly now. I can't believe how I've treated my body. It's like I wanted something terrible to happen to me. And now it will.

I stare at her. "Where's my juice?"

I take a step backward. She steps toward me. I take another step back, this one shaky and unsteady as I begin to lose my balance, and she comes closer.

"Liz, you can't tell anyone. You'll ruin everything. You'll get in trouble." She swallows. "You'll get *me* in trouble. It's not fair."

"I have to tell someone. I'm going to tell Mr. Riley. He'll help me. He'll understand. Josie, I can't live like this anymore. I feel like it's killing me to keep this secret."

I teeter backward, trying desperately to regain my footing, and the edge of my boot catches on the side of the dock. I hold my arms out toward Josie, trying to grab on to her.

She gazes at me for what feels like a very long moment, even though it's only a few seconds. She does nothing.

I fall into the water. For a moment, my entire body disappears. Then I surface, splashing loudly, screaming for her to help me.

The water is freezing at night by this time of year, undoubtedly cold enough to knock me into sobriety. I continue to splash around for a few more seconds, trying to grab on to the edge of the dock, to pull myself up. My stepsister only stares, watching, thinking. Deciding.

Then she gets onto her knees. She extends her arms, like she's going to pull me to safety, and for a moment my expression shifts to relief as I reach for her, grateful for the help.

Josie puts one hand on my shoulder, and the other on the top of my head. She pushes me underwater. She is silent, tears brimming in her eyes, a look of steely determination on her face.

She holds me beneath the water for a very long time. Eventually, I'll have to breathe. Even as I'm watching, I remember it so clearly. It's almost like I'm living it all over again. Water in my lungs, in my nose, everywhere. It burns so badly, my mouth open in a silent scream underwater, the whole world going black behind my eyes.

Tonight, on the eve of my eighteenth birthday, I die.

Josie stands up. She's wearing a tank top and denim shorts, so she's barely wet at all. Her arms are red from the cold water. She goes inside the boat, into the bathroom, and quietly dries herself off. She stares at her own reflection in the mirror, takes many long, deep breaths before leaving the bathroom, shutting off the lights in the boat, and climbing under a blanket on one of the beds.

She lies there for a while, eyes wide open, gazing at the ceiling of the boat. Then, only a few minutes before I'm officially supposed to turn eighteen years old, my stepsister falls asleep.

When I open my eyes and look at Richie, I can tell immediately: he understands. He might not have seen everything as I saw it, but he felt me. He knows.

"You," he whispers, jumping to his feet, backing slowly away from Josie. "You killed my Liz."

Josie presses a single index finger to her closed lips. She doesn't say anything.

"Why did you do it?" Richie asks, still whispering. "Why would you hurt her?"

"She had everything." Josie's voice is so calm that it frightens even me. "She was beautiful. She had you. And she had our father. Everybody knows I'm his daughter, *everybody*. But he'd never admit it. Even my mom told me it was true. But Liz got all the attention. Liz was the prettier one. Liz was the queen at school. It was so easy for her. It was never easy like that for me. She had everything, Richie. She had everything even when she didn't deserve it."

Her voice grows louder as she speaks, gaining more

conviction with every word. "You barely knew I was alive before you found out she was cheating on you. Maybe it wasn't *really* cheating, but it was close enough. Richie, I wouldn't have done that to you! Don't you understand? Life follows a pattern. Liz was like her mother. I'm like my mother. You're like my father. Do you see? We should be together."

Richie looks around, like he's trying to come up with an exit strategy. But there's nowhere to go. All he can do is listen.

"Liz had everything," Josie repeats, "and she was going to throw it all away because of one stupid, drunk night." Her voice begins to waver, just a little. "And she was going to take me right along with her. I love my dad, Richie. And I love you. I loved Liz, too. She was my sister. But she had a good life. It was time for someone else to have a turn." She closes the baby book, puts it aside. "It was my turn. She was going to tell on us, tell on *me*. I wasn't driving that night. I didn't hit Alex. I didn't deserve to get into trouble for what she did."

"You didn't want to get caught." Richie's eyes are wide. "That's what this is all about, isn't it? Admit it. She was going to tell the truth, and you couldn't have that."

"Yes." Josie appears feverish. She nods in agreement. "Sure. I guess that's right, Richie."

"You're sick," my boyfriend says. My Richie. The love of my life.

Josie nods again. "Maybe so."

Richie leans over, taking deep breaths, trying to collect himself. As he's staring toward the floor, he notices something.

I follow his gaze. I gasp.

There, around Josie's ankle, is her "Best Friends" bracelet. She's still wearing it. Even though she killed me.

In one swift motion, with more anger in his expression than I have ever seen before, Richie lunges toward her. Before Josie has a chance to pull back, he grabs the bracelet and yanks it from her ankle, snapping the chain.

"What are you doing?" she shrieks, pulling her leg away.

He holds the bracelet in his fist. There is genuine rage in his gaze, along with so many other emotions—pain, heartbreak—but no compassion. No pity for Josie.

"Give that back," my stepsister breathes, staring at his closed hand.

He shakes his head. "No. You'll never wear it again. Never."

There is a light tap at the front door.

"I'm guessing that's the police." Richie is short of breath. He doesn't move.

Josie looks calm, but her breathing is deep and heavy. Her eyes are glazed with emotion, even though her tone is flat. "Aren't you going to let them in?"

"Liz would have done anything for you."

"Liz was going to ruin my life."

"So you killed her instead."

Josie blinks. "Let them in, Richie. I'm tired of waiting." She sighs. "Life is boring without Liz. If I'd known that beforehand, maybe things would be different."

Twenty-five

I remember everything so vividly now, my whole life a series of clear memories stretching before me like a slide show. I can access any of them anytime. There are no gaps anymore. There are no blanks. The feeling of helplessness that has plagued me since my death, the frustration of not being able to remember, is gone.

I remember being twelve years old, on the first day of seventh grade, when Mr. Riley noticed my lanky frame and asked, "Have you ever considered running cross-country?"

"You mean distance running?" Even then, I was already a spoiled girl. "My dad always says he doesn't run unless somebody's chasing him." I pause. "But my mom was a runner."

At first, like anything new, it was difficult. My body had never found its rhythm until that first afternoon, I realized. And then I understood why people fell in love with running, just as I fell in love with it: for the first time in my life, I felt like I could do anything. As my legs found their stride and I grew to understand how to comfortably pace myself, I learned how it felt to have my mind go completely blank. To spend hours thinking about nothing. When I was running, I didn't have to worry about how I looked or who might be more popular. I didn't worry about the rumors that circulated constantly, in town and in school, about the affair my dad and Nicole had been conducting before my mother died. I didn't wonder if Josie was really my half sister. I didn't think about my mother, unconscious, dying in a pool of water and blood and glass. I simply pushed forward, breathing in and out, putting one foot in front of the other. You can't imagine how free I felt when I ran.

But after I killed Alex, no amount of running could erase the image of his dying body from my mind. I tried so hard; I ran harder and farther than I ever had before, doing the only thing I knew to clear my head. There was no escape. Even before Alex found me in death, he was everywhere. That last breath. Those eyes gazing up at me. There was no forgetting, no matter how many miles I went.

I ran until my feet were bloody and blistered. Until even Mr. Riley told me it was too much, that I was driving myself into the ground and I had to let up. By then I knew it wasn't working anyway.

Why did I wait so long to decide to confess my secret? What was I so afraid of? Anything, I know now, would have

been better than having the end of Alex's life on my conscience. Anything—even my own death.

We were a happy family once. For more than seven years,
my dad and Nicole, along with Josie and me, lived as normally as possible under the circumstances. Acknowledging
that my father and Nicole were almost definitely having an
affair before my mother died makes me angry now, but it
doesn't make me love my dad any less. It makes me feel so
sorry for my mother. Maybe, probably, if Nicole had never
moved back to Noank, or my parents had never come back
here after college, everything would be different.

But then I never would have met Richie. And if there's one
thing in my life I don't regret, not for a moment, it's Richie.

It is a beautiful day in late November. In a few days, it will be
Thanksgiving. I don't know why I'm still here, to be honest. After the police took Josie away, I expected to fade into
oblivion, to go wherever Alex went. But nothing happened.
I've been here, still, for weeks. I'm waiting for something,
surely, but I don't know what.

So much has changed, yet so much has stayed the same.
Once they got over the shock of learning that Josie was responsible for my death, my friends fell easily enough into their old
routines. Caroline's father has found a new job, which is apparently even better than his last one. Out of all my friends—even
Richie—she is the one who visits my grave the most. I know

she must be so relieved that everybody knows the truth about what happened to Alex and me, and that she no longer has to carry her suspicion alone. When she visits me now, she never says much. And when she's finished, she walks across the cemetery and visits Alex. Despite all her flaws—the stolen money and pills, her fixation on popularity and status—she remains a good friend.

Mera and Topher are exactly the same as they've always been: Topher still smokes, then brushes and flosses obsessively; he and Mera are still the golden couple of the school. Their affection used to make me feel endlessly annoyed, but it doesn't bother me so much anymore. I'm happy for them. They deserve to be happy.

And then there's Richie. On this particular morning, he steps out his front door and leans against a post on his porch, stretching his hamstrings. He's become quite the runner lately. I can understand why.

He looks down the street at my old house. Since Josie won't be finishing the school year at Noank High, my father has said he wants to sell it quickly. Already he's had a few offers, but he's rejected them all. I don't know why. He and Nicole barely speak to each other anymore, and I'm guessing they'll get a divorce sooner or later. Once, shortly after Josie was arrested, my dad confronted Nicole to ask her if she'd known that Josie was responsible for my death. She insisted she had no idea. I want to believe her. I really do. But I can't be certain. For years, she pretended to be my mother's friend, while she and my father were having an affair. What kind of person does that? In my heart, I know there's a chance that she had an inkling of Josie's act. If she *did* know, I'm certain she would have stayed silent to protect her own daughter.

More than any other feeling, though, my heart breaks for my father. In one lifetime, he has lost two wives and two daughters. How does a person move on from something like that? I can't imagine what he'll do. For now, he still spends most of his time on the boat, even though it's freezing in Connecticut, where winter comes early and almost always overstays its welcome.

Richie begins to trot down the street. As I'm watching him, I feel a familiar twitching in my legs. It's the desire to run, I know; I've felt it every day since I died. But this time something's different. This time, the feeling is encouraging instead of frustrating. It feels possible.

I slip off my boots. I've done it plenty of times before, but until this moment, I've never been able to keep them off. I'd look down and there they'd be again, pinching my toes, the pain so constant and sharp that I never got used to it.

But not today. Today, they stay off. I wiggle my toes with excitement, unafraid to run barefoot. I bite my lip and smile, hopeful. Then I start running, following Richie down the street. He's still slow. I'm much faster. Before long I've caught up with him, and I'm right beside him. The stones on the road against the bottoms of my feet don't bother me a bit.

When Richie reaches the end of my street, he pauses. If

he goes right, it will take him into town; if he makes a left, he'll be heading toward the beach, but also toward the boat docks, where he and I are both looking at my dad, sitting on the front deck of the *Elizabeth* in a sweater and coat, sipping from a flask, staring at the water. Just staring. *Oh, Daddy.*

Richie looks around. For an instant, he looks directly into my eyes. Even though I know he can't see me, I give him my biggest smile. "I love you, Richie Wilson," I tell him. "Always have. Always will."

That's when he decides. He makes a left, jogging toward the docks. When he reaches the *Elizabeth,* he stands wordlessly before my father, the silence awkward, even though the two of them have known each other for years. At first it's like my dad doesn't even see him. But then he looks over, puts down his flask, and says, "Richie. Hi."

"Hi, Mr. Valchar." Richie catches his breath. "I saw you sitting down here, and I just thought— Well, I don't know. I thought maybe you could use some company."

Richie has been in my house a thousand times, shared countless conversations with my dad over the years. But right now it's uncomfortable, the two of them staring at each other, so much unspoken pain between them.

"I like being alone," my dad says. "Just being out here . . . it makes me feel closer to Liz sometimes." He pauses. "Not all the time. But sometimes. And that's enough."

"Mr. Valchar," Richie says, "I've been wanting to talk to you for a while. I wanted to tell you that I'm sorry. If I hadn't taken Liz to that garage to get her car fixed, she never would have met Vince Aiello. Everything might have turned out differently." He stares at the dock. "Sometimes I feel like it's all my fault."

"You can't think that way," my dad says. "It's over now. You didn't know everything. You were only trying to help."

Richie shades his eyes from the bright sun as he looks at my dad. "Still. I'm sorry. I wanted you to know, I think about her every day. What happened between me and Josie, it was nothing. It was just that I felt comforted by her, you know?" He shakes his head. "I can't believe it, but it's true. Knowing the two of them were half sisters—"

"They weren't," my dad interrupts, suddenly alert.

"What do you mean?" Richie is confused. "We all thought— I mean, even my parents thought you were Josie's dad."

My father picks up his flask again, takes a tiny nip. "When you kids were young, they didn't have things like DNA testing yet. Nicole always told me she wasn't sure, and when she and I got married, since Josie's father moved so far away—I mean, *he* certainly thought I was her dad—I don't know. We all thought it would be better if we didn't know. I thought Josie deserved a real dad. I tried to be that for her. I thought there was a good enough chance. But after . . . after she got arrested, I asked for a blood test." He shakes his head. "Can you believe it? All these years, and now I find out she's not mine." He takes another drink, wincing as he swallows. "Liz always loved having a sister. Ironic, isn't it?"

Richie doesn't say anything.

"So all that bullshit Josie believed about destiny, about things happening for a reason . . . Josie thinking she was gaining something when she hurt Liz, whatever the hell she was thinking she was destined for. And the way she went after you. Like she wanted to be just like her mom. Like it would have mattered, or been okay, even if she *were* my daughter! It was all bullshit. There is no destiny. No soul mates." My father looks around. "There's just a bunch of death."

Richie takes a slow breath. "I'm sorry, Mr. Valchar, but I have to disagree with you on that. Liz was my soul mate. She was the only girl I ever loved. I wanted to love her forever. I *will* love her forever."

My dad nods. "I know you will. So will I."

There is more silence. I close my eyes for a moment, thinking of Richie. He might have been the love of *my* life, but he still has plenty more living to do.

"How are you doing?" my dad asks. "I mean, I know things are hard for you, but do you think you'll be okay?"

Richie looks like he wants to cry. "I've been doing a lot of running," he says, not exactly answering the question. "It helps me to clear my head. Sometimes when I'm out there, I'll go for whole stretches of time without hurting. Without thinking about Liz." He pauses. "It helps. For a long time, I didn't think I'd be okay. Not ever. But now I think . . .

I think it's possible. Maybe someday." He studies my dad. "What about you, sir? Will you be okay?"

My dad doesn't answer right away. Finally, not looking at Richie, he says, "Liz would want that, wouldn't she? She would want us to go on. She would want us to live our lives, to remember all the happy times we had together." He takes another sip of liquor. "It's hard to remember them sometimes, but there *were* lots of happy times. Weren't there?"

"Yes." Richie nods. "There were so many."

Since my death, people have often commented about what I might want for them. Plenty of times, they were wrong. But my dad and Richie are right. All I want is for them to live. To go forward with the understanding that every moment is precious; every day is a blessing. To see life for what it truly is: a series of endless possibilities, not just for great pain, but for great joy.

Finally, I understand why I'm still here. To let them go.

"You'll be okay, Richie," I whisper.

My father leans back in his seat. He gives Richie a sad smile. "Life goes on."

For now, I know, his words will have to do. They aren't exactly an answer to Richie's question. But they're enough.

There is a long pause. Richie asks, "So you're moving?"

"Looks that way. We'll see what happens." My dad shifts in his seat. As though he's only realizing now how cold it is outside, he shivers. "You should get on with your run, then, if it makes you feel better. I don't want to keep you."

"Okay. I'll see you around, sir. Right? At least for a while?"

"Right." My dad manages another smile. "Go. Run."

I watch Richie as he makes his way back along the docks and onto the street, breaking into a jog once he hits the pavement. I don't feel any desire to follow him.

My dad puts his flask into his coat pocket, gets up like he's preparing to go inside.

"Daddy," I say to him, "I love you."

He doesn't pause or flinch or give any other sign that he's heard me. But once he's disappeared inside the boat, I feel the most amazing sense of calm. Like I've done everything I can to make things better. The rest is up to them.

Without knowing it, I've stepped to the edge of the dock. It is almost the exact place, I realize, where I fell into the water the night I died.

The sea is calm and clear. I gaze downward, expecting to glimpse my reflection.

But it's not there. Instead, I see my mother's face. She is young, happy, smiling at me. She looks healthy.

There's no need to hold my breath. I look around one last time. I wiggle my toes, so grateful that they are finally free.

I jump into the water. Everything is warm and bright. I am not afraid at all.

Acknowledgments

This book would not have been possible without the help and support of so many people who have believed in it from the very beginning and who have been such amazing cheerleaders as it evolved into the final product. My sincere thanks to my editor, Stacy Cantor Abrams, who continues to be one of my favorite people to work with, and to my incredible agent and great friend, Andrea Somberg. I also want to thank Rebecca Mancini for her amazing work, as well as Deb Shapiro and everyone else at Walker. I am so, so grateful to be part of your wonderful team. In addition, I want to express my gratitude to Rachel Boden for her fabulous insight. This book would not be what it is without each of these individuals; I am so excited and proud of all the work we have done together!

Catherine M. LoChiatto

JESSICA WARMAN is also the author of *Breathless*, *Where the Truth Lies*, and *Beautiful Lies*, which have received six starred reviews among them. The idea for *Between* came from an actual incident from her childhood, when a local boy went missing after a party on a yacht (he was eventually found, alive). Jessica lives in Pittsburgh, Pennsylvania.

www.jessicawarman.com

*T*wo identical sisters tied by a psychic bond—

—— until one disappears . . .

beautiful Lies

JESSICA WARMAN

Read on for a sneak peek
of Jessica Warman's new haunting,
page-turning literary thriller.

CHAPTER ONE

It's one of those cool, crisp fall nights that make you feel like the air is ripe with possibility, like anything could happen. From where we stand on the jogging trail, my sister and I can see the whole city stretching out around us. On the farthest end, all the way across town, there is a dusk-lit celebration taking place, a huge tent holding overlapping threads of bodies, the sounds of their voices carrying across the wind, all the way to us.

"Ah. Oktoberfest at the Yellow Moon," she says to me, squinting, standing on tiptoes in her scuffed ballet flats, like if she stares at the party long enough she might absorb some of the excitement, which feels almost electric as it seeps from the crowd.

She looks at me, her face shadowed by the almost-darkness. Her lips are outlined with crimson liner and filled in with a deep shade of cherry gloss. "Don't you wish we could go?"

I wind a strand of long red hair around my finger, thinking. Someone nearby on the path is smoking a cigarette. I can smell it even though I can't see him, but he's in the shadows somewhere, probably close enough to hear us. "We're only eighteen." I smile at her. "We can't drink yet, Alice."

She smiles back. "You know that wouldn't matter." We have fake IDs. And even if we didn't, Doug the bartender would give us drinks. My sister and I work at the Yellow Moon as servers a few nights a week.

"It wouldn't work. Everyone would recognize us," I say. "Half the town's probably there. If we got drunk, we could get in trouble." We've stopped walking for the moment, pausing to gaze at the lights across town. In the moonlight, my sister looks ready for anything: she is confident, calm, her dewy cheeks flushed with anticipation.

"Wait," I say to her, "your eyes."

She bats her lashes. "What's the matter with them?"

A family strolls past: a mother, father, and a daughter who can't be older than maybe four. The little girl has three purple helium balloons tied around her wrist, bobbing in the smooth night air as she walks, her pink-and-white sneakers dirty, almost blackened at their edges with dust from the trail.

The family pauses to look at the two of us. My sister and I are standing face-to-face, our identical noses only a few inches apart, our dilated pupils aligned. The space between us feels alive, almost humming with invisible energy.

The mother wears cutoffs and a red tank top, even though the air is cool enough for jackets. She looks tired but happy, holding her daughter's hand. "You don't see that every day," she says to us, squinting through the dusk to get a better look. "You're identical. Yes?"

I don't break away from my sister's gaze. The corners of her eyes crinkle in a soft smile. She is my favorite person in the world. Tonight, even our breath seems to be in sync. "Yes," I say, "we're identical."

The mother kneels beside her daughter. "See, sweetie? They're twins."

She's right. Even though we're dressed differently, and even though my sister is wearing heavy makeup—while my face is bare except for some light blush and powder—we are an unmistakable matched set.

The little girl gazes at us, openmouthed. We both smile at her.

She looks at her parents. "I want to go home." She seems almost ready to cry.

Her mom and dad give us an apologetic look. "Kids," the dad says. He flashes an embarrassed smile, and I feel a surge of unease when I see that his teeth are crooked and yellow. I'm not sure why exactly; there's just something about him that makes my stomach turn. As the family begins to stroll away, it almost seems like the earth is tilting beneath me, moving my surroundings a hair off-kilter. I can almost taste the cigarette smoke in the air, rancid and thick. It smells toxic; I have the overwhelming urge to get as far away from it as possible.

As she's walking away, just once the little girl looks over her shoulder. She seems afraid. But of what? Of us?

"I think we scared her," my sister whispers. She giggles. "We're freaks."

"We aren't freaks." It's getting darker by the second. "Let me fix your eyes."

She begins to look through her purse, digging around in the contents to find a tube of black liquid eyeliner. She hands it to me.

"Hold still," I tell her. "Alice. Look at the stars."

She puts her small hands on my shoulders to steady herself. I take a step closer to her—so close that I think I can hear her heart beating, close enough that I can see the faint pulse in her neck and feel the warmth of her breath on my face. With a steady hand, I reapply the liner with smooth strokes. Even when I reach the inside corners of her eyes, the inky applicator tip almost touching her tear ducts, my sister does not flinch.

"There," I say. "Finished."

I can see a touch of anxiety behind her smile. "How do I look?" she asks.

I still smell cigarette smoke. The family from a moment ago is far away, three bodies bobbing against the horizon, growing smaller with every step. Soon they'll turn a corner and disappear altogether. I don't like being alone out here, so close to whoever is standing in the shadows, maybe watching us. I know I'm getting upset over nothing, but I can't help it; the air reeks of disease. "You look like Alice," I tell her. "You look like yourself."

"We could go home," she offers. "We could stay in tonight."

I frown. "A minute ago you were ready to sneak into Oktoberfest, and now you want to go home? What fun would that be? We said we'd go out. You wanted to come. Our friends are waiting for us."

"*Your* friends," she corrects me. "They don't like me anymore. Remember?" She looks around, sniffling. I know she can smell the smoke too. "I'm nervous," she says.

"Don't be. Everything is fine. You'll be great."

She looks at the lights from Oktoberfest across town again. "Bet they're having more fun than we will at the fair. We could go. I have my ID."

I follow her gaze, imagining how it would feel to be silly and drunk, the thrill that comes from truly getting away with something. She's right; it *would* be more fun.

But we have plans. "We already talked about this. We're going to the carnival. I'll be with you the whole time, Alice," I say.

Her lips—full and shiny, identical to mine except for their deep stain of color—form a slow smile. "I know you will, Rachel."

More confident now, she starts walking again, heading

toward the fair. When I look at her, the last few beams of sunlight almost completely below the horizon now, all I see are shadows against her profile, her sharp features softened, almost seeming to dissolve.

She glances at me, smiles again. "All right, you've convinced me. Now come on, before I change my mind. We'll be late." She tugs me along, our fingers still laced together. The gesture feels as natural to me as breathing. She is mine. I belong to her. This is how it has always been, even before we were born.

∽

On our side of town, only a few hundred feet down the path we're walking on, there's a whole different kind of crowd gathered for the annual autumn festival at Hollick Park. I can smell it before I see it, the gross odor of cigarette smoke replaced by whiffs of cotton candy, funnel cakes, and hot dogs.

"I want a candy apple," my sister says, holding my hand more tightly as we walk down the hill, toward the field crowded with people and vendors' booths. At the far edge of the park, there's a tiny carnival set up, a cluster of rickety-looking rides crowding the horizon. In the center of them, a Ferris wheel spins slowly, its metal beams strung with twinkling white lights, the structure towering so far above the rest of the fair that, at its highest point, the wheel almost seems to graze the moon.

"Rachel." I hear someone calling us—calling me. "Rachel and Alice! Behind you!"

We both turn around. "Here we go," my sister murmurs.

"Shh." I give her a look. "It's okay."

The voice belongs to Kimberly Shields, who we've made plans to meet up with tonight. Everybody calls her Kimber. She waves at us, beaming, her bright green eyes flashing beneath the fair's lights. She's still in her cheerleading uniform, obviously having just come from a football game. She's with two of our other friends: Nicholas Hahn, whose dad owns the Yellow Moon, and his girlfriend, Holly Willis, who goes to our church and volunteers in the nursery every Sunday, and whose family leaves their Christmas tree up year round.

At almost eighteen years old, Kimber Shields is an honest-to-goodness sash-wearing cookie-selling Girl Scout. A few weeks ago, when she was at the mall, an elderly man had a heart attack in the bookstore, right there in the Crafts and Hobbies section. Kimber was a few feet away, paging through a book on knitting. Without any hesitation, she got down on the floor and gave the man CPR until the paramedics arrived. She saved his life.

The five of us stand in a semicircle beside one of those games where you try to toss a ping-pong ball into glass bowls filled with water. One out of every five or six bowls has a fish swimming around in it; if you sink one, you get to keep the fish.

"Charlie would love this," I murmur, looking at the fish. Charlie is our cousin.

My sister stares at the game. "It's two dollars for four tries," she says. Her heavy black eyeliner gives her face a hollow look, making her blue eyes seem bigger than they actually are, their lids filled in with dark gray shadow, the effect both dramatic and kind of unsettling in its allure. Her beauty is different from mine tonight: more arresting, more intimidating somehow. When she's all made up, out and about, she has a presence that commands attention, and she knows it. Tonight she wears a plain, fitted white T-shirt and a denim miniskirt that's so short I almost can't believe our aunt and uncle let her leave the house in it, even if she is wearing tights underneath. Despite the way she faltered a few minutes ago, she is nothing but confidence now. Men who pass by us stop to look at her, even if they're with their wives or girlfriends. They can't help themselves.

"So? It's only two dollars." Nicholas—nobody *ever* calls him Nick—looks into his open wallet, thumbing through a bunch of ones. "You ought to try it, Alice. Win yourself a fish or something."

Nicholas lives a few blocks away from us, in one of the biggest and nicest houses in our whole city. In addition to the Yellow Moon, his dad, Mr. Hahn, also owns Pratzi's, which is a hoity-toity restaurant uptown. Nicholas's dad drives around Greensburg all the time in a silver Mercedes with tinted windows, blaring classical music, a lit cigar between his lips. People say he has ties to the local mafia, but I've always doubted it; I can't imagine that our town even *has* a mafia connection. Anyway, I know that Mr. Hahn is a jerk. For one thing, he's an awful boss; he's always flirting with the waitresses, making sleazy comments about the way we look, his gaze raking over us like we belong to him. And supposedly his first wife—Nicholas's mom—left because he used to beat her up all the time. He never got arrested for it or anything, but that's what people say.

Despite his family drama, Nicholas is a nice enough guy, well liked by pretty much everyone, cute in a nerdy kind of way. I'm actually surprised he and Holly decided to come out with us tonight; lately they've been devoting most of their time to geocaching, which is kind of like an elaborate treasure hunt using GPS. I don't know much about it beyond that, but Holly has told me it's a ridiculous amount of fun.

"For two dollars," my sister tells Nicholas, "I could go to the pet store and buy myself a goldfish."

"But the fun's in trying to win," Holly says. I can see her breath suspended in midair as she exhales; that's how chilly it is.

"I bet they're scared," I say, staring at the fish as they circle endlessly in their tiny bowls.

Nobody says anything. We all look at the game, its edges crowded with little kids, their parents standing behind them looking bored.

Finally, Kimber giggles. "Rachel, you're so funny," she says. "Fish don't have feelings."

My sister is chewing pink gum. She blows a bubble, snaps it loudly against her lips, and says, "So what you're telling us is, if a fish needed CPR, you wouldn't help it."

Kimber seems confused. "Alice, fish don't—you aren't—" She frowns, looking from my sister to me in frustration. "I earned my Good Samaritan badge for that."

"I know." I try to smile warmly at her. Kimber responds by frowning again, bringing her fingers to her neck to grasp a tiny golden cross dangling from a thin chain.

Kimber is a good person—she deserves all the happiness she can get. Back in the first grade, before I ever knew her, her parents went through a messy divorce. One night while she and her mom were sleeping, her dad set their house on fire. He went to prison, and Kimber was in the hospital for months. I've seen her getting changed in gym class; she has horrible scars all over her back and shoulders. She never wears tank tops or goes swimming with the rest of us in the summer. She's never even been on a date, even though plenty of guys have asked—she's too ashamed of the way she looks.

There is a noticeable unease among my friends, who are doing their best to be kind to my twin. Things used to be different among us, but in the last six months or so, she has broken away from our group, preferring to spend her time alone. She's gotten a real taste for alcohol lately—pot too. As a result, her reputation has disintegrated to the point where some of our friends aren't even supposed to be around her anymore. This fact pains me, because I know her better than anyone. I know she's not a bad person. She just wants some peace, the opportunity to quiet her mind, which always seems to be working against her. She wants to silence her thoughts, but she doesn't have any idea how to do it aside from drinking or smoking until she can't string together a sentence anymore.

Sometimes I understand exactly how she feels.

We are essentially the same, she and I. Her and me. My sister, myself. When she takes off her makeup and brushes out her hair—when we first wake up in the morning, or right before we go to bed in the evening—nobody in this world can tell us apart just from looking at us. Only we know who is who. Knowledge like that, shared with only one other person in the world, can feel exhilarating. It's like we own a secret that nobody else will ever hold the key to, for as long as we both live.

∽

Don't miss any of Jessica Warman's
richly **compelling**, critically **acclaimed** novels . . .